TURKEYS
NOT
BEES

by Martin Knox

First Published – 2022
This edition published 2022 by Novel Ideas
Brisbane, Qld Australia

Copyright © Martin Knox 2022

Typeset in Times New Roman 12pt by Donna Munro Graphic Design.
Cover artwork by Donna Munro Graphic Design.
Printed and bound in Australia by Ingram Spark.
Copyright © Martin Knox 2022
htttps://www.martinknox.com
mpknox46@aapt.net.au

DEDICATION

This book is dedicated to my family: Zoe, Tessa, Amani, Uly and Dorian, hoping that my writing will help them to respect, understand and conserve the World they will inherit, with care for individuals, through philosophies of freedom, voluntary responsibility, reason and science. I appreciate their support but opinions and any errors are my own.

ACKNOWLEDGEMENTS

I am indebted to the following.

I have put formatting, cover design and publishing, in the capable hands of Donna Munro. She has also helped with cataloguing my posts on my blog.

I attended reading groups with the University of Queensland Students Philosophy Association, led by Sam Adams, David McGovern, Chester Stadler, Cas Maclean and Louis Altena, in which we discussed Heidegger, Debord and other philosophers' writing. The students were innovative and responded helpfully to ideas I proposed for my novel.

Miles Whiticker contributed political background to philosophies and events in the novel.

Writers of Seville, led by Nancy Cox-Millner and Robyn Martin, are my writing group where I tried out several pieces and received helpful critical feedback.

Led by Garth Sherman at U3A in Brisbane, the discussion group Thinking About Current Issues considered some of my themes when I aired them at meetings. Besides feedback, the discussion was rich in ideas I used in my story.

Brad Ahern involved me in walking to protest a potential government mandate of Covid vaccination. He encouraged me in researching the dynamics of the nanny state and in concluding how this would affect individuals.

Dave Jones discussed some of the story ideas and philosophies with me, providing invaluable help.

Ken Chandler provided encouragement and was a source of literary ideas.

Dr Tom Richardson, School of Biological Sciences, University of Bristol, made available his biological experience of teaching and learning in social insects.

Dr Tessa Knox, my daughter, who works for WHO in Vanuatu, commented on the chapters where the coronavirus epidemic and vaccination are discussed.

Dr Zoe Knox, my other daughter, who works for Leicester University in the UK, is a distance runner and commented on training and physical fitness issues.

Dale Bampton, BL, who is a distance runner, encouraged my applying of flow to athletics.

John Leonardi was generous in providing me with a place to write during flooding of the Brisbane River in March 2022. He helped me with discussion of issues of Australian Government responses and initiatives during the coronavirus pandemic.

REVIEWS

REVIEWS OF MARTIN KNOX'S PREVIOUS BOOKS

ANIMAL FARM 2 (2021)

Reviewed by Divine Zape for Readers' Favorite.
Review Rating: 5 Stars

Fans of Animal Farm by George Orwell will adore Martin Knox's Animal Farm 2, a fable with strong hints of political satire set on a farm on tropical Caruba, an island in the grip of the Social Republic. It is set within a cold war between the Social Republic and the Democratic Union. After successfully leading an animal revolution, the pigs take over control of the farm and put the animal workers under unacceptable and harsh working conditions. When coal is discovered on the farm, it attracts the attention of the superpowers who are in it for their own interests. The animals find themselves embroiled in a war of climate change, where they have to decide to shut down the power station and the coal mine or use renewable energy. But the consequences will be dire for the animals including the loss of jobs. So, the only option they have is to fight for their freedom from totalitarianism. But can they win?

This is a cleverly plotted story with interesting characters, and readers will relate to the animals that behave like humans; the anthropomorphism is brilliantly executed. Readers will encounter animals such as pigs (Lords Napoleon, Natalia), cattle (Tosser, Earl, Henry, Arnold), sheep (Sharon, Trudy, Sophie, and others), goats, llamas, horses, donkeys, mules, and more. Animal Farm 2 is open to several interpretations with political manipulation, abuse of power, superpower interests, and those who bear the brunt of political manoeuvring. It is a fable, but it is the same story that we see being played out too often in the political world. The novel features relevant and deftly written political themes, a debate on climate change, and the effects of totalitarianism. The characters are elaborately written and readers can see in them a portrait of what politicians do. The satire is biting, ingenious, and written in a context that readers can relate to. Martin Knox's satirical novel is a work of great imagination.

TIME IS GOLD (2020)

Readers' Favorite 5-stars December 11 2020
Reviewed by Romuald Dzemo

Time is Gold by Martin Knox is a brilliantly plotted and well-written novel that centers on a strong and original concept. Maxi Fleet wants just one thing: to run faster than any female has ever run before. She is training to beat the world. Stan has offered a lot of support, supervising and guiding her as she trains to compete in a future marathon. Maxi is determined to push herself beyond the limits and achieve her dream, and there is a strong support system to help her as she pursues this dream. Jack Cram is a PhD student in physics who is working on a revolutionary concept of stretching time. In Maxi, he finds the best opportunity to experiment on his theory, and if he succeeds, it will be a breakthrough for him and the scientific community. Can his idea of "extreme-flow" improve Maxi's performance and produce the desired results?

This is a wonderful story with elaborately developed themes, including love, ambition, hard work and pain, the drive for success, performance, and friendship. Set in the future, it has strong psychological and scientific underpinnings. The story is told in an absorbing first-person narrative, a style the author uses with mastery and it establishes a real connection between readers and the characters. The story has a premise that got me hooked right off the bat and I loved the bold ideas developed in this novel, especially the concept of "extreme-flow." This concept stipulates that anyone can perform better by getting into the flow that is extremely engaged. Hence marathon runners and others who embrace endurance with cognitive vigor can bolster their time, bit by bit, crossing finishing lines earlier, inserting additional accomplishment and staying younger. Time is Gold is a classic novel, speculative in style, hugely engaging, and featuring tight and excellent writing. While I loved the plot points, it was the depth with which the characters are written that had me turning the pages.

SHORT OF LOVE (2019)

Readers Favourite, August 5, 2019
Review by K.C. Finn Rating: 5 Stars

Short Of Love is a work of picaresque satirical fiction penned by author Martin Knox, which explores the notion of love and relationships, and how we treat other human beings when we view them as commodities for love rather than as individuals.

Author Martin Knox has created a fascinating parody of modern love and its effects on life, whilst also managing to stay true to the nature of many relationships where competition becomes a feature over compassion. Overall, Short of Love will interest any reader who enjoys dissecting relationships and the notion of romance itself.

PRESUMED DEAD (2018)

Readers' Favourite January 6, 2019
Reviewed by Grant Leishman; Review Rating: 4 Stars

Presumed Dead is a classic "whodunit" and author Martin Knox does a very credible job of describing in detail the investigative techniques of crime scene analysis that the character had developed in his years as a police forensic scientist. The story is well constructed, with possible "red herrings" thrown in at appropriate points.

The two principal characters of Jane and Phillip are well drawn and easy to relate to and empathize with. It is interesting that, as in real life, Knox has sought to bring two people with polar opposite personalities together in a romantic relationship. Jane, the firebrand extrovert with a passion for politics, and Phillip, the quiet, methodical, introvert who struggles to relate to people on a personal level.

I particularly enjoyed the political undertones of the story and the ideals of what truly constitutes democracy. The idea of scrapping political parties and independent politicians voting on their conscience every time has been floated often and I think even trialled occasionally. It brings a real modern-day relevance to the story – one only needs to look at the political turmoil in the US at present to see the dangers of partisanship and party politics. All in all, a very satisfying read and one I can recommend.

LOVE STRADDLE (2014)

Reviewed by Ian Lipke, October 4, 2014.
Editor of Media-Culture Reviews at Queensland University of Technology; author.

This novel by Martin P. Knox is vast in scope, scintillating in the brilliance of its conception and staggering in the creation of its hero. This is the work of a major talent

The concept is a straddle, a manipulation of the market in commodity futures:

'...an investor in commodity futures wants to spread the risk between commodities that are substitutes for each other... when the price of one goes down, the other goes down as well.'

Selwyn then applies such a concept to women and their affections to comical effect. It is in the teasing out of this idea into human behaviours that the originality of Knox's writing appears.

The last words in this review have to be delivered by the irrepressible Selwyn. Vicki has given him his marching orders and he has taken up with Helen.

'Vicki knows what I'm like. Her place in my straddle allows her full freedom. If it becomes possible, I still want to close out my short on her and exchange my love for hers, at my best price.

Until then, I also have a long position and am invulnerable.'

What a hoot! This book is recommended very highly. Get hold of a copy from Amazon. You'll enjoy it as much as I did.

THE GRASS IS ALWAYS BROWNER (2011)

Reviewed by Venero Armanno, December 10, 2011.
Lecturer Creative Writing, University of Queensland;
author of 9 best-selling novels.

'Martin Knox is the type of writer who knows how to tell a wonderful story and pose thought-provoking questions about life and the future. In his book The Grass Is Always Browner, Knox has managed to craft a political thriller, a romance and an allegorical tale of one man's prophetic journey towards enlightenment, all within the umbrella of a deeply satisfying work of speculative fiction. This is a novel to savour and Martin Knox is a writer to watch.

AUTHOR BIO

Martin Knox grew up on a farm in Somerset England. He graduated from Birmingham University as a chemical engineer and worked in the petroleum industry in Canada. He researched alternative systems of government at Imperial College, London. He emigrated to Australia and was employed in mining development. He became a high school teacher and wrote science textbooks published by the Queensland Department of Education.

He has been writing fiction novels full-time since 2013: speculative, love, politics, crime, sport and satires. He is involved in public policy-making, has proposed an underground railway for Brisbane and a new paradigm for climate science. He discusses current issues at U3A and reads philosophy texts with students at the university of Queensland.

He pole vaulted at school and writes about training elite performers in athletics and education. He writes 'in flow' and blogs about energy supply and covid restrictions. He was vaccinated voluntarily but protested against mandatory vaccination of others. He writes letters, plays the guitar, sings badly and does outdoor gym.

He is divorced with children and grandchildren.

LIST OF NOVELS PUBLISHED

Available from Amazon in Australia, USA, UK and Canada

The Grass is Always Browner (2011)
Love Straddle (2014)
Presumed Dead (2018)
$hort of Love (2019)
Time is Gold (2020)
Animal Farm 2 (2021)
Turkeys not Bees (2022)

Contents

COMING OF AGE

CHAPTER 1 MAVERICK

I slipped my face mask down and looked around the circle of half a dozen friends, sitting around our home barbeque, drinks in hand. They helped themselves to food from a side table and ate with plates on their knees. They were university people. I had returned to the university two years previously after 6 years in industry.

Megan was my girlfriend, a psychology PhD student on an athletics scholarship. She had recently won a gold medal in the 2032 Olympic Games in Brisbane, our home town. We were agreed not to have children until we had completed our PhDs. We had both caught coronavirus at the Games. Now we were celebrating her discharge from hospital at the rented house where we lived. I had been detained at home by police, for leaving quarantine without discharge.

'Can you go out, Chance?' asked Don, like me a physics PhD student. His unusually level gaze searched mine. He was serious, rather po-faced. His quiet opinions were well-informed, moderate and widely respected.

'No, I must stay here,' I said between mouthfuls. 'They're keeping tabs on me with this.' I held up my phone. 'They call me from the police station several times a day, using a GPS to check I am here. It's nanny state over-control. I don't deserve this.' There was anger in my voice.

Our garden had an enormous leopard tree. A flock of rainbow lorikeets flew in and commenced a deafening racket of excited shrieks.

The group looked at me as I ate, curious. They had heard me rant before, but not about the 'nanny state'. It was the first time they had seen me angry. I was 28, with 3-day stubble, tall and fit looking, wearing a long-sleeved shirt, blue with vertical white stripes, hanging loosely over blue jeans and running shoes. No-one said anything. They might not understand what I meant by 'nanny state'.

'Is it right they can treat me like a nanny correcting a child?' I said, shouting to be heard.

'Perhaps you blew it when you broke quarantine,' said Don, shouting above the din.

'The quarantine time had ended,' I said. 'They should have discharged me.'

'Where does your detention allow you to go?'

'Nowhere.'

'Can you have visitors?'

'More than 1.5 metres away and wearing a face mask. Does anyone mind that I am not wearing mine?'

It was hanging around my neck. A few were wearing theirs.

'Why aren't you wearing it?' asked Don. He wasn't criticising me. He knew I was making a statement and that I would welcome his question.

'How could my mask protect you, if your own won't?' I responded. 'Me wearing mine won't make any significant difference to you. The fabric is a coarse weave. It could reduce the number of virus particles I inhale slightly, but I'm prepared to take that risk.'

No-one disagreed with me but they weren't entirely convinced, because virus transmission processes were not public knowledge. My unmasking was petty, but it symbolised my dissent from the conditions of my detention. No-one seemed to mind.

The lorikeets left as abruptly as they had arrived.

'What are they on?' someone asked in a quiet voice that seemed loud. 'Hemp?'

Everyone laughed.

'If people fear I will infect them,' I said, 'making me mask up is not the answer. They can distance, or stay at home, wearing their masks if they wish. I have agreed to wear a mask with visitors. That would protect you, achieving for me a benefit of altruism, as if you were kin. The philosopher Immanuel Kant would require that if I wanted you to wear a face mask, I should wear one myself, because not wearing a mask would be selfish, irresponsible or merely thoughtless. But I don't want you to wear a mask. I don't care if you put down your masks. If you agree, I will keep my mask lowered and take my chances. Is that okay?'

Most of the others slipped down their masks.

'Why did you leave quarantine without being discharged?' asked Nick, from under his Stetson.

He worked as an environmental scientist, doing impact assessments for infrastructure development. He was a hippy with an obsession for American country music, which explained the Fu-Manchu moustache and cowboy hat he wore everywhere.

'I had waited to be discharged but they were delaying and it seemed interminable. It was possible they were delaying hoping to pressure me into accepting vaccination.'

'Could you have been more patient?' asked Don. 'Maybe they were held up.'

Before starting a PhD in physics, Don had worked for a construction company, testing structural strengths of buildings. His authoritarian views were the antithesis of the anarchist Nick's.

'I was like going crazy,' I said. 'I'd been shut in the Olympic Village for a week and when I had tested negative I had to get out of there. Quarantine is oppressive, preventing exercise and fresh air, creating guilt and illness where there was none before.'

'You seem to have entangled with petty officialdom,' said Nick. 'I can see they have ground you down. You have been through a lot. I'm sorry this happened to you, Chance.'

'Could you have been infectious?' asked Don trenchantly.

'No. I had tested negative.'

'Didn't they accept that?'

'No. They arrested me for breaking their rules in going to see Megan who was in quarantine.'

'What did you expect?' said Don. 'Their job is to protect everyone.'

3

'They are authorised to control spread of infection and I wasn't a risk,' I said. 'I had done my quarantine. I was demanding my rights to leave as a free citizen. There's no law preventing a hospital visit. It was nanny state over-reach.'

'What the hell is a 'nanny state'?' Don asked.

'It has many controls,' I said. 'Some countries like Singapore are reputed to have many more regulations and restrictions on citizens' lives than in other countries. Germany was freest in a recent survey of regulation of alcohol, tobacco, food and vaping in 30 European countries.'

'Maybe Germans are least well off.'

'Many are within their rights to want to be without those regulations. Governments have legislated to control thousands of products and situations unnecessarily.

'I use the term 'nanny state' to describe regulation by all federal, state and local governments in Australia today. When I don't wear a mask, it is not just being contrarian. It's contempt for over-protection by Australian governments.'

'It seems like you are breaking restrictions allowed by emergency health legislation.'

'I have explained why not wearing a mask is of no significant consequence,' I said. 'People should take personal responsibility for their health, not foist it onto the community.'

'You are out of step with the rest of us,' said Don.

'Getting out of step could help to halt a march to doom,' I said. 'A Canadian journalist and magazine publisher said:

'. . .Australia is becoming the world's dumbest nation . . .(because of) the removal of personal responsibility and the increase in the number and scope of health and safety laws.' Tyler Brule, 2015

'He argued that Australian cities were over-sanitised,' I said. 'Many of the laws have been implemented in the expectation that they will reduce violence or improve health and safety. In many cases the excessive laws are being accused of restricting freedom,

4

ruining livelihoods and small businesses, turning the nation into a nanny state.'

'We're steeped in nanny state laws,' said Don, with his hands behind his head. 'We have mandatory bicycle helmet laws, gun control laws, prohibitions on alcohol in public places, plain packaging for cigarettes, pub and club lockout laws and permits for picnics on a beach. These are only a few. They are ridiculous. A senate enquiry investigated laws and regulations that restrict personal choice 'for the individual's own good.' It is an oxymoron. Australia's criminal legislation has gone too far.'

'Our gun control laws are reasonable. Other nations envy us.'

'That may be an exception. A nanny state excessively controls, monitors, or interferes with people's private actions or behaviours that are deemed unhealthy or unsafe.'

'What is state-like about a nanny state?'

'The term is an echo of 'nation state', which is a political entity whose domain is an independent state. A nanny state has a nanny figure parodying a monarch. The government is inflated and domineering, resented by the people.'

'It could be worse. You could be in prison.'

'This is a kind of prison. They've taken away my freedom. I have not broken any laws. I oppose their takeover.'

'What freedom?'

'My right to go where I want and help Megan compete. She could miss the World Championships.'

'She did brilliantly at the Olympics.'

The Olympics had been held in Brisbane earlier that year, 2032.

'She did. The Australian Olympics Committee wanted to stop her using our flow technique, but the IOC allowed her to compete.'

'Why did the AOC want to stop her?' asked Don.

'She wouldn't accept their coaching. When she was successful coaching herself, they tried to ban her technique.'

'At least you and Megan are together now,' said Don.

'Have you been vaccinated?' Don asked.

'No, neither of us have,' I said. 'It could be why they wouldn't discharge me.'

5

'Why did you refuse?'

'There is not enough evidence of benefits and too much risk of side effects.'

'But suppose a vaccine was available with strong evidence that it was safe. Would you accept vaccination?'

As usual, Don's view was moderate.

'I would do what's reasonable,' I said. 'If it would protect me and others from infection, or reduce the severity of illness and there was no risk of side-effects, I would take it.'

'Doctors have advised getting the vaccine,' Don said.

'I want more facts before I make up my mind,' I said.

'What if everyone made up their own mind?'

'Then I would be a fool not to.'

I said it as a pun, but no-one laughed. They didn't believe I would want to conform. My reputation was as a maverick, unorthodox and independent-minded.

'What will you do?' asked Don.

'I'm stuck here for two weeks. After that I will be free to campaign.'

'Will you get the jab?' he asked.

'No, I will oppose any coronavirus mandate,' I said. 'Doing the right thing' means continuing my life in good health, with a free conscience, as an individual. One jab wouldn't be the end of it: it could be the start of a series of vaccinations and treatments that could have serious repercussions. Once the nanny state has the upper hand, all kinds of forcible treatments could follow.'

'What treatments are you talking about?'

'Of the mentally ill, including euthanasia.'

'Some treatments might be of benefit.'

'Some might be harmful. My objection is institutional rather than technical. The nanny state is overbearing. I may accept other treatments but my stand is against the threatened vaccination mandate, a totalitarian proposal. I must consider carefully what to do.'

'Why don't more people refuse the jab?' asked Don.

'There are reasons for and against. Not many of us can keep an open mind, as if Schrodinger's Cat is both alive and dead, waiting for conclusive information. Most people plump for having a jab, accepting there can be harmful consequences.'

'Why do you say a mandate would be totalitarian?' asked Nick.

'It's a system of government that is centralized and dictatorial and requires complete subservience to the state,' I said.

'We haven't gone that far yet,' Nick said.

'We are getting there,' I said.

'Hopefully the pandemic will be over soon,' said Megan.

'I hope so too, but unless we oppose it, the problem of nanny state totalitarianism could be permanent.'

CHAPTER 2 RECKLESS

I had met Nick studying physics in our first year at university. He was a left-leaning hippy and I was a rebellious anarchist. We were allowed another subject and I chose a philosophy unit, while Nick opted for environmental science. Drawn together by unorthodox common interests, we became friends. We lunched in the cafeteria with a lot to talk about. When his father was out of work and Nick was short of money, I shared my food with him.

We had parted when I went to Canada after graduating. We had kept in touch and when I returned to do postgraduate studies, we usually met for lunch. Nick worked as a volunteer for an environmental group and didn't earn much, whereas I had saved money from my well-paid job. I continued to pay for his food.

'How's your family?' Nick asked as we ate at the Museum.

Nick had gone home with me to my family for several weekends at our farm near Toowoomba in Queensland, Australia. I had an older brother and younger sister. I told him they were all well.

'Why did they call you Chance?' Nick asked, as we shared a basket of chips.

'My mother was sure she was going to have a girl and when I was born a boy, my father said it was chance. I was named for good fortune. Providence smiled on me and all I had to do was wait and rewards would come my way.'

'You have been fortunate,' Nick said.

'I guess so. I was like: wild, unmanageable and irresponsible, counting on good looks and good luck to get by until well into my twenties. I used to do stupid things.'

'Why?' asked Nick.

'My parents over-controlled me, I was frustrated and caused trouble. They stopped me doing almost everything, like going to school friends' homes or taking a girl to the movies. I resented it and acted up.'

'Why were they like that?'

'I suppose they were trying to protect me. I played with my brother and sister when they would play with me. There were accidents and I was blamed because I was rough. They thought I was dangerous. Our pet animals knew it too: the cat, puppies, chickens and a tortoise couldn't get away from my tormenting fast enough. I had fights throwing fallen apples at my siblings in the orchard, until I ran out of apples and started throwing rocks.

'Apples are too tame. Let's have a proper fight!' I said. 'See if you can dodge.'

But the others pulled out.

'I practiced gymnastics, jumping over hay bales in a barn, or somersaulted and landed softly on huge bales of wool, or into loose grain.

'I played mostly by myself, throwing stones, spears and knives, firing catapults, ballistic weapons, bows and arrows at imagined enemies. When our father wasn't around, I sometimes took aim at and injured farm animals. I knew it was wrong, but I was provoked to misbehave by frustration. I was desperately unhappy.'

Nick said: 'Simone De Beauvoir (5) quoted Descartes as saying:

'Man's unhappiness is due to his first having been a child, finding himself cast into a universe which he has not helped to establish, which has been fashioned without him, and which appears to him as an absolute to which he can only submit.'

'The worst of being a child is that you don't have a say in anything important. The best was I enjoyed impunity and felt privileged with time and opportunities. I modelled myself on characters in my books: explorers, outlaws and sheriffs. I was unhappy when I couldn't equal their feats.'

'Was your childhood really unhappy?' Nick asked.

'Our family pretended to be happy. Our parents were without choices and we kids were expected to present an appearance of happiness.'

'When I was very young, I lacked consideration, became uncooperative and mum would fly into a temper and beat me. I would jump off the garden wall on to my forehead repeatedly, to get attention. My dives brought bruises and little sympathy.

'I can't take you anywhere,' mum said to me. 'They will think I've been hitting you.'

She did hit me, slapping me hard around the head. My hearing recovered, but I wanted a kinder mother and I became withdrawn and uncooperative.

'I was always in strife. You are more trouble than the other two put together,' she told me. My father was kind and attentive to me, so I didn't make trouble with him.

'I was about 5 years old when loud screaming attracted my attention to the cutting of a pig's throat. It was dragged to the knife, squealing its protest. It was an annual event, to supply meat for the house. The bloodied corpse made me aware of death and I understood why they mustered the ewes and picked out the sturdiest lambs to be trailered to the slaughterhouse. I supposed that the lambs' feelings would be like my own and that in death they would suffer terribly physically and psychologically. I was complicit in brutal murder and it upset me.

'Did you take risks as a child?' asked Nick, eating my chips.

'It's my life to do what I like with,' I said. 'What did you used to do?'

'I went sailing with my family and fishing with my dad,' said Nick. 'Those were great times. We towed our trailer sailer to the Bay and cruised out to the islands. If we caught enough fish to eat, we stayed out for a week.'

'What kind of fish?'

'Bream and whiting mainly.'

'Were you in any storms?'

'When the wind got up, we would run to shelter behind an island,' said Nick. 'It was cosy down below and we would play cards until we could open up the hatches.'

'Who was with you?'

'Just my parents and my younger sister.'

'What's she doing now?'

'She's in second year at university.

'Was your childhood happy?' I asked him.

'Usually I was happy enough,' said Nick. 'Our parents were like best friends, thoughtful and kind. Now tell me about your school days. Did you like being a teenager?'

'Not much,' I replied.

We walked back from the cafeteria to the university. Jackaranda trees lined the boulevard, soft, almost fern-like in appearance due to the dozens of tiny leaflets that made up each compound leaf. The complexity of their leaves astonished me. It would produce clusters of fragrant purple panicle-shaped blooms around exam time.

It was good to be back at the university after so many years away.

CHAPTER 3 TROUBLED

'I was a troubled youth,' I told Nick, as we ate in the university refectory. 'According to Simone De Beauvoir adolescence is a crisis with unpleasant vacillation, which she called 'assuming subjectivity'. I think she meant appreciation of others' viewpoints varies in adolescents, from time to time.'

'Our family was nominally Anglican, but our attendance at church was irregular. When I was 13, I went to confirmation classes with our vicar, who explained the intricacies of dying and going to heaven or hell. It was theoretical and didn't interest me. My mind was on the girls present.

'I was an altar boy, whose job was to help the vicar enrobe. I carried the salver of wafers and the silver chalice of wine he administered to rows of kneeling communicants. I went to a bible college for summer camps, where my faith was tested in long prayer sessions. I was distracted by the girls. My interest in the church never got off the ground.'

'Are you religious at all now?' Nick asked.

'No, not at all. But I understand how people can think God is caring for them. You aren't religious, are you?'

'No way. No higher power is caring for me.'

'At age 14 I was allowed to use a 0.22 rifle to shoot hares and rabbits. I hunted pretending my life depended on obtaining food. I stalked through scrubby brush upwind of my prey, with my rifle held in front of me, crawling commando style. The thrill of sneaking up on an unsuspecting animal and killing it appealed to something primal in me. Dad insisted that every animal I killed had to be brought home to be eaten. I grew tired of skinning and gutting my kill.'

'Did you ever accidentally shoot anyone?' said Nick.

'No, but I thought about it. As a teenager, I was angry to be stuck in a World with bad problems, without being able to do anything about them. I took sight on planes going over but I didn't pull the trigger. One time I almost killed myself.'

'What happened?'

'I was unhappy at home. I put the barrel in my mouth but I couldn't pull the trigger. It wouldn't be fair to my parents.'

'Did you have anyone you could tell how you were feeling?'

'No. I wasn't that friendly with anyone. At school they stopped me playing cricket because I was dangerous, so I turned to field events, jumping and throwing, which I practised alone. Then I discovered pole vault. The school's athletics coach had little experience and left me alone to learn the technique by trial and error. I liked being upside down metres in the air, held up by a pole that could snap.'

'You're going to break your neck,' the other boys said. 'Are you crazy or something?'

'When I was a teen, death was something that happened to livestock. I would be careful up to a point. When a friend passed his driving test, crashed and was killed, I analysed his life to determine if divine retribution was at work. I couldn't be sure if he had it coming. I wanted to find out what to avoid. The stakes were different to falling off my bicycle into a ditch, as I did regularly after quaffing pints of ale at the pub after tennis.

'I won't die until my time is up,' I thought.

'Did you ever feel that you had nine lives like a cat and were using them up?'

'No. My luck was the same on every throw of the dice.'

When I got older I was allowed to take risks that had been prohibited when I was younger. As an adolescent I wasn't afraid of danger. I climbed tall trees to birds' nests or scaled cliffs. I sometimes fell. Once I needed stitches, but nothing worse.

'What else did you do?'

'I was fascinated by the possibilities of water. I built a dam across a creek that flowed through the farm, raising the water level to a height that submerged the farm roads and prevented land rovers and tractors going to work. The obstruction deeply satisfied my need to be an engineer, until dad ordered me to release the flood water.

'My father bought me an unbroken hill pony. He was fiery and we broke each other. He threw me off every time I rode him. He would get the bit between his teeth and bolt. I had no instruction in how to train him and it was a contest of strengths and willpowers. I was lucky not to be badly injured.

'I took risks whenever I could. In the gym at school, I enjoyed box work, vaulting and summersaulting, imagining I could fly. The rubber mat always caught me. Nor was there much chance of dying on the rugby field. I was often at the town hospital's emergency department after a game, with concussion or a suspected fracture, but nothing serious.

'I wanted to be intrepid and forgot safety, by leaping over farm gates, walking across barn rooftops, climbing up cliffs, jumping across streams, hurtling downhill in billycarts, standing on the seat of my bicycle and generally taking risks as if everything was a game. I was angry that so many things were banned as unsafe. I opposed the caution of those who rejected my right to determine what risks I could take. I was assuming subjectivity, as Beauvoir described. But I had no masterplan for my personal development, other than to finish school and go to university.

'Is that like coming of age?'

'Yes. At school I was interested in science and was accepted to do physics at university. Meeting you in first year was pretty good.'

'You seemed very independent.'

'You knew a lot about the environment and politics.'

'My parents involved me in campaigns.'

'That was when I ceased to revere parents and teachers as gods,' I said. 'I realised they had contradictions, hesitations and weaknesses. I was growing up. I had begun to use discretion in setting up my own character.'

'Did you have a plan of how you wanted to be?'

'No, nothing,' I said. 'I winged it until third year. In first year I drove an ancient Volkswagen beetle. Do you remember it? It offered new opportunities for risk taking. At the wheel, I felt powerful and free. The steering wheel was on the left, the wrong side,. I couldn't overtake because I couldn't see past the car in front. I would stamp on the accelerator, swing across and force oncoming cars aside to let me pass. Somehow, I avoided crashing and escaped with the certainty that my continued existence was privileged and at the whim of a benevolent God.

'As a young adult my self-image included seeking and performing feats of daring. I had accidents but suffered only broken limbs and unconsciousness and was undeterred. I fearlessly walked along parapets of high bridges and did unsteady handstands above precipices. I didn't care about safety. I imagined I was immortal *a priori*: I had survived so far, therefore I must continue to survive.

'My bravado was 'macho' In Spanish, or 'having balls', like a real bad boy. I wanted to be heroic. Everyone said that being brave and cool would attract girls. Girls could be feisty or sassy, but I never found one who took risks like I did.'

'Being with you was risk enough.' Nick said.

'Haha. I supposed girls would prefer a guy who's used to danger because he would be braver protecting them. I took risks but avoided fights, because winners had more experience of fighting than me.'

'Your adolescence sounds more troubled than mine was,' Nick said. 'You were lucky to survive.'

CHAPTER 4 RESPONSIBILITY

'In our hall of residence at university, where we met, I had my first relationship with Julie, a French language student. We studied together, kissing and cuddling. She wouldn't have sex with me, wanting absolute commitment. It was an unacceptable trade and towards the end of first year I stopped seeing her. I had love, but not enough.

'I was too young to accept responsibility. My studies in philosophy had introduced me to the writings of Simone de Beauvoir (5). She described eight personal dispositions: child, adolescent, sub-man, serious man, passionate man, nihilist, adventurer and existentialist. I kept her book and used her nomenclature to identify stages in my educational career. In my freshman year I thought I must be a 'sub-man', because I suppressed my emotions, although I wasn't aware of doing this at the time.'

Now, years later, I was having lunch with Nick.

'What stage are you now?' he asked.

'I could be an existentialist, or a nihilist,' I said. 'What about you?'

'I could be an existentialist,' he said. 'But in first year I was probably a sub-man too.'

'We matured between first year and second year,' I said, 'with employment.'

'What did you do in the first long vacation?' he asked.

'I got a job in the UK, arranged by my uncle. I had gone over and worked on his farm in the school holidays. My father had emigrated and we all went back and visited his relatives every couple of years. A massive nuclear power station, Hinkley, was built next to the farm, looming over it. My uncle was friendly with the manager and asked him if he had a job for me for a couple of months.

16

'I emailed the manager that I had worked on the farm and was now a science student in Australia. I said the university required me to get practical experience in the vacation, relevant to my studies in physics.

'I received a phone call in Australia from the manager of the power station's science laboratory.

'Would you be able to monitor water quality, collect samples and do tests on them?' he asked. 'There isn't much physics, but the power station is large and nuclear powered, with a laboratory staff of 10 scientists. They monitor for any radioactive leaks into the environment, by testing samples of liquid and gas effluents. Your work as an intern would bring experience in radiation physics.'

It seemed ideal.

'I replied: 'I'm very interested.''

''When can you start?' he said.'

'We fixed a date, I travelled to the UK and began paid employment. My job was to collect condensate in the turbine hall and bring it to the laboratory, where I measured its oxygen content. High oxygen would mean there could be corrosion and the condenser gas would have to be purged.

'The manager told me to check the chlorine content of seawater in the cooling circuit. Sea water flowed into a caisson offshore to cool the station's condensers, through an intake tunnel two metres in diameter. Chlorine gas was supposed to be pumped in, to control growth of crustaceans inside the tunnel on the walls. I found no trace of chlorine. I reported this to the laboratory manager.

''See if you can find out why the pump has stopped,' he ordered.

'When I fiddled, it started.'

''Well done,' the manager said. 'Now there'll be chlorine going in.''

'Two hours later, there was a loud boom, a roar shook the glassware in the laboratory and the turbine hall was enveloped in a cloud of steam. I thought it was a reactor meltdown explosion and crouched under a bench to escape from ionising radiation.

''The condenser water tubes have been blocked by something,' a scientist said.

'Just then the phone rang and the chief scientist answered.

'Fucking hell,' he said putting down the phone. 'The control room guys think we have blocked the condenser tubes with barnacles, stopping steam from condensing. They are blowing down steam to stop the turbines exploding.'

'One of the scientists explained to me: 'Barnacles are filter feeders and the sea water washing in through the tunnel brings them food and creates an ideal environment for growth. We inject chlorine to stop them growing. The chlorine pump could have been down for a week and nobody noticed. The barnacles could have built up on the walls. When you restarted the chlorine, they let go and were swept into the condenser manifold, blocking water entry to hundreds of cooling tubes. Without cooling water, the tubes couldn't take away heat fast enough to condense the steam and the pressure built up until the safety valve popped.'

'The steam thundered out all afternoon, until they shut down the turbogenerator set. To remove the barnacles, hundreds of bolts holding the manifold had to be undone manually. This took until the next day, when generation resumed.

''Did you have any idea of the havoc you would wreak by restarting the chlorine pump?' the chief scientist asked me.

''No. I didn't know what the chlorine was for.'

''Well, now you know. How does it feel to have shut down a nuclear power station?'

''Not good.'

''It's not your fault,' the manager said. 'I should have known this would happen when I told you to fix the pump, but it had never happened before on my watch. I didn't realize the chlorine had been stopped for weeks.'

''I thought that the manager had tried to put the blame on me, a green vacation student, as the 'fall guy',' I said.

'The barnacles had to be cleared and there was no other way?' said Nick.

'He told me it wasn't my fault,' I said. 'He probably told his bosses that it was my fault. When something goes wrong, people try to distance themselves from blame.'

18

'I learned from this incident to take responsibility for my actions, finding out consequences beforehand,' I told Nick. 'My other learning was that a nuclear power station can only be as safe as the operators, who are human and make mistakes.

'So that's what I did in the vac. What did you do, Nick?' I asked.

'Nothing as exciting,' he said. 'I was taken on by an environmental consultant to measure air and water quality at a coal-fired power station.'

'Did you find anything interesting?'

'There was heaps of pollution and no-one seemed to be doing anything about it.'

'They had probably done all the cheap things. Reducing pollution is expensive.'

A year later, for vacation employment, Nick and I went to work in a Montreal oil refinery in Canada, arranged by Nick's father. He was friends with the oil refinery manager through his work as an engineer. Our parents paid our fares to Boston and we caught the bus up through New England in the Fall, passing maple trees in all their glory. It was a long way from Australia and Nick was lucky that we went when we did, before his father lost his job.

The Laboratory Manager, Francois Dumas, assigned us to take gasoline samples from the product pipelines. We tested them in the laboratory with a chromatograph, recording concentrations of volatile hydrocarbons. If volatiles were insufficient, the gasoline wouldn't ignite in engines and would have to be reprocessed.

'If you measure a sub-spec sample, call the control room immediately,' manager Dumas said.

We took samples every two hours, climbing ladders between hot pipes and distillation columns. The stairways were steep and tiring. In the laboratory, we analysed the samples. It was hard work and it soon became tedious.

The work wasn't much related to physics and perhaps that's why we found it boring. It wasn't ideal vacation employment but we didn't quibble. We planned to sightsee around the USA by

Greyhound bus afterwards. We liked being there because Montreal was wonderfully vibrant and we met locals who showed us around.

We printed each day a table of our laborious results, but no-one seemed interested. After several weeks, we had not found any sub-spec gasoline and our work seemed pointless.

'There's no lack of volatiles.' I said. 'It's summer and cold starts aren't going to be a problem anyway. '

'What we are doing is meaningless,' Nick said. 'No-one gives a tinker's cuss about our findings. They wouldn't know the difference if we used the same sample for every test, saving ourselves the sweat of collecting samples and testing them.

'We have to produce an analysis for every sample.'

'If we fiddle with the chromatograph, we can get analyses from a single sample, that are different enough and no-one will ever know.'

This would be blatant cheating. I tried to live honestly and I didn't like it.

'We should do what we agreed to do,' I said.

Nick was blasé. 'C'mon, Chance. Wouldn't you rather read a book than waste your time with this shit?'

Reluctantly I agreed. We concocted credible analysis reports and reclined in armchairs in the general manager's office, reading and snoozing.

One night, when we arrived at the laboratory, we were surprised to find the manager waiting for us. We followed him into his office. He kept us standing. Something was wrong.

'What happened last night?' he asked, looking from one to the other of us suspiciously.

'Nothing unusual,' I shrugged. 'Why?'

'A heating element in the main fractionating column burned out about midnight,' Dumas told us. 'The product was sub-spec. It should have been recycled and rectified. Instead, a large slug of gasoline has been piped to Chicago and another loaded into a lake tanker. Several trainloads have gone west and the remainder has been trucked to service stations all over Ontario. The fault was not recognised until 9.15 am when the switchboard was jammed with complaints from the public who couldn't start their vehicles. There were so few volatiles that even in summer the cars wouldn't start. We are currently recalling the entire delivery. As we speak, there are hundreds, even thousands, of service station mechanics draining and refilling vehicle gas tanks across Canada and America. Some customers will never trust this company again and will take their business to other suppliers. Your job was to find out this problem while it was here at the refinery. What happened?

Nick and I looked at each other and shrugged.

'We don't know.'

'Now, tell me exactly where the samples that you tested came from.'

We admitted faking the sampling, everything. We had not realised that our results were used for anything and we were sorry. We hung our guilty heads.

Dumas' voice had an edge that would cut glass. 'I told you when and where to get the samples and you cheated. I told you the control room wanted to hear about off-spec results, but you thought you knew better and that there couldn't be any. You didn't do your work. Normally, I would fire you both. However, Nick's father is a mate of mine. I feel sorry for him, that he has a son like you. I'm giving you another chance. Remember this: I trusted you and you let me down. I am very unpopular around here just now and it's your fault. Get out of my sight, you lazy cheating smart-asses.'

I was embarrassed. Nick had led me astray but that was no excuse. I had allowed myself to be led. I had behaved immaturely. It wouldn't happen again.

'We are fortunate Dumas knows your old man,' I told Nick.

'Do you think so? Dumas is sure to tell him and he will go mad at me.'

'We're not kids any more,' I said. 'Your old man's anger is less than we deserve for this. Would you have wanted the company to sue us for fraud?'

No.'

Now, years later the incident haunted me.

'Do you think our cock up rebounded onto your father?' I asked Nick.

21

'My father lost his job later that year,' Nick said. 'Shit.'

'I want to live virtuously,' I said. 'I want to be honest. According to Aristotle, honesty is halfway between habitual lying and hubris.'

'We aren't habitual liars,' Nick said. 'I'm not sure how close we came to hubris.'

'Very close,' I said. 'When people have asked me why I believe my work is good, I have always told people science is honest. We have been caught cheating, I know that my 'honesty' was faked, boastful and ugly. It was hubris.'

'Hypocrisy,' said Nick.

I recalled Nick had persuaded me to take part in the ruse, but I couldn't lay the blame on him. We had led each other on.

Before graduating, Nick and I reflected on our career prospects.

'I don't want work that is routine, like sampling and analysis,' Nick had said.

'You probably think I'm wild,' I said. 'But I want to live my life with courage. Nelson Mandela said *'Courage is not the absence of fear, but the triumph over it. The brave man is not he who does not feel afraid, but he who conquers that fear.'*

'Do you have a cause to conquer?' asked Nick.

'I want to confront something that threatens everyone's future and overcome it by reason and strength.'

'The future has plenty of fears for everyone,' said Nick. 'Which one are you going to overcome?'

'Unless I go out on a limb, I am never going to reach the best fruit,' I had said. 'It won't get any easier by waiting fearfully, dying slowly. I want to take the most worthwhile risks with the biggest prizes.'

'I don't much like your chances of finding much worthwhile risk as a scientist,' said Nick. 'From what I have seen, scientists like to choose the common denominator having least risk and run with the herd.'

'That's not fair,' I said. 'Sometimes scientists avoid dealing with problems of human behaviour, ethics, politics and economics because they lack confidence or feel unqualified. Going against the herd takes courage.'

'They won't take risks,' said Nick. 'If you are going to stick your neck out, the herd will be against you. You could need all your courage.'

'I agree. Bertrand Russell once said:

'Collective fear stimulates the herd instinct and tends to produce ferocity towards those who are not regarded as members of the herd.'

'Having courage is when you overcome timidity by mustering many small acts of defiance into a single act of resistance,' I said.

'Risk taking is unwelcome in workplaces,' Nick had said. 'When we were young we were protected from the safe conformity demanded by the world. Now we have to conform. Forget about resisting. Your plan is dangerous.'

After graduating, my job in Canada had demanded more subservient conformance than I could tolerate. I had disregarded Nick's advice and maintained a critical mind set in employment, becoming a secret socialist. He had been right, resistance was impossible. I had returned to Australia and worked for a different company, but the pattern had repeated and I returned to university to get more qualifications.

Nick worried about me. I was reckless and active whereas he was cautious and passive. He followed me around, persuading me to avoid unreasonable risks. He was a good friend.

CHAPTER 5 TWYLA

Nick and I listened to music in my room in hall and smoked joints Nick had brought. Feeling mellow, we reflected on our undergraduate days eight years earlier.

'When you met Twyla in second year, you seemed to change,' Nick said.

'When you meet someone, they can cause you to have a different view of yourself. Twyla set off an epiphany, a flash of deep realisation of my own free will, that my life was mine to control,' I said. 'I became determined to make a difference.'

'I remember you had some big ideas,' Nick said. 'You seemed to change them pretty often.'

'You were there when I met Twyla,' I reminded Nick. 'I was over Julie by then. Twyla was beautiful. She got me interested in art and politics. I admired her inventiveness. I wanted her badly but I wanted a relationship without strings. Do you remember the great conversations we had sometimes when the three of us ate together?'

'I don't know who was crazier, her or you,' said Nick. 'She wanted the whole world run by women, alternating with men year by year.'

'I had never met anyone like her before,' I said. 'She made a difference in my life. Her home country was Cape Verde archipelago in the Atlantic Ocean, 600 kilometres off the western coast of the African continent, near Senegal. It was a colony of Portugal until 1975. They speak Portuguese, also English.

'She was beautiful, exotic, with her oval face, small neat features and perfect dark skin framed by tightly woven corn plaits in a meticulous pattern. She told me all about her family. She had several siblings. Her father was harbour-master. She had left home to finish her schooling and lived with an aunt in Lisbon. She was awarded an

Australian Government scholarship, in a competition between Portuguese speaking school students, for the best student to study in Australia.

'Why Australia?' Nick asked.

'Her scholarship allowed her to study international development. She was very bright, had gone to a good school in Cape Verde and studied incredibly hard. She could be a credit to Australia in an international career.'

'My family made Twyla perfectly welcome, but I seldom went home and I grew away from my family and upbringing. My interest in socialism provoked my parents to argue with me, but I made up my mind independently. My visits home were strained.

'For the first time in my life I decided consciously what to believe in and who to befriend. Ambition stirred within me and I harnessed my free will to take me somewhere, to a destiny now concealed, which I was confident would soon emerge.'

'What happened with you and Twyla?'

'She was my girlfriend from early in second year. By the end of third year, we were still living separately in halls of residence and I used to sneak into her room. We had no verbal commitment but sleeping together occasionally ended the torture of abstinence, without me feeling I had crossed the line into a permanent relationship. I knew I was leaving at the end of the year and our planning didn't go any further than that.'

'I saw less of you in third year,' Nick said. 'I guess that was Twyla's influence?'

'I was very fond of Twyla. Our relationship was unusual because of the racial divide. In Brisbane in those days there weren't many black and white couples and there was a lot of prejudice. When we were together on the street, drunken youths called out: 'Wog fuckers!'

'What did you do?'

'Nothing. They were trying to annoy us. We ignored them. I was a sub-man, rejecting the passion they aroused in me. In retrospect, I regretted it.'

'Why did you regret it?'

'Twyla would have liked me better if I had punched them. Me ignoring it, probably widened the racial divide between us.'

'Ignoring them was probably the best way to defend her,' said Nick.

'Twyla didn't feel safe in Brisbane. It spoiled things for us.'

'It would have been upsetting for Twyla,' said Nick. 'It upset me too. Everyone who dealt with Twyla had quickly realised how lovely she was. I am ashamed that Australians rejected her.'

'Yes, she was a powerful distraction, but I worked hard,' I said. 'At the end of the year, I was offered a job with an oil company in Canada to help plan development of a project to exploit the Athabasca tar sands. Emigration meant parting from Twyla. She was starting third year. I couldn't take her to my job and I didn't want to stay in Brisbane with her, or with anyone. I was 20 and unprepared to commit to a relationship.

'Because I was a sub-man, I made myself blind and deaf to her attractions, without love and without desire. It was fear in the face of existence, unable to face the risks and tensions which love implied.

'We decided that if we really had what it takes to commit permanently, we should test it by separating for a year or two. We were both in our first relationship and I wanted more experience. It was difficult to know if there was a line between what we had and true love. That was why we were separating.

'Twyla came to the airport to see me off. My parents were there. Our parting was sad, for our plans to get back together were vague. We had been together for two years and we were very affectionate.'

'I hope you'll write often,' she said.

CHAPTER 6 TAKING RISKS

In my first job in Canada, I missed Twyla with constant craving and realised that what we had was special for me. We wrote regularly and I imagined that we would get together at some time in the indeterminate future. I threw myself into my work. I became a strong contributor to a project team, earning a good salary.

'Your physics skills will enable you to help prepare our feasibility study,' they said. 'You'll soon pick up the engineering jargon.'

I was learning an exciting new profession in a well paid job and could afford adventurous recreations. I learned to fly light planes at an air force base near my work. I loved aerobatics, but loathed the tedium of checklists, navigation and flying straight and level. I discovered from several near accidents that I was better suited to low routine activities and tried free-fall parachuting, hang gliding, wind surfing and base jumping.

I met Tembo, a base jumper.

'Where do you jump?' I asked him.

'In the mountains,' he said. 'There's a cliff in the Rockies.'

'How do you get there?'

'We drive in and then go up in a helicopter.'

'How many jumps have you made?'

'Heaps.'

'Tell me about it.'

'Last weekend I jumped down 2 kilometres vertically,' Tembo said. 'I wore a lycra bodysuit with a hood and a parachute pack. The suit has stubby wings under the arms. I ran and dived out from the top of the cliff, steering with my wings and going down through a chasm. I sped down a valley beside cliffs until I soared over the landing ground, pulled the rip cord and landed on my feet.'

'How long did it take?'

'About 40 seconds.'

'What did it feel like?'

'Out of this world,' said Tembo. 'It seemed to last for ages. There's nothing like it. It's tremendously exciting. Your mind races but time crawls, with mountains rushing past and the ground looming up. It drives everything else out of your head.'

'Is that why you do it?'

'I get a rush, a huge buzz, beyond anything else,' he said. 'It's like being reborn with new awareness of the world.'

'Is it like a near death experience?'

'Maybe it is: I could have died.'

'So is it the danger that attracts you?'

'No,' Tembo said. 'It's fun and no more dangerous than crossing the road.'

'What are the risks?'

'Your chute might not open properly, or you could get tangled up. A beginner might fly into the mountainside, or freeze, not pull the rip cord and crash.'

'Could there be winds?'

'We don't jump when it's windy,' said Tembo. 'But sometimes there are gusts.'

'Have you ever been frightened?'

'I was petrified the first time, but now I'm used to it.'

'Falling 2 kilometres vertically in 40 seconds is 180 kilometres an hour,' I said.

'It's terminal velocity, as fast as air resistance will let you go.'

'How quick did it seem?'

'It was serene, not quick at all,' said Tembo. 'Those 40 seconds went on for longer than any other 40 seconds I have ever lived.'

'Did they last as long as four 100 metre sprints would take?' I asked.

'It seemed longer: unhurried cruising.'

'It is an illusion,' I said. 'We're beguiled to believe we operate constantly. Because you seem to be speeding up as you get closer to the ground, it seems like it is taking longer than it really does.'

'That's right,' Tembo said, nodding. 'It's the Kappa effect. People overestimate elapsed time when stimuli are repeated with increase of the spatial distance traversed. I assumed I was going faster than I really was.'

'It made your experience of time seem unreally long?'

'Yes. Chance, you are one cool piece of work,' said Tembo. 'Your mind is doing physics all the time.'

Tembo invited me to jump with him. The next weekend and we jumped in tandem.

'It was an experience I wouldn't have missed,' I said afterwards, 'but I won't go again, thank you. I have found out what I wanted to know: which is that perception of time can vary. I am going to investigate time perception in other situations.'

I strove to be a serious man, as described by De Beauvoir. My base-jumping experience was done responsibly. I had freedom but I subordinated it to the rules of base-jumping because there was too much anxiety and doubt without that. I had chosen for my recreation a physically constrained world and forgotten my goal was freedom. Plunging from cliffs denied my freedom, making me a serious man in a limited universe. I willed myself to be a god; but I was not one and knew it. Had I been more active and experimented at base-jumping, I could have become a demon in surreal revolt against conventional morality. I had begun responsibly, but in other compartments of my life I continued to blunder.

I had been in Canada two months when Nick wrote that Twyla was pregnant. I had been oblivious to this risk. It was a huge shock of responsibility. I phoned her.

'Nick said you're pregnant.'

'Yes.'

'What do you want me to do?'

'It's not yours,' she said.

'What? Whose is it?'

'You don't know him.'

'How could this happen?' I thought.

'Were you going with him when I was there?'

29

'No. Afterwards.'

'What is he going to do?'

'I don't know yet but you don't have to worry.'

'I will worry. If he doesn't do the right thing, I will.'

'Thank you but it won't be necessary. You don't need to be concerned about me.'

She ended the call.

It was unexpected, without my understanding, on the other side of the world. I was hurt that Twyla had betrayed us so soon after I left. It wasn't like her to suddenly have an affair. I had thought if she did, she should have written to tell me.

It seemed possible that the child could be mine and recalling how I was set against having a baby and I didn't want to be committed. Perhaps she didn't want me to know. Possibly she had made up her story to hide having a termination.

The thought that she could be removing my child from me broke my heart. Overriding it was the guilt, loss of her trust and grief at the termination. I tried phoning and calling without success for several weeks. Then I found out she had left the university. It was a tragedy, for she was a promising scholar. I felt my support for her had been deficient and her rejection of me unfair. I was hurt and it changed me. I became depressed, unable to sleep, manic, going into care for two months.

Afterwards I was serious, always. I wrote to her a couple of times, but she didn't reply. Her memory faded and I took up with a girl I met. It felt like double-timing and I couldn't write to Twyla again. It took several years to stop wanting her.

For recreation, I skied and played rugby. I read Steinbeck and Hemingway action novels. I also dabbled in the environment and political matters. My views clashed with those of people on the political left. I despised unions, because in my view they enabled freeloaders to ride on the backs of diligent performers. But I was blind to capitalists riding on the backs of workers and my views were often at odds with both workers and managements. I was a lone dissenter.

30

I read Ayn Rand's novels 'Atlas Shrugged' and 'The Fountainhead' and was seduced by her idea that selfishness was 'virtuous concern with one's own interests'.

I took venturesome vacations from my job to exotic locations. Responsible and careful at work, on holidays I took risks others refused.

In Peru, on a backpacking visit to Macchu Picchu, I walked at night along a narrow uneven trail winding around a precipitous Andean gorge. It was a moonless night and a friend and I were one step from stepping off the footpath and plunging down the vertical mountainside. I held on to his belt in front of me, to stop him falling from the trail. Then it was my turn in front. We stumbled along for three hours, blindly risking certain death. The sensation of peril was entrancing, as if this experience would strengthen my hold on life. Afterwards, I felt elated, as I did after landing from a stormy passage in a yacht. The proximity to death made ordinary existence seem mundane and the uncertainty sublime.

Another time, I was crewing on a yacht cruising up the coast of Brazil to Recife. When we arrived in the shallow harbour, we moored a kilometre out from shore. Our crew of 7, composed of 6 men and 1 girl, Nina, together rowed to the yacht club in the ship's tender to get provisions and quaff sundowners. At dusk we rowed back blithely drunk, overloaded with provisions, with little freeboard. We were fooling around, rowing through breaking waves, when we capsized half a kilometre from shore. We were in the sea surrounded by floating bottles of beer and packages of groceries. I had started swimming to land, when I heard the girl's voice.

'I can't swim,' Nina spluttered.

The others were out of earshot and I went back to her. Under her, with her arms around my neck, I swam backstroke, until I was exhausted. I tasted oil and heard a shout from the darkness ahead.

'There's an oil slick. If you follow the beach to your right, there's a way through.'

31

With Nina kicking too, we eventually reached the beach and walked back to the yacht club, where we used paper towels and diesel oil to wipe off the black muck covering us.

'Be careful with the diesel,' Nina said. 'It can poison you through your skin.'

But I didn't listen and later I collapsed with heatstroke. I lay on my sick bunk in a serious condition for two days and it seemed I might die.

I was barely conscious when I heard the captain say: 'We'll put the hippy overboard.'

I began to get better immediately.

I had enjoyed rescuing Nina and it had been worth it. Taking risks had compensations.

Gradually I became more discerning about which risks were worth taking.

I had spoken with steel workers when they descended to the ground from erecting skyscrapers and bridges. They had safety equipment but neglected to use it when it inhibited their movements. They were accustomed to hazardous work. Their attention was on what they had to do, rather than on what could go wrong.

I was independent and liked to make up my own mind about risks. I resisted when others tried to make decisions for me. I deplored being herded like a sheep. I would dance across city streets, without using zebra crossings, teasing oncoming vehicles like a toreador in a bullring. I crossed against pedestrian lights, jinking and side stepping. It was my role in life to defy fate, dodging and dancing away from danger.

'I can do what I want with my life. No-one has any liens on me,' I said.

The chances I took were calculated risks, by weighing up the frequency of consequences against expected costs. If benefits would exceed costs, I would do it. I tried to be rational but my evaluation could be affected by my mood. When the outcome excited me, I accepted more risk.

I had by now learned my company's technology and planned my work with confidence. When I accepted to supervise an earthworks project, I believed it would be easy.

'I can do this,' I said, without qualms.

The task was to excavate, with a contractor's scrapers and a dozer, a ramp down to the seam of mineral for a new open-cut mine. For a mining engineer, it would have been a small task. But I had inadvertently taken on more risk than I could manage. Noticing I was a novice, the scraper drivers drove crazily fast and could have rolled their machines, killing themselves. I was responsible for their safety and would be blamed. I had no experience of supervising this type of machine, nor men like these. When I ordered them to drive sensibly, they drove even faster.

I worried and didn't sleep for several days, becoming unable to function. My boss came and relieved me of my responsibility. I took two weeks off work with emotional exhaustion before returning to work. I was ashamed that I had failed my supervision assignment. Later, when they needed supervisors for other tasks, I was not selected.

I liked to think I was not driven by my ego, but it had been my ego that accepted the supervision task. Chance was my name and I was a player in the game of life, taking risks naturally. I should have said: 'I don't know how to do it.' I had wanted more responsibility and seized the opportunity because I was feeling unfulfilled and unloved in my job. The risk enticed my ambition, despite the gamble it entailed.

Chance is not simply the drawing of lots, but raising the stakes in every attempt to master chance through the will to power, and giving rise to the risk of an even greater chance.
Foucault (9)

I took risks of trial and error that gambolled with my personal well-being, until I learned to be circumspect and approach new situations with caution. I had been lucky to escape from immersion in oil with heat stroke. I had worried unnecessarily at the mine, bringing mental exhaustion. Subsequently, I became more careful, a serious man, with growing confidence of my efficacy and worth.

The stigma I suffered in mining supervision put a damper on my ambition to be a project manager. I realised I had limitations. I wasn't sure what to do with my life. I took a year off from my job to travel and hoped that I would discover a new mission.

Now I avoided uncertainty and unfamiliar situations.

'Once bitten twice shy,' I said to explain my risk aversion.

The unpleasant consequences of my risk taking precipitated me into wanting self-mastery and control of my work environment. Nietzsche tells how the spirit of the *camel* grew to want to dominate the lonely desert like a *lion*, going wherever he wanted, leading a heroic life existentially.

CHAPTER 7 NAIVETY

Taking leave from my engineering job in Canada, I headed south in my station wagon, destination Panama. I stayed in a basic hotel at Oaxaca in Mexico and tried to locate the type of hallucinogenic mushrooms The Beatles were said to have eaten there. On the first evening, at a cafe in the town square, I met two American girls and invited them and a couple of hippy guys back to my hotel room. I was an adventurer ready for new experiences.

We smoked a couple of joints and talked. Then the guys said they were going to crash and left. The two girls stayed and I thought I might score with the friendly one. We chatted and after a while the other one left to go to her room, leaving the two of us together. I put my arm around her and tried to kiss her, but she pushed me away.

My experience of Australian girls had been that their resistance was token and could be overcome by persistence. When I tried to hold her, affectionately, this girl from New York reacted as if I was going to rape her.

'Back off,' she screamed. 'I don't want you. Haven't I made that plain? Don't you have any respect?'

'Sorry,' I said.

It was the opposite of the amorous result I wanted. I had offended her and she stormed off to her room.

The next day I ran into her in a cafe, where she gave me a deep freeze.

'I am really very sorry,' I said abjectly.

'Okay,' she said, her face softening, but she made it plain she wanted nothing further to do with me. It was a salutary lesson. I liked her and I never ever again tried to hold any girl without her permission. Never had I experienced such vitriol. I had been naive and I blamed the Australian girls who had let me get away with it. I supposed the American girl was more liberated, having a different perception of her rights. Australian girls' resistance in my youth had been passive, wanting to avoid confrontation. Their wooden responses had been enough of a turn off for me. I had wanted to be gentle and the girl's complaint had hurt my pride. She had dealt with me as a tyrant, who cared only for my pleasure and glory. I concluded American girls were more assertive, in the same way that when their men were frustrated they punched walls, doors and cars. Perhaps Americans were more definite — leaving less to chance than Australians.

The incident left a bad taste in my mouth. I drove on to the Pacific coast, where I slept in a hammock on a beach for two weeks and body surfed. I was with a couple from Australia and together we bought several kilograms of Acapulco Gold, potent marijuana grown locally. We smoked, talked, slept and surfed in rotation. It was blissful. I was so spaced out; I didn't care what happened to me. When waves tumbled me under, I had difficulty finding the surface and was lucky not to drown.

When I resumed my travels, I stashed a kilo under the dashboard, among the electrical wires. An American traveller stopped with us for several days and secreted several kilos under the floor of his camper van. He said he was wanted in the US for taking pot across the border.

'The FBI are hunting for drug runners in Mexico, killing them at will.'

Undeterred, he departed for the USA with his cargo. A few days later there was a newspaper story with a picture of his van burned out by the highway. A body had been found beside it. I was chilled.

A person's response to danger is decided in a marble-sized part of the brain, the amygdala, under the back of the head. In adolescents and young adult males, it responds weakly to danger, but with age it puts out adrenalin to freeze, fight or flee. After age 30 males become more adept at avoiding danger by these strategies.

I was 24 and my peril barely registered with me. I drove across Mexico, through Yucutan and down through the jungle into Belize. I was aware my stash could be penalized crossing the border, possibly as a capital offence, but the risk seemed low. I did not fear the FBI or consider what the Australian government's response would be if I was caught. The grass-like stench in my vehicle made my hiding place obvious but I continued because I was an adventurer, seeking kudos from other hippies by law-breaking. They knew of my adventures and I imagined they admired me. Now, decades later, I doubt there could be any danger to me from writing about my drug trafficking. No kudos remains.

Much to my relief, the border guards let me in without a search.

In Belize City I met some locals returned from New York, wanting drugs to take back. They carried flick knives, threatened me and discovered my kilo. I gave it to them willingly, glad to see the back of it, because it was compromising my safety. My amygdala was active at last and I realised I had been lucky. I stayed away from bulk drugs after that and continued to Panama, then around South America by plane, trains, yachts and buses.

In further adventures, until I was 30, running risks was ritual with minimal caution. I had good fortune. I often travelled alone, but had interludes with companions. I travelled without tangible goals, enjoying escapades in exotic locations. In Central and South America I was hosted by Peace Corps volunteers and indulged in pot-induced nihilism with them.

My naive adventuring was solipsistic, an extension of my risk taking and irresponsibility when I was younger. I was aware of my trend towards bigger and bigger risks, but I did not imagine what could happen next. I had grown from a child, through adolescence, then as a teenager, to adventure as an adult, without a cause. But that was about to change.

ALLEGORY

CHAPTER 8 SPIRIT

I had studied the adult psychological types of De Beauvoir (5) and Nietzsche (12) in my philosophy class at university. These were the only books I took to Canada with me. I looked in them to find patterns emerging in my experiences there.

On my return to Canada from South America, my spirit had matured. I wanted my life to have continuity beyond the stages De Beauvoir described, following the pathway of Nietzsche's *spirit*. I began to emerge from the unfeeling De Beauvoir sub-man, with the despair of my blighted career path, becoming serious and adventuresome, eventually becoming Nietzsche's lion.

In the countries I had visited, I developed a passion for democratic government and I became caught up in activism for socialist government reform. My understanding of socialism was limited and my passion for it did not fulfil itself genuinely. I planned to study socialism and realize my passion when I returned to my job, knowing it would have to be a secret interest because the corporate ethos of my employer was adamantly anti-socialist.

On return to Canada, my spirit had been restored and I had a new understanding of my job. My experiences had opened my eyes. I was cynical and shunned the hamster wheel of remuneration and consumption. It was all too predictable. I had started as a lowly project engineer in a tall office building. My office space had a desk, a filing cabinet and a crudenza. Others near me did similar work in similar cubicles. Some of them had a carpet, or a picture on the wall, as rewards for conformance. There were meeting rooms and tables for viewing maps, collaborating and conferencing. I was always under surveillance, not just by my supervisor, but by co-workers. They pressured me into their recreational activities, preventing my escape from the intensely normative environment.

'Are you coming with us to Hawaii at Christmas?' a co-worker asked.

'No, I don't think so.'

'Most of us are going. We have a great time. You should come.'

'That's exactly why I wouldn't go. I would want to get away from work.'

'You'll be the odd one out.'

'Bugger off.'

My lifestyle centred on my occupation. I lacked friends and I felt isolated. My spirit was like a sheep in Nietzsche's parable, in a flock moving through savannah foothills, being transformed into a *camel*, a *lion* and finally into a *child.* Niezsche told of distinct parts in a life whose spirit evolved. I used the story to anticipate stages in my career.

'My spirit has to become a beast of burden, a *camel* who slaves, before transcending into a *lion* who is king of his domain,' I wrote to Nick in Australia.

'It will be a change for you to slave,' he wrote back. 'You are used to doing what you want.'

In my job I knew I was being conditioned by expectations of superiors and colleagues but I only slowly became aware of how very extensive was this influence. By reading the post-modern theory of Foucault (10) I realised that I was conditioned by performance standards, rewards, reprimands and remediation. In my annual review, my performance evaluation was average, as if I had been tolerated. After doing my utmost to please, it was disappointing.

Looking back, my subjection was unconscious. The power that reformed my behaviour was invisible and ubiquitous. I suppose I must have been aware of some of the influences and my attitude gradually took on some passive resistance. My colleagues were all in some degree less than assiduous in following leaders' directions and expectations. My behaviour was modulated from conformance to acceptable efficiency. Others had negative performance evaluation too and it was a loss for the company, productivity being only a fraction of the potential.

There was nothing I could do to improve my position except to defend myself from other denizens of the desert. I had wanted to be creative and esteemed. To survive, I had to look out for myself and this meant doing whatever my supervisor wanted. His control demanded I do certain tasks, at certain times, performing for his colleagues, who would approve or reject my performance.

'I can hardly believe how powerless I am,' I thought.

Frustrated at work, I was wild playing rugby and at club parties.

My magnificent old Jaguar Mark VII had a footbrake that didn't work. I was unable to obtain in Canada a replacement for the brake master cylinder. It was a heavy car and to slow it down, I had to resort to stemming across its trajectory, as one does on skis by turning sideways to check progress. In a straight run downhill, without an intersection, I weaved with tyres howling. To avoid traffic lights, I sometimes had to turn abruptly on to a side road.

My escapades, laughing at private danger, relieved the frustration of my careful job. My position was in the herd, undistinguished yet.

CHAPTER 9 HERD

My spiritual progress emulated the life stages in *Thus Spoke Zarathustra*. At first I imagined my spirit was desperately seeking recognition but finding only nihilism. I was conscious of my lack of achievement and my position was lowly. My sheep had to become a camel before I would be useful to the corporation.

With growing experience, I identified as member of a *herd*. The others wanted to be burdened as little as possible, caring only to reach abundant pasture, content with lives that were safe, quiet and relatively wealthy, without surprises. Held together by mutual interest and little affection, having an aversion for any kind of risk, we relied on our unelected herdsman CEO to tell us what to do.

Our herd was crossing a vast hostile, unforgiving, lonely and dangerous desert. Nietzsche's allegory could be set in the Serengeti Desert, where wildebeest wended between grazing places, stalked by lions. I had few opportunities, many hardships and stiff competition to move up the shallow hierarchy of the herd.

I was one of a project engineering species. My peers were mainly boomer generation, with strong work ethics, self-assured, competitive, goal-centred, resourceful, mentally focused, team oriented and disciplined by managers. I wanted to ascend to be a herd leader, but the desert in Nietzsche's story had only a few oases where herbivores watered. In between, there was little opportunity for advancement. Fierce predators pulled down the weak, unless the group defended them. Colleagues who deviated, or had bad luck, quietly disappeared. In retaliation for a misdemeanour, they moved in the walls of a colleague's office until he quit. There was depressing intellectual aridity, little hope of promotion and cynical suspicion of my physics training.

I was socially shy, concealing my feelings and lacking empathy with the others. Their efforts were half-hearted. They declined work when they could and relied on their managers to indicate activities that would bring easy rewards. I was one of a few who put in more than minimum hours. Most did their hours, took their pay, took their holidays and took their superannuation, without ever imagining they had other choices and could delay gratification. Most herd engineers simply took care of their families, went to work and conformed.

In my thoughts, I remained independent from the herd, nursing secret passions from my travels for socialist reform of governments. My ambition now was to achieve a high position in a private or public organisation. I could not proclaim my passions for peace and world government. Social reform remained my unfulfilled subjectivity. I was frustrated and alienated. Earlier, I had been an adventurer, caring only for my pleasure or my glory. Now my ego was involved and I was not getting the fulfilment I badly wanted.

After a year, I landed my first professional assignment, but the task was menial. My role was to adopt our group's working methods, moving with the herd, avoiding accidents, avoiding unnecessary risks and respecting authorities.

I wanted work that was more interesting and more responsible, but good engineering projects were few and far between. Engineers competed fiercely, but covertly, to be assigned to exciting projects for leverage up the hierarchy. They could gain: managerial privileges; assistants; high pay; innovative projects; external assignments; kudos; overseas travel; and an expense account.

The best assignments were few and hard to come by. Opportunities were not widely known and ambitious engineers touted their curriculum vitae to managers who could inform them of openings and influence their selection. Rivals eyed each other jealously and rushed in an undignified mob to stake their claims, crowding the most popular prospects with their bids in a Matthew Effect. Mischief-makers started rumours and lemming-like rushes occurred, sometimes over cliffs when illusions were discovered.

Hoping for promotion, I applied to sit the company's management aptitude test, completing a questionnaire at my desk.

The questions were multi-choice and some were puzzling. I was asked 'Which would you prefer, to work as a truck driver, or as a ballet dancer?' Another was: 'Did you ever want to have sex with your mother?'

Puzzled by the relevance of the questions, I spoke to the human resource manager administering the test, a psychologist.

'How will they decide which answers indicate management aptitude?'

'There are no right answers', he said. 'We pick out oddballs. If your answers are similar to the others', you are suitable. If yours are weird, management is not for you.'

'So a manager should be able to predict how the group will respond on moral and ethical issues?'

'Yes, exactly. A good manager has to be able to anticipate underlings.'

'Won't applicants' answers merely show their sycophancy rather than their moral values?'

'Managers' empathy with the hierarchy is most relevant.'

'That is a prescription for autocracy in a stable environment. But ours is dynamic, with changing tasks, development and innovation. Managers need to have creative leadership abilities.'

'Sorry, we don't test for that.'

My concern was ignored and my oddball status confirmed when I was not selected. My peers' attitudes were unknown to me in my isolation. I had to be content to be in the herd as a project engineering sheep. I despised the dullness of management.

I was allocated a desk sharing an office with a middle-aged geologist who explained to me the company's exploration methods. I became friendly with him and he had time to answer my rookie questions. I wondered why he was sidelined.

He swigged milk throughout the working day.

'I have an ulcer,' he said. 'It could kill me. It's my nerves.'

He was off sick for weeks at a time.

He gave me career advice.

'Take it easy or you'll end up with an ulcer like mine.'

I was habitually anxious, unable to relax as I struggled to conform. It was oppressive and I began getting stomach pains.

My doctor was not reassuring.

'Stop worrying about your work,' said the doctor. 'Get used to it. Unless you stop worrying, it will kill you.'

The sombre prognosis came as a shock to me. I worried about becoming a mindless drudge running on the corporate hamster wheel. My health was affected, until I stopped churning my frustrated thoughts endlessly and pointlessly at home. I was anxious about my failures and others' successes but I didn't know what I could do differently. I put my head down and worked as hard as I could, hoping things would improve.

I was held back from prominence in the herd because I was a passionate man. I cared and was emotionally involved in everything. My affectation for social reform was not wanted, and would be opposed if it was known. My secrecy was disloyal and made me anxious.

CHAPTER 10 CAMEL

My *camel* spirit emerged from my growing identity as a serious man.

It took me several years to master my employer's business. I studied academic subjects at night, supplementing my on-the-job learning of engineering with humanities and other disciplines that could help me gain promotion. I helped co-workers, giving advice or assistance when needed, always taking on heavy loads. I did not seek recognition and because I was discrete, my presence became relied on and valued. I knew what everyone was doing and I used my understanding for the benefit of the group. They relied on my memory of what had happened and accepted my narratives of the group's history.

My spirit was like a camel's, rejoicing in strength of body and mind, carrying the herd's heavy burdens across the desert, serving it loyally and reliably, becoming the most valued individual.

I kept my vaunting ambition hidden from the animals of the herd, to reduce competition. I strove to earn the esteem of my manager and my group, by prodigious hard work. I gained a reputation as a man of the world. I was so useful, I couldn't be replaced and they kept me down with the herd in menial roles, without promotion.

'You do a good job,' my manager said, 'because I manage you.'

'I don't need you.' I said, because we were friends.

'You need me more than you realise. I protect and nurture you. You would be lost without me.'

'I want my own show or I'm leaving.'

I was determined not to follow in the footsteps of the geologist who shared my office, ulcerating on the company treadmill. I resented the corporate control system, with surveillance in glass-walled offices, normalised by a morally aggressive office culture and evaluated by opaque self-serving supervisors. The pay was good but insufficient to induce me to run in their hamster wheel, under surveillance like a prisoner in Jeremy Bentham's panopticon.

I resigned.

I would resume my journey as a *camel* with another organisation. My experience was portable and would stand me in good stead. My employer was loathe to see me go.

'You have a bright future here,' my boss said. 'A management position is in the offing.'

But I had shot my bolt. If I stayed, having threatened to resign, I would be despised for disloyalty.

'No thank you,' I said.

I returned to Australia, where I obtained a position in a Brisbane petroleum consultancy.

I was quickly accepted by my new employer in menial roles essential to their engineering business, familiar to my experience as a *camel*. My position was clerk in their head office, without line responsibility, coordinating administration. I knew the procedures and etiquette for consulting other specialties, stakeholder organisations and governments.

The project engineering teams I coordinated moved with me, like Nietzsche's *camel* in a caravan, across the commercial landscape, with profitable cargoes. Routes were well established and I pioneered new business. But the limited scope of my responsibilities continued to frustrate my ambitions.

My role was to hold and improve my company's position in profiting by exploiting petroleum resources and drilling rights granted to us by the government.

'Our main resource is Government relations,' our CEO proclaimed.

I was assigned to use my financial analysis skills to obtain tax concessions and minimise payment of corporation taxes. My physics wasn't wanted. In our engineering circles, innovations discussed were mainly financial. They had little interest in developing any technology, preferring to import it.

I was almost crushed by the mundanity of my tasks, but survived in the desert, gaining self-confidence with experience. I accepted my burden, increasingly taking command and organising the other engineers, strengthening the consultancy. My behaviour was always honourable and for the benefit of the group.

I studied at night Nietzsche's writings and rejoiced in my strength, in my will to power and the way others trusted me. I was egotistical, longing to control the domain and hankering after higher education to develop my abilities and achieve a glorious destiny. But I couldn't apply my wide learning without having higher qualifications in the core business, engineering.

The desert was lonely and I no longer wanted to promote plans that were not my own. I desired to unburden myself and take control of my own destiny, asserting *'I will.'*

Nick James, my friend from undergraduate days, was still in Brisbane and had become a long-haired disciple. He worked as a volunteer for an environmental organisation, evaluating government energy policies, preparing campaign materials in visual and print media. He supplied me with pot and followed me everywhere. We smoked together at home.

My manager welcomed my usurpation of coordination but kept management control from me, which was frustrating. It was natural to want to be elevated to where I could serve from a command position. I dealt successfully with the company's problems and I gained confidence, asserting my will in the territory I knew so well, where I had slaved ignominiously.

Domination was denied me. Opportunities to develop the engineering prowess I needed were taken by engineers with higher degrees. Exciting pioneering tasks were snapped up by PhDs on secondment from the corporate research centre, who were given precedence. I was confident of understanding the organisation's terrain and I had theories that could change production, but I was without a PhD and my analytical skills were overlooked. I was the strongest contributor in department meetings and forums, but I was left with the tedious work to do, as reliever of others' burdens, fighter of others' battles and collector of scars. I supported others, holding the consultancy together. Glamorous leadership was the province of the hierarchy and it was denied to me.

In Homer's story in the Iliad, Achilles was a warrior who could choose to live a short, unhappy, but glorious life and be remembered for all eternity. Or alternatively, he could live a long, happy, peaceful life, but would soon be forgotten. Achilles chose to strive for glory.

My *camel* would go for glory too, even if the path would be short and unhappy. I wanted to be remembered for contributing to the community. But I was valued as a *camel*, a beast of burden, having physical strength and useful skills, but it was a menial role that lacked opportunities to express my creativity.

To achieve a *lion* role, I needed to obtain a personal domain and hold it carefully.

I had learned that freedom could not be obtained at the expense of others. Privileges had to be earned.

I worked hard for my employer and gained respect as a serious man. I had failed to fulfil the trust placed in me earlier as a mine supervisor. Now I avoided taking risks. I may have been deluded in feeling my self-importance growing, but I was getting closer to my goal of obtaining an independent territory. People knew what I stood for and my zeal was almost fanatical.

Nietzsche tells how the spirit of the *camel* grew to want to dominate the lonely desert like a *lion*, going wherever he wanted, leading a heroic life existentially. To achieve a *lion* role, I needed to obtain a personal domain and hold it carefully.

CHAPTER 11 LION

It took me a year to grow into Nietzsche's *lion* role. I cultivated a *can do* image and became widely respected.

I lived alone and enjoyed being a bachelor and going on casual dates. I continued to play social rugby, vying with the players for women who watched our games. My team position was in the scrum, with body contact an outlet for my aggression. Collisions and head knocks were frequent, on one occasion narrowly escaping disabling spinal injury. My skill was in tackling. After our games, my bruised shoulders couldn't support my arms to steer my car and I had to be driven home. Gradually I learned from painful experience to appear willing, but to minimize my exposure to violence. I hung back in loose play. I took care of myself, drinking little, being gentle with our girl followers. I played responsibly.

'Chance, you're becoming staid,' said one of my team mates.

I had realised that freedom and risks should not be at the expense of others.

'Once bitten twice shy,' I said to explain my caution. How I conduct myself is none of your business. Go f**k yourself.'

I met Georgina at work. She was a manager in the systems department. She was conducting a workshop to update the consultants with a new computer system. I was impressed by her good looks, high rank, succinct talk and well-informed content.

'I try not to be pedantic,' she said when I complimented her on her presentation. 'When people want to know something, I find it best to let them ask.'

'That supposes you have the answer.'

'I wing it and hope for the benefit of the doubt.'

'You fooled me. I look forward to your next session.'

'Me too. Bye.'

I went to several other events she ran and we became friendly. She was my favourite manager, interested in my work.

One morning as I arrived at work she rode up in the lift with me.

'We could go for a drink after work,' she suggested when we were alone.

'I'd like that,' I said.

On our second date, I took her home to my bed. She was an energetic lover, but not unpleasantly so. I began to have plans for her. She could help me in my campaign to be a *lion*. Her help could be useful for guiding my climb up the hierarchy. Later I realised she was taking over my career.

Georgina's management position gave her a wider perspective of corporate issues than mine. I was fascinated by her experience of the traditions, ideologies and moral values in everyday decisions, such as promotions and new products. Through her insights, I was becoming a better *lion*.

The business vista she opened up to me was a spectacle of capitalism, corporate greed and management self-interest. It was the autocratic reign of the capitalist economy identified by a Frenchman, Guy Debord (14). His 'spectacle' was any procession of images, promulgated by media, that served to keep consumers asleep or totally unaware of their material reality rooted in exploitation.

She also gave me an insight into corporate disaffection for government.

'Every type of primary industry in Australia is involved in rapacious profiting from natural resources and government largesse,' she said. 'Government mismanagement gives handouts that put private business earnings from production activities in the shade. Consequently, skilled personnel like you are assigned to investment analysis instead of using your skills for technological development to benefit society.'

Georgina's cynicism revealed to me the 'spectacle', as a double tragedy of unhappy workers in shit jobs, earning money to sublimate into shitty purchases that don't bring happiness, both groups sponsored by and kept in misery, by middle class capitalists. Debord's theory assumed workers were alienated as workers and purchasers: he wanted more lower class revolution, as an adjunct to Karl Marx's theory in Das Kapital (1867) and the Russian Revolution. But Debord's concept of a revolution would be cultural disruption, rather than uprisings and strikes or violence.

I tried to interest Georgina in opposing the spectacle, but she was an apologist for capitalism and wouldn't accept the premises of Debord's spectacle.

'People make a free choice whether to engage in or disengage from the spectacle,' she said. 'Workers would have the most freedom. In theory, the spectacle could deliver a utopian society based on capitalism. The spectacle could be the main thing diverting people from bloody revolutions like the Russian and French Revolutions.'

'If you believe that, you are missing Debord's message,' I said. 'He was concerned about lack of freedom:

"The consumer spectacle is the most efficient way to pacify the working class and to make workers shut the fuck up about their shitty lives of exploitation and alienation. Everybody is working their asses off to be able to go home at night and watch TV, with advertisements depicting idyllic scenes colonizing social life.'

'The spectacle is a cynical idea, that people are manipulated to attend entertainments and purchase food and other goods, not by pleasure, nor by social rivalry, but by the suppliers' sensational propaganda in media, that present images to lure customers with advertising,' said Georgina. 'The peoples' real desires, for community and intimacy with loved ones, is neglected.'

'The tragedy is that the spectacle, commodified as different products obtained at various venues, is the only experience the lower class get,' I said.

'The Australian lifestyle keeps most workers consuming happily and going to work to pay for it,' she said. 'They can't imagine having more freedom. There is no possibility of a revolution soon.'

I realized Georgina and I were intractably opposed. She promoted the spectacle in my territory as an agent. She threatened my reform of the capitalist system. It was in her nature to fight me and any change I wanted. I accepted her challenge. We were locked in ritual combat, mitigated by our lustful sexual relationship.

I maintained a vigil over the boundaries of my projects and kept out invaders from other projects, asserting my dominant will, seeing off competitors with prodigious roaring. I could say '*I will*' to whatever I wanted, because I created my own values, with freedom to fulfil my destiny.

At last I was away from the herd and the desert was mine. The desert my spirit ruled over was empty, the way I wanted it, fighting when necessary to keep it under my control. My spirit was free and I could climb the hierarchy to the top by any means. I was much happier now.

CHAPTER 12 DRAGON

Nietzsche's allegory (12) predicted the *lion* would be opposed by a *dragon*. Georgina was a middle class opportunist without beliefs or allegiance to anyone and I was left in her wake. I had realised she opposed me and now this was a problem.

My mind was on my job and I was content to be a fuck buddy. When Georgina connived with my mother for us to marry, I was having difficulty at work and didn't notice until it was too late. My mother did not allow for my not wanting to be married. I was reluctant because it would divert me from my work, which was my main interest. I foolishly agreed and we had a small registry office wedding and moved into an apartment together.

'I am not going to worry about you any more,' my mother said. She meant well, assuming my wife would care for me, but Georgina was only interested in herself.

After marrying, a new phase of my life began. Whenever I tried to take control of a task, either at work or at home, Georgina would interfere. I learned too late that managers and their subordinates do not have stable partnerships. Co-workers can idly interfere with the couple. Georgina had little liking for me and tried to dominate me. She was the very devil of a dragon.

I had married hastily without knowing her private self. She pursued leisure with her friends, leaving me to repent.

'After they married me to her, I realised I didn't want her,' I said to Nick.

'You married a manager,' he said. 'You didn't know her as a person.'

Georgina was demanding, unpleasant and intent on destroying my self-possession. She attacked me without provocation, openly criticising those things I cared most about, especially my work.

Living with her was like a nightmare without escape. As Nietzsche had predicted, she was a *dragon* who contested the *lion's* territory. She wanted control over him personally, not over territory.

Her challenges to my control infuriated me. She raided my ego like a terrorist. I reacted by surrendering, sulking, counter-attacking or raging. She was a more powerful adversary and usually I was the loser.

Her assumption that her seniority at work should give her precedent authority at home was irritating.

'I don't want you organising my things,' I said.

'But they're all over the place.'

'That's the way I like them. They stay in my space and I know where they are.'

Her unreasonableness had removed all joy from my life, driving a wedge between us. I strove to spend my time collecting and analysing data, using it to dominate my domain.

I put in long hours at the firm and lost sight of the individual I wanted to be. My life should have had bold designs and bright colours, not the tepid fare of Georgina's company. I lacked the recognition and self esteem I needed to shore up my failing ego.

Instead of helping me, Georgina had jackbooted into my work like a storm trooper. When I spoke formally in public, or informally at parties, she was always the first to display lack of interest or opposition. She would go behind my back, bad-mouth my ability and deride my respect for others. She took sides with authorities whose ideas contradicted mine, creating enmity.

My *lion* had subdued all those in the corporate desert, except the incumbent lord, the *dragon* Georgina. My spirit clashed with hers, still opposed after centuries of fighting each other. Her antipathy was ancient and enemy of my self-mastery. She embodied the tradition of all the values that had come before us that the *lion* required her permission to thwart. Neither of us would ever compromise. To become lord of the desert and win his freedom, the *lion* had to vanquish the *dragon*.

She was a barrier to true freedom. She blocked my *lion's* will, saying *NO* when I contested values created previously.

My skirmishes with Georgina entrenched our hostility.
'Why are you starting a degree course in psychology like mine?'
I asked her. I had started studying online.
'Why shouldn't I?' she said grinning.
'Are you trying to compete with me?' I asked her.
'Why would I do that?' she said.
I didn't reply but thought: *To try and dominate me.*

It crossed my mind that she could be insane. Georgina the *dragon* was a feminist driven by opposition to patriarchy and antipathy to males.

My career had commenced learning to serve others, using my strength to carry heavy loads, like a *camel* plying across the desert. I grew wanting to be in control and Georgina's opposition was destructive. I had fought to make the desert territory my own, but fighting her was futile. We had nothing in common. It was a tragedy that I hadn't recognised our fundamental opposition, until after I was married to her. I had been blinded by her work persona and blamed her for deceiving me about the rest. The worst part was her lack of affection.

After moving in, she changed to a new type of IUD. I had made my disinterest in having a child clear to her.

'Thank you for taking care with contraception,' I said.

'It's okay for a short time.'

'No, it's for the foreseeable future. We are not going to have a baby and we need contraception until I have finished my PhD,' I said. 'We agreed before we were married.'

My contest with Georgina for control surfaced when she dropped a bombshell.

'I want to have a baby now,' she said.

I would not be pushed like this. My *lion* asserted its indomitable will to power assigned by Nietzsche.

'Not yet! You agreed to wait until I had finished my PhD!' I roared.

Having a baby would be a grounding experience, whereas I wanted to be able to think abstractly in tranquillity. I had several years of my PhD before me and if we had a baby, the interruption would derail my work. My nights would be disrupted by noise and my days by visits to medical specialists.

Still she persisted in wanting a baby.

In the ensuing struggle, I tried to develop my role as an overman. I reminded her of our agreement when she moved in. I sensed betrayal. She was trying to seize sexual control beyond our agreement. At first I had enjoyed socialising as a couple but Georgina's conversations were dull. I missed dating single females. My life became unpleasantly certain. I tried to hold on to personal control, but alone and vulnerable I slipped into a dark place. In the industrial desert I had become a coordinator and manager, but with the obstacle of Georgina in my way I couldn't be the *lion* I wanted to be

I quit my job at the consultancy and applied for a national grant to study for a PhD in physics, at the same university where I had done my first degree.

'You've returned to Go,' said Nick when I told him. He was still working in environmental science. 'You always did like physics.'

'You didn't ask me about quitting your job,' Georgina said.

'It's none of your business,' I said. 'I changed because you were not respecting my control at work.'

'I was trying to help you.'

I recalled her gossiping with my colleagues.

'I don't need that type of help,' I said.

Fighting with her was futile but finishing with her would admit failure. I hardly knew her and I was focussed on her shortfalls. Our relationship had become unpleasant and there was no way back.

'I want you to move out,' I told her.

After Georgina had left, my freedom as a postgraduate student was wonderful, a relief from the nastiness between us.

I moved my things into a different bedroom and had nothing more to do with her. I was relieved when she left. The hurt was sharp, like pulling off a sticking plaster but after it was done it felt like a heavy weight had been lifted off me. Without Georgina, I was happy and could indulge my curiosity in a playful learning posture. It took a year to get a divorce.

CHAPTER 13 CHILD

I was accepted into the university's postgraduate programme. As a PhD student, I felt playful. I imagined a '*child*' figure as the culminating stage in Nietzsche's allegory of his spirit's emergence, metamorphoses and transcendences.

'*The true object of all human life is play. Earth is a task garden; heaven is a playground.*'
(G K Chesterton,1874-1936)

I had become a '*child*' of no particular age or experience, an existential being in a learning posture. It was not clear if this would be my end state, whether I could revert to earlier incarnations and past conditions, or I could continue to develop, into a form yet unknown to me.

My free spirit was like a child at play, forgetting what came before, discovering the world for the first time. The *child* was curious and filled with wonder, making up his own values and existing in a liberated state of free creativity and play. He was not weighed down by rules and values, discovering for himself the meaning in things. The *child* shouted the sacred 'Yes' that affirmed life. He simply existed and created.

My spirit had its own will and had won its own world. I was a risk taker who had opened a door to a world where my risk taker's view counted most, overcoming the opposition of those whose mantra was 'No.'

The university's Physics Department had more freedom than the job I had quit. They gave me enough rope to hang myself and by overworking, I almost did.

I obtained a room in a university hall of residence and a research room at the university, moved in and started work. On the day I commenced my studies, my whoop was the roar of a *lion* who had won kingship of his domain. I had a definite intellectual place in this new academic desert that I would defend against intruders.

Before starting a PhD, I had to complete a one-year master of science course. There was a continuous programme of lectures and regular assignments requiring long hours of study. The burden of course work was more demanding than any job I had known. I was stressed. By Christmas, my concentration was shredded from respecting tight deadlines. I needed a holiday.

For the first time, I felt my ability was limited but Don said the high workload was deliberate.

'The course philosophy is to prepare students for hard work by overloading them,' said Don. 'Like a body builder who overloads his muscles to tear the fibres and have them grow back stronger, this course is strengthening your brain for heavy lifting.'

'It comes as a shock, is all,' I said. 'I need a holiday.'

I booked a week's skiing in Austria with Gareth, a rugby friend. I drove to Heathrow airport alone, intending to leave my car in the long term car park and meet up with him at the check in.

When I drove up to the long-term car park, there was a sign: 'Long Term Car Park Full.'

Cursing, I drove to the medium-term park, where there was another sign: 'Medium Term Car Park Full'.

My heart sank. The only other car park was short term but the cost of parking there for a week would be more than the cost of my holiday. If I drove to a car park outside the airport I would miss my flight.

I was a planner and prided myself on avoiding problems, but trouble had found me out.

Cursing my bad luck, I drove around the airport looking for somewhere to leave my car. I saw a fenced compound with a sign 'Pilots Car Park'. There were few cars parked there and much open space. I thought my car might escape notice if I parked in there, in an unobtrusive position. I put on the back seat, prominently, a peaked and badged cap, like a pilot might wear. It was a memento from a casual job I had as a security guard. There was a chance they would see the cap and not the car, assuming they were legitimate.

I went to find Gareth and check in at Departure.

The flight was filled with skiers, many of them students. By the time we arrived in Innsbruck Gareth and I were friends with two girls staying at the same guest house. We skied together and by the end of the week we were sharing beds. I was concerned that Marion could get pregnant but she assured me she was protected and I believed her. I liked her, but I was not looking to commit to anyone until I had finished my PhD in about 3 years time.

I had worked hard and now I played hard on this holiday. Skiing was a metaphor for how I wanted to live my life: on the edge. On one side was dull conformity and on the other a tantalising tussle with out-of-control. On skis, I went too fast and was often a foolhardy danger to myself. I liked the exhilaration of the struggle to stay in control at high speed without crashing. It was a sport like no other, with thrills and spills aplenty.

On our last day, I misjudged a steep snowbank and buried my skis in it, injuring my knee. I was fortunate that my leg wasn't broken but I could hardly stand on it and I did no more skiing.

At Heathrow, when I limped to the Pilots Car Park, my car was gone. The airport police had it in their compound.

'Your car has caused a furore,' they said. 'We thought a pilot had been abducted when we saw that cap. We traced it to your employer and they told us you were on holiday. You are not popular and you will be charged.'

My knee was very painful. A hospital examination revealed a torn cartilage.

'Your operation is scheduled in two years time,' they said. 'There's a waiting list.'

'I can't tolerate the injury for that long,' I said. 'If you have a cancellation, I can come in within an hour.'

The next day they called me in and the torn cartilage was removed that day. Walking was very painful for several weeks. They told me the meniscus would grow back but I wasn't game to test it. I never skied fast again.

I received a summons to appear at Richmond magistrates court, where my 'Parking Offence' would be heard. I could speak in my defence. I felt wronged and prepared a statement of mitigating circumstances.

I was standing in the court when I read my statement.

'The long and medium car parks had signs, saying they were full,' I said, with indignation. 'I had no choice.'

'They have never been full,' lied an airport official.

I received the maximum possible fine for a parking offence, several times the cost of my holiday, taking the last of my savings. I was shocked that an authority would lie brazenly in court. Presumably they wanted to hide their deficiency of provision.

I had resumed course work at the university when there was a disaster. Marion phoned from the city where she lived, that she was coming to visit me. I wondered what she wanted, until she told me she was pregnant. It was a profound shock that tested my integrity. It was like discovering that my target practice had accidentally used live ammunition and badly injured someone. Sex suddenly had unwanted consequences. I wanted neither a child nor a permanent partner.

Gareth was unsympathetic.

'You have to face up to your responsibility,' he said. 'You don't have the right to choose otherwise.'

But Marion agreed to a termination. I drove her to a clinic and paid half the cost. I was sad, not least because Marion forgave me. But Gareth became unfriendly. I resolved to quit chasing girls.

My holiday had been a chronicle of irresponsible misadventure. I had parked illegally, skied recklessly and bedded Marion, all with childish abandon. I had taken risks and lost, with only myself to blame. I resolved to be more careful in future. To be accepted as a responsible person, I must lead an impeccable personal life.

My lifestyle now consciously avoided risk. My happiness would now have to come from something other than the rewards of good luck.

CHAPTER 14 PLAY

At the end of the year, I wrote up my thesis for a master's degree, guided by my supervisor Jack Montand. He was an existentialist with a carefully trimmed beard. His PhD had been in the metaphysics of space and time. He read gloomy novels by Thomas Mann.

My topic was risk-taking. I reported that my experiments with traffic lights had indicated when drivers were hurried, for example by orange lights, drivers became more vigilant and calculated risks more carefully. Jack submitted our paper to a journal. When it was published, it attracted some attention from academics, mostly favourable.

I had developed an image of bohemian individualism. I was chairman of the students' committee and had locked horns with the department head on the issue of reducing our students' workloads.

'Overloading is a valid training strategy,' I said, 'when it develops muscle. But our coursework has little muscle development and much suffering. If we were theological students learning about Jesus, the pain could validate the workload. But we are not and we request that the workload is reduced or made more relevant to our careers.

'Subsequently the course was improved.'

I chose campaigns carefully. I was more cautious and circumspect than in the reckless days before my accidents. I wanted to be a big success at university and this meant gaining respect.

With my master's course completed, I began searching for a PhD topic. I could choose research topics, contrasting with the rigidity of my former employment where I had been valued only as a lackey. Now I was respected for my ideas.

I steered away from fields in which I lacked experience.

'I am most interested in solving problems about things, not about people,' I told Nick.

I could choose from several disciplines and I diversified, exploring thoroughly the humanities collection in the university library. I had graduated in physics and my PhD was in that discipline, but I was fascinated to learn about topics in philosophy, psychology, sociology, social psychology, anthropology, political economy, management and ethics. These disciplines could add weight to a thesis argument in physics.

I loved developing my PhD topic. I had emerged from the challenges of my career blessed with childish innocence and open-mindedness. I was like a child with a new toy. I turned my topic over and over in my mind like a Rubik's Cube, looking at it from every possible angle for patterns. My spirit now willed my own will, with the power to conquer.

It took me six months to discover my main interests. I was most interested in motivation in sports.

'Existentialism is depressing.,' I said to Jack. 'Kierkegaard and Nietzsche's ebullience is often leaden and the writings of De Beauvoir, Sartre and Camus sometimes have a suicidal tone. Individuals are insufficiently aware of how their own unique qualities control what they do.'

'I agree,' he said. 'You are in monist territory and you need to tease out situations that interest you, where body and mind are considered as one.'

I explored various philosophical threads. One of them interested me greatly.

'I want to find a phenomenon I can open up like a Russian doll, exposing Kant's noumenal world beyond experience, with intention and meaning. His noumenon was the thing-in-itself, as opposed to the 'phenomenon' — the thing seen doing what it is supposed to do, an important difference.'

'I want to know why high performers are more able to take risks, from their point of view. It could help others to perform better.

'Could this be the difference between an athlete's goals and their performance. Why not investigate these as the phenomenon?' I said.

'Interesting,' said Jack. 'Mind-body dualism expects the mind to be distinct with a role separable from the body. Your investigation of risk-taking could discover how top performers' minds and bodies work together. You should make a thorough search of the monist literature. You have time. You should find Heidegger's ideas enlightening.'

The literature search of research articles concerned with both mind and body was a huge task but I enjoyed it.

I followed Kant's idea of a noumenon into the philosophy of phenomenology pioneered by Husserl and Heidegger.

'Why are you interested in phenomenology,' a colleague asked me.

'I like it.'

'We can't just do what we like!'

'Why not? Phenomenology is for me like gaining perceptiveness that has captured my imagination. It sits well with my experience. Could there be a better reason?'

'Most of us do what we do to pay the bills.'

'I don't have a family. I live simply. I do what I want.'

My answer didn't tell how I could make a living from it, but I hoped I might be able to one day. My ideas could attract others who would provide for me.

Through long summer days, my mind played with ephemeral ideas as I looked into athletes' purposes and risk taking. I became quite detached from practical matters. It was extraordinary to have nothing to do except to read and develop original ideas, about ideas that had escaped attention from philosophers and scientists, that I could now claim to have uncovered.

Seeing past the trees to glimpse the whole wood was daunting and however much I read, there was always more I needed to read. All I could do was to cut away the underbrush and reveal the large timber, to revere it, or plan to fell it, to make space for new ideas to grow.

'In my view, aiming at simplicity and lucidity is a moral duty of all intellectuals: lack of clarity is a sin, and pretentiousness is a crime.' Karl Popper, 1972

My work was like play and I felt privileged to have this freedom. Assembly line workers, have mental freedom to think about and plan private activities, such as what to do after work, whereas my thoughts were concentrated on the meaning of what I was doing. I didn't do much other than work.

As predicted by Nietzsche's allegory, I was like a precocious child, creative and demanding. I had little consideration for others. My relationships with others naively played the ball, not the man, without bothering about feelings or what came before or after. I didn't make many friends at this time.

'If your subject person is going to act from will-to-power, you must know his ultimate goal,' said Don.

'Nietzsche's will to power left original purpose open, except for 'telos'.'

'Could that final purpose of power be to influence others?' asked Don.

'Yes, if you like.'

'Influence is posteriori,' he said. 'It comes afterwards. It isn't there beforehand. How could something influence power, before it happens?'

'Like with all goals, it is imagined,' I said.

'I'm not convinced a person can imagine influence beforehand,' said Don.

'Why not,' I scoffed. 'People lie awake at night imagining controlling others.'

'Until they get control, they might not have influence,' Don said.

Ultimate goals were elusive. Our arguments sometimes continued for days, were resolved agreeably, or agreed to disagree. Failure to win an argument could upset me and I would sulk for hours before rebounding with enthusiasm. But setbacks were surmountable because my research had a positive focus. My ethos was that difficulties could all be overcome by intelligence and diligence.

Nick came round and smoked pot with me. Together we listened to music and laughed at our good fortune.

I went into the university regularly for progress meetings with Jack, my supervisor. I tried to take him to my ontological places, with some success, keeping a written record of our discussions. My spirit having transcended completely through the cycle predicted by Nietzsche, I could continue in in the *child* role in existential freedom, as long as I could obtain research facilities and funding.

Life was good. But something could happen.

'I had used my magic age as if it were a wand, with every crazy day bringing something new to do, never seeing the waste and emptiness beyond.' Song by Glen Campbell.

PHENOMENON

CHAPTER 15 DATES

My diet of reading, thinking and imagining research changed me. I became child-like in temperament, enjoying existential freedom, absorbed in my research project. Wanting to share my freedom and happiness, I looked for a partner.

I met Nicola at a party. She was a friend of Don, working at the university's social sciences research centre.

'Are you still with Georgina?' she asked, when we met for a date.

'We've separated.'

'What happened.'

'We weren't compatible,' I said.

'I'm sorry,' she said, waiting.

I couldn't elaborate without revealing my disinterest in long term relationships. She could find that out later.

'I'm sorry to,' I said. 'Thank you.'

I was interested in Nicola. Her clothes were loud and she was brash. She seemed like a positive force, which was what I wanted.

'What do you do, besides social science?' I asked her.

'Fringe theatre,' she said. 'When they put on a play big enough for my skills, I take a part.'

It explained why she struck poses and declaimed quotations and soliloquies from Shakespeare's plays. She was a show off, but I let it pass without comment. Many people show off their skills.

'Do you go to theatre?' she asked me.

'Sometimes. I like Shakespeare, Chekhov and Beckett.'

'I prefer less formal stuff,' she said. 'Modern plays.'

'What do you do at the social sciences research centre?' I asked her.

'I explore the unknown, ' she said.

'Do you know what you are looking for?' I quipped.

'I'll know it when I find it,' she said.

'Touché,' I said.

I hoped she would rise to my allusion, that you can't find something, without knowing what you're looking for. But she didn't seem to notice it.

Her self-affirming intuition was riddled with tautologies. I was impressed when she told me of her penchant for hitch-hiking, thumbing rides to the next suburb, or interstate.

'Do you accept every ride you're offered?' I asked.

'No,' she said. 'I have a sixth sense for danger.'

It was a bit too trite. Her creed seemed to be her intuition. If I had met her before my accidents, I would have been rapt, because I had been a hitch-hiker and intuitive when younger. I had learned to be suspicious of intuition by being misled. She seemed reckless and wanton. I wanted a more reliable companion but the main problem was she seemed superficial. Realising we were incompatible, I politely moved on.

'It could take a while to find a suitable partner,' I reflected. *'But I'm not in a hurry.'*

Finding dates was easy and I met Tania at a book launch. She worked as a marketer for a book publisher. She did yoga and Pilates, also Tai Chi for defence training. We had a date and made a lengthy search for a suitable restaurant, inspecting menus and kitchens. Most ingredients were unacceptable to her. She seemed obsessive, rejecting many foods on dietary grounds, such as cholesterol, gluten and sugar, until I realised that she was a hypochondriac. Her fastidiousness was annoying, because I wanted to experiment with new foods.

She was a demanding person. One evening we chose a restaurant and she spoke to the waiter at the desk.

'The music is too loud,' Tania said. 'I want you to reduce the volume.'

'Yes Madam.'

We sat down.

A few minutes later she said to me angrily: 'It's still loud.'

She thumped the table top hard with her fist, bouncing the cutlery, utensils and crockery noisily. Every eye in the restaurant swivelled onto us.

'Turn the fucking music down!' she spat.

The volume reduced. I was impressed with Tania. This woman seemed to offer the solidity I wanted.

She ordered calamari.

'This is overcooked,' she complained. 'It's like rubber. I want it freshly cooked.'

They complied.

On our second date, she made a scene at another restaurant about the service. She seemed nit-picking, pedantic, with entrenched attitudes, rants and harangues. Her conversation had a whining tone and her meditation was dogmatic rather than spiritual. She was too focussed on the minutiae of life, to embrace my aesthetic interests.

'Can you afford to be so picky?' said Nick when I told him about her.

'You are overlooking my good qualities,' I said. 'There has to be someone for me out there!'

'It would take a strange woman to want you!' said Nick.

Nick was beginning to get on my nerves. The problem was that he hero-worshipped me and followed me around. I detested charisma in others and in myself most of all. Undeserved admiration embarrassed me. My self-deprecation was an obstacle in finding a girl who would like me enough without fawning.

I was discovering the variety of the world again, after my sojourn in the desert. I wanted life-affirming experiences with limited risks, unlike my social play with siblings and weapons as a child. I wanted to live simply and honourably. Our parents had instilled in me honest dealing and I would consider only one girl at a time. When I finished with a girl the ending would be agreeable and decisive.

My search for a girl friend was methodical. I drew up a checklist of the features she should possess: looks; physical attraction; willingness to negotiate; understanding of my work; and independence.

I showed my list to Don.

'You haven't included honesty,' he said.

'No,' I said. 'In our post-truth world, the most I can hope for is she doesn't lie often, because they all tell lies sometimes.'

'I hope you treat them kindly,' he said. 'Nicola hasn't had time for me since you finished with her.'

'I don't know why that would be,' I said. 'We parted as friends. Thank you for introducing us.'

'I don't have an infinite supply,' he said. 'I know one who might tick your boxes. My Sophia has a girl friend: Megan. She's a performer.'

'Stage?'

'No. Athletics. She medalled at the Nationals.'

He raised an eyebrow and I smiled, declining a facetious retort. Don was a recreational runner and had followed Megan's performing career closely.

'What sort of person is she?'

'Single-minded but pleasant. Megan has recently broken up with someone. She is beautiful in a spare way.'

'How old is she?'

'25 I think.'

'A year younger than me,' I thought. *'Ideal.'*

'Would you like to meet her?' Don asked.

'Yes please.'

I was interested that she was an athlete. Although I hadn't achieved anything prestigious in athletics at school, I had enjoyed competing immensely. I would be thrilled to meet a woman performer and looked forward to discovering her achievement.

CHAPTER 16 MEGAN

I went with Don and his girlfriend Sophia to a pub, to meet Megan. She was gorgeous, in a rather imperious way, with alert blue eyes that sparkled with good humour. She had physical presence, crossing and uncrossing long beautiful legs self-consciously, with glimpses of shapely thighs.

'Why Megan?' I asked her.

'It's Welsh and means 'pearl'. My father is Welsh. Our family name is McLean, a Scottish clan name. Is Chance an English name?'

'It's English for good fortune.'

'You have had the good fortune to meet me,' she said with a self-deprecating smile.

'I think so too,' I said.

She was too good to be true. Although I was a scientist, my thinking sometimes reverted to the fatalism of my childhood, inherited atavistically. The idea of a God or a higher power pulling my strings like a puppeteer was anathema, but for me to maintain a strict deterministic outlook was difficult when I was confronted by unexpected occurrences, such as meeting a girl as delightful as Megan.

'What research are you doing?' I asked her.

My mind was on her long legs, imagining them wrapped around me.

'I'm doing a PhD.'

'Do you have a philosophy?' I asked.

'More than one. My first degree was in philosophy,' she said.

'I did physics with a unit of philosophy,' I said. 'Do you have a philosophy of life?'

She told me she had started thinking about the nature of reality at school, asking questions, such as: What should she do with her life?

71

What should she think? Who should she relate to? What possessions did she need? When she couldn't find answers by asking, she looked in philosophy books. Her parents had encouraged her interest in debating and she became captain of her school's team.

I was fascinated. At our end of the table, we were engrossed in each other. Don and Sophia didn't seem to mind our preoccupation with each other. Don gave me an encouraging look.

'I was interested in Plato's harmony between the three parts of the soul: reason; spirit; and appetite,' said Megan. 'I also read some of the Stoics.'

'You were comprehensive.'

'I wanted to know what to do with myself.'

Megan said she had discovered Descartes (1694-1778) and became self-aware that her body and mind were separate but operated together. Her school science studies helped her to know what her body could do, but she worried that her mind was not under her control.

'I used to think my body existed to carry around my head. What was inside my head was a mystery.'

'Because your 'soul' was spirit and unknown to science?'

'Yes,' she said. 'Christian stories mention the soul, but the Bible is an opaque and ambiguous book. Freud described the id as part of the soul with important instincts and intuition.'

'I imagine you are not happy your id is beyond your control?'

'A whole layer of my experiences is beyond my understanding.'

'What research are you doing?'

'Social psychology.'

'Are you finding out what is in people's heads?'

'I am finding out how to motivate people to seek employment.'

'Like going along with the crowd?'

'Haha. Fear of missing out is a negative motive,' she said. 'I am using Maslow's hierarchy of needs to look for the positive threads people follow into employment.'

'Like needing shelter and love first, before needing to belong?'

'That sort of thing. It's an old theory but it works.'

'Interesting. Imran said you have been in a relationship?'

'I'm over it now.'

'What happened?'

'He was a pole-vaulter and we trained together,' she said. 'When I improved and he didn't because he was lazy, it came between us. He imagined he had enough natural talent to succeed. When he didn't, he was jealous of me and tried to prevent me training. We broke up.'

I wouldn't ask her age. If she was my age, as Don indicated, I wondered what she had been doing during the four years I had been employed in industry.

'Did you get to stay on after graduating?' I asked her.

'I got a part-time job as a research assistant in psychology. After three years, my experience in the job and my philosophy degree were accepted to do psychology research. I had continued pole vaulting since school and was winning high level competitions. I won a combined athletics and research scholarship. I am supposed to divide my time equally between athletics and research. I am funded for three years, to do a PhD. The university benefits from my publicity and they pay for my research.'

'It is generous. I wasn't aware of postgraduate athletics scholarships. They must like you. Imran told me you're good.'

'It's my pole vaulting that clinched it,' she said. 'I get a lot of publicity.'

'How did you get into pole vaulting?'

'I started at school and it became a passion.'

'You must be very good. You've the right height for it. Did you hear about the pole vaulter who walked into a bar?

'Go on.'

'She was tall!'

'Haha. That's a tall story.'

'Imran said you medalled at the National championships. Did they throw you out?'

'Haha. I got the bronze, the same as last year.'

'I am investigating risk and endurance,' I said. 'Does your event have those?'

'Yes. Not much risk, but plenty of pain, exhaustion and failure.'

73

'I expect your training is tough. I did some pole vaulting at school.'

'Then you know training can be an ordeal, but there's fun too.'

'It was fun. What motivates you?'

'Everything. The possibility of winning. The health benefits of training. Meeting other people. Travelling to places.'

'Pole vaulting is said to be the most risky of field events,' I said. 'Are you making a statement?'

'I've tried running, throwing and jumping, but vaulting is most thrilling. I get a buzz out of jaw-dropping achievement.'

'You get high on fiberglass!'

She laughed.

'I plant it, swing up on it, fly away and feel the rush!' she said. 'I get as high as I can!'

'Performing seems to be your passion.'

She nodded. I was relieved. Passions were sometimes religious.

'Ideal,' I thought. *'She could be too preoccupied by either athletics or her research to seek permanent commitment from me.'*

'What will you do afterwards?' I asked her.

'Maybe a postdoc somewhere or a HR job.'

I cut to the chase.

'Doing a PhD is like going into a time warp for several years,' I said. 'Will you ever want a family?'

'That's a forward question. Are you looking for a wife, or sumpin'?'

'Not until I have finished, in maybe 4 years time.'

'You're a cold fish, aren't you?' she said. 'If you met the right person, would you delay?'

'It might be possible to delay, with understanding.'

'And agreement.'

I felt I had arrived. *'Megan is like me, doing a PhD and interested in philosophy. She seems ideal.'*

'Schopenhauer regarded passion as *'a sickness of the soul,'* I said. 'But Kierkegaard said: *'The conclusions of passion are the only reliable ones'.* I guess you prefer Kierkegaard.'

'I do. Schopenhauer was a bit weird.'

74

'When you hurl yourself into space, what are you thinking?'

'Am I doing it right? Is it the way I trained? Am I giving it everything I have? I'm not over-confident. Is my answer what you expected?'

'I wondered if you ever think what could go wrong.'

'No, not me. I expect my passions to turn out well, like Kierkegaard's leap of faith. But enough about me. What about you? I would like to hear about your research. What are you doing?'

'I'm interested in risk,' I said.

'What type of risk?'

'I'm investigating several: Nietzsche's philosophy of daring to be great; burn-out with sub-optimal performance; brinkmanship; endurance.'

'I like Nietzsche.'

'An individual can try to dominate others, with an urge for fame, power, and riches. But the will-to-power is also for inner forces that drive a person to act in the world, about achieving their goals in a never-ending quest for self-improvement, for knowledge and for creativity.'

'Do you think his philosophy could bring improvement to an ordinary person's living?' she asked.

'Yes, it could,' I said. 'Everyone performs in some way. I am interested in enjoyment as a motivation, so performances are less demanding and more rewarding.'

'With better endurance?'

'Yes and less risk.'

'I am doing my PhD fulltime and it's a dry diet,' I said. 'You're lucky to be able to switch to performing for a change.'

'What motivates you?' she asked.

'It varies from task to task,' I said. 'I extend my knowledge by reading. Sometimes I vindicate my theories by gathering data and writing articles for publication. I have a blog to get attention to my work and I get some feedback from followers. Sometimes I investigate questions and puzzles I have come across. Sometimes I try to advance my position within the university, for the money and the esteem. Sometimes I make a bold move, just for the excitement.'

'Like what?'

'I have submitted a research paper,' I said, 'to read at a conference soon.'

'Has it been accepted?'

'Yes, for next month.'

'I'd like to be there.'

'I'll give you details.'

'What are you best at?'

'Figuring things out,' I said. 'Investigating.'

'What else do you do?' she asked.

'I play social rugby sometimes.'

'Do you socialize during the game?'

'Hardly. Just insults and threats.'

She laughed deeply, holding her sides and I joined in.

When we had first been introduced, her looks had seemed pleasantly distinctive rather than pretty. Only certain views revealed her beauty. Now I had studied her face, she seemed alluring and in certain views, distinguished.

We talked about our other interests, friends and activities.

We rejoined conversation with Don and Sophia. I parted with Megan having arranged a date at a local restaurant that weekend.

Afterwards her magic lingered and I felt vulnerable, because I would be hurt if she broke our date. Although I had nothing to fear, I was invested in her and could lose badly. But we met as planned and I was a happy man.

Being with Megan was easy. We dated several times. In her company time flew. She had similar interests and seemed an ideal partner. I wanted to find out more about her as a performer. When I was with her, my spirit gambolled, discovering her likes and wanting to entertain her.

'Megan would make a fine playmate,' I thought.

When I returned her to her hall of residence in Prince's Gardens, I kissed her and she kissed me back. It was the best kiss of my life.

'Which hall is this?' I asked her.

'Greer.'

'Are you a feminist?'

'No. But don't try me or I might come out.'

'Have you lived here long?'

'Since I started a PhD.'

'Will they let me in?' I asked.

'No, not now. Visitors have to be out by 10pm.'

Waiting to sleep with her seemed less like a penance and more like an imminent reward. I said goodnight.

Over the following week we had several dates, went to a movie, to an art gallery and to a restaurant with Don and Sophia. We talked a lot. She was fun and a delight to be with.

She was a respectful person and stated her thoughts openly. Doing similar work, we were supportive and helpful to each other. The meaning of our liaison was mutuality. When we talked, what to do was easily decided.

CHAPTER 17 PERFORMER

'What do you think of Megan,' I asked Nick, because I was besotted and needed a reality check.

'I like her,' Nick said. 'She's single-minded about both her athletics and her research.'

'That's an oxymoron.'

'I meant she does both seriously.'

'She's determined alright. She'll suit you, if you can stand the competition.'

She was formidable, but I didn't feel threatened. We did not criticise each other's work and tried to help each other.

We had dated several times when I took her to a Japanese restaurant for dinner. We ordered Bento boxes and chatted drinking glasses of rice wine as we waited. I had started my research project and wanted to find out how she self-rated her pole vaulting.

'I'd like to watch you competing,' I said to her. 'How good are you?'

'I'm not sure I'm still rising,' she said. 'I am usually in the first three.'

'What would it take for you to improve?'

'I wish I knew. Maybe a new technique.'

'Do you have a coach?'

'Yes. I go to a sports centre and do track work with a coach. I go to an indoor performing facility and workout in the gym with several others each week.'

'What's your coach like?'

'Adamson has retired from performing. He came second in the National pole vault 5 years ago. He is demanding, rather terse and short-tempered. I get on with him well enough.'

'I'd like to watch you competing.'

'The Southeast Area Championship is next month. Australia's best performers will be there and some elite internationals. You could come to that if you want. It's at the Gold Coast. My father is driving down. You could ride there with us.'

'I'd like to very much.'

'What's your father like?'

'He used to be a PE teacher. Now he's a science teacher at a high school. He'll be interested to meet you. Penny will be coming too, with her friend Lily.'

'Is your sister older or younger?' I asked.

'We're twins,' she said.

'Identical?'

'No. Opposites.'

'What does she look like?'

'She's shorter and has dark hair.'

'Is she an athlete?'

'She plays cricket.'

'Cricket? That's different. Are you dissimilar in other ways?'

'Yes,' said Megan. 'Penny is like my mother, socially inclined, trying to blend in, calm and composed, rarely gets flustered, immaculate, matter of fact, trustworthy, traditional, moral and humble. She goes to church. She is serene on the surface but paddles her religion beneath the surface like a duck. She is suspicious that passions are weaknesses.

'I'm more like my father, Michael, proud to be different and egotistical.'

'You're the academic one?'

'Penny is an expert in a good job.'

'How well do the two of you get on?'

'We go our separate ways but we clash sometimes. You'll have to meet her.'

'Yes, I'd like to.

'She's coming to the Area Championship,' said Megan. 'You'll meet her then, if not before.'

'It's good of her to give her support.'

'Yes, my family gives me encouragement,' she said. 'It makes a difference.'

Our food came. We admired the neat Bento compartments, each with a different food. We were silent as we sipped the miso soup. We savoured the delicate strips of sashimi. There were sushi rolls which we dipped in wasabi, hot horseradish sauce. Then we started on the teriyaki, strips of beef with vegetables, marinaded with a sweet and tangy sticky sauce. There were other vegetables, ginger and rice.

We talked as we ate.

'How determined are you to get to the top?' I asked her.

'I always try my best.'

'Do you believe in free will?'

'I am thankful for what I have,' she said. 'I would like to have a stronger will, but science doesn't leave much room for it.'

'What do you mean?'

'My actions are almost totally determined by what my body can do, by scientific processes I have trained to use. Free will doesn't get much of a look in.'

'You are mostly right,' I said. 'Kant (1724-1804) believed that the key to knowledge and understanding of the world of experience in space time had now been placed into our hands by science. Anyone who genuinely believes in determinism, as applied to human beings, is committed to it causing every consequence. However, there seems to be no-one who believes it.'

'You mean no-one believes what happens to us is pre-determined?' Megan said.

'Everyone believes people have free will to choose, at least some of the time. If what happens has been determined, there would be no point in our complaining if others treated us with vicious brutality, because it would have been impossible for them ever to do anything else. They would have had no choice. So we have to believe there is such a thing as free choice, or free will, at least some of the time.'

'We punish criminals because their free choices were bad ones. We have to blame ourselves. It is up to us what we do.'

80

'It is decided by the free operation of our will, determined personally. The laws of science determine part of it, an unknown amount and we overlook that.'

'We are always responsible,' she said.

'We have agency,' I said. 'The bonus is we can choose our lives.'

'My psychological personality type is an Enneagram Type 3 adventurer,' she said. 'What are you?'

'I too like adventure,' I said, ' but I'm probably a Type 5, an investigator. My Briggs Meyer is INTJ, a Mastermind. I want to create ideas like an artist, to attract interest and stimulate conversations.'

'I like new experiences most,' Megan said.

'Are you a butterfly, sipping here, sipping there?'

'No. I have sipped and settled in a good few places.'

'Perhaps you won't settle anywhere?'

'I'm still looking.'

We told each other experiences of situations with free will.

I was trying to imagine Megan, performing her lived experiences, as a phenomenon with intent, or free will. I wouldn't mention phenomenology until I had seen her perform. I would ask what her performing meant to her. Her vaulting could be expected to be existential and different to more familiar events, such as sprinting.

We finished with our boxes and ordered lychees.

Our talk now became playful, wanting dinner to continue, simply because we were getting on so well. They brought the lychees and the flavour balanced the wasabi taste, which had lingered.

We began kissing. She was irresistible and although kissing was fun, it was torture too.

'Could we go somewhere with a bed?' I asked.

'Sweetly said,' she replied with sarcasm. 'Do you think we are ready for that?'

'How would I know if I'm not?'

'Do you know where this could go,' she asked.

'We could be a couple and live together.'

'I thought you told me you didn't want to settle down until your PhD is in the bag.'

'I don't, but I would make an exception for you.'

'You hardly know me. You could change your mind.'

'I'm trying to get to know you,' I said. 'Having sex would be friendly.'

'What if it's not good enough?'

'Waiting could make it worse.'

'How could waiting make it worse?'

'Our psyches could wrap around each other,' I said.

'Like a strangler fig?' she asked. 'Yuck! That's horrific. It would be unpleasant and difficult to undo.'

'Then you agree waiting could be worse,' I said. 'You should come to my room.'

'Good idea.'

We had sex for the first time. It was beautiful, with gentleness and patience. I was surprised when she would not see me during the week and I lived in a half real world of not knowing her intentions. We had met in passion but afterwards it seemed that she had finished with me. I was hooked like a fish after an angler has struck in the barb. There was no escape. I thought she might be playing with me but there was nothing I could do to stop it.

I wanted to spend time with her outside my work, but she seemed to prefer being alone, which was hurtful. If she was playing hard to get to provoke my interest, it was working, because I was infatuated.

She had never suggested I join her on a training run, so I suggested it.

'Are you sure you're fit enough?' she asked.

'I run at rugby,' I said. 'It depends on how fast you go.'

'You would have to keep up,' she said. 'You can join me tomorrow morning, leaving my hall at 6.30 am.'

'Okay,' I said, gulping. Getting up at that time would be a shock.

We met in the car park. She was wearing top, tights and fluorescent orange running shoes. I had on stretch shorts and a loose T-shirt with a sun hat. We set off along the running track around the campus perimeter, with Megan setting the pace.

I hadn't run this fast before and struggled to keep up.

She allowed me to come alongside her.

I was blowing, while she breathed easily.

'Can I suggest a couple of things?' she asked. 'You are slapping your feet down noisily, heavily and loping along. It is more efficient to run silently, lightly and smoothly, with a minimum of body movement. Your body should lean slightly forward, keeping time evenly with your forearms like horizontal pistons.'

I watched her and tried it, but I couldn't keep up with the astonishing pace she was setting.

'This is too fast for me,' I told her. 'I'll see you back at hall.'

I continued a short way and went back. She came back half an hour later.

She made light of it.

'You can't expect to keep up when you start,' she said. 'I have been running for years.'

There was no shame in it. I didn't suggest running with her again and nor did she. I stuck to my rugby. I had had my first lesson in Megan's performing: she was outstandingly good.

I had imagined she might be what Nietzsche had designated an ubermensch, an overman or, in Megan's case, a superwoman.

I thought *'She might possibly want to be a national hero, Australian of the Year, earning praise from critics, gaining recognition for her sportsmanship and earning a place in posterity, with a State funeral and buried in a cathedral.'*

There was no doubt in my mind that she had a bright future.

Megan paid little attention to positioning herself in the public eye and despised pomposity. She seemed more interested in personal achievement.

I suspected she had existential dreams and role icons she didn't talk about.

'When you perform, do you have a goal?' I asked.

'I'm no superwoman. I am not in it for the prize money, even when there is some. I am encouraged most by the glory of winning. Improving my personal best is a nice idea but it doesn't motivate me the way it does my brother.'

'Is he older than you?'

83

'One year older.'

'Is he a performer?'

'Yes, golf. He tries to improve on every hole and lets the winning look after itself. I can't compete like that. Improving his personal best inspires him.'

'Is he a professional?'

'He will be within a year or two. He trains on a driving range with a personal coach.'

'It sounds as though he knows what he's doing. Could you have a more cognitive approach to your performing?'

'Cognitive meaning knowing?'

'Yes. Could you video your performances?'

'I have to share a coach and get one of the girls to point the camera. My practicing is dull. I prefer learning by the trial and error of competition.'

I was surprised that Megan had come so far without more goal direction. Her aim was only partly quantified and could not be a guide for continuous improvement.

'You need personal coaching.'

'I would like it but I can't afford it.'

'How does your brother afford it?'

'Golf coaching.'

'I'd like to meet your brother.'

'Why?'

'I am trying to find out your training needs. He could help me understand you.'

'He has some weird ideas and he is not at all flexible. He lives with my parents. You can come and meet him and them. They all think they know what's good for me. But they don't.'

She smiled ruefully.

I had realised that Megan was an unusually determined performer. When I asked her to go to a movie with me, she politely declined.

'I need to study,' she said.

I had to be content with fragments of her life.

'She could be preoccupied with her interests, or playing hard to get,' I thought.

I felt our relationship had not quite arrived. Her frequent unavailability could not be a ploy, because it lacked resolution. What we had together was a rather thin relationship in which I wanted her companionship but was frustrated. Megan was elusive and I was often disappointed. The merry-go-round of our encounters often brought me emotions other than love and her perfection changed in my mind to a character made more interesting by flaws.

CHAPTER 18 WATCHING MEGAN

I had driven down to the Southeast Area Championships with Megan, her father, sister Penny and Lily in Penny's cricket team. Lily was medium height and fit, gorgeous, with red hair and long legs clad in patterned leggings.

'You should do well today, Megan,' Lily said in the car, laughing nervously. She used her prettiness to charm people, hiding her lack of self-confidence. 'Last time you may have choked a bit.'

'What do you mean?' said Megan, indignantly. 'I did my best.'

'It wasn't up to your usual standard,' said Lily. 'On your last jumps, after the winner got over, you seemed to hold back.'

'Give me a break!' said Megan bluntly. 'Pressuring me won't help.'

'Sorry, Megan. I was trying to help,' said Lily self-effacingly.

On arrival, Megan limbered up at the trackside watched by Lily and coach Adamson. When Lily's boyfriend Hugh arrived, Lily put her arm around Megan's waist.

Lily leaned on the barrier, talking intently with Megan, enjoying each other. I wondered what was going on between the two. Megan's gaze was calm and purposeful, her determination grim, without self-satisfaction, absorbed in self-improvement. I supposed she and Megan would be talking about the competition. I was jealous that Megan had time for Lily but not for me.

Megan was the 10th of 15 women to perform. Adamson spoke to her at length before she went out. She stood poised at the start of the runway, her pole resting on her shoulder, with the far end on the ground. She concentrated, gazing at the bar with fierce intensity, breathing deeply and steadily. I was reminded of a bird fishing, a heron, poised motionless in the shallows, ready to stab downwards. She lifted the pole to incline upwards and sprang forwards, accelerating with knees lifting high and pumping downwards, torso leaning as she drove forward, her blonde ponytail swinging, increasing speed, with the pole tip descending smoothly, until she planted it in the box and swung up into the air. As the pole bent into a C shape, the straightening pole propelled her upwards into a hand stand, with her legs and body passing over the bar. As her torso went over, she turned to face the bar, curling around it, almost touching it, dropping down to land on her back in the centre of the foam landing mat, bouncing up to a standing position and moonwalking off.

If we had to choose one human to represent the best of human physical abilities, it should be a female pole vaulter. She would combine amazing speed, strength, coordination, agility, grace and also be capable of reproduction. Such distinction goes unrecognised because few people have had the opportunity to pole vault and are unable to appreciate its superiority over the other events. A woman pole vaulter could be the best candidate to be sent into space to found a new civilisation of superhumans.

'She is very good,' I said to Michael. 'I love watching this. Elite performances inspire me.'

'Do you perform at something?' he asked.

'Just at living my life. With ambition.'

'That's nice.'

'Did you ever coach her?' I asked him.

'I got her started with sprinting in primary school.'

'She looks like a sprinter.'

'Looks don't count. A pole vaulter has to be fast,' he said.

We talked, stopping to watch her perform.

The arena was serene under a blue sky, with seagulls scooting robotically in the throwing area. When they startled, they flew around mewing until they settled again.

Penny, Michael, Lily and I went down to the barrier to watch Megan perform. Penny was silent as she observed her sister. Megan had started at 4m85 after several others had been eliminated. Each performer could knockdown up to three times at each new height.

I saw that she was following proceedings closely, but when Megan succeeded she didn't applaud with the rest of us. Only four of them remained. I wondered if there was rivalry.

When Lily came back to sit down, Penny made space for her and monopolised her attention. Penny was normally reserved but she sat close beside Lily, obviously wanting intimacy.

'Those two could be gay,' I thought. *'Lily is popular with the twins, as if they might be competing for her attention. I hope Megan's interest in her is merely friendly.'*

From my seat in the stand, I kept a jealous eye on Megan and Lily. I went down to the barrier to talk with Megan between rounds. She was chatting with Lily about the jump. I overheard her reflecting on her last jump and analysing it.

'I only just got over,' she said. 'I need to be faster and spring up earlier.'

She was preoccupied and reluctant to talk to me. I wanted to question her about her goal achievement and perception of risk, but it was not the time. She had to perform again shortly. She had programmed her actions days ago and was now on automatic, uncommunicative.

'Does she desire me?' I asked myself endlessly. There was plenty of evidence she didn't, but just when I was on the point of despair she would acknowledge me by coming over, smiling or waving, rekindling my hope.

They put the bar up 5 cm to 4m90. Only two of them cleared it, Megan and Ingrid, from Sweden. They put it up to 4m95. Megan narrowly missed with her third attempt, getting silver, Ingrid succeeding with her second attempt, winning gold.

In the car on the way home, Penny was at the wheel. She talked to Lily beside her, but her attention was on the conversations behind her, where I sat with Megan and Michael.

'You were terrific Megan,' I said. 'I want to know what it's like for you. My first photo has you ready to start your run and the last has you on your back on the mat. What was in your mind in between?''

'A performance begins earlier than that,' said Michael. 'Tell him Megan.'

'Before I start my run, I mentally prepare and limber up,' she said.

'How long does that take?' I asked.

'I plan it with my coaches during training,' said Megan. 'The night before, when I am in bed, I rehearse it in my mind, imagining it in slow motion, to see it and feel it. Before the event I warm up, getting my body ready.'

'Then you have a lot to think about when you concentrate,' I said. 'Do you imagine what could happen if you fail?'

'No. I think about my goal and I imagine myself succeeding,' she said. 'When I start my run, I need to be brimming with self-confidence. There is no room for hesitancy. I know I can fail, but I do everything I can to succeed.'

It was the first competition I had seen her in and I was being careful not to give Megan my opinions. I recalled that Lily's earlier comment about choking had annoyed her. It was a lot for Megan to bear, hearing advice from Adamson, Lily and Michael, with their different points of view. Her science offered her a glimmer of independence. Nietzsche's 'will to power' probably decided most of what she did.

There was a lull in the talk.

'Should I try to improve from how I seem to others, or from how I seem to myself?'' asked Megan.

There was silence as we grappled with the question.

'That is a great question,' I said. 'Philosopher Immanuel Kant made it his life's work to answer it. He conceived of a thing as a phenomenon, as it appeared to an observer, whereas the thing-in-itself was a noumenon, in a world beyond experience and could be an idea, an ethic or moral, called free will. What you do is determined by the material world, or alternatively, by your free will. Your performance could have both.'

'The physical world controls almost everything,' said Megan. 'Does my free will explain only a little of my performance?'

'It adds a dimension of intention to your every action,' I said. 'It is the part you can control.'

'Do you mean I can add as much free will as I want?'

She was sceptical.

'Or as little. You might not have enough. Free will is like electricity from a car battery. If the car stays in the garage, the battery will go flat and it won't start. If you run the car regularly, the battery will charge up and have electricity even for a tough cold start.'

'I see. Does this mean my performance depends on regular wilfulness and that I can leave out practical science, religion, coaching and team advice?'

'No,' I said. 'Free will is only one part of your mind. You will need to train other parts too, such as science, goal focus and engagement.'

'Practice brings it all together,' said Michael.

I was pleased Megan was interested in my general ideas. I wanted her to be a subject in my investigation of risk and endurance.

'Megan is unusually wilful,' I thought, *'She is tempered by a higher purpose that is keeping her disassociated from me and her friends, as if she wants only limited intimacy. I wonder if she has suffered in a previous relationship and is keeping her distance.'*

'Free will is false,' said Penny, 'because it's too individual. Rousseau wanted us to be guided by collective will. He thought free will is unsavoury, a low animal behaviour that leads to chaos. Megan, you should emulate the aesthetic aspect of human performance, celebrated in the sculptures of Michelangelo and Da Vinci. The human spirit seeks elevation to collective values, that escape the loneliness of individuality. The individual has volition and also integrity. When you perform, don't you feel serene doing something everyone regards as elegant?'

'Yes, but that's not enough for me to want to do it better.'

'I am interested in how you concentrate intently before each performance, before you start your run up,' I said. 'What are you doing when you are concentrating?'

'When I step onto the runway, there isn't much time,' Megan said. 'First I shut out all the distractions and remember my routine, my plan and the steps I must follow. Then I steel myself to explode down the runway and grip the pole with all my strength.'

90

'Do you have a different goal for each attempt?' asked Penny.

'I have the same performance goal, but modify my actions to correct for my most recent attempt.'

'Megan is a proficient performer, with family and friends in support,' I thought. *'She could be a champion.'*

'Chance, are you thinking of taking up performing?' asked Lily.

'No. I'm interested in it as a risk-taking activity. I did some pole vaulting at school.'

'What happened?' asked Penny.

'I was outclassed,' I said.

'Because you were all about ego?' asked Penny.

'No. I just wasn't competitive.'

'If I don't win, I don't care,' Megan said. 'I do it for fun.'

'If you were always last, would you quit?' I asked.

'Probably.'

'Did you enjoy competing today?'

'Not much. I was carried along by the spectacle, by the programme of events and by the hype of the media. The organisers were making money out of audiences and our unpaid training.'

'Do you feel you were exploited?'

'Yes. In the track and field business, a medal is all I get. I won't get anything else to sustain my motivation until the next event, the State championships, other than bling. No pay or prize money. Imagine a profession where you need to be in the World top 10 to begin earning a decent wage. It is humbling. Not to mention the minimal, smelly changing rooms and minimal refreshments.'

'But didn't the applause mean anything to you?'

'They have turned adulation into a commodity,' Megan said. 'The media promote favourite athletes and personal sensations to attract audiences who they expose to advertisements and promotional images. It's an industry built around the spectacle of athletic achievement.'

'What industry?'

'Selling and supplying hosting benefits, travel fares, tourism revenues, stadium ticket sales, media rights, athlete interviews, sportswear advertising, motivational conferences, promotional appearances, fanware promotions and so on.'

'Today's event was small. Millions are invested in facilities and audiences are glued to their screens being persuaded to buy drinks, foods, bling, cars and holidays. I like genuine applause for high performance but often it is the spectacle that is being applauded.'

'Is the spectacle an objective reality?'

'No. It is not even a visual image. It is the subjective multisensory engagement people experience, most like being in a crowd engrossed, in a culturally rich movie.'

'Debord said the spectacle is the most efficient way to pacify the working class and to make workers shut the fuck up about their shitty lives being exploited and alienated. Everybody is working their asses off to be able to go home at night and watch TV. The spectacle is what serves to keep consumers asleep or totally unaware of their material reality rooted in exploitation.'(15)

'What Megan is saying is that the audience were excited and sounding off, not affirming high achievement. It didn't mean much to her. Is that right Megan?'

'Yes. That's how I see it as a performer. Audience participation is obscured by hype, by cheerleaders, by bands and by media sensationalism. It doesn't reward me much.'

'Penny, how did you think she did today?' asked Michael.

'Terrific and that's not hype.'

'Thanks Penny,' said Megan.

'When's your next cricket match?' Michael asked Penny.

'Saturday.'

'Where?'

'We're playing Easts at Norman Park.'

'I'd like to come,' he said. 'How about you Megan? Chance?'

'Okay.'

We would both go.

'I'll see if Hannah wants to come. We can take a picnic.'

CHAPTER 19 WINNING EGOTISM

I stayed for dinner at Megan's parents' home, with her brother George, Penny and Lily.

'When did you move out from home?' I asked Megan.

'When I started my PhD,' she said. 'Studying is easier in hall.'

'I am in hall too,' I said. 'I can concentrate better.'

'How's the food?' asked Hannah, her mother.

'Your dinners are wonderful,' I said. 'I love coming here.'

'Thank you. I meant the food in hall?'

'It's pretty basic,' said Megan. 'It's fish and chips or chicken curry. It keeps the wolf from the door. Your dinners are feasts compared.'

I spoke to Hannah.

'Megan told me you are a lawyer?'

'I am a magistrate in the family court. Do you do athletics, Chance?'

'I did some at school and went to the state championship, but I didn't continue at university.'

'Do you do any sport now?' she asked.

'I play rugby with the uni 2nd XV. It's a lot of fun.'

'I'll bet. So what did you think of Megan today?'

'I was blown away. She's very good. You must be proud of her.'

'We are, although sometimes we worry she'll hurt herself.'

'Oh, Mum!' said Megan interrupting. 'It's as safe as houses.'

Megan's brother had not spoken so far.

'Megan is very competitive,' George said to me. 'She will try to beat you.'

'Beat me how?'

'Anyway she can. She's a narcissist and wants all the attention.'

The room went quiet and everyone looked at Megan. She was smiling.

'Is this true, Megan?' I asked.

She nodded. Michael and Hannah were smiling too.

I felt like a fly caught in a spider's web. I reviewed what I knew about narcissism. A narcissist has an inflated sense of self-importance with an excessive need for admiration, disregard for others' feelings, an inability to handle any criticism and a sense of entitlement. It wasn't Megan at all.

'You're having me on,' I said to George. 'Haha.'

They all burst into laughter. Megan had been correct: her brother George was weird. He filled my glass, trying to make amends.

'Megan is too self-centred to be a narcissist,' Penny said to me confidentially. 'She doesn't care what anyone thinks of her.'

'I don't find her self-centred,' I said. 'She is an egotist, which is appropriate for an elite performer.'

I hadn't known anyone as famous as Megan and I revered her. Her family's interest in me was flattering.

'Megan has adopted Voltaire's philosophy, that free will has precedence over reason,' Hannah said. 'She is very determined.'

'Megan is certainly self-centred but her family don't see it as a major problem,' I thought.

Michael and Penny dominated the conversation.

Afterwards I said to Megan alone: 'Penny seems to have assumed control.'

'The others control her more than it appears,' Megan said.

I realised that living at home, Penny had less autonomy than Megan.

'Why doesn't Penny move out?' I asked Megan.

'She gets waited on hand and foot,' she said. 'Why would she want to move out?'

'To be more independent, like you.'

'She has egoistical relationships with everyone, trying to get control,' Megan said.

'Her social relationships limit her,' I said. 'Penny wants control. You demand it.'

'Do I seem big-headed to you?' Megan asked.

'Not at all, but you need to avoid hubris syndrome. When you are a champion you can be an empress by entitlement for a short time. At others, you need humility and recognition of others, family for instance. You have to keep over-confidence in check and learn to avoid the mistake made by Icarus.'

'The god whose wings melted?'

'He flew too close to the Sun.'

'Do you think I'm over-confident?' asked Megan.

'A little, sometimes. Like me. I don't want to go overboard with my free will. I need to hold something back.'

'What?'

'I'm not sure,' I said. 'I need to go beyond Nietzsche. He wanted to replace religion but he didn't entirely succeed. I sometimes feel I have too much freedom and am slightly out of control.'

'In what way?'

'I could be less critical of religion, more sceptical and accept a humanitarian ceiling.'

'I don't have too much freedom,' said Megan. 'I want more.'

Our discussion had been frank and I was getting to know Megan. She had revealed herself to me and disclosed difficulties she was dealing with, beginning to trust me. My feelings sang when she was friendly, because more than anything I cared what Megan thought of me.

'Here you go, old chap,' George said refilling my glass, as if we were best of buddies.

'I want to tell you about my golf,' I said to George, smirking inwardly. 'I love the excitement and uninhibited freedom of the game. I'm rather good at it. When I am on a golf course, whether I am on a tee, smashing the ball out of sight, paddling in a lake to retrieve it, or nudging it gently towards the hole for a tenth attempt, I cannot resist the challenge. It never seems too easy to me. Whenever I play, I always explore new territory, getting into woodland, rough heaths and sand traps. Part of the physical challenge is lugging around a bagful of clubs that I seldom use. I take my putter for most shots and carry the bag as a workout.'

I had bragged deadpan, concealing my sarcasm.

George's face was part smile, part scowl.

'Golf is good for me,' I continued. 'It exercises my muscles in carrying and walking. I need precise control of my club to stop the ball taking off in any direction. I have found the best way to find my ball is to search along radii around the tee at increasing distances. Keeping track of the ball exercises my vision. It's forbidden to swim out into the deep part of lakes to retrieve balls and I have to trek back to the pro shop to buy more balls. Playing a round involves walking several times that distance.'

Now George had realised my sardonic self-deprecation and was beaming.

'Golf is a social game and when I can find someone who will play with me, we take turns and I have time to find my ball,' I said. 'Players normally stay with their opponents while they play shots, to stop them cheating. After losing a ball, dropping a ball into a favourable lie is an important skill I have.'

'You mean nudging it?' said George.

'No. Moving it's against the rules. Dropping it takes skill. Disputes while playing a round are not usual, but can be settled in the clubhouse bar.

'Part of the fun for me is to ignore abuse when I am being closely followed. While I am mishitting and searching for a lost ball, other players can demand to play through. I cheerfully acknowledge their gesticulations and shouts, which are a part of the excitement of the game.

'I once achieved a 'par' result for a hole I played. Numbers of strokes for a hole are labelled with names of birds: birdie: eagle: double eagle or albatross: bogey: double bogey: triple bogey and ace. There could be a duck too. A bogey is not a bird. I don't know what all those names mean. I won't worry about them until I am below 10 strokes per hole, which may not be for a while, but I am looking forward to it.'

'If I were you, I wouldn't bother,' said George. 'Stick to rugby.'

'Playing golf has been valuable to me in family relationships, at work and socially,' I said, undeterred. 'I have developed concentration and keen observation, able to size up situations before letting fly. When I miss badly, or am found out taking a short cut, I have learned that losing my temper or breaking my equipment won't help. At my office job, I stalk success as I do on a golf course. People leave me alone to plan my approach, to select the best strategy without getting lost. That's why I love golf. It expresses deep optimism about life and the need to get over losing my balls.'

I paused. George giggled.

'Chance, you are a bit of a card,' he said.

The conversation continued over dinner, with everyone joining in discussion of some old chestnuts and a few new ones. Five voices overlapped, in a chorus of responses, continuing until the next topic was broached. The twins and Lily tried to outdo each other in responding to the following conversation topics:

Is participation in athletics declining?

Should more athletes get university places?

Is testing for drugs in sport a sufficient deterrent?

Should athletes get more encouragement at school?

Should teachers advise students of sports and athletic of events that could suit them?

When competitiveness has declined, is a career in athletics possible?

Do athletes make good citizens?

Are girls closing the gap with boys in competition?

Which sports and events should be unisex?

The discussion was amiable, a sharing of perspectives, mostly with wide agreement. Family members held many views in common. They were polite in hearing my ideas and replying.

Lily was a charming and interesting conversationalist. She was a freelance journalist who wrote lifestyle articles for newspapers and magazines. I sensed that Megan and Penny were pitching for her attention. The others knew each other well and my presence was somewhat overlooked. Only George seemed not to be under Lily's spell and I wondered if he had failed in intimacy with her.

97

'You'll have to come to dinner again,' said Hannah.

'Thank you. I would like to,' I said. I wondered idly if I should invite Nick to meet Lily. He might find her too much of a handful. She was attractive and a focus of male interest. I could introduce them later.

That evening I went with Megan to a movie. She was relaxed and content with her performance earlier.

'Silver is my usual,' she said. 'Perhaps I'll get gold next time.'

I sensed that Megan was without the momentum needed to improve and had lost her way.

'I thought you were great,' I said. 'Winning isn't everything.'

I wanted to discover her view on the importance of winning.

'You equalled your personal best today,' I said.

'I had wanted higher, but equalling it was good enough,' she said.

'You did well.'

On the following day at the university, I asked Jack: 'How would it be if I investigated performers' improvements in flow?'

I told him I had experience earlier of coaching a marathon runner in flow (1).

'Did it make a difference?'

'Yes. There have been several investigations with flow giving positive results.'

'Flow has been investigated to death,' Jack said, 'but the causality and mechanism have not been discovered.'

'Not in psychology,' I said. 'Phenomenology is metaphysics and would cast a wider net. I hope to find new opportunities for athletes. Phenomenological analysis from the performer's viewpoint could assess their risk-taking intentions.'

'How can performers record their experiences while they are fully engaged?' he asked.

'It may be possible to prompt their recall with videos,' I said.

'What does your girl Megan think?'

'I haven't started her with flow yet. I want to set her up with phenomenology first.'

'How can you set her up?'

'She would have her own view of what she is doing and understand it.'

'Trying to change a performer's lived experience with flow could be difficult,' said Jack. 'Some psychologists regard flow as an escape from consciousness. It can't be both lived experience and unconscious at the same time. You could be chasing your tail and end up back where you started. But it's worth a shot. If you don't get anywhere, we can switch to something else.'

Jack had agreed to supervise my research into flow for a PhD. My research proposal was accepted. I had cleared the first hurdle, but I still had to run my race.

CHAPTER 20 CRICKET

I watched with Megan and Michael in the four row wooden stand, as Penny strolled out from the pavilion with the home captain and umpire. There were a dozen spectators. We were at a club in Sunnybank, a Brisbane suburb, with a bare patch of wicket in the centre of a manicured cricket oval and an ornate white pavilion. Penny wore a white shirt with cream flannels, a baggy dark green peaked cap and white boots. Her strong build and dark good looks matched the traditional captain's role she was playing. The trio reached the wicket. The umpire spun a coin.

'Visitors, what's your call?' she asked.

'Heads.'

They looked down at the ground.

'Heads it is. Will you bat?'

'No,' said Penny. 'We'll have them out inside 25 overs.'

'Visitors will bat. Captain, would you place your team, please.'

They went back inside.

A brush turkey, with its guilty head hung low, ran furtively to and fro inside the wire netting perimeter fence, seeking an opening to get out.

'It keeps repeating in the same place, like a needle stuck in the groove,' I said. 'It doesn't seem very smart,'

'Smart enough to be a turkey before there were wire fences,' Michael said.

'Should we help it?'

'No. Let it learn for next time.'

Penny and Lily led out the home eleven and Penny directed them to fielding positions.

'Have you watched before?' I asked Megan.

'Several times,' she said. 'I usually come for the area finals.'

'Why didn't you take up cricket?' I asked her.

'Penny loves the pageantry,' she said. 'She's an extrovert and in her element. There isn't enough action for me. I haven't the patience.'

Megan was more judgemental than perceptive, preferring objective issues rather than the subjectivity and passions of team competition. It was a clinical outlook, similar to my own, although I was more sceptical and agnostic.

Batters clumped out in pads, pulling on their gloves, waving their bats confidently to us in the stand. Guided by the umpire, they carefully marked their creases.

Passive traditions nauseated me. The futility of intelligent adults involving themselves in a pointless game repelled me. I had come to watch Megan's sister play cricket. I hadn't thought through that I would have to appear interested in all the other nonsense. It would have been pleasant to sit in the sun if the spectacle had appealed to me more.

'It's like watching opera,' I said to Megan. 'The stage has actors in traditional costumes performing well-known roles.'

I was predisposed by my reading of Debord to find a spectacle with domination of the lower class by middle class interests. His objection was that workers were exploited for profit by capitalists, alienating them. But the cricketers here were unpaid, presumably taking part from love of the game. There couldn't be much exploitation here.

I had known workers who far from being alienated, took pride in their work. They were amateurs. There was little evidence that the genteel culture here served capitalist interests. The ground and pavilion were supported by informal donations and bequests. No revolution of the lower classes was imminent here.

Megan said to me: 'This is a lovely cricket field, don't you think, Chance? There is a story that an American asked a groundsman at Cambridge University: 'How d'ya get the grass to grow so dang even?'

"We have watered it and cut it every day, for 500 years,' the groundsman said. The American changed his concept of the game from tribal contest to ritual.'

I laughed.

'Cricket is steeped in tradition,' I said. 'The batsmen, fielders and spectators, all seem drowsy in the sun, performing routine activities in slow motion. It's more about following the rules than about winning.'

'I agree,' Megan said. 'Penny likes order. That's why she is religious.'

'Which did she take up first, religion or cricket?'

'Religion.'

'Could playing cricket be like following a religious order?'

'Probably. They both involve a surfeit of pointless activity,' I said.

Penny opened the bowling, hurling the ball down to bounce at the batter's feet. The batter blocked each ball. Bowling switched to the other end for the next over. A spin bowler tossed twisters. The batter failed to connect, but the balls missed the stumps, with groans from the fielders.

'Do you like it?' Megan asked me.

'Penny is a good bowler,' I said, changing the subject.

The game continued at a leisurely pace in full sun. The only sound was the smack of the ball on willow and occasional shouts of 'Howzat.' They made 154 runs, with four batters bowled out, three catches and one run-out. There were five boundaries, one went over the pavilion and was found by a spectator. There were five dropped catches.

For lunch there was cold chicken and salad with mayonnaise, with lemonade or ginger beer. It had been brought by rostered home team players: Dawn and Jane. Penny's family had brought sandwiches and we all sat at a table with Penny and Megan, with Lily between us. The girls laughed and joked a lot and I was left out. Penny had her arm around Lily, while Megan flirted with Lily. I wondered if Megan had a lesbian interest, or she was trying to attract Lily away from Penny.

102

'It could be high spirits,' I thought. *'I can't be sure that Megan's hitting on Lily isn't to compete with Penny's lesbian pitch for her.'*

I had no experience of lesbian women and was repelled. I learned that Megan had other friendships and was jealous.

'How did you two come to be so different?' I said to Megan and Penny.

'At school,' Megan said, 'we both studied the philosophy of John Stuart Mill (1806-1873). According to him, an individual can have any liberty that does not adversely affect others. However, I was a competitor and wanted to adversely affect others. My liberty is wilful. I cannot be tamed. Mill's control is confining and unacceptable. Participation and winning are a part of human living and for Penny, 'playing the game' is everything. She wants rules to bring order and equality, with winning of less importance, whereas for me competition cannot be fair because individuals are different. That is how Penny and I are different.'

'Penny would find equality hard to achieve,' I said. 'Egalitarianism, or equalitarianism, is the doctrine that all people are equal and deserve equal social rights and opportunities.'

'We have a semblance of equality,' Penny said. 'Everyone is listed in the batting order and fielders have a say in their field positions. Assignments are selected for the common good. The competition is between two sides who are nominally equal. We have more equality than in other sports, such as athletics.'

'Athletics competitions equalise opportunity,' said Megan. 'They have equal rules to distinguish performances.'

Penny let it go.

During lunch, a young man, Lily's boyfriend Hugh, arrived. He played rugby with me in the winter.

'Sorry to miss the first half,' he said. 'I've been training the youth team. Have you batted yet?' he asked Lily.

'No. I'm in after lunch.'

Lily seemed indifferent to Hugh. She paid most attention to Megan. He looked put out.

103

When the lunch things were cleared away, the Home captain said: 'In you go Visitors!'

Penny and Lily walked out to open the batting. They quickly ran up 80 runs. Penny was caught behind for 42, ending a partnership which had some intimate moments.

'Penny is not hiding her affection for Lily,' I thought. *'If Lily hadn't flirted with Megan, I would think she and Penny are a couple.'*

I mused that Megan could have befriended me from social convention, rather than affection.

Lily made 45 and was caught out. The team scored 155 for six, which made it a win for Penny's side and the game ended. Everyone shook hands and some of them hugged. Then we had cucumber sandwiches and tea brought by Celia. After a modest but enjoyable tea, Penny stood up and thanked Dawn, Jane and Celia for the refreshments.

Penny was self-confident. I surmised her religion gave her life security and meaning.

I had watched Penny and Megan hitting on Lily and feared Megan had a lesbian interest in her.

CHAPTER 21 RELIGION

I talked with Megan and Penny as we waited for dinner at their parents' place.

'When you were at school, did you go to church?' I asked.

I wanted to find out if Megan had any religious or spiritual interest in her sport.

'For many years we went as a family,' Megan said.

'Then what happened?'

'I refused to go and they went without me.'

'Did you continue Penny?' I said.

'Yes.'

'I was the bad daughter,' said Megan. 'They said my wilfulness was my downfall. My parents accepted Schopenhauer's philosophy that free will encumbers human striving and causes lust, greed and misery, in a Hobbesian state of nature. They deduced I was dangerously wild and seeking liberation.'

'You were a sinner,' said Penny. 'They had evidence . . .'

'Not much,' said Megan interrupting her. 'They wanted me to take refuge in doleful religion, guided by religious claptrap:

'Willpower is to the mind like a strong blind man who carries on his shoulders a lame man who can see. Arthur Schopenhauer (1788-1860)

'I did not want to be carried by any religion, only by my strong belief in myself and my willpower,' said Megan. 'I was not lacking in vision, nor lame and could look out for myself without guidance. They tried me on Rousseau's collectivism too, but his freedom was all appearance:

'There is no subjection so perfect as that which keeps the appearance of freedom.' Jean-Jacques Rousseau.

'Rousseau (1712 – 1778) prevented personal freedom, not allowing an individual to deviate from the general will,' said Megan. 'Kant evaded the issue with a duality that our free acts of will take place, not in the phenomenal world, that has scientific laws, but in the noumenal world, which was inaccessible to scientific understanding. My free will, vital for my performing, was beyond understanding. It was acceptable but unknowable.'

'I accepted a leap of faith. That's where we parted company,' said Penny.

'Kierkegaard's (1813-1855) 'leap of faith' and his 'living with passion' acknowledged Free Will existentially,' Megan said. 'He seemed to cling to religion as a last desperate attempt to keep God in the picture, provoked by the assault of the heretic Nietzsche, who brought free will to prominence undeterred by rationalism or God.

'It must seem like I was a renegade,' said Megan, 'but I was genuinely frustrated and yearned for direction. I admired Penny's trust in her faith and Kierkegaard's passion, but I was looking for a perspective to guide development of my performing. That was when I discovered Nietzsche and I seemed to come home.'

Megan paused and looked at Penny and me apologetically.

'I hitched the philosophical compass of my motivation wagon to Nietzsche's daring,' Megan said. 'His will-to-power was existent self-expression and seemed at first able to contain my enthusiasm for performing. It was like looking through the wrong end of a telescope, reducing to a smaller field of view, making it easier to focus. But the outlook was too separate from others and lacked helpful perspectives of what competitors were doing.'

Penny had listened to her sister's account of her doubts without comment. Now she told how her own religious beliefs had evolved.

'Megan's beliefs have accommodated her yearning for personal control and omitted concern about others,' said Penny. 'For me, religion has put concern for others at the core of my spiritual life.'

106

'That's not fair,' said Megan. 'I don't display my concern for others as publicly as you do yours.'

Penny continued undeterred: 'I read Kierkegaard at the same time as Megan and took a 'leap of faith'. I worshipped with our parents and carved my life around a religious tradition. I learned how to lead a pure and good life through virtue and reason.'

'Your goodness and morality are not without critics,' said Megan scathingly. 'Your church has not endeared itself to those who want drug control laws repealed. I don't want to argue about that here. How about you, Chance, did you have a religious upbringing?'

'I toyed with religious devotion,' I said. 'I spent weeks of summer camp on my knees at bible college and I hated it. I was like Groucho Marx, who wouldn't join any group that would have him as a member.'

'Do you mean you were too individual to join the religious group?'

'I didn't want to be in any group, religious or otherwise.'

'Faith requires subscribing as a member to share in a purpose. It took me years on my knees, before the mystery of my religion was revealed to me,' said Penny.

'You made me seem wicked,' said Megan. 'You have been narrow.'

'I had a boyfriend for a while, but it didn't last,' said Penny. 'I looked inside myself for approval and found it. My faith is a leap that cannot be justified rationally. God is the reference point in my life.'

She sang quietly: 'Then sings my soul, my saviour God to thee,

'How great thou art, how great thou art.'

'That song tells my belief and happiness,' said Penny. 'I doubt non-believers have as much reverence for whatever they follow.'

'You make us non-believers seem like simpletons,' I said, 'but some of us are grounded in objective reality. A supernatural deity cannot be rationally proven and faith cannot rely on sound logic alone.'

'My posture towards my God is humility and contrition,' said Penny. 'Non-believers' seem less oriented towards reflection and learning.'

'Kierkegaard's leap of faith was romantic and fanciful,' Megan said. 'My own belief is that I must be master of myself, with rights to individual judgement.'

'What's so special about you?' Penny said.

'I am unique,' said Megan. 'Religion subordinates the individual, who must move from social to egoistic relationships in order to escape subjection. I must avoid subordinating myself to others and escape from being 'dragged along' by my appetites, as you inevitably are Penny, living at home.'

'Are you saying my religion is socially conditioned?' said Penny.

'I think Megan means that it easier for her to dispense with a religious belief, because she is alone,' I said.

'Isolating yourself in a hall of residence, Megan, does not remove your need for direction in your life,' said Penny. 'Your beliefs seem unduly egocentric. My idea of religion is not what I am to know, but what I can give my life to believe in because it's 'right' or 'true'. 'My individuality is not mine by right, but by faith, which is a force without reason from within me, personal and passionate. I choose to believe.'

'I can't imagine having faith,' Megan said. 'I find the notion disquieting, like when friends in the dressing room brag about having sex and I have had none. I wonder how they can be so sure they have found the real thing.'

'Do you try to find out?' Penny asked, seeming curious about Megan's sex life.

I looked at Megan and raised an eyebrow. Megan sometimes surprised me with her atheism and scepticism. I wondered if I was imagining her, because she seemed too good to be true, like a stuffed toy with only an outside to be seen.

'I don't need to,' said Megan. 'Their experiences may not be the real thing. I'd rather not know. '

'Penny, you have chosen to subordinate yourself to an ideal,' I said. 'Megan has not shut the door to it.'

'There is much more to it than that,' Penny said. 'Sharing a faith is part of belief. I am trying to live virtuously with others, whereas Megan has mere egoism, that respects no-one and is anarchy.'

'I have sceptical science, not nihilism as you suggest.'

'Megan, you are preoccupied with a small part of what being human is all about. People have feelings too.'

'Feelings are a fickle task master,' I said.

'Feelings won't disappear by ignoring them. They work in your subconscious. When I am in batting at cricket, I am not afraid because I trust in God to protect me. I face all things in my life like that.'

'You are no more feeling than me,' said Megan.

'It's arguable,' said Penny. 'You have cut yourself off, whereas I go to God.'

Megan was indignant.

'When I perform, I try to be totally in control of myself and fearless, knowing things can go wrong, because my mind is set on doing as well as I can.'

'I do that too,' said Penny. 'My posture in all things is like batting, depending on my senses and skills to stay in.'

'I am not so defensive,' said Megan. 'My goals achieve something. That means everything to me.'

'Is clearing a high bar important, or did I miss something?' said Penny.

The conversation had become acerbic.

'Girls, girls,' I said. 'Can there be a compromise between you?'

'Our differences don't need to be reconciled,' Penny said frostily.

'I am not comfortable to be with passionate persons,' I said. 'Penny, I would like to persuade you to give up your plunge into dark faith and to adopt self-interest. It is more reliable.'

'Aren't you suspicious of self-interest?' she said, scoffing. 'Hasn't self-interest been exploited by the worst kinds of political brigand? Cults revering individuality have no future in civilised society. Their anarchy will bring chaos.'

109

'Perhaps it's the political process that has been at fault, not the ontology of self,' I said. 'Self-interest and egoism are consistent with stability, whereas false leaders can lead idealism to chaos.'

'You are wrong,' Penny said. 'There is no way to compromise rule by God with rule by Godless individuals.'

'That seems unkind,' I said. 'Megan, Lily, Hugh and I have not experienced your God epiphany, but that doesn't make us godless, bad people.'

'No,' she said. 'Your godlessness is scepticism, not evil. But scepticism doesn't get you anywhere, as Schopenhauer pointed out:

'Scepticism is an impregnable fortress from which the garrison can never sally forth.'

'In other words, you can have your doubtful cake, but you can't eat it,' Penny said. 'Your scepticism is not a practical philosophy for living.'

'You are being offensive,' said Megan. 'You are trying to pull out from under me my hopes and the science that sustains them. It is a weakness of my position as a sceptic that I can't dismiss the nonsense of you religious believers.'

'Penny has a right to her religion and to criticize ours,' I said. 'She can expect to be criticized, but she should not have her beliefs dismissed as nonsense. I hope we can stay friends. I have to go to a lecture. We'll have to continue this discussion another time.'

'I enjoyed it,' said Penny. 'Goodbye Chance.'

CHAPTER 22 MOTIVES

I went every afternoon to Megan's athletics ground to watch her train. I was inconspicuously investigating how she could improve with more awareness of risk-taking and more understanding of her motives.

Motivation was a preoccupation in both my own and Megan's research. I had drawn her attention to the theories of Nietzsche.

'The motives Nietzsche admired were elite,' said Megan. 'His father was a Lutheran pastor and Friedrich became a privileged and radical intellectual. He was a university professor at age 24, when he became an atheist. He aspired to have influence beyond the reach of ordinary people.'

'He lived in solitude and simplicity, without friends,' I said. 'His woman friend left him. He wanted to show people how to get everything they could from a godless, meaningless and pointless world.'

'Nietzsche's ego was somewhat sublimated and wilful, typical of society's elite at that time,' Megan said. 'It was his rejection of religion and traditions that spoke to me.'

'He would have approved of your new personal best at the State Championships,' I said. 'He would have perceived you as a ubermensch, overcoming your inhibitions, daring to be great, with the sky as your limit.'

'Would critics say I was elite, or exclusive?'

'Neither,' I said. ''You don't have a lust for fame.

'Unfortunately I do,' I thought. ' *I have wanted to perpetuate my memory with academic achievement. It would be better to have more tangible and less selfish goals.'*

'Nietzsche would have admired your unstoppable daring,' I said. 'Achieving your personal best was in the right spirit. It was a better result than coming second.'

'That's how I see it. When I compete, I turn my dial to full on. My run-up is flat out. I don't muck about.'

'You make the most of yourself in every muscle,' I said. 'Let's have lunch.'

We ate at the kiosk in St Lucia, near our work. She bought a salad focaccia and I had a ham and tomato sandwich. After eating, we strolled along a campus boulevard treed with Poicianas, magnificent shade trees with clusters of fiery-red fan shaped flowers with dangling seed pods.

'For Nietzsche will was everything,' Megan said. 'He emulated Napoleon and influenced Hitler and Stalin. My will is not monstrous, nor do I need to win. I am at pains to reconcile my daring with reasonable goals. Nietzsche would have expected more from me. He wants everything. It is too much.

'Psychologist Abraham Maslow was more believable,' she said. 'He was from a working class Jewish family and his theory of psychological health and self-actualisation explained the people he knew. They were people who had needs, as do the unemployed I am investigating. They are ordinary people seeking rewards, living austerely and avoiding punishment.'

'Fair enough,' I said. 'I don't see rewards motivating you, but perhaps I don't know you well enough.'

'I don't need external rewards,' Megan said. 'What motivates you?'

'I want to make a difference for ordinary people,' I said.

This was my stock answer, when really I am in it for myself,' I thought.

'Why?' she asked.

'To do the greatest possible good, which Aristotle called Eudaimonia.'

'What is the greatest good?' she asked.

'It's happiness that is seized, like Nietzsche's daring,' I said.

'Is it the happiness of the *carpe diem* motif?'

'Yes, but obtained from other people. Nietzsche dared us, like the Roman Poet Horace, to 'seize the day' and be great,' I said. 'He rejected Descartes view of reality split into mind and matter, subject and object, observer and observed, knower and known. Nietzsche asked whether man is a result of the erroneous work of God or God is the error of man.'

'I don't get it,' she said. 'Are you saying Nietzsche wanted us to pursue lofty causes?'

'Yes, but not God. Husserl took this further in examination of consciousness without a dualistic split and its objects as Lebenswelt, 'life's world'. Heidegger, his student, united the observer–observed dyad to include existential concerns: awareness of intent, meaning, objectives, curiosity, idle talk, ambiguity, thrown-ness, fallen-ness and provenance.

'Did Heidegger want recognition of nuances of meaning in the performance?'

'Yes.'

'Who was to do the recognising, the coach or the athlete?'

'Either or both. He described the performance and left it to us to decide how to organise it. Observer awareness of the subject opened new vistas of fulfilment. Subject awareness of the observer created other dimensions of performance.'

'You want me to observe matters I have been unaware of,' said Megan. 'Could that be a problem?'

'They could, if I had an agenda, but Heidegger prescribed a method to avoid that, called 'bracketing',' I said. 'He excluded potential for observer bias with attention to the phenomenon.'

CHAPTER 23 ANALYST

Megan's athleticism was astonishing. At the Southeast Area Championship she had cleared a height within one percent of the Australian record. Her *dasein* was as an elite performer, a role with special being. Heidegger used the term 'dasein', translated as 'Being there', to emphasize that a human existence is a subjective activity, more than a state or condition. To analyse it, I needed to stand in her shoes, fully understanding her position. She explained to me what she did, but I was not nearly able to understand it from her perspective. Any help originating from my own experience of pole vaulting could do more harm than good.

'Nietzsche's will-to-power impacted the world as a monism, with the subject and observer having the same view,' I said to Megan. 'What an observer sees doesn't matter. First Husserl and then Heidegger tried to see the subject's situation from her own point of view. Phenomenalism transfers responsibility from the observer to the subject, with achievement on the subject's own terms.'

'Heidegger repositioned the observer to look at the world over the subject's shoulder, instead of from the independent viewpoint of an observer. The observer is less self-important and more sensitive to a subject's intentions, meanings and needs, which can be original. The view is not of an unfeeling subject, like an inanimate object, but a view of a *being there*.

This meant a dramatic change in feedback to Megan from her performing. It was a huge shift for Megan to forego independent coaching. Control became internalised in her. It would take time for her to accept her new more responsible perspective and I would have to be patient.

'You look nice,' I said when I met her for lunch at the Museum.

She was wearing a colourful frock with bare arms and legs.

'Thank you.'

'I want to remind you to do your own analysis,' I said to Megan. 'After today, I will be more like a facilitator of your training. I won't be imposing my views at all. Your locus, or place, of control has moved from coach-centred to student-centred.'

'What's the difference?'

'Your coach has been directing you. Now you are in charge.'

'Wow. What if get it wrong?

'You won't, but in case you want to blame yourself, remember yours is the most relevant and immediate experience.'

'Won't I need others' advice?'

'You will still have the benefit of others experience, when it is relevant. Others' pole vaulting experience and scientific experience may not be relevant. We will follow the procedure of Husserl (1859-1938). To prepare to help you, I must erase my own memories of pole vaulting and put aside my scientific understanding. I will 'bracket' them by telling you my experience, so you can correct me if I persist with any of it.

To set aside my performing experience I must spend some time reflecting on my experiences, as I am doing now.'

'Can't you just forget them?' Megan asked.

'The experiences are ingrained in me, even after all this time. To bracket them, or separate them, I need to revisit them.

'I did some pole vaulting, many years ago,' I said. 'I want you to imagine I gained my experience in ways you have been learning to perform here.'

My earliest memories of the event I call 'performing' was in PE classes, grappling with the pole and the difficult and unforgiving nature of the technique. I had experimented at home with stilt-walking, ladder-balancing, tight rope walking, whip-cracking, bareback pony riding, box-vaulting and trapeze. I had seen them at circuses and practiced them in the farm barns with ropes hung from beams. My attention was on gaining enough speed to be lifted by a wooden pole. A low bar lacked kudos, so I was overly ambitious and most attempts failed. After a series of knockdowns. clearing the bar was euphoric.

'I had set my sights on being a fast bowler at cricket. After my full toss struck a batsman on the head, the coach of my school's First XI cricket team ordered me to cease bodyline bowling.

'Don't bowl so fast — it's dangerous,' he said. 'Aim for the wicket, not the batter.'

'I ignored his warning and continued to bowl quickly, at body height. I didn't recognise the ban on speed. Bodyline was not against game rules, but it could be stopped under an umpire's authority. I was dropped from the team.'

'That was harsh,' said Megan.

'I had been warned before,' I said. 'Even so, I was chagrined that I had been rejected despite being good at taking wickets. It was humiliating for me, but I was glad to stop spending Wednesday afternoons waiting in the pavilion, as last man in the batting order, when I was itching to develop my physical skills. I had been thwarted and I was angry.

'I applied my athleticism to field events with a couple of others who also lacked cricket finesse. I had a strong arm and could throw the javelin and pole vault. Perhaps the sports teachers thought a self-discipline experience would do me good.'

'The PE teacher who supervised us lacked ability to demonstrate pole vaulting skills and my development was mainly by trial and error. There were many possible errors and I suffered sprains, cuts and abrasions from impacts with the uprights, bar and unpadded ground. My improvement was slow and I managed a height of only 3.5 metres.'

'3.5 metres isn't much,' said Megan.

'It seemed like a lot at the time.

'I didn't have a coach and took responsibility for my own learning. I competed against students from schools with experienced coaches. I went with our team to compete in the area sports carnival. My poles were rigid tapered aluminium, revolutionary in their day, but no match for my rivals' bendy polycarbon-fibre poles. They could store more energy and flipped the performer much higher. I began at 3.5 metres and cleared it, but when they raised it to 4.0 metres, I was eliminated.

'Although pole vault was my preferred field event, I was frustrated and switched to training for javelin. Javelin required speed and brute violence. My friend Jude was a kindred spirit, a reject from cricket, with a chip on his shoulder. He practiced at javelin with me. On our school's Performing Day, Jude revealed psychopathic intent.

'I am going to spear me a teacher,' he said.

He almost impaled a teacher who was judging from beside the landing sector. Jude was disqualified and expelled from the school.

'After that, I threw the javelin alone. I lacked coaching. I learned that to succeed, hard work and practice are needed. With my academic subjects, I had more guidance and had success. In pole vaulting, without guidance, my success was limited.

'So that's my experience of performing,' I said to Megan. 'I am putting it all aside, bracketing it, so I can help you analyse your performance from your point of view.'

'I need you to get me started,' she said.

'I'll be pleased to,' I said. 'But I won't be coaching you the old-fashioned way. You will have to assert your viewpoint with confidence.'

'That's my inclination,' she said. 'I don't like being pushed around by anyone. For me the worst aspect of being coached has been coaches' preoccupations with their pasts, their so-called experience, while ignoring my wants in the present.'

'It won't be like that,' I said. 'I will leave out my experience and help you to understand your present. I will be there when you need me. I won't criticize you."'

'Looking at my performance from the inside is daunting; but having you with me is reassuring,' she said. 'Thank you.'

As we left the Museum, we looked at a model of a Shakespearian royal court scene in a display case, with figurines in intricate costumes.

'Performers' have set roles,' I said. 'You are the performer in scenes where you are the focus of the drama. We will work out who else is there and what we can do to bring out the best in you.'

117

CHAPTER 24 PHENOMENON

I drove to the Queensland Championships at Nathan in Brisbane, taking Megan and Lily.

'I'll watch you when you get to the National,' Penny had told Megan the night before at dinner.

'You won't want me there,' Michael said to me. 'You said you want the focus on what she is doing to come from herself.'

'I would like you to be there, in the stand,' said Megan, disappointed.

'I'll come to the National,' he said.

He seemed a little put out. It was a change in Megan's performance after many years with her father watching and coaching.

Lily and I watched Megan from the stand. I went down and videoed Megan's vaults from the barrier, shooting from several angles, because her phenomenon was multi-dimensional.

'Why are you videoing her?' Lily asked me.

'I want to describe what she does,' I said.

'But you can see what she's doing.'

'It is her view of herself that I want and the video will help her tell me.'

'What do you want it for?'

'As a basis for her to improve.'

'Oh,' Lily said.

There were 17 competitors and the event lasted about 4 hours.

Megan's winning jump was 4m95, equalling her personal best at the Area Championships.

'It's a good result,' I said to her.

118

'The record is 5m00. Perhaps I choked, with a ceiling at my personal best. If I had jumped over 4m95 in training, I might have broken the record.'

'You came close. Well done.'

I had videoed her jumps and was looking forward to analysing the recordings.

Afterwards, I said to Lily: 'I need to talk to Megan alone, while it's fresh in her mind. Do you mind waiting for us for 15 minutes?'

I led Megan to the back of the stand where it was quiet and we sat together. Lily was curious and positioned herself where she could see us.

I told Megan: 'The philosophers Husserl and Heidegger identified how to observe a subject's individual lived experience, considering it as a phenomenon. I want you to regard your performance just now as a phenomenon.'

'What difference will it make?'

'A huge difference. The change in perspective could affect how you perform in future, by existential awareness of your actions and personal awareness that you haven't noticed, nor observed, nor recorded before.'

'Do you mean my perspective has been incomplete?'

'Exactly,' I said. 'It is not a personal failing, but a common flaw in training. I need you to imagine 'being there' and describe your jump in minute detail. The other day we bracketed my performing experience. That excluded my familiarity and clears the way for you to record your experience and then analyse it.

'Please recount your thinking from the start, to the end, including any reasoning or evidence you recall having at the time.'

'Okay,' said Megan, sitting back and closing her eyes. 'I'll tell you about my winning personal best jump just now at 4m95.'

'Tell me your dasein, your lived experience, exactly as it seemed to you at the time, what it meant to you. When you contemplate your intentions, you should refrain from judging or holding back information, so the validity of natural attitudes is not negated. Hold off from world-views and give as much detail as you can.'

I placed my phone on the seat between us.

119

'Are you okay with my voice recorder?' I asked.

'Are you going to quote me?'

'I wouldn't quote you without your permission. You can approve the transcript.'

'What if I change my mind?'

'You will be able to correct the transcript. But you won't be held to anything. Your attention should be on distinguishing appropriate perceptual structures.'

'What does that mean?'

'If you find yourself telling it to someone else, mention who. For example, you might imagine addressing another performer, who you could tell your 'being there' to.

'You could say something like: 'Lisa, I am trying to spring up the way you do.'

Lisa Hemmings was the current World Champion.

'Okay,' Megan said.

'Ready?'

I switched on the recorder and Megan began her account.

'There were 17 of us . . .'

'Present tense please. Say 'There are 17 of us . . .''

There are 17 of us competing. I opted to commence at 4m90, my personal best. My goal for this competition is 5m00. There are only two other girls remaining. I had cleared 4m90 and so had they. With the bar at 4m95, we all knock it down twice. Next will be my last attempt.

'That's fine, Megan,' I said. 'Can you be more definite about what you experienced so that others can put themselves in your shoes. For example, names of objects and numbers of things. Give your impressions, telling your understanding. Imagine we want to reproduce the situation in a model and we only have your words to go on. Tell us your intention, what you are doing and what it means.

'It's my 4th jump in this competition and I am warmed up. I jog around waiting for my turn, keeping my muscles warm. My head is clear, alert. When the stewards are ready for me, I step onto the runway with the pole forward from my shoulder, resting on the ground. The other girls are watching. I want them to see me do a new personal best. I play images forward in my mind of the sequence of actions I will take and how I will feel, right through to landing on the mat.

'My other marker is 24 running paces along the runway, before the box, where I will spring up holding the planted pole above my head, at arms length.

'My goal is foremost in my mind: the bar is at 4m95, 5 cm higher than my personal best. I concentrate and imagine clearing it.'

'I am poised on the runway. I try to ignore the other competitors talking near me. I know you are videoing me. I focus on my goal and my body. I rock to and fro, several times, beginning my routine. If my run isn't precise, my pole plant will be wrong, a no-jump. Even small differences in my take-off could make the difference between sailing over and getting tangled up with the bar and uprights.

'The runway is 40 metres of multi-layer, springy synthetic material with a waterproof sealed surface. I spring forward and stride with maximum effort, pushing with my toes. I have been weight training every day, overloading for strength, ignoring muscle pain. I can feel the right Achilles tendon I injured 3 months ago. There is a risk it could start up again but I cannot wait any longer for healing. It could need a year to regain full flexibility. It feels good enough. Today it will get a full load.

'Terrific so far. I have been totally with you. You are equivocal about whether your Achilles' is sufficiently healed. It's a threat to your performance. Did you make any concessions to it?'

Not consciously. My second stride, off my weak right leg, is shorter than I wanted. I am annoyed and briefly consider starting the run again, but it's not too short and I continue. I will be behind my plan, with insufficient momentum, unless I am strong enough to catch up.

Megan's provision for her injury was impressive. She was objective and calculating.

'You seem conflicted between your original run-up plan and the need to adjust it for taking-off early?' I asked. 'Because you were annoyed, did you expect this to detract from your performance?'

'No. I was in automatic and the annoyance was fleeting.'

'You told me about your injury in the past tense. Would you use the present tense, please?'

'Sorry. I am running with the pole in front of me. I gradually lower it into the box as I accelerate up to maximum speed at take off. If I run faster, my torso would not be steady, the pole could waver and I might miss the box.

'My body feels good, taut and ready, slicing through the cool air. As I run up, my mind is sensing any fine-tuning needed for my sub-goal of a strong take-off leap from my weak right Achilles. Would I be early? Was my correction enough?

'I imagine the wrenching pain from the stopped pole unless I spring up in good time. I know from experience a shoulder dislocation would be extremely painful.'

'How do you anticipate the pain?' I asked.

'They say that pain is weakness coming out. I ignore it.'

'Your comments about the pole are revealing,' I said. 'The pole is an essential accessory to your 'being there' and you have a top priority of controlling it. Could you foresee having any other problems with the pole?'

'It could snap; or my hands might slip down; or it might spring out of my grasp. This pole is quite new. I have done grip-strengthening exercises. Some adjustment of my hands could be

needed. Now I spring up powerfully, bending the pole, my shoulder muscles braced for a shock. I am gripping the pole fiercely, with the help of the tack I smeared on my hands, I dread having my hands skid down the pole and landing on my bum.

'As I feared, my take-off is a little short. I can still do it. I have sprung early and too much of my momentum is spent impacting the box, rather than bending the pole and storing energy. As always, I fear that the pole has bent so far it will snap. Relief when it doesn't.

'I hold on to the bent pole and feel myself being lifted in slow motion, enjoying the ride, looking around, judging exactly when to swing up into a handstand on the pole. I must conserve sufficient momentum and elastic energy to reach the bar. I must convert my energy into height potential over the bar, without risking falling back.

'I have practiced it many times and this time I try to push myself higher than ever before, making the movement continue longer, taking my time, going up and up, the sweetest time, with my body held up as if by magic, going higher than ever, without me changing hand positions, which would be a foul.'

'You are aware of your technique in relation to the rules for this event. Are you in danger of breaking the rules of hand position?

'The rule is that my hands must not change position up the pole and I grasp it strongly. Out of the corner of my eye I can see the bar silhouetted above and behind me. I am looking down the pole as I push down on it, straightening my arms, obtaining a few more centimetres of height for my body to pass over the bar, feet first, in slow motion, legs, torso then arms. Then I am falling down, recumbent, to sink into the soft landing mat. The pole clatters down nearby. I stand up and wade off the mat, with the watchers loyally calling 'Yay, Megan!'

'It's good to have their acknowledgement.

''Too easy,' I say, sardonically.'

123

'Your idle talk reveals you are pleased to achieve a personal best,' I said, interrupting her.

'I was pleased to achieve my own standard. It wasn't a perfect jump but it is a new personal best of 4m95 and I feel euphoric. Cool.
'I watched the other two girls fail and knew I was the winner.
'Then I could attempt the record. I tried but knocked it down. I didn't mind — there would be other opportunities another day.
'I feel terrific, pleased with myself. The striving and hurt of training had been worthwhile. That's all I can think of.'

'Thanks,' I said switching off the voice recorder. 'I'll transpose it into a script and let you check it.'

'It's a big task for you,' she said. 'I talked my head off.'

'It'll be a guide for things to look for when we watch the videos.'

'Can we look for ways I could improve?'

'We need your record of an unsuccessful performance for that. This one will familiarize us with your thinking when it was fulfilled. Your account is more than a description; it asks questions and poses hypotheses. Your perspective is unique and existential.'

'Won't it lose its value with time?'

'Yes. We have to do it soon.'

'I think you've hit on something important with this recording,' Megan said. 'Thank you.'

'No problem,' I said, hooking my arm through hers. 'Let's go.'

We went to where Lily was waiting and then back to my car to drive home.

'Does she know what's she's doing?' asked Lily.

'Yes,' I said. 'Her self-awareness is impressive.'

'Megan is cool,' she said. 'With her, every moment counts.'

'Her account revealed her intentions and how they affected her actions,' I said. 'It will be a pleasure to analyse it.'

It was a phenomenological analysis of her personal lived experience. My first idea had been that Megan could improve her performance by Nietzschean willpower but Megan's intention went far beyond daring to be great. To be great was her intention but her deliberation was less cognitive and more visceral. She was driven partly by will, but she had added self-expression, as if she enjoyed exploring her limits.

CHAPTER 25 BEING THERE

At the wheel on the way home I said to Megan: 'You should be feeling pretty good about today. Are you still euphoric?'

'A little,' she said. 'You sound conflicted that I am emotionally involved in my performing.'

'Aristotle regarded courage as a mean between fear and reckless confidence. Consorting with an honest candid type like me will restrain your impudence and any overconfidence.'

'What impudence?'

'Could you have been a little precocious?'

'He's right,' said Lily.

'Coy would be a kinder word,' said Megan.

'How about cute. What do you think, Lily?' I asked.

Her crush confronted, Lily was embarrassed. 'Yes, cute, definitely,' she stumbled.

It was my jealousy that had asked the question. As usual, I had strong feelings and Megan was cool and calm. My feelings were for her, but as usual she was acting detached.

'Some people don't form close attachments,' I thought. I had found out from the Internet about a condition called disassociation. It could explain how Megan kept at a distance from everyone, including me.

She had recounted her winning performance and I had recorded it. Her account was thoughtful and its appeal to me went far beyond cognition and into a realm of passion. My affection for her lacked objectivity, having adoration I had never felt for any human being before. I was numb and tongue tied.

'That was amazing,' I said, my words stumbling. 'Your understanding of the physics is excellent.'

'Dad helped me.'

'I may be able to help you improve some more.'

Her silence could mean that I was being tedious, clumsy and insensitive to her. My desire for her was genuine, but my authenticity might seem awkward.

She looked at me doubtfully.

'You?' she said. 'Improve how?'

'With physics and metaphysics.'

I wouldn't tell her my ideas about flow yet, until I was sure it could help her.

I had been without any girlfriend since Georgina, Nicola and Tania. Having a sincere relationship with Megan, without long term commitment, seemed contradictory. I wanted to be involved in other compartments of her life. Despite the distance between us, I had become infatuated with her. I wanted her and could think of nothing else but seducing her.

Summoning my courage, I took her back to my place and into my bed. Our shyness had gone. Our coupling was intense with sensitive attention to each other, seamy, steamy and moist. I had been close to partners before, but never as close as this. It was an experience that changed me forever.

Afterwards, we lay side by side and talked about this and that.

Presently I said: 'Do I seem like I want to be your coach?'

Megan hesitated and I knew she did not want that. She knew that I did not want to wear the mantle of a traditional coach.

'You?' she was incredulous. 'You are too deferent. Coaches are assertive. Is it important for you to be my coach?' Megan asked.

'No. You don't need an assertive coach. I want you to take over your training. I'll show you how to look through the wrong end of a performance telescope and clearly see everything important.'

'I'm not sure I want you sitting on my shoulder.'

'Isn't that what I have been doing so far? You may not have noticed, but I have helped uncover some important aspects of your performing.'

'What was important?'

'Your ultimate goal, meaning and intention,' I said.

'Why are they important?'

'Heidegger went into great detail teasing out those features of a phenomenon and how to reveal them,' I said.

'Like what?'

'I have tried to apply Heidegger's principles to your performing, but his text has complex ideas in German. I think I understand well enough to apply them. For example, he requires any discourse about the phenomenon should not be idle talk, nor ambiguous, neither fallen, nor thrown and always curious.'

'Whoa! One at a time, please. Should I refrain from idle talk?' she said.

'Yes. The phenomenon description has to be authentic and idle talk would detract.'

'Why would chat be inauthentic?'

'I suppose when we articulate our experiences, it sets in our minds the concepts we will enact. Our talk shouldn't be frivolous or it could instil false ideas.'

'I can see how being sincere and unambiguous would be necessary by the same reasoning,' Megan said. 'How about avoiding being 'fallen'? What does that mean?

''Being there' can 'fall' away from its authentic potentiality, by absorption in Being-with-one-another. Heidegger's antidote is curiosity, which enables intelligibility and learning, preventing fallen-ness.'

''What about being 'thrown'?' Megan asked.

'I think his idea is to avoid naivety and not have an arriviste mindset. You have been thrown into pole vaulting. You need to be familiar with the world of your phenomenon,' I said.

'Fair enough.'

'Those are the qualities your phenomenon needs to be authentic.'

'It's like a checklist of dos and don'ts for me to be aware of,' Megan said. 'Do I have to know them?'

'It will take some time. I'll help you.'

'I'll try to remember.'

'It is most important that your body is ready for optimal achievement, like an instrument that has been tuned. Heidegger's nuances of mental posture are like fine tuning.'

'Does that leave anything for you to do?'

'Haha. You need to be more aware than me, but I can prompt you. I'll be there in support.'

'What is my ultimate goal?' Megan asked.

'According to Heidegger, in the end we will all die. We need to live our lives keeping that in mind.'

'How depressing.'

'Not necessarily. Death could be the crowning achievement of a life of accomplishment, the greatest moment of one's career. Life is part of a phenomenon of living. Heidegger's logical response was to live with one foot in the grave and the certainty of death.'

'Wouldn't it be more logical to imagine one's life like Schrodinger's Cat: alive and dead at the same time?' Megan asked.

'That would focus one's life on an uncertain existence, less inclined to be distracted by things that don't matter. It could be deflating and depressing, even absurd.'

'I suppose waiting for certain death could be more pleasant than living precariously,' she said. 'Living with that cat would cause me anxiety. I think I would prefer being in Heidegger's terminal state.'

'It's for you to try,' I said. 'I can't show you how you will end up or when, but I can help you focus on things that matter.'

'How did you come to Heidegger?' Megan asked later in the journey.

'I had never liked science's dualism,' I said. 'The balance between an observer and a subject is arbitrary and too artificial for me. It is uncreative because an observer has to already know what he's expecting to observe. However well-prepared he is, he can miss a lot.

'In a famous experiment, an audience is watching a basketball game. They have been instructed to observe and keep a record of players who score. During the game, a person wearing a gorilla costume walks onto the court, across the playing area and away. When questioned afterwards, no-one saw the 'gorilla'. The unexpected was not observed.

'I want to observe and record your unexpected. It could be important. Heidegger's phenomenalism attends to the subject's meaning of events and her intentions, rather than the observer's.

'Heidegger's abstract ideas are difficult to interpret, because his writing is long and dense. I do not claim to understand it well. I have glimpsed his philosophical postures of contemplation and thinking, in observers and their subjects. Heidegger describes precisely how to apply them in practical contexts. That is what I have been trying to do with you.'

'Do you want me to look for gorillas when I'm performing?' Megan asked.

'Yes. There could be other things going on too,' I said.

CHAPTER 26 EVALUATION

The following day I met Megan mid-morning at the research centre's coffee bar.

'Do you still think my jump yesterday was okay?' she asked.

'It was perfect,' I said.

'Really?'

'You cleared 4m95, a new personal best.'

'It wasn't perfect,' she said.

'It seemed perfect to me.'

'Well, I should know,' said Megan. 'It didn't feel extraordinary enough.'

'Well observed,' I said. 'It is your evaluation as the performer is what counts. Robert Persig in his novel The Art of Motorcycle Maintenance (7) had a protagonist who evaluated what was good for him as 'quality', an elusive and existential entity, fundamental to contented living. If you can discern the quality of your performances, you can train to attain high quality, like tuning a motorbike. He relates this approach as a precondition for rational problem solving. The romantic approach focusses on being 'in the moment' and is unable to apply rational analysis and depends on others for problem solving. He is unable to tune his motorbike.'

'But isn't it higher quality when I reach a greater height?' she said. 'I don't need to evaluate my performance.'

'No, the height you achieve is a romantic outcome and you may not have it by safe, efficient, reproducible processes,' I said. 'A low quality jump could be a personal best, but technically a cul-de-sac without a future. A high quality jump could be a knockdown, but full of promise. Evaluation of quality has a wider view than the outcome of any one jump.'

'Wow! What a mind blowing concept!' Megan said. 'What is 'quality'?'

'Persig is ambiguous and says quality cannot be defined because it is recognised by informal thinking.'

'So why bother with quality?'

'A jump has many qualities but there is no simple formula for distinguishing high from low quality. We can take various aspects into consideration without being able to reach an overall conclusion.'

'Why do it then?'

'To fine tune your performances,' I said. 'Let's start on that now.'

'All three jumps were knockdowns,' she said. 'Does their quality matter?'

'Your best knockdown could be your starting point for next time.'

'I may leave out something important.'

'Tell what you can recall,' I said. 'Let's go to that table over there.'

We changed to a corner where we wouldn't be overheard.

'Okay,' I said. 'Tell your experience, please.'

'I'll try,' she said. 'Here goes.'

I switched on my voice recorder and Megan closed her eyes as she recounted.

'It was the Queensland Championship and I had won with a personal best of 4m95. They allowed me to attempt the record of 5m00. That was my goal I had trained for. I could have three attempts. After I had knocked it down twice, this is my final attempt. Although I was unsuccessful, it's etched in my memory.

'I took my longest pole . . .'

I interrupted. '. . . Present tense, please. We need your lived experience. Stay in each moment, until you have sucked out the relevance.'

I am using my longest pole because my normal pole had only just reached 4m95. It's quite a bit longer and requires more speed. I have done 6 jumps today and am feeling tired after competing for 2 hours but I am desperate to achieve my goal. This is the first time with this pole in competition. It's an experiment. I'll ask the stewards to bring the uprights forward adjacent to the plant box, so I won't need as much momentum.

'I commence my run up half a pace back, to allow for the extra pole length. I am thinking 'This is my last attempt,' I put everything into it. I notice that my take-off is a little early, with the pole too flat and bending too much, so that my forward motion slows. I am lifted almost straight up. I get my legs over the bar but I'm too slow and come down on top of, it instead of over it. I like to finish on a high and now I feel encouraged because I almost achieved it. I was thinking my run-up had let me down . . . I can't remember. Another day, when I am fresher, with a better take-off, I'll get over. I rack my pole and go in for a shower.'

'What did you think you could have done differently?'

'I seemed to need more momentum. The longer pole reached, but I needed an earlier take-off. More weights work could have sped me up with the heavier longer pole. I'll have to do better to achieve a personal best of 5m00 at the National. What did you think?'

'Could you have misjudged where the bar was and thrown back the pole too early, before you had reached the bar?'

'I let go when I was vertical and about to fall back. If I hadn't pushed the pole away, I wouldn't have reached the bar.'

'Your account figures,' I said. 'We can see if it matches the video. I agree that at the bar, you had traded off momentum for height. I want to talk with you about your conception of momentum transfer and energy conversion. You sometimes use the terms differently from me. Your ideas could be more correct. Tell me, what is your idea of what the pole is for?'

'When I bend it, it has recoil and throws me into the air.'

'Correct,' I said. 'The recoil or spring converts your horizontal kinetic energy into vertical potential energy.'

'Hang on,' she said. 'I don't like energy to be invisible. I prefer it that momentum is conserved because I can imagine the momentum changing direction from horizontal to vertical. It's a better explanation I think.'

'Momentum is an old-fashioned concept,' I said politely. 'Inertia separates mass and velocity more readily.'

'Momentum is easier for me to understand,' she said, assertively. Her voice had taken on a metallic timbre. 'I can imagine myself having momentum.'

'I'll try to remember to explain with momentum,' I said. 'Momentum is conserved by the bending of the pole and straining its elastic fibres. The fibres are elongated and their elastic memory exerts a force trying to return to their original lengths, straightening the pole and imparting momentum to you. Is that explanation acceptable to you?'

'Yes, that's okay. Picturing the fibres helps,' Megan said. 'My skill is to strain the pole fibres so when they recover they lift me up. The fibres could eventually become brittle and snap.'

'Would a new pole be more elastic and throw you higher?'

'It could do. My long pole is almost new.'

'Maybe the elasticity helped you more than you think.'

'Do I have other misconceptions about the physics?'

'Mostly you're good. I could help you deconstruct and reconstruct one of your performances.'

'How would that benefit me?'

'With constructivism, you could rebuild your understanding on an empirical foundation.'

'Wouldn't that just take everything apart?'

'No. It builds up alternative solutions logically, from understandings. For example, I agree that you had enough height to get over but you came down too early. I'm not sure your take-off was short or whether your Achilles affected you. There was a lot happening at once. We need a model to match your movements in the video so you can consider changes. I'll look around for one.'

We continued to evaluate her failed jump, agreeing what had happened and how improvement could occur.

'Now you are in charge; your interests are paramount,' I said. 'If I seem pushy, it is because I see myself sitting on the same side of the table as you. I am making suggestions, not giving orders. It's good that you want a discussion because I want that too. Your next

134

task is to include in the transcript your experiences relating to the things we have talked about. We will then analyse it for you to plan what training you need to do.'

'Will you criticize me?'

'When you ask me to.'

'And if I don't ask you?'

'You will be without feedback that could be helpful.'

'Fair enough.'

Megan had definite goals and could deduce from the analysis what training activities she needed. I was a facilitator now, rather than the bully I had been.

'It is good not to be an object to be observed, pummelled and bullied into shape,' Megan said.

For her, phenomenal analysis and student-centred coaching was the end of the road to her individuality. Until now she hadn't had confidence that anyone else understood what it was like to be hurled into the air. I was making it my business to understand. She was a phenomenon, by her own account and others'.

Despite our intimacy, getting Megan's full attention continued elusive. Her standoffishness seemed like a betrayal. After all my devotion and caring for her, I wanted to demand to be loved by her. I didn't, telling myself to be patient.

She didn't respond to the transcript of our interview I sent her. I wanted feedback and it was exasperating. Perhaps she didn't value what I was doing. I liked to watch Megan training. There were usually friends and fans watching and she wasn't able to spend much time with anyone. I sometimes felt neglected and jealous.

I confided my frustration to Nick when we had lunch at the Museum.

'Are you saying Megan has clammed up and won't cooperate with you?' asked Nick. 'It sounds like you need her more than she needs you. Imagine how she feels. You have eviscerated her performance with your verbal picture.

'Are you saying she might not like it?'

'Yes, I am. Some American Native Indians believe that a photo or a video can take away a piece of their soul. She may subconsciously feel that her performance belongs to her and she could resent your efforts to capture it in words and recordings. Could Megan believe your phenomenology has pillaged her essence?'

'No, I don't think that's likely,' I said. "The sad part is the reverse is possible. I have put something of myself into recording her carefully in words, as well as in video and I have taken artistic licence. She may not value that I am adding anything worthwhile.'

'But you told me the Megan phenomenon would not have an observer or an observer effect?'

'I did and I have tried to be scientific. But it has not been possible to entirely exclude myself,' I said.

'I think she would expect that,' said Nick. 'The problem could be after years of virtual slavery, Megan has realised she is in control of her training and can do whatever takes her fancy. She feels like a new person and it could be shyness inhibiting her, like an emerged butterfly waiting for her wings to harden. You shouldn't be quarrelling. You need each other.'

CHAPTER 27 HOMING

I wanted Megan to realize my commitment to her and invited her to go with me to my parents' home, for a weekend visit.

'I'd love to come,' she said. 'Do they live on the farm you were telling me about?'

'No. They moved in near Toowoomba,' I said.

'When did you last see them?'

'Last Christmas. I visit them about once a year and my phone calls are weeks apart.'

'What do they do?'

'My father designs irrigation systems and my mother is a radiographer in a hospital.'

'Where are your brother and sister?'

'They live and work in Brisbane,' I said. 'Would you like to meet them?'

'Yes, I would like that.'

'Everyone is going home for Sunday lunch, so they'll be there at the weekend.'

'Have you taken a girl home before?'

'No. Why?'

'They might not like me.'

'I'm sure they'll like you very much. Don't try too hard. They're easy going.'

It was a pleasant visit. Megan talked with my parents. They were interested in her performing and her research. Sunday lunch with my brother and sister was our first family gathering for several years but by the time the third bottle of wine was flowing, the conversation had relaxed. They liked Megan and she fitted in well.

I took Megan on a tour of the district, visiting my favourite places. I showed her a pond in a park where I had sailed my model yacht. I talked with some model enthusiasts. Then we walked in the hills overlooking the city.

'These are native bees,' I said. She saw the small black bees visiting Callistemons with their blood red bottle brush flowers

'They also bring pollen from Grevillea and Eucalyptus flowers. They probably have a nest in a tree hollow.'

'When they return to the nest, honey bees do a waggle dance to tell the others where the pollen is, with a dance inside on the comb. watched by the others.'

I made a short pass trotting, waggling my rear end, then looped back and repeated.

'My run direction shows the others the direction to fly relative to the Sun,' I panted. 'My waggles were quick, showing the food is close by the hive.'

'Cool,' she said. 'Bees have a language, of sorts.'

It was a sunny day, with skylarks pirouetting above us. I gazed at the cityscape and horizon, trying to remember the names of places I knew. I shared my knowledge of local history with her, recalling how indigenous people would have looked out from here at settler wagon trains and rushed away to alert others and enlist in a defensive force.

We sat in the garden of a pub, sipping beer and cider, looking out over the countryside.

'I feel safer with a panorama.' I said. 'In the city, there is no horizon and there are places where nasty things can lurk.'

'You told me when you were young you were into risk and adventure. What happened?'

'I grew up. I had more than enough adventure.'

'I asked your father if he missed the farm and he said he did. Why did they leave it?'

'There was a drought and they couldn't afford to stay,' I said. 'It was a tragedy but common enough. Farming has risks that can go on for years, scarring lives. Leaving was the best option.'

'In athletics, competition is no cake walk.'

'We are fortunate to have academic careers that are reasonably secure,' Megan said.

'Prospects can change without warning.'

'We need to get finished as soon as possible.'

'I'm with you all the way,' I said.

All too soon our visit was over. We had enjoyed each other's company. Being with her made being by myself seem dull.

CHAPTER 28 RISKING SAFETY

Regulating risk could possibly make athletics safer but athletes and officials would have less freedom and the nature of competition could change.

Megan and I watched a videoed documentary about an attempt on the world marathon record. The runner was accompanied by a team of pacers who shared the burden of the lead between them, until the favourite took over and finished in record time.

'She probably kept her speed just below bonking,' I said. 'She knew the signs.'

'Could she really stay at the edge of bonking?'' Megan asked.

'Hitting the wall is real,' I said. 'At record speed her body would be signalling danger and she would be over-riding it. The safety margins could be large, but inadequate preparation could result in her body failing and even permanent injury.'

'There isn't much burning out in the pole vault, even in training,' said Megan. 'I don't think about physical risks when I'm performing. My greatest risk is when I don't reach enough forward momentum on the pole and get tangled up with the bar, bringing it crashing down.'

'Just because you don't think about it doesn't mean you can ignore the risks.'

'Changing my action to improve would be alluring. Going higher puts greater stresses on my muscles and if I haven't exercised at this level, muscle strain and tearing of the fibres can result. I don't know consequences until afterwards. It happens when I don't have enough running speed or take off badly. My risks are mistakes, not choices.'

'Perhaps a risk is a wrong choice?'

'At the time it seems like the only choice. That is the mistake.'

At this time I was exploring my relationship with Megan, uncovering the treasure of her extraordinary nature. She was intuitive, solving difficulties from her experience, out of hand. Her judgement was spontaneous and usually correct. For example, when shopping she accepted amounts billed without demur.

'The price is right,' she would say. 'They have a standard charge.'

'I want to check it,' I said, always the investigator. 'They might do it for less if we ask.'

Megan was venturesome in bed too. Of the two of us, she was the innovator who wanted to try new things. We made love in the afternoons, in a darkened room, dissolute and dizzying. Sex with Megan was love and never boring.

I discussed her risk taking in performance with my tutor, Jack Montand.

'Megan does not consciously weigh up risks,' I said.

'Could she train to do that?' Jack asked. 'Perhaps you could make her aware of menus of alternatives.'

'She has her own algorithm,' I said. 'It is specific to her possibilities, like a car driver's propensity to run orange traffic lights depends on age.'

'Is there an age that takes more risks?' asked Jack. 'Aren't young males the culprits, until their amygdalae develop?'

'I heard experienced drivers who are middle-aged run the orange more often.'

'They could have become blase'.'

'Increasing the orange light time may not avert collisions,' I said. 'It might be better for lights to go from green directly to red, without any orange at all. '

'Then why are orange lights used almost everywhere?' Jack asked impatiently.

'I suppose some people want leeway,' I said. 'Red and green alone are too binary and nerve wracking. People want to have a margin for error.'

'A coloured light has subjective meaning. In China, when lights were first used, drivers sped up at red lights because red is commonly associated with positive action. They stopped at green lights, meaning peace.'

'I'm not sure what this has to do with risk-taking,' said Jack studying his fingernails.

'Athletes could be signalled when to go, when to hurry and when to stop.'

'Sport and athletics have only a few safety regulations. Soccer has yellow card warnings for reckless play. Reckless force gets a red card and sent off. Some sports have penalty boxes or sin bins.'

'Regulations anticipate danger and protect people,' I said.

'I suppose when a football player breaks their back, if there has been no rule infringement, the audience would want a new rule introduced,' said Jack.

'Without orange lights, traffic lights would be more anxiety inducing,' I said.

'You mean having a long orange light makes red more acceptable?' his tutor asked.

'Yes. It is a warning.'

'In some sports, spectators expect to see injuries. In motor sports, boxing, gymnastics, ski jumping and ice skating, errors can have dramatic consequences. Reducing the errors would reduce audience interest.'

'Would it be possible to protect people in those sports from injury?' asked Jack.

'Probably not,' I said. 'Personal safety is ultimately the responsibility of the performer. It relates to rewards and risks.'

'That's interesting,' said Jack. 'Your investigation of risk has reached an impasse, between more regulation on the one hand, or on the other, having performers accept more responsibility. You need to resolve the dilemma somehow. Let's stop there for today. How about we talk about sports injuries and accidents next week? You're making headway and I'm looking forward to hearing your ideas.'

'Okay.'

A week later we met again in Montand's office. He always had seasonal fruits. He gave me a persimmon.

'Wait a few days until it softens, then cut it in half and scoop out the inside with a spoon.'

'Thank you,' I said.

'Continuing from last time, are you proposing athletes have green, orange and red regulations?'

'There could be warnings to prevent injury to themselves or others when conditions become dangerous.'

'Wow,' Jack said. 'That's stretching the traffic lights analogy a bit far, isn't it? Could dangerous conditions be detected by monitors, for example heart rate. Then athletes who exceeded their maximum levels could be disqualified?'

'How would maximum levels be decided. Every athlete is different. Could they be tested?'

'Maybe,' I said. 'It would slow down performance times. Competition could change to finding who could go closest to the heart rate limit without disqualification.'

'Testing your hypothesis would require data about injuries with and without regulation and it could be difficult to control because it's unethical.'

'How unethical?' I asked.

'No authority could decide safe levels. Most risks are currently self-regulated,' Jack said. 'Relinquishing those rights to a regulating authority would be resisted.'

'Injuries would have to be analysed for their intentionality,' I said. 'For example, bonking could result in different situations. An athlete might not recognise they are about to hit the wall, or they could want to accept the risk as a cost of winning.'

'What if they ignore the signs and warnings?'

'There are many sports where competitors are at risk of injury, unless they hold back,' I said. 'Self-regulation can be a winning skill. For example, in extreme sports, endurance, running, weight lifting and jumping, participants assess and limit risk of injury, without jeopardising their competitiveness.'

'How could there be rules to prevent injury that are fair to everyone?' said Jack.

'By observing outcomes.'

'Everyone is different. Observing outcomes with injuries or near injuries would be difficult,' he said.

'I agree. It's too difficult. I have come around to wanting athletes to self-regulate.'

'It seems obvious,' said Jack. 'Can a pole vaulter be told anything about how to avoid injury that she doesn't know already?'

'I can help Megan self-regulate,' I said. 'I have been looking into phenomenalism as an alternative. Phenomenalism views outcomes of observer-relative sensory phenomena as a patterned collection of sensations. Intentionality matters, for interpreting limits to performances and sanction them if necessary. It's a whole new field of performance evaluation.'

'Could it be in use already by top performers?' asked Jack.

'Enlightened coaches may allow elite athletes to self-regulate,' I said. 'Phenomenalism widens the scope of risk evaluation. It begins with conscious experience as a whole, not split between subject and object as it was by Cartesian dualism.'

'How is the phenomenal perspective different?' Jack asked.

'The meaning of an action can be changed by intentionality, in the same way that a change in intonation alters the meaning of speech,' I said. 'For example, a pole vaulter could have intended to clear the bar, but realised she cannot succeed and intends to knock it down. The meaning of her actions would be different.'

'Self-regulation is a better way of evaluating,' I said. 'The observed individual has control. An observer who says that a cat is smiling is saying more about the observer, than about the cat.

'You mean the cat may not be showing affection: its smile could be something else, such as solicitation.'

'Yes,' I said. 'To change the cat's smile you would need to change the cat in relation to the observer, for example, by her feeding it.'

'An action in pole vaulting that is dangerous may not be intended, simply misjudged,' said Jack.

'An umpire couldn't call it,' I said. 'Performers have to regulate themselves.'

'Could looking at traffic lights be barking up the wrong tree?' asked Jack. 'Risks with athletes are less predictable.'

144

'Maybe not,' I said. 'To win, an athlete probably takes on more risk than her rivals. Elite athletes need to be savvy with their body's safety limits. I want to investigate safe limits to regulate against accidents. Athletes need to know how far they can go.'

'Regulation isn't the answer,' said Jack. 'One size won't fit all. I can't see the nanny state regulating sport and athletics.'

'They're trying to do that.'

'Bloody hell,' Jack said. 'I hope they recognise that each athlete perceives risks differently.'

'Phenomenology can improve performance by self-regulation.'

My supervisor nodded. 'Good choice. You will have the athletes' input and it's they that control the outcome and who have to live with the risk. External regulation is not needed.'

'The Australian Athletics Association has mooted introduction of safety regulations,' I said.

'It could be just nanny state talk,' Jack said. 'The nanny state is rampant. Following the campaign to expose sports players accused of sexist, drugged, provocative and violent behaviour, the government is proscribing all aggressive on-field behaviour. Body contact sports will become fakery, like wrestling.'

'It goes beyond concern for injury, into promoting exemplary responses to aggression, ostensibly to be a model for reducing domestic violence,' I said.

'Sport is not a laboratory for interpersonal relations,' Jack said. 'Why not focus on cleaning up politicians' behaviour in parliament? They should model peaceful interaction.'

'The nanny state is trying to prevent athlete self-regulation,' I said.

'The Australian Athletics Association (AAA) could oppose giving athletes autonomy because it would put their coaches out of a job,' said Jack.

'The spectacle in sport will be regulated by capitalists, who allow audiences as much violence as they want,' I said. 'Athletes will not have any say in it.'

'Athletes will push back against regulation of risks that opposes fundamental traditions,' said Jack. 'Events have long histories that athletes will not allow to be disrupted, regardless of demands for change by spectacle capitalists.'

'I agree new external regulation in athletics will be resisted,' I said. 'Sport is a popular mass spectacle. The nanny state could want to maximise its popularity by making it accessible to everyone and forcing elite athletes to follow specific performance requirements.'

'The phenomenal approach devolves risk interpretation to athletes. It opposes the thrust of the nanny state into regulation. Are you sure you want to go through with this?'

'Yes. The nanny state is wrong. The centralisation trend against athletes is doomed.'

CHAPTER 29 AUTOMATICITY

'Do you need help planning your training programme?' I asked Megan.

'It should be me that does it,' Megan said. 'I want to be responsible for it. Until now I have been left out, as if my views don't matter, when they should be the starting point. You, Coach Adamson and others can input ideas, but I know my weaknesses and what activities to train at to overcome them.'

Increasingly she relied on herself. The phenomeno-logical viewpoint had unleashed in Megan a psychological makeover that shook her to the foundations and kept her learning by experimenting, either on her own, or as suggested by me, or Adamson.

'Relying on my own judgement of what is good or bad is a new experience,' she said. Sometimes I want to be told what to do but deciding myself has taught me to take responsibility for myself and I am able to concentrate on my performance

'Heidegger's phenomenology (2) was a method for exploring human experience and defining its nature, requiring transcendence of cultural conditioning and understanding of self and consciousness. He explored the meaning of the verb 'to be' and 'dasein' or 'Being there'. His existentialism was new, concerned with the concept of being and being in the world.'

'Why phenomenology?' Megan asked.

'It has a performer's perspective and enables you to analyse what you are doing,' I said. 'The other philosophies don't give enough respect to the performer.'

'Do you give me enough respect?' she asked.

'I certainly do. Right now I am going to take you out for lunch.'

'Why?'

'Because you are special and deserve respect.'

We drove in my car to the yacht club at the coast. I parked and we walked through the avenue of majestic Alexandra palms, tall and bearing prominent leaf scars. Each graceful crown had 8 to 10 pinnate, feather-like fronds. I know, because Megan counted them. We ate slowly, watching the boats go by.

I felt that Megan and I had something special happening. By choosing phenomenology, we had declined the perspectives of the existential philosophers: Saussure, Russell, Wittgenstein, Sartre and Simone de Beauvoir. Their perspectives assumed that existence preceded essence, as if Megan's actions were her reality rather than her whole person. These dualist views had a limited understanding of Megan, because they could not see everything she was doing at once. They were limited by signs, words, symbols and structures, variable definitions and different meanings, depending on context. They lacked the universality and practical applicability of phenomenalism.

'Phenomenalism is a monist view that regards all existence as one and the same reality,' I said. 'Your perspective of risk takes precedence over mind and body, registering in one consciousness. Without synthesis of the two, neither a scientific, nor an existential perspective, is adequate.'

'To express my understanding of my performance, I need your physics and its language,' she said. 'I will learn it.'

A few days later, Megan handed me the transcript she had checked of her performance at the Queensland Championships.

'I've made some changes. It's the best I can do. I want you to tell me how to improve.'

We set about refining the analysis using my videos.

I had never stood in an elite athlete's shoes before. Megan told me she had specific actions at definite moments, such as when she planted her pole at take-off. She explained these pivotal instants to me and her intentions at each. Each of her performances was different, with an enigmatic and experimental quality that made it difficult to predict what would succeed or fail.

After work, we walked beside the Brisbane River. It was getting dark and flying foxes passed overhead, going to feed on fruit and nectar. They came over in thousands, spread out like silent bombers on a raid, the gaps between them wide. Their flight was solitary, heavy when they were carrying young. Silent and unhurried, they laboured steadily through the heavy air.

The flyway was hundreds of meters wide, coming from over the horizon, going past and out of sight down river. Some stopped to feed on flowering fig trees en route, crash landing in, climbing around in the upper branches, squeaking querulously with their helium voices, flapping noisily about, until they flapped away, merging into the tide of passing bats.

Watching them, their individuality seemed to have transcended into a group purpose. I mused that a difference with humans was that we went in many different directions.

I was aware of my emotional involvement with Megan, but kept it aside. She was my lover and close friend, with a growing spiritual connection that was central to our relationship.

Megan was confident. One of the new breed of gung-ho athletic heroes, she was prepared to push the boundaries. She was a hero to herself. When I thought of Megan, it was as a complete phenomenon, with attractive qualities, physique, intentions, actions and emotions. These different parts formed a coherent whole, with an effect on me that was profound, making me feel I knew the wonder of her completely.

'Heroism is a Nietzschean preoccupation,' I told her. 'You can be my hero. Phenomenology can identify your actions while performing. We can concentrate on the intent of each action.'

'My intent is to perform my best,' she said.

'Your phenomenon is a narrative of thoughtful performance,' I said to Megan. 'I imagine every performance as a phenomenon with daring and determination. Heidegger would identify each performance as all those things you have intended and controlled in 'being there' or 'dasein'. The perspective is cerebral activity driving your attention from action to action in a series. When your attention is taken from your goal, the impetus you are capable of is reduced. You maintain it by goal automaticity.'

'I am beginning to understand phenomenology,' she said. 'My lived experience is goal seeking.'

Heidegger investigated language and nuances of expression in existent contexts by leisurely contemplative scholarship. He wasn't concerned with keeping abreast of the latest publications and public discourse. His writings teased out nuances of meaning in observer and subject interaction that others had interpreted hastily. He revealed them carefully.

The elements of a phenomenon that yielded to his scrutiny were dasein and time, but he gave them individual meanings that prevented generalisation. An athlete's dasein could be unique, affected by local presence and transformative experience. Her time was personal.

Heidegger wrote his exposition in descriptive prose in the present tense. Like other philosophers whose works are still available, he was a writer rather than a talker. He was involved in National Socialism, joined the Nazi party, becoming the National Socialist rector of the University of Freiburg. After World War II he was forbidden to teach for six years. Phenomenology did not depend on the Nazi ideology. Martin Heidegger wrote:

'. . . he who thinks great thoughts often makes great errors.'

He showed no remorse for his Nazi error, remaining faithful to the party. He died in 1976. To dismiss his phenomenalism because of his political activity, would be like dismissing nuclear fission because it was used to make bombs in WWII. He discovered something others abused.

I hadn't yet told Megan about flow. I had hinted at it in talking about 'goal focus'. She had been adjusting to the phenomenal perspective and I was excited at the prospect of flow boosting her performance.

CHAPTER 30 PAIRS

Nick came and we sat in the stand together watching a cricket match. Penny and Lily were playing on the same side. They had met Nick previously, at a party. I asked him a question that had been bothering me.

'Am I imagining it, or are the girls unusually friendly?' I said. 'Megan seems to have taken a shine to Lily, but Lily is following Penny around. What's going on?'

Megan was standing beside Lily with a possessive hand on her bottom.

'I don't know,' said Nick. 'I had noticed it too. It could be high spirits.'

'Perhaps they have an attachment of some sort,' I said. 'They could be closer than I want.'

'My money's on you and Megan,' Nick said. 'Do you know Coase's Theorem? It rates relationships by absence of conflicting externalities, obstacles difficult to negotiate. You and Megan seem compatible.'

'Interesting,' I said. 'There are four possible couplings: Megan with me; or Lily with Megan; or Lily with Penny; or Lily with Hugh. Some of the couples could have conflicting loyalties.'

I tried to rate the relationships to find which was most likely. Coase would rate the feasibility of the pairings by neither love nor affection, but by the mutuality of the externalities. Externalities could be easiest to negotiate by sharing of a sport, or a heterosexual relationship. I thought about which pairings had compatible externalities.

I considered two types of externality: +1 for compatible sports, -1 for incompatible sports and +1 for gender difference, because difference of gender conformed to the heterosexual norm. I rated homosexuality -1 because same genders could be incompatible in deviating from the traditional model for couples.

My rating of Megan and I was +1 for heterosexuality, with +1 for compatible sport, total +2

Lily with Megan was -1 externality for homosexuality, with -1 externality for sport difference between cricket and performing, total -2.

Lily with Penny was -1 externality for homosexuality, with +1 externality for compatible cricket, total 0.

For Lily with Hugh, there was +1 for heterosexuality, with -1 externality for incompatibility between rugby and cricket, total 0.

In summary, I was relieved that Megan and I had fewest externalities to be reconciled, whereas Lily and Megan had most. Lily was incompatible with both Penny and Hugh.

'Megan and I are relatively compatible,' I told Nick.

'Then you haven't got anything to worry about,' he said.

The analysis eased my concern about Megan's standoffishness, that had marred the previous weeks. Penny and Lily seemed trapped in a doomed relationship. I felt sorry for Hugh.

My calculations had left out the key ingredient of affection. However well our sporting and social interests coincided, we could never succeed as a couple unless Megan wanted to be with me. I had wondered if she was leading me on and would leave me when I was of no further use. My work with Megan had made me useful to her and I hoped our relationship would improve. We disagreed about small things, such as setting the dishwasher cycle. I wanted a quick wash, for efficiency but Megan would reset it to slow, for a better wash. I let it go, as our relationship now seemed on a better footing than when she was playing hard to get.

My affection for Megan increased steadily as I got to know her. She was undemonstrative and I had to go for days without a sign of affection, except when we made love most nights, with mutual oral stimulation, after a bath to eliminate sensory overload. Her attention was wonderful and appeased my qualms.

FLOW

CHAPTER 31 WHY FLOW

'(Flow) is the way to learn the most, that when you are doing something with such enjoyment that you don't notice that the time passes. I am sometimes so wrapped up in my work that I forget about the noon meal.' Albert Einstein (13)

'It is interesting that Einstein, who was a guru of time metaphysics, acknowledged a flow condition had time-bending effects,' I said.

'Is flow induced by smoking pot?' Michael asked.

'Some runners claim pot helps them get into the zone, but I doubt that pot helps their performance. There are many reports of runners getting a lift or a buzz and calling it flow.'

'Where did the name 'flow' come from?' Michael asked.

'Achieving success is sometimes called 'flow' when it's easy and enjoyable,' I said. 'Some psychologists have posited that flow is the state most akin to happiness. In fact, flow does not carry you along. It has goal-focussed striving. Coaches and psychologists sometimes misrepresent it as relaxed and indistinct, because it does without traditional coaching techniques. Flow is the opposite of domineering, bullying and fear, sometimes called coaching. Flow is liberating.'

As we talked, a family of Mynah birds flew in to takeover a bottlebrush in the garden, searching for nectar and insects. They peered at us inquisitively.

'Is flow a sensation?' asked Michael.

'It occurs when three conditions are present: goal focus, mental engagement and automaticity of skills. It's a psychological state.'

'It's not physics,' he said.

'I hope to discover the metaphysics of its timelessness.'

'It must be interesting to research something so mysterious.'

I glanced to see if this was sarcasm, but his interest seemed genuine.

'My hypothesis is that an athlete's performance could improve in flow,' I said.

He thought for a moment.

'How could you test it?'

'Because the condition is self-observed, testing would be partly subjective. I hope to find objective indicators that link the condition to performance.'

'Good luck,' he said, standing up. 'I think lunch is ready.'

Although Michael had reservations about flow, he was interested. I hadn't told him I planned to persuade Megan to try it soon. There seemed a fair chance of flow improving her performance.

CHAPTER 32 FLOW

One evening I asked Megan: 'What shall we do tomorrow?'

I knew she had her usual Monday training but I had a new activity for her to try.

'Would you like to do something different?' I asked.

'What?'

'I would like you to try 'flow'. Do you know about it?'

'I know it's good. Athletes say it helps them. I didn't know it was something I can do when I want to.'

'You can learn.'

'Learn when?'

'Starting now. It will take some time, maybe weeks. Flow gets talked about in changing rooms, as an achievement. Experiencing flow is an achievement but it is much more. It can be an aspiration of how to perform and a philosophy of how to live your life. Flow is a headset. You can try it on next time you train.'

'What if it doesn't fit my head?'

'It will. The theory is described in a book 'Flow' by psychologist Mihaly Csikszentmihalyi. Here, you can borrow it.'

She took it from me and read the cover blurb.

'I can't even say his name.'

'No-one can. The theory is not complicated. You have to be goal-focussed. What is your goal for your next competition?'

'I want to do 5m00 at the Nationals next month,' she said.

'Are you sure you can do that?'

'I'm capable. I've done it in practice.'

'Most athletes discover flow when training,' I said.

'What happens?' she asked.

'They get a buzz that resonates, even for hours. I want you to try getting into flow at every performance, by striving for the three conditions: goal focus, engagement and automaticity.

'I thought being in the zone applied only to longer lasting activities, like running and tennis?'

'True, flow is more easily recognisable in activities that last longer, but you can stretch your performance in flow to last from the beginning to the end of the competition,' I said. 'A musical virtuoso can perform an entire piece in flow with timeless intensity.'

'Are you sure my performance has enough activity to benefit from flow?'

'Yes. Flow makes its own time. Your performance can be totally absorbing, timeless, highly skilled and enjoyable. A professional golfer can stay in flow for hours, with hits at long intervals apart. '

'I have felt some timelessness! What causes it?'

'It's a psychological condition. It has been experienced not only in performing, but in sport, music, art and stage arts. It may be possible to stay in flow for one jump, between jumps, or during most of a competition. Have you ever been on a high in competition?'

'Yes, sometimes I am in automatic and the time slips by without me noticing.'

'Great! It sounds like you have experienced flow.'

'A few times, maybe. Do I have time to get into flow when I'm performing?'

'How long can you delay to start an attempt?'

'I am allowed one minute on the runaway before starting.'

'It isn't much, but you can be ready for it. Your preparation has been underway long before. You can have your skills ready, honed to automaticity in training. You can switch into flow on the runway.'

'How can I practice?'

'You take charge of your time. Tomorrow you can try ways of getting into flow during training exercises and staying in flow as long as possible.'

'Will I do my exercises, keeping in mind: goal focus, engagement and automaticity?'

'That's right. You will build them up gradually, until your preoccupation is overtaken by enjoyment.'

'It seems easy enough, but I bet it isn't for everyone, or more people would be doing it. Is it like mindfulness?'

'The meditative posture is similar, but the difference is that your mind has to control your body too, for optimal achievement.'

'We'll see.'

We stopped then and I made dinner. We ate out at restaurants regularly, but I made dinner for the two of us at home sometimes. I cooked stir fry or pasta or curry and for dessert there were strawberries, raspberries and blueberries with cream.

Megan read some of Mihaly's book. It was organised like a textbook but I could see she was interested and was taking seriously my proposal for her to get into flow.

The next day I went with Megan to the track.

'Where shall I begin?'

'What's your first exercise?

'I'll jog two laps, to warm up.'

'Then what?'

'I'm going to do a set of ten 40-metre dashes. Then sprint 5 laps of 400 metres.'

'Okay, do your warm up and then come back here.'

When she returned, I said: 'Listen to this Zen checklist and repeat it back to me.'

I recited from memory:

Relax breathing.
Get into the rhythm and cadence you have practiced.
Listen to the music of your feet.
Breathe with the rhythm of your feet,

She repeated it back.

'Apply it now to your dashes, taking a minute for the checklist. I have written the checklist on this card which you can read before each run.'

157

After the dashes, she did five sprints around the oval.

Then we walked over to the vaulting pit. I helped her drag out the landing mats and put up the standards and bar.

'What now?' I asked her.

'I'm going to start at 4m50 and work up in 10 cm steps, repeating when I knockdown, until I reach my goal of 5m00.'

'I want you to use the same Zen checklist, with extra steps of visualising and poising on the runway. Repeat after me:

Relax breathing.
Visualise running up, jumping and finishing.
Poise, then commence with correct movements.
Get into the rhythm and cadence you have practiced.
Listen to the music of your feet.
Breathe with the rhythm of your feet.

After three attempts she could recall most of it.

'Here's a card. Use it while you are waiting to step onto the runway, then recall the steps as you poise for a minute and run. You must remember the steps until it becomes automatic. Recite it to settle your nerves and get you into 'flow'. Think FLOW at the start.'

At the start, Megan cleared every time, as I put up the bar. At 4m90 she knocked down and took 2 attempts. At 5m00 she knocked down 3 times.

'That's all for this morning,' she said. 'I'm tired.'

'It was a pretty good workout.'

'How much practice could I need?'

'It could take weeks or even months to learn to get into flow on demand and stay in. Are you interested?'

'Yes very, if you're sure it'll work.'

She was verifying I was sincere, but her trust in flow to improve her performance was limited because so far she had little or no benefit.

'It'll work, I'm sure,' I said. 'I want you in your mind to decompose your performance into your subgoals: first your run, then the plant, the take-off, then swinging up, then the fly away and clearing the bar. Imagine the six parts in turn and how you will perform them.'

Mental training was only one aspect of improving her performance. In the days following, Megan did weight training, for strength, acceleration and pole work. She practiced gymnastics exercises for dexterity. She went to Zen archery classes to improve her mental coordination.

In the afternoons, Megan worked on her research. She interviewed unemployed people and analysed the data to find motivations.

'Your flow idea has been useful for conducting interviews,' Megan said to me. 'I have the questionnaire off pat.'

'Good, your mind is under your control,' I said. 'Your mind loves to make the most of your body. They are separate but not indifferent. Your body strives to do what your mind wants. Zen will bring your mind and body to act as one, without thought, judging subjectively and passionately.'

'Are they in symbiosis?'

'Yes they live in close physical association and their interaction advantages both.'

'Often, but not always?'

'As often as possible, with Zen coordination. They are not dependent. With both you will be able to have your goal in the forefront of your consciousness. It has to be meaningful, achievable and decomposable into definite stages. What goal do you have?

'5m00 at the National.'

'It's the same goal you had at the Queensland Championships.'

'Yes. I'm going to achieve it this time.'

'You need to decompose it into the six parts and plan each one.'

When a week later she was running 40 metre intervals, holding her pole, at the training track, Megan hadn't said anything to me about flow. I was watching her, as I usually did. I could see she wasn't in flow by her lack of concentration and half-hearted efforts. There wasn't anything more I could tell her about the importance of getting into flow. It was as if my enthusiasm was being wasted. I

159

could have retaliated by withdrawing, but I knew that in her own way she would be trying. I trusted her absolutely. I sensed that she needed me, so I continued to watch her training, waiting for a boost in her lived experience.

She was doing sprints when I talked with her at the track.

'How are you getting on with flow?' I asked her,

'Do I really need to be in flow?' Megan asked, panting. 'I haven't experienced anything different yet.'

'Keep trying.'

'Is it scientific?' asked Megan. She knew it wasn't. It was her way of protesting her training ordeal.

'If you get into flow, you can expect your performance to improve. It's scientific enough.'

'Do I want to be in flow only when I'm performing, or anytime at all?'

'Anytime, in training, or whenever, but not when you're feeling frazzled. Getting into flow requires great peace of mind.'

'Why?'

'The only thing in your mind must be flow.'

'Okay, I'll try it.'

She changed from running intervals, to repeats along the 40 metres runway.

'I am turning the dial on perceived pain to full on,' she said. 'It's maximum pain in my thighs at every stride, each one longer than the last.'

She did 10 run-ups, running on through the sand pit and out, carrying her pole. Then she changed to vaulting. I helped her setting up. She vaulted well, equalling her personal best.

A week later, in the same exercise, she jumped up off the landing mat and ran up to me, excited, her face flushed and eyes agog.

'I know what flow is now,' she said. 'When I was on the runway, it all came together automatically. My feeling of being there went outside myself, easy and fun, on automatic, like a series of obstacles I could jump easily. It flowed like magic. Suddenly, I was over the bar and it was the best feeling of all. A new personal best of 5m00.'

'Congratulations,' I said. 'It was flow and it could be the first of many such experiences!'

When she came out of the changing room I gave her a gift-wrapped box.

'What's this?' she asked.

'A present for you. Open it.'

'Chocolates! I never eat chocolates,' she said, pleased.

'This is a special occasion. A treat.'

'Thank you.'

Our project was underway and I was ecstatic. The problem was, after that when she achieved for the first time something important, she expected me to give her chocolates. The first time I didn't, she asked 'Do you love me?' and wanted a kiss when I answered 'Yes.'

But this first time, the chocolates made it simple. That night when we made love, our interaction flowed, with a new sense of purpose, engagement and automaticity.

'Would you like to go on top?' I asked her.

'Okay.'

It was more than okay. She applied her athletic prowess and we were lovers, 'rolling like thunder under the covers', until I asked her to stop. My orgasm was long and deep with exquisite pleasure. Then I engaged tenderly with her doggy fashion. Resting connected with her lean firm body was erotic. Then she climaxed. We lay side by side exhausted.

It was timeless, until our hungers were satisfied and we sank back replete.

In the weeks leading up to the National, Megan practiced getting into and staying in flow.

Her improvement was impressive.

'It's different from the lackadaisical vaulting I am used to.'

'You are making good progress,' I said. 'You are just in time to use flow in the National.'

'Have you told Adamson what we're doing?'

'No. I asked him if he knew about flow and he said it wasn't science. End of conversation.'

'He'll change his tune when he sees your improvement.'

Megan had mornings at the Institute of Sport, training with Adamson's group of performers and afternoons at her Psychology Department.

'Let's spend a week in Sydney for the National,' I proposed. 'You can take a few days to acclimatize. Afterwards you can reward yourself with a couple of days timeout, as a tourist, with me.'

'If I don't win, I won't enjoy a reward,' she said.

'You will be celebrating being in the National. It's a huge achievement . . .'

'. . . just being there!' she said, agreeing with me.

CHAPTER 33 NATIONAL

Megan's first outing armed with phenomenology and flow was to the Australian National Championship in Sydney. I flew down the week before with Megan and Coach Adamson. A group of family, friends and fans had flown down with us. When we arrived, a crowd of media and fans greeted us noisily at the airport. She was renowned for challenging the record at the Queensland Championships and there was speculation she would break the National record. Megan was a celebrity, extensively interviewed, her photos in the news, besieged by autograph hunters.

'It's part of being a commodity,' Megan said. "Girl athletes jumping in bikinis' is a powerful image, promoting a spectacle of international competition seen worldwide. Interviews with me speculating about the competition will have the capitalist tills ringing.'

'What would we do without the spectacle?' I asked.

'Life would go on but less dramatically, without spectacular events and hype. Without the glitz, dazzle and cameras it would be different. The event could not be held at this venue without selling of tickets to a mass audience.'

'Couldn't the event be less professional, a friendly community gathering, such as a corroboree?'

'Investors would move in, advertise, enlarge and commercialise it, as a spectacle.'

'Debord (16) wanted to counter the spectacle with cultural disruption, preferring non-violent societal change to outright revolution. A revolution could end the capitalist exploitation of the spectacle, with people receiving the jobs and goods they really want.'

'Hmm. He was an optimist. What's the real harm in it?'

'The spectacle is artificial and bloated by commercialism. The only people who get much real enjoyment are investors.'

'But audiences love to scream for their favourites and their country.'

'I am not sure tribalism is deeply rooted in people, or whether they are just letting off steam.'

'It seems superficial. Could there be better ways to gain emotional relief?'

'If there are, the spectacle would be on to them.'

We stayed in a hotel by the harbour.

'I am expecting a big improvement in your performance,' I said, as we lay side by side. 'You need to get into flow in your first jump and stay in flow until you have won, or until you have been eliminated.'

She didn't reply. I realised I was repeating what I had said previously. Megan would find my repetition dull or annoying. What did she really think of me: stupid? I needed to smarten up my act, get some new lines, or I would lose her.

Then she replied.

'How can I stay in flow, with my mind focussed and engaged, for three hours, when I am sitting chatting with the other girls?' she asked.

'You could space yourself out, ignoring distractions, avoiding idle talk, letting disruptions go by, keeping your mind focussed and engaged. It will take practice because flow thrives on constancy and your performance has bursts of activity followed by watching others compete. You need to keep your mental flow humming between attempts, right through to the end.'

'Isn't getting into flow for each jump enough?' Megan said.

'Switching in and out could be more difficult in an all-day competition,' I said. 'But you can train for flow on demand, by developing focussing routines you can call on when you need them.'

Megan trained at a sports ground with other pole vaulters, about half locals and the others from overseas.

She trained hard everyday.

On the competition day, she performed consistently well and won with 5m00. It was a well-deserved win, close to the national record of 5m10.

'Superbly done,' I said.

'I was in flow most of the time,' she said. 'I was floating. Thank you for your encouragement. Flow is a wonderful technique.'

'I know. I use if often in my research work,' I said. 'I set a goal to write a first draft and concentrate my efforts. After that, I write oblivious of time, until I am done, at a pace as leisurely or frenetic as I feel, in sessions that often go on for hours.'

For three days we explored Sydney City centre and Darling Harbour. Megan was an enthusiastic tourist and we took frequent selfies. We rediscovered the pleasure of walking along beaches with bare feet, feeling the surge of waves. The next day we went to Circular Quay and to an exhibition of European Masterpieces at the Gallery of Modern Art. We discovered we had different tastes in art.

'The best art generates most discussion, I think,' I said.

'Aren't you ever spell bound?' asked Megan. 'Van Gogh's paintings leave me speechless.'

'We are different,' I said. 'We can have different interests provided we are truthful with each other and can negotiate compromises.'

We browsed the galleries together, discussing paintings we liked. It was fun reaching agreement.

CHAPTER 34 MODEL

After returning from Sydney, we continued using Megan's testimonies and my videos to analyse her performances. But we had no way to bring all the data together.

'We need a computer model of your performing actions to explore what you do in slow motion,' I told Megan. 'We can build a model of your biomechanics to simulate each jump. We can use it to find out causes and sequences and adjust your actions.'

'Elite runners and throwers are using models,' she said.

I got into contact with John, a researcher friend at another university, who showed us the digital kinesics model he had developed.

'I developed it to model a long jumper,' he said. 'But you could adapt it for the pole vault. All I need from you is credit for design of the basic model.'

'Thank you,' I said. 'That's generous.'

He helped me modify the code to match Megan's performances and we measured her physical dimensions precisely. I had learned to write computer code in my job in Canada and we developed most of the features in a couple of months. The model had a dynamic stick figure propelled by voluntary muscles, accelerating with a pole, storing momentum by bending the pole when she took off, lifting her with enough energy remaining to pass over the bar. The forces and movement were represented by equations that calculated, at intervals of one second her speeds and heights.

Megan loaded the model with measurements of her body size and weight taken from videos taken in front and on both sides. We had to make do without an overhead view. We overlaid the video images with a grid, to estimate lengths of 24 bones she used most often. We also estimated for a stick figure held together by bones and joints, the weights at centres of gravity of her limbs and torso. We installed muscle data for variable effort forces causing movement and inertia. The computer screen had images of her body changing position continuously and smoothly in a jump. Megan took a copy of the model on her laptop and spent hours exploring effects of changes. She was able to accurately predict consequences of her actions on her vaulting performance to match her performances.

'It's realistic,' I said. 'We can learn a lot from this model.'

We ran and reran it many times, calibrating it to match her performances in competition. She adjusted the data and rewrote the equations until we had a fit. To get it, she sometimes had to deconstruct her ideas of her actions and reconstruct real connections that explained the data better.

'So *that* is what I have been doing,' she said when she saw the model of herself in action. 'I hadn't realized.'

It took several months to get the precision we wanted and test effects of changes. We learned to avoid predictions having too many degrees of freedom, with so many unknowns, predictions would have confidence too low to be worthwhile.

'Garbage in, garbage out,' I said. 'Only accurate data will tell us what we need to know.'

'I have learned to predict most results from the model by calculating them in my head,' she said.

'Excellent! You have developed a mental model, subconsciously setting constants and variables to match your performances,' I said. 'That's terrific.'

'Does the mental model have to converge with the actual results?' she asked.

'It will if the model is any good,' I said. 'You will be able to rely on its predictions and work out how to counter problems as soon as they arise.'

'I am becoming like the model: detached, logical and timeless,' she said. 'I am a pole-bot.'

'You are one cool tech head,' I said.

'I have tested pole holding positions on the model,' Megan said. 'I have marked the best hand positions on the pole for fast, medium and slow speeds. I'm not leaving it to chance.'

'How do you know if you are fast enough?' I asked.

'The pole angle has to be right to slide into the box.'

'What can happen?'

'I may not have enough momentum to bend the pole,' Megan said.

'A stiff drink could do it,' I said.

We both laughed at the innuendo.

'I love it when you talk dirty,' I said.

Mostly we were serious.

Our love-making had become protracted and uninhibited, with licking, tasting, liking and sucking, culminating in shagging and fucking. Our familiarity with each other's body and preferences was comfortable but innovation was never the same twice and brought new excitements.

Megan's work with the model was time absorbing.

'It's time for a break now,' I said when she had spent several hours exploring online.

'I just want to try out one more thing,' she said.

'What are you doing?'

'I am finding out effects of varying timing of my take-off.'

'Your commitment to developing the model is amazing,' I said.

We had both become efficient programmers, working in flow for long sessions.

We had setbacks but we persisted until we succeeded. Megan was more stubborn than me and I worried that she could injure her brain. With patience and persuasion I tried to slow down this headstrong woman.

'Come and eat,' I told her. 'The model will still be there when you get back.'

We ate at one of several small restaurants near the university. Mostly we ate in companionable silence because we were absorbed in the model. Persig (7) had pointed out that respecting detail was fundamental to 'classical' technical work rather than 'romantic' more casual involvement with technology. He wrote that the romantic approach was usually less successful. Megan's flow training had classical goal focus and engagement. There was little romantic imagination in her repetitive training for automaticity. She was determined to succeed.

Our modelling work was intimate. Megan stayed at my place often. She had clothes and other belongings there and it seemed like a small joint residence. We were considerate in how we shared the bathroom, kitchen and bed. I liked her being there a lot.

At training, Megan had become adept at focussing on her goals and had increased her mental engagement.

'We still have to bring Adamson in on flow,' I said.

'He hasn't said anything about my steady improvement,' Megan said.

'What is causing it?' I said.

'Flow, I think,' she said. 'It isn't science. Will we ever know for sure?'

'Adamson might claim credit.'

'So long as I am improving, does it matter?' Megan said.

'It matters to me,' I said. 'Flow needs credit to gain respectability.'

'I don't feel comfortable grafting flow practice onto my training without him knowing,' Megan said. 'Should I tell him?'

'We have to be cautious,' I said. 'He has already rejected flow, saying there isn't scientific evidence. Could you present it as a proposal by a PhD student to improve your performing through his training?'

'Adamson can't stop me,' said Megan. 'Roosevelt said the way to negotiate is: 'Speak softly and carry a big stick.' I am in the right. Adamson should know it's in the spirit of my dual degree to try new psychological techniques. I can insist on training how I want, or I will pull out. I will compete in flow when I want to.'

Would Megan be able to change her relationship with her coach, or was it wishful thinking?

CHAPTER 35 MOVING IN

I worked with Megan, developing the model, usually for an hour or two each day, in the mornings. In the afternoons and evenings, I watched Megan training at the track. Each of us valued independence but our mutualism was like a coral's, with the two different individuals in harmony. We loved each other, thinking and doing for each other, agreeing easily, relishing sharing our lives. But our sharing was about to move to a higher level.

When we were dining at the Green Olive, a pasta house, we made the final decision.

'I'll pay the deposit tomorrow,' I said.

'It's a big step,' Megan said.

We had decided to rent a semi-detached house in Brisbane's West End. Living in hall separately had been convenient but it was too inhibiting and we wanted to live together.

'We know each other well enough,' I said, 'unless you have been hiding something.'

'Not me. The only risk is of having too much of a good thing.'

'If you can handle it, so can I,' I said. 'Anyway, this is a trial, isn't it?'

'A trial of what?'

'Living together permanently.'

'You make it sound like life imprisonment,' she said.

'Sorry. I am a little anxious.'

It was a big step to take. Would we fit together well enough? I didn't know what to expect.

'I thought you were a risk taker from way back,' Megan said. 'What's happened to your daring do?'

'Since I have been with you I have become used to constancy.'

'Living together won't change that.'

'Your performing could change. You will be away a lot of the time.'

'Can we face that when we come to it?'

'Okay.'

Just then Penny and Lily came in.

'Over here,' called Megan.

We all sat together and ordered drinks and food.

'We're moving into an apartment,' Megan said.

'Congratulations,' said Lily and Penny.

'How are you two getting on?' Megan asked.

'Okay,' said Penny. 'I'm still living at home. It's not ideal. Maybe we'll copy you.'

'Ours is a trial,' said Megan. 'Chance is wary.'

'I don't blame him,' said Penny.

'That's not very nice,' I said. 'What do you mean?'

'Your performing, Megan, is hardly a vista of endless tranquillity.'

'Chance is more concerned it will be too dull when I'm away,' said Megan. 'Aren't you Chance?'

'Quite the opposite,' I said. 'I am a little wary that your career could take-off and leave me behind.'

'My real worry is she won't relax with me in a homey way,' I thought. *'She is too restless, always moving on to the next thing.'*

'Oh,' said Megan. 'So it's my career you're worried about. It could be a male ego thing, wanting to be in control?'

'You're settled aren't you Megan?' asked Penny intrusively.

'Competitions are overseas and take up to a month each,' said Megan. 'Unless I go to the big ones, I could get squeezed out. Staying in the elite group is gruelling.'

Our food came. As we ate Penny and Lily bragged about their cricketing exploits.

'I hit one into the pavilion,' said Penny. 'It rattled around and smashed some china. I seized the opportunity to declare. Our team was more interested in fielding than in watching me score runs.'

'Wouldn't they prefer to sit in the pavilion, rather than going out in the baking heat?' I said.

'Sometimes,' Penny said. 'But it was a cool day and we wanted to get them out, so we could go home.'

'When are you moving in?' Lily asked Megan.

'Next week.'

'We're watching you, jealously,' said Penny. 'Lily and I could move in somewhere together.'

'What would Mum and Dad think of you moving out?' Megan asked Penny.

'They'd be glad to see the back of me. I embarrass them.'

'They've never said anything like that to me,' said Megan. 'You could be imagining it.'

'We'll see.'

Going to live with Megan was exciting. Megan's love raised my awareness of her strengths and weaknesses, as she had engaged with mine. It was a little unnerving to be so invested in another person with the possibility they might withdraw. It added tentativeness to our proceedings, as if they could stop suddenly.

We tried out the bath and explored oral sex for the first time. I had reservations about where I breathed because I had a friend who almost died from a respiratory infection he attributed to inhaling fecal matter.

'Yuk,' said Megan when I told her. 'That seems very unlikely. Fecal matter is benign. They feed it to people in probiotics.'

'Digestive systems can deal with it, but respiratory systems can develop bacterial and viral infections, even lethal ones.'

'Our bath will remove any risk.'

We washed carefully and I performed my subjugation ritual to her satisfaction, evident by her yelling. Then it was her turn, with her intimidating incisors sheathed. I avoided thinking how a female praying mantis could bite off her partner's head during copulation. We were trustful and I enjoyed more stimulation than I had ever known.

Our new living arrangement was a success and both of us grew in confidence.

CHAPTER 36 COACH

Megan respected coach Adamson and wanted to inform him of her interest in flow, but when she had mentioned flow to him, his response had been negative. We had put off taking our proposal to him. She raised it with him again after a training session.

'Coach, I want to train using flow. I . . .'

'You already have a full programme,' he said. 'What will you leave out?'

'Nothing,' she said. 'Flow would be a psychological veneer over my training with you. It would be cognitive, motivational and attitudinal. It wouldn't change my activities. My programme with you would be unaltered.'

'If you won't be doing anything different, why bother?'

'Flow could improve my performance.'

'Says who?'

'My partner Chance Finething wants me to add flow to my mental training. He's a PhD student. He is investigating effects of flow. Since I have been using it, I have improved. I would like you to meet him.'

'Have you changed my programme?'

'No, I am doing everything you wanted.'

'Is it his idea to include flow?'

'No, it's mine. He wants to work in with you. We would plan this with you. We have been meeting daily. I am improving.'

'Your improvement might not be due to flow,' he said scowling.

'I have been training hard.'

'To reach higher, you will need extra strength and fitness.'

'I agree. We want to graft flow onto my programme with you, not replace it. I would continue to train as I have been.'

'I am worried that your friend will distract you.'

'Could we both come to talk with you, about exactly what our proposal could involve?'

'Okay, if you don't take too long.'

'Can I get him to phone you to arrange a meeting?'

'The best time to get me on the phone is between 10.30am and 11.00. I look forward to hearing from him.'

'Thank you coach.'

That evening, I was having dinner with Megan, her parents and her brother and twin sister, at their house.

'How is your training going, Megan?' Michael asked.

'I have been getting into flow,' she said. 'Chance and I are hoping Coach Adamson, will allow me to merge my flow training into his programme.'

'He won't be interested,' Michael said. 'His coaching is traditional. He chooses what you are to learn, how you will learn it and how he will assess your learning. He initiates activities, while your role is student, who follows his directions.

'Your phenomenalism and flow are radical new approaches,' he said. 'They change the coach from an authority to a facilitator. Few coaches would allow Chance or his ideas into their domain. Coaches rule absolutely. For most coaches, another coach would be a threat. Older coaches often disdain psychological and spiritual techniques like flow. They are authoritarians and won't adapt to a one-on-one relationship, as friend, mentor or guardian. Their ego is too fragile. Their technique is basically bullying, using verbal abuse and shaming athletes to do what they otherwise wouldn't do.'

'That's negative,' said Megan. 'I usually want to do what Adamson sets me.'

'You might not be aware of other better activities,' said Hannah. 'He may be a bully preying on your self-confidence. He may be neglecting your abilities and funnelling your success to validate his instruction. You may not be learning as much from him as you are capable of.'

'Coaches traditionally claim to know best and assume the right to impose on athletes,' said Michael. 'They may not respect an athlete's autonomy, as if their experience and wishes are irrelevant.'

'Adamson talks with me to know some needs he can't see,' said Megan. 'But you're right, he often ignores what I tell him.'

'Self-directed learning has become common in golf,' said her brother. 'I practice driving at a range with video self-analysis. There is a coach, but I learn independently.'

'The bullying mind set is still common in coaching for all ages of sport, music, performance, education and training,' Michael said. 'Coaches are able to bully students by techniques such as discrimination, ridicule, isolation and favouritism.'

'But Chance, you said flow doesn't have objective evidence?' said Megan.

'It doesn't,' I said. 'There is objective evidence of your performance and you will be able to join the dots to infer effects of flow. You are already using a student-centred approach called constructivism, in which you build understanding from objective evidence. You are gaining confidence from flow and from using our model. You are ready to take over.'

'Should I look for another coach?' Megan asked.

'Let's see if Adamson would move over,' I said.

When we met with Coach Adamson, he asked me to explain my theory.

'It's not scientific,' he said cutting-off my explanation. 'You'll never get a PhD with that.'

His sledge-hammer negativity was confronting but I tried to be conciliatory.

'A thesis with evidence that flow improves performance could be accepted,' I said. 'But I agree there could be opposition and that is why we are asking to work in with you in our investigation of Megan's performing.

'We will make sure we don't interfere with your work. Adding flow is like boosting her performance. I would like to show you on my laptop the progress she is making.'

I opened my laptop, showing a simulation of Megan vaulting and knocking down the bar.

'This is a simulation of a jump she did yesterday in training.'

Adamson watched the simulation in silence.

'How does it know how she would move?' he asked.

'It calculates her speed and position from Newton's laws of motion and other equations.'

'You must have used her mass, body lengths and muscle forces. Where did you get the data?' Adamson asked.

'We've recorded and measured everything we can and estimated the rest,' said Megan. 'We tweaked the model to match her knockdown.'

'What will this model do to help her win?'

'We can find the effect of holding the pole 5 centimetres higher.'

I keyed in the change and ran it.

We watched as the pole failed to reach vertical and Megan's legs knocked the bar.

'I could have predicted that,' said Adamson.

'Good,' I said. 'We have developed the model to make her aware of her actions and consequences, also her intentions. It's a method called phenomenology.'

'You have done a lot of work,' Adamson said. 'What benefit do you expect?'

'We can answer questions such as: What if I have a longer pole?' Megan said.

'You would have to try it,' Adamson said.

'Let's see what her past performances tell us,' I said.

I ran it again with the longer pole. We watched the stick figure clear the bar.

'The answer is, with the longer pole you gained a few centimetres.'

Adamson seemed impressed.

'Megan should keep up her physical training,' he said. 'Simulation is like masturbation, you can get to like it better than the real thing.'

Megan looked at me and rolled her eyes, as if to say 'What a prick!'

'Megan won't be doing any less jumping,' I said. 'I agree with you she needs more strength, automaticity and mind control. What do you think about doing some Zen training, Megan?'

'With Zen it could be even better. I have done the Zen archery introductory and it was great, I'd like to do more,' said Megan.

'How will that help?'

'With the model I have fewer errors and fewer knockdowns. I have more training time for repetition and optimisation.'

'It's interesting,' said Adamson. 'I'm not convinced flow or Zen are necessary. Let's see how you progress up to the Asian Games.'

'How should we do that?' I asked.

'Megan can coordinate with me,' Adamson said. 'You can tell her when you want her to do something and she can discuss it with me. Your model reminds me of artificial intelligence robots that design dance steps. The designs are mechanistic and don't understand all the dimensions of human performance, such as limits of movement of joints and interpretative art. Dance has turned away from them.'

I didn't like Megan being controlled by Adamson but it was better than having him standing over her and trying to muscle in on my flow project.

'We have yet to add to the model all Megan's musculature and when we have, we can program Megan's movements to be artistic,' I said to Adamson. 'We will round out the stick figure to look like her.'

'It's just cosmetic,' said Megan. 'The connections, pushes and pulls will be inside.'

'We believe this model has helped Megan improve,' I said.

'She has improved physically for sure,' Adamson said grudgingly.

'Would you agree some of the improvement could have resulted from mental training?' I said. 'Could working with this model be helping her mental processes?'

Adamson shrugged. 'Hmm. It's possible, I suppose.'

'Thank you for your interest in our work, Coach,' I said. 'This model empowers Megan and it's up to her to use both of us as best she can.'

'Megan has to be careful not to waste my time on this,' said Adamson. 'Good morning.'

He left.

'What a grouch,' I said to Megan when he had gone. 'He suspicious of what we're doing. If you improve your performing, he will claim it.'

'If I improve, that's the last thing I'll worry about.'

'You have plenty to think about,' I said. 'You are going to be busy.'

CHAPTER 37 TRAINING

Megan's personal best had improved steadily in training and we attributed it to optimal achievement in flow from her learning with the model. Several of her club friends had copied her and taken up flow, training with focus, concentration and repetition. But others were unwilling to make the effort required and her new technique was resented.

'You are over-training,' one of them complained to her. 'Just because you bust yourself at training and do some fancy vaulting here, doesn't mean you'll be any better in competition.'

Megan didn't have a ready reply.

'How much training should I do?' she asked me, as I watched her lifting weights at her gym.

'A body builder would exercise to change body shape. You don't need to grow muscle but you do need to rehearse using your body for competition. There has been evolution in training practices. In 1954 in England, training was regarded as unnecessary and tantamount to cheating. Specialism and professionalism conferred unfair advantage over the prevalent amateurism. Roger Bannister had no coach and was preparing to attempt the 4-minute mile record with little training, until the Americans caught up to his time.

'The dilettante culture Oxbridge gentlemen had enjoyed was losing. He was a medical student and could only get a couple of hours a day off from his ward rounds. He stepped up his training effort and began running intervals, the latest technique. He began to be coached. When he broke the record, it was a triumph for dedicated training.'

'Have you noticed the African Acacia tree outside this sports centre?' I asked Megan.

'No.'

'It has leaves in thin plates, spreading out high up on a tall trunk, like a parasol.'

'I've seen it.'

'Whenever I see it, I am reminded of Lamarck, who held that a giraffe was merely an antelope whose progenitors had strained their necks toward higher and higher branches of this tree. The trees had grown beyond reach, in layers pruned by feeding giraffes.'

'Hang on,' said Megan. 'The long neck wasn't from straining. The shorter necked animals starved and the survivors bred longer necked offspring.'

'Yes, natural selection is partly right,' I said. 'But there is renewed interest in Lamarck's theory and epigenetics is becoming popular. Changes in our bodies and perhaps our minds, can be passed to offspring during our lifetimes. Your offspring could inherit the body and abilities for pole vaulting you have strained to produce.'

'I'm not planning on having any offspring,' she said. 'The only spring I'm interested in is my take-off. Does epigenetics have any relevance to my training?'

'Your straining can change you. You could grow longer arms and a smarter brain.'

'I won't count on it,' she said.

Megan and I went for coffee.

'I am feeling pretty stale with all the training I have been doing,' Megan said, sniffling.

'Do you have a cold?'

'No. I'm fine. I have been training too hard.'

It would be unlike Megan to admit she was unwell.

'Could you cut down your training for a while?'

'I don't want to,' she said. 'There doesn't seem to be an orthodoxy about how much training to do. How much training do my competitors do?'

'The USA and Soviet squads train full-time, paid from national funds,' I said. 'Performing is professionalised, like in other sports.

'Sergey Bubka, a Ukrainian state-funded professional, set the record for men's pole vault at 6m16 in 1994.'

'How can I compete with professionals?' asked Megan. 'I earn nothing and have to support myself from my PhD grant. I have stepped up my training until I am doing as much training as full-timers.'

'Superpower nations' athletes are also advantaged by having a larger population pool, more competition, better organisation and more money for travel.'

'I just want competition to be fair,' said Megan. 'I don't have to win.'

'It's fair when any competitor could win by equal striving,' I said. 'It isn't fair when more favourable funding and more experience makes a difference.'

'But that's what happens!' she said.

'Competitors can be unequal in many ways,' I said. 'All you can do is make the most of your ability.'

'Must I turn a blind eye to differences that are not exclusive, such as a nation having an intensive athlete development programme?'

'Yes, because Australia could do the same. Who's to say how best to develop athletes?' I said.

'I'm doing the best I can,' Megan said.

'My view is that your training for the Asian Games should rehearse achievement of your goal,' I said. 'I'm not sure you are committed to it.'

'What's your rationale?' Megan asked.

'You can't count on doing better in competition than you have achieved in training,' I said. 'When you compete, your goal should be familiar to you by experience.'

'Competition can bring out better performances than in training,' Megan said. 'Won't I be aiming too low?'

'Not if you perform better when you reproduce experience, than when a packed stadium applauds you.'

'Wouldn't that depend on how ambitious I am when setting my goal?' she said. 'I need to set a goal that stretches me, but not too far.'

'In flow, there is intense focus on an achievable goal,' I said. 'Performance is not an adventure.'

'I must rehearse goal achievement from now on,' she said. 'I can forego the rare moments of unrehearsed success when I think I'm immortal.'

I recalled that Australian athletes' training conditions were difficult. Megan's American opponents, better supported than she was, had scholarships worth tens of thousands of dollars. Athletes could win prizes too, in certain events. At the Tokyo Olympics in 2020, the United States Olympic and Paralympic Committee awarded $37,500 to each athlete winning gold, $22,500 for silver and $15,000 for bronze medals. Famous marathon competitions had bigger prizes. In the Boston Marathon, the winners of the men's and women's open divisions each took home $150,000, with $75,000 for second place. In the Dubai Marathon, first place winner received US$200,000 and an additional US$100,000 bonus for achieving a world record.

Australian medal winners were awarded less. Field athletes received less than endurance runners. Megan's research scholarship was barely enough to live on. She couldn't afford specialist coaching, gym memberships, workshops, equipment and holidays overseas. Her main expense was rent on the house she shared with me, paying from her scholarship.

Megan and I had settled in.

'We've been together for a month,' I said.

'How good for each other are we?' Megan asked

'It is working for me,' I said.

'Me too,' said Megan.

'Have you had to adjust?' she asked. 'I have.'

'Have you had problems? I didn't realize.'

'Nothing I can't handle. I am used to being alone. It's harder to relax with someone in my living space all the time.'

'We have heaps of space. That can't be the issue.'

'I am not used to having anyone overlooking me.'

'I didn't realize. I'm sorry about that. Maybe I should go out more, or stay away.'

'No, as I said, I've adjusted. What about you, do you have any problems with me?'

'I usually like the clothes you wear, except when you wear fraying jeans with holes at the knees.'

'Oh. What's wrong with that?'

'It looks impoverished. Why don't you wear good quality clothes? You have plenty.'

Megan bristled. 'It's a fashion. Even well-off people wear rags. How is it a problem for you?'

'I am embarrassed. I want to be recognised as a person of some means.'

'I'm sorry if you're ashamed of me. I'll dress more conventionally,' she said bitterly. 'I want you to be proud of me. I didn't know you hankered after affluence.'

'I don't. Let's not quarrel.'

'Now I'm wondering what else you have stewing. Perhaps we need to have a free-for-all and tell each other exactly what we think of each other?'

'No. I don't have anything else to complain about. Do you?'

'Not right now.'

'We need to keep open the option to talk about our differences.'

We had few differences. Our new home was comfortable and we would open a bottle of wine and drink it on the patio which overlooked trees and a park. Dazzled by the colourful plumage of Rosellas and Lorikeets, feeding on nectar they took from the flowers of wattle bushes, our difficulties faded.

Since moving in, we had seen less of Penny and Lily and I had Megan to myself, which was what I wanted.

CHAPTER 38 COMPETITION

Megan was in training for the Asian Games. Her intense training and use of flow was resented and denigrated by some other athletes and coaches.

'Psychological training can endanger athlete health,' they said.

'Flow training is a technique for optimal achievement and does not endanger athlete health,' I said.

'Flow training can reduce perception of warning signals, causing injury.'

'No. It heightens attention, reducing injuries.'

Some athletes and coaches holding down jobs opposed full-time training and pressured Megan to quit her intensive flow technique.

'I can't afford to give up my day job,' said a rival. 'Training for field events doesn't have to be intense.'

In field events, some opponents wanted natural ability to hold sway, tempered by regular practice. Megan's arduous programme was regarded as unnecessary and unpleasant for the athlete.

'What's the problem?' Megan asked a team member.

'The others worry that too much training can lead to staleness and underperformance.'

'It's nonsense. Automaticity is an asset not a liability,' she said. 'Training can be enjoyable.'

Megan's diligent training was producing good results.

'I'm the same person,' she said, reflecting on her success in training. 'Maybe my body is stronger and fitter. Is all.'

'Your improvement has needed a stronger body but the mind that commands it has reached new heights.'

'My mind is the same.'

'It has adapted and become reflexive,' I said. 'You have spent a lot of time rehearsing until your skills are precise and automatic. You have learned to adjust what you do from our model. Your Zen classes have taught you to coordinate your mind with your body. Flow has taught you to be goal focussed and mentally engaged. Your mind has developed in many ways that enables it to control your body better.'

'Oh,' she said. 'It's a theory. But I'll believe you anyway.'

We had come a long way together. I still watched her train most days, but she had become independent in planning her training. She worked steadily, increasing her flow skills.

'This morning was magic,' she said when we met for lunch. 'Getting to my third jump was so smooth it surprised me.'

'What height did you achieve?'

'A new PB of 5m20.'

'Well done! Were you in flow throughout?'

'Not in my first and second. In the third I locked in flow on the runway and sailed over. Afterwards, I was too excited and failed at 5m25.'

'Are you surprised to be near the world record of 5m30?''

She thought for a moment. 'No. I'm just getting started,' she winked.

A week later she was disconsolate.

'I haven't been able to get any nearer the record in training.'

'Is something wrong?'

'I haven't been able to get into flow. The other girls have been distracting me. They call out comments during my run-up, to break my concentration.'

'What comments?'

'They jeer 'Meagre beaver.' Or 'Chancy of the overflow.'

'Their hostility would be off putting,' I said. 'but you don't have to notice it.'

'It's anti-elitist,' I thought. *'In Australia, the 'Tall Poppy Syndrome' refers to the expectation that poppies should grow together, and if one grows too tall, it must be cut down to size, unless it has its own group.'*

'Adamson might have put them up to it. He doesn't like you locking in on flow.'

'When I told him I had improved, he warned me to stop using flow.'

'What did he say?'

''Keep your mind on what you're doing. Forget that flow nonsense.' He didn't congratulate me on my new personal best. What sort of a coach is that? He said that I had perceived a ceiling of 5m00 and now I had merely broken through it, as if I had been choking. That is so untrue!'

Megan began weeping angrily.

'He is being unfair,' I said. 'He phoned me and said that some other coaches have complained about you. They said using flow was giving you an unfair advantage and I should stop working with you or you would be banned. A sticking point is they believe you could be in a hypnotic state — but they don't have any evidence.'

'Everyone mentions time distortion,' said Megan. 'Is that like time dilation?'

'I do have a neuroscience theory that the intense mental engagement of flow can cause time dilation and timelessness. But its not hypnotism. Time dilation is explained by Einstein's Special Relativity theory. The jeerers don't understand time dilation and they are making flow into something insidious when it's glorious!' I said. 'Anyone who wants to can train in flow. It is not unlike their own concentration. At the conference, I told the coaches' about your flow.'

'They can't compete except by pulling me down,' Megan said.

'People have some strange ideas about equality,' I said. 'There is a movement that wants to equalise all competitors on a level playing field, despite every individual being different. There are too many differences to make the challenges the same for everyone, as they try to with horse handicapping.

'The social levelling that is achieved by socialism and secularism can be engineered by the state. If we empower the state to this degree, then the state effectively dictates reality and tends to move in the direction of totalitarianism. The logic of totalitarianism is that there are only two classes of actors in the society: the state and the individual. The individual is expected to serve the purposes of the state. Although the close of the 20th century saw the early threat of totalitarianism blunted, we must understand the part played in its rise by enthusiasm for social levelling. And we must continue to oppose it as it returns with ever softer and friendlier faces.

'Levelling mental differences is going too far. Standard conditions, such as standard runway times for pole vaulting, can be controlled but differences in performance technique can't.'

'Handicapping athletes for equal outcomes would be impossible,' said Megan.

'Absolutely,' I said. 'Some competitors are more qualified than others. Nature herself has already applied screening in getting them to the line. No-one should tamper with the line up. Here is the view of the philosopher, Ayn Rand:

'Since nature does not endow all men with equal beauty or equal intelligence, and the faculty of volition leads men to make different choices, the egalitarians propose to abolish the 'unfairness' of nature and of volition, and to establish universal equality in fact — defiance of facts.

Ayn Rand, Return of the Primitive: The Anti-Industrial Revolution.'

'They can ban flow, but they won't be able to test for it,' said Megan. 'A ban on flow can't be enforced.'

'Governments do what they want,' I said. 'St Augustine pictured some governments as bands of robbers with official uniforms of state.'

'Social levelling is wrong,' she said. 'It assumes that equality can be ordained by people without authority in that sphere and imposed by constraining competition that can only be fair when it is free of unequal constraint.'

Megan was angry. She recalled her years of dedicated training, to achieve values that were being arbitrarily replaced. She recalled her discomfort, performing in conditions of cold, heat and wet. She recalled the hours she had spent travelling to, participating at, or returning from, athletic events. She didn't grudge her time but it had been predicated on the continuation of conditions that were now under threat. Athletics was in turmoil.

Competitions have rules that pronounce behaviours in a competition fair, or unfair,' Thought Megan. *'It is fair for pole vaulters to be disqualified when they climb up the pole. It is unfair when competitors or spectators jeer, during a performance. Judges are needed to ensure standards of fair conduct are met.*

These were anxious times for Megan, due to the uncertainty of competition rules. She was alternately dispirited and angry, but I consoled her in bed, entering, pushing, thrusting, pulling and pumping, enabling her to forget her problems and sleep soundly.

NANNY STATE

CHAPTER 39 NANNY STATE

I was a regular for dinner at Megan's parents' place. They kept up with current issues and there was always lively discussion around the dinner table. Hannah was a magistrate and proposed topics of general interest.

'Does democracy still work?' Hannah asked. 'Do we have enough say in public policies?'

'Which public policies?' asked Michael.

'All of them,' she said. 'When people are left out, or treated like children, they sometimes get resentful and angry.'

'We have what they call a 'nanny state,' Michael said. 'It has the appearance of protecting vulnerable people from bullies, who would grab more than they should, like a nanny controls greedy unruly children.'

'According to Mark Fisher (15), capitalism fosters impulsive and hedonistic appetites,' he said

'Capitalist greed can certainly be a problem, but over-reach by the nanny state can be worse. In principle, a nanny state is benign, suppressing individual desires, but I detest overreach that diminishes personal responsibility, replacing it with ethics and morality,' I said, moderating my voice from shrillness because I was too excited. 'A nanny state can become a police state.'

'You're right,' said Michael. 'It was tried in the Soviet experiment but it failed. If the collectivism you speak of takes over, will it fail again?'

'Last time, instead of openness bringing reform, people lost confidence and the Soviet economy crashed in 1991,' I said.

'This time it will be different. Capitalism nurtures the id and removes its limits and individuals can operate wantonly, especially when corporate interests remove boundaries,' said Michael. 'Optimistically, a nanny state that curbs it could unleash a harmonious general will in a liberated way.

'A government could protect us from the bad effects of competition, or absence of competition, on individuals' rights, parity and the public good.'

'Nanny state provision is costly to the public purse and does not bring equality to needy people,' said Penny.

'The term 'nanny state' is used to malign collectivism,' said Michael. 'People regard it as over-protective, smothering individuality, fostering freeloading, growing like a malignancy.

'A nanny state can have benefits,' he said defensively. 'Australia's nanny state has provided personal welfare envied in other countries. People have had a say and our nanny state provides things most people want.'

'A nanny state has to compete with individualism,' I said. 'I am an avid believer in individual interest as the locomotive of volition. I am deeply suspicious of the motives of collectives of do-gooders.'

'Individualism and social inequality have been fostered by existentialism and utilitarianism, displacing religion,' Michael said. 'The nanny state is an antidote. You are using the term nanny state pejoratively, but that is a minority and libertarian perspective. The classical liberal view is of government that provides services missing from the market and promotes economic growth. You are supposing the nanny state imposes unwanted goods and services. Sure, there may be some excess, but that is not the whole story.'

'Most people want to leave social policy to experts,' said Megan. 'The bureaucrats do what they like - which usually isn't what I like.'

'People want a charitable nanny state to let them off the hook of their Christian consciences,' Michael said. 'People don't want to give to beggars on the street when the nanny state has responsibility.'

'Many people wrongly assume the nanny state knows best,' I said. 'Its role has grown insidiously.'

'It isn't a conspiracy,' Michael said. 'The nanny state is an appearance, together with capitalism, in its various manifestations, as the primemover of Debord's spectacle, soothing lower class yearnings with goods and services. The nanny state aids the capitalists by mediating the spectacle.

'That's the subtlety of Debord's analysis of the spectacle: he blames capitalism for the spectacle and wants to clean it up to achieve worker emancipation,' Michael said. 'He adopts the Marxist belief in alienation of the lower class and portents of revolution to overthrow the middle class. Social reformers have opposed capitalism but they have been unrealistic:

'It is easier to imagine the end of the world than the end of capitalism.' Mark Fisher (17)

'The context of the spectacle is totalitarian control,' I said. 'It is associated with dictatorship, central control, persecution and one-party rule.'

'We believe the government has to provide services and goods for survival,' he said.

'A neoliberal would say that central control and surveillance are needed to help the corporations and the economy,' I said. 'A Marxist wants the same police oppression but against ideological enemies, capitalists and fascists.'

'In Australia we have some of that, but not enough for a totalitarian state,' he said.

'Not yet, but we're getting there,' said Michael. 'Hannah Arendt, Heidegger's student, lover and friend, traced the origins of totalitarianism (4) to arbitrary leader ideology, central domination, an atomised population, fear in the masses and individual superfluity.'

'Arendt was very successful as a philosopher and writer,' said Megan. 'Do you think Heidegger helped her?'

'For sure,' said Michael. 'Help with what?'

'Phenomenalism,' said Megan. 'Her ethics of ambiguity has a phenomenal approach.'

'His methods could have realized her dasein,' I said. 'She personally experienced the subjectivity of the Nazis.'

'Heidegger's antisemitism didn't clash with her Jewishness, because she helped him recover when he was stigmatised as a Nazi,' I said.

'She was remarkably tolerant, finding Eichmann's crime was banality,' said Hannah. 'Her insight was that totalitarianism is wrong, whether of the political left or right, by people who are otherwise ordinary.'

'Today's totalitarianism of the left and of the right is similar,' I said. 'There is extremism and polarisation.'

'It is a political morass,' said Michael.

'It may be perpetrated by ordinary people, but the schism is consequential.'

'It might be more concerning if it was bridged,' I said.

'Or pole vaulted,' laughed Megan.

'Haha', I said. 'Civil society is decaying, communities are declining and the nanny state is taking up the slack, making provision for collective care.'

'People have become disaffected and are too fearful to look after their own interests,' said Hannah. 'In the family court, people expect me to resolve matters they could resolve themselves, if they were less dependent. When asked for an opinion, or to make a commitment, they cringe.'

'Do they cringe in fear or is it deference to expertise?' asked Megan.

'Both,' said Hannah. 'They won't accept risk or responsibility. Many people want a nanny state to keep them healthy, find them jobs, feed them and provide them with housing. State provision of health and education has been popular. Provision of disability services and tertiary education has run into opposition. Outcomes of over-protection and free-loading are being countered by making individuals responsible for themselves.'

During the discussion, Penny and I had cleared the table and loaded the dishwasher.

'Let's go for a walk,' Hannah suggested. 'We can talk as we walk.'

We moved as a group and the discussion continued. When we reached the park, we watched a family of tree creepers on a stand of eucalypts. They were medium-small, mostly brown birds with patterning on their underparts, looking for insects on the bark.

'In a park near here, there are ridiculous signs saying: 'Beware falling branches!' Hannah said. 'The sign doesn't protect; it merely exculpates the park manager. A park is supposed to have some natural hazards, it's part of the fun of going there. We need to preserve our natural instincts. A sign says: 'Do not throw stones at this notice.' The precaution is over-protective and offensive, as is nanny state intrusion. It angers many people.'

'There are two sides to caring,' I said. 'Public care empowers authorities and arbitrary controls. When public care is relinquished, people have to accept individual responsibility. '

'Perhaps a sign saying 'Beware falling branches' is the antithesis of a nanny state,' said Michael. 'It notifies people of personal responsibility. Where there are no signs, would the nanny state accept responsibility?'

'No,' I said. 'The sign merely prompts individual responsibility.'

'That is what the nanny state does best,' Michael said. 'It applies moral consciences to keep the impulsive and hedonistic id inside us in check.'

'It is state care,' I said. "I don't like that sign because it invites atrophy of my personal responsibility.'

'Does it take anything from you?' Michael asked.

'By reading that sign I will be alerted and have my natural caution reduced,' I said. 'The message can't be undone.'

'Is it overreach for an independent person like you? asked Hannah.

'Yes,' I said. 'The recipient has to want to be cared for. It's not for me or others to tell Megan how to be careful, how to train or what regulation she needs. The other side of care is responsibility. If Megan cares for herself, she has to accept responsibility.'

'Chance, you seem to have done a U-turn!' Michael said. 'You began with a nanny state approach to athlete safety, investigating how to protect athletes from danger. Now you are reverting to individual responsibility. What happened with you?'

'I have realised Megan is a unique individual and she shouldn't be required to behave like everyone else, without choice or self-regulation,' I said. 'She should be able to do what she wants.'

'If everyone did what they wanted,' said Michael, 'we would soon degenerate into a dog eat dog world, a state of competition that would descend to the least common denominator of anarchy and chaos.'

'Get along with you. People are not that bad!' said Megan.

'They are. They can't help themselves,' said Michael. 'They are stupid and easily led.'

'That doesn't mean they need a nanny state to overreach,' I said. 'Or totalitarianism.'

'The middle class keeps the lower class feeling fearful and superfluous,' said Megan. 'Debord's analysis describes the situation as society existing within a spectacle which is capitalism. The spectacle has media which obscure the lower class's alienation from capitalist systems of both production and consumption. The public news channels are unrelenting in diverting attention to issues that worry us, such as climate change. The spectacle is a mad grab to escape an unpleasant reality. Society is driven by existential fear to consume escapist media entertainment, to consult services that reassure, to buy protective products and to take anaesthetic drugs to dull the pain. The fear industry is huge, profitable and totalitarian in its effect.'

'Marshall McLuhan in Understanding Media (16) proclaimed 'the medium is the message'. Debord agreed media were important in people's lives and he dug deeper to uncover who profited from, invested in and controlled the media,' Michael said. 'Debord parted company with the Marxists, accepting media would be capitalised, rather than wanting middle class control ended.'

'Woke folk are angered by the abuse suffered by the lower class and want revolutionary workers' councils to oversee improvement,' said Megan. 'That seems unlikely in the athletics industry, because the movers and shakers in the AAA have distinctly middle class tendencies.'

'We have to make do without a revolution,' I said.

'De Tocqueville argues that it's only natural for the masses to allow an aristocracy to take control,' I said.

'In order for the revolutionary intellectual anarchy to disappear, the majority of civilians must exercise their reason. But the author himself recognizes that the power that directs the mass will always be aristocratic because, as he says repeatedly, it's impossible for all men to have the time and leisure necessary to occupy themselves with works of the mind.
De Tocqueville (8).

'Perhaps privilege is the genesis of the nanny state - deference to elite reason,' said Hannah. 'It used to be called noblesse oblige. We now want people to sacrifice themselves for the welfare of the community, for example by changing from cheap to expensive electricity. Care for others is romantic but selfishness is more reliable.'

'The nanny-state is idealistic and romantic, but not everyone wants that.'

'Foucault (12) suggested that people *consent* to act in a certain way, not necessarily from free choice. Consent is manufactured in controlling mechanisms that produce norms, constitute interests and shape behaviour. This is how a nanny state operates, by consent.'

'People want a nanny state when they are fearful,' said Megan. 'They scan the news continually for dangers.'

'The spectacle promotes the nanny state.' I said. 'Only approved dangers can make headlines, Mass media have taken upon themselves to censor controversial sources, using text bots to censor even well-authenticated sources.

'The media interest is to exclude extreme opinion that would turn some of an audience away.'

'Extreme opinion can be distasteful but it can also alert people to matters they want to be aware of, including media hegemony.'

'The media interest is to create a news churn that won't offend and alienate audiences from subscriptions and advertisements,' Hannah said. 'Their touchstone for news coverage is to show items that are net earners.'

'The spectacle does not have free speech,' I said. 'The text bots crawl through and censor anti-capitalist content.'

'There is a role for censorship,' said Michael. 'A small one. Some dangers are difficult to avoid. It's necessary to have roads divided to protect people from erratic drivers approaching, but in most situations people need to retain the ability to evaluate risks for themselves and take precautions.'

'I agree,' I said. 'By the time they reach adulthood, people should have taken responsibility for themselves in most situations. Instead, wherever I go I am directed about what to do and what to buy. They assume I want to be told, when quite often I don't. I resent having to read signs and ponder the labyrinthine minds of bureaucratic sign posters, advertisers and scamsters. No-one reads the terms and conditions that come with products and services. It is a device to dominate customers, a part of the spectacle..

'I don't like it that the nanny state is taking us towards a narrow Disney world of thoughtless stereotyped behaviour and neglecting the challenge of contemplation, exploration and discovery. Parents and teachers know that without challenges, their children won't achieve much. When exposed to reality, humans can grow up during all of their lives.'

I stopped and drank some wine.

'Bravo,' said Megan.

'Not everyone would agree,' said George, who had been silent up to this point. 'There is a type of human who declines taking any responsibility for risks.'

'Homo patheticus,' Megan said.

'Spoken like a performer,' said Hannah. 'But supposing you were struck in the head by a golf ball and reduced to a wheelchair, wouldn't you want the state to protect you, relieving your family from responsibility and looking after you forever?'

George nodded. 'That's right.'

'Wanting to relieve others is not the same as declining responsibility,' I said. 'A Nanny state can absolve the community from responsibility by shutting down activities in which injury can occur, but that goes against human nature. Humans have always taken risks. Our ancestors used to live with risks constantly, leaping from tree to tree. If risk-taking is stopped, we could become like sloths, slow and vulnerable.'

'Sloths do okay,' Megan said.

'How do you know that?' I asked.

'They don't go around causing trouble, do they?' she said.

They laughed at that. I felt welcome with Megan's family. I was impressed by their reasonableness and good humour.

On the way back we saw a possum just out of reach up a huge blue gum.

'The loggers must have left this one,' I said.

'It could have grown since they came through about 100 years ago. It has been protected for the last 50 years.'

'The nanny state is not without successes.'

CHAPTER 40 OVERREACH

Talk continued in the McLean's family dining room over coffee.

'The nanny state goes too far,' Megan said. 'It over-protects. My poles have a warning sticker affixed. It says:

'Use of this pole can cause serious injury or death. Beginners should not use it without a coach present.'

'That notice makes my flesh crawl,' she said. 'I don't dispute that accidents occur from recklessness. It's questionable that a pole has significantly more danger than learning to ride a bicycle, throw a javelin, shoot an arrow, drive a car or boil an egg. Unexpected dangers should be labelled. Vulnerable people may not be deterred by warnings. Many people learn about dangers by trying new things.'

'I agree. Caution goes with intelligence, not regulation,' said Michael.

'Don't we need to protect stupid people?'

'Of course, but it is a question of degree,' he said. 'Without protection, we have survival of the fittest, in a Hobbesian state of nature, red in tooth and claw. Everyone wants protection from the worst dangers.'

'Hidden dangers are banned, for example drugs,' Megan said.

'The overreach of the state can go beyond protection when it has power to interfere,' Hannah said. 'The stolen generation of children is an example. Australian governments, in a fit of cultural hegemony and moral certitude, encouraged by religion, removed children from poor families 'for their own good'.

'They received an apology from a Prime Minister, as if the mistake was racism against 'blacks', but 'white' children from poor homes were also taken,' Michael said. 'Had the nanny state provided practical help for parents struggling to raise their children, it would have been less divisive.'

'We place too much faith that the nanny state will look after everyone,' I said. 'Australia's nanny state is taking over and individualism is threatened.'

'The threat to individuals is removal of personal choice by state control,' I said. 'The nanny state could bring hellish living conditions and mind numbing jobs. The Soviet experience went further, into totalitarianism.'

'The nanny state reduces choice,' said Hannah. 'Frank Chodorov, (1887–1966) pointed out that egalitarianism is not only doomed, but undesirable, because it threatens freedom.

'Freedom is essentially a condition of inequality, not equality. It recognises as a fact of nature the structural differences inherent in man - temperament, character, and capacity - and it respects those differences. We are not alike and no law can make us so.'

'Equality is okay in principle, but there can never be equality of outcomes,' Michael said. 'Some idiocy has to be assumed. In schools, teachers are indoctrinating students with consolatory assessment. For example: $2 + 2 = 5$ is rated as 'a reasonable attempt' and encouraged. The student may not know of his error, nor how to correct it. Employers complain that millennial workers, when they are corrected, walk off the job, because they were consoled at school and haven't experienced criticism. Consolation has been overdone. Resilience and lifelong learning are needed.'

'Employee resilience is at an all-time low,' said Megan. 'School leavers trained within the consolatory curriculum may be traumatised. Workers quit and are left on the bottom rung of the earnings ladder.'

'There is talk about government enforcing a universal wage,' said Hannah. 'Could there really be equality? Workers would have to learn to meet work standards or leave that job.'

'Opposition to negative discrimination may have gone too far,' said Michael. 'A popular Canadian psychologist has said there is excessive intolerance for inequality:

'America is besieged by 'postmodernists' who wish to build an economic system that will guarantee 'equal outcomes' for all individuals.' Jordan Peterson.

'He predicts disaster for a system attempting to make outcomes equal,' said Michael. 'Equal opportunity is different from egalitarianism, which is the doctrine that all humans are equal in fundamental worth or moral status, opposing competition. People who are down-rated should be helped to improve, for the benefit of all, not allowed to drag down their betters.'

'We need to oppose the nanny state's sponsoring of immature adults, unable to solve problems by thinking and reasoning,' he said.

'The nanny state has evolved in size and complexity,' I said. 'State care may have begun with protection at some time after voting began in Greece about 500BC, but devolution of power from kings, oligarchies, tyrants and early democratic rule, has taken a long time and remains an issue in politics today. The idea of a 'nanny state' that protects those in need, emerged with the concept of a welfare state, commenced in the UK by the utilitarians, including Jeremy Bentham. There were various ideas about how the greatest good of the greatest number should be calculated.'

I paused as Hannah poured from a pot of fresh coffee.

'The welfare state is one of the UK's most successful social reforms. Bentham and the utilitarians set up a series of rewards and punishments to civilize human behaviour. Regulation of health, penal and education systems spread to Australia. Bentham strongly believed that education should be widely available, particularly to those who were not wealthy or who did not belong to the established church. He opposed the idea of natural law and God-given rights, believing that however rights are defined, it needed a government to enforce them.

'Bentham created 'panopticon' prisons with continuous surveillance by removal of prisoners' privacy,' I said. 'Their rehabilitation was supposed to result from isolation. The experiment was abandoned as inhumane. Employees were in many places supervised like prisoners. As an office worker in Canada and London, I had suffered under an excess of employee surveillance, both physical and psychological. I had quit my profession to escape it.

'For most workers, Foucault (10) described surveillance during working hours, social conditioning by behavioural and language control. Debord associated surveillance with worker alienation within his spectacle. Autocratic management practices have been displaced by overreach of the nanny state.'

'Did the spectacle emerge from utilitarianism?' Megan asked.

'Yes, half a century later,' I said.

'We should not be too critical of the nanny state,' said Megan. 'In Australia, public welfare systems have delivered clean water and sanitation, limited drink driving, required safer vehicles and regulated road safety. Besides providing universal health care, states have been responsible for child protection, educating the masses, supporting the homeless, electricity supply, product safety, food safety, environmental health, financial management, social services and vaccines.'

'I agree,' I said. 'In Australia, the nanny state has done much good. Nevertheless, nanny state over-provision and over-protection are indisputable. Australia has large, but not the largest, state-funding of economic and social services.'

'Norway and Sweden have more public funding and pay higher taxes to administer soft capitalism,' said Hannah.

'American hard capitalism has lower taxes, less government health care, less infrastructure provision by government and fewer public holidays.'

'Disaster support is a community expectation. Australians support disaster victims with public finance for: floods, cyclones, earthquakes, bushfires, droughts, erosion, disease and pandemics,' Megan said. 'Farmers receive state payments for economic hardship

201

declared to be disasters. When adversity strikes, businesses, property owners and workers expect help from the nanny state, especially when insurers become reluctant to provide coverage and pay claims. The nanny state has had to pick up the tab for temporary housing, evacuation and supplies. Help for disaster victims from compensation is widely supported, gets votes, is profitable and re-elects governments. The spectacle goes from strength to strength.'

'The nanny state wants to protect us from potential problems,' I said. 'There is a stream of claims for nanny state help with opportunities for research and technology, for example to mitigate global climate change hardship.'

'Nanny state policies proposed by the left are opposed by the right,' Megan said. 'The partisan interests are aligned. Industrial leaders oppose nanny state actions when they oppose their accumulation of capital and wealth.

'Independent individualism is more deeply rooted in the human psyche than equality,' I said. 'I have been unpleasantly aware of the nanny state taking away my liberties and reducing the quality of my life. This has been apparent on urban streets, where I have been hindered by unwanted traffic lights, traffic calming islands, roundabouts, pedestrian crossings, pedestrian crossing lights, unnecessary road signs, parking zones, parking meters, no-stopping zones and one-way systems. Officialdom in other spheres has grown a morass of websites and complex forms of correspondence claimed to benefit a majority, but they disadvantage me. I must benefit others at a higher cost to myself than is reasonable.

'The nanny state has taken over the middle ground from libertarian conservatives with the prosperous market economy on one side and the impoverished socialist welfare state on the other,' I said. 'The nanny state lies between middle class wealth and lower class poverty.'

'Nanny state intervention in sports is recent. A sport is respected for its explicit rules of competition, as a microcosm of a society wanted to be a free from corruption,' Megan said. 'Sport and elite activities have critical audiences including people of lower ability who need to have their interest in participating represented, even if they cannot compete themselves.'

'A nanny state has to care for all her charges,' said Penny. 'How can the nanny state represent people with disabilities when it needs to?'

'There is a move to widen participation, with more equality of opportunity. New rules are being proposed to allow participation by disabled individuals previously regarded as unqualified, who can now win,' said Megan.

'Elite athletes would quit rather than compete against disabled athletes,' I said. 'Is it in the interests of all to throw the baby out with the bath water?'

'Sport and performing have traditionally fostered competition,' said Penny. 'Are you saying that could end?'

'It's possible,' I said. 'There could be other ways of being involved in sport and performing that do not result in humiliation and elimination. There are people who resent others' physical ability who would prefer more sedentary or alternative participation in sports.'

'Megan has more than one string to her bow,' said Penny. 'She could tell pole vaulting stories.'

'All elitism is under threat, not just in athletics,' said Megan. 'The spectacle of nanny state levelling in sport is motivated by the government's political agenda. The political parties are relating public social goals to relations between athletes. Everyone is supposed to be equal. The term *elitism* may be used to describe a situation in which power is concentrated in the hands of a few people. This may not be fair to the others. A select group of people is perceived as having intrinsic quality, high intellect, wealth, power, notability, special skills, or experience — they are more likely to be regarded as constructive to society as a whole and therefore deserving of more influence or authority. Is it wrong-headed to suppress those people?'

'Perhaps not, but levelling down the tall poppies could head off a change like Mao Zedong's Cultural Revolution,' I said. 'Doing farm fieldwork, the elite would quickly lose their skills. Such extreme levelling could reduce civil society.'

'More levelling would be desirable for some qualities than others,' said Penny. 'Levelling of wealth and property ownership would be very different to levelling of athletic performance abilities. There would be a lot of resistance, because it is cultural change.'

'Levelling could be our revolution, like China's,' Megan said.

'It could be disastrous to devalue education,' I said. 'I am biased.'

'Even so, a large change to create equality could be attempted,' said Michael.

'Leave me out of it,' said Megan.

'With a rampant nanny state, anything can happen,' I said. 'My research into competitive risk-taking indicates overreach can get badly out of control, with the nanny state promoting the spectacle. Business and the nanny state have committed to profitable growth from private and public capital.'

'Can individuals oppose it?' Megan asked.

'They might not be able to,' I said.

'Many people will object to changes to the rules of sport,' said Megan. 'Me for one.'

'Me too,' I said. 'We must oppose the nanny state before it's too late.'

'Also the spectacle,' Megan said, 'We must oppose it, if possible.'

Megan and I thanked her parents, said goodnight to Penny and George and went home.

The talk of rules changes was worrying. We could have to fight for our rights, an unpleasant prospect.

CHAPTER 41 EXCLUSION

Megan had won a place in the Australian athletics squad to go to the Asian Games in Seoul. After the National, her training was taken over by a AAA national coach: Gordon Barker. Megan was paid to go to Barker's training camps where she had to conform to his strict programme. Between squad training, she continued to work out at the university under coach Adamson. Adamson obsequiously adopted Barker's programme and tried to curtail Megan's flow work with Chance.

'Your programme has frequent changes in activity,' Adamson said. 'You won't be doing anything for long enough to get into flow. Pole vault action is brief, spontaneous and flexible, not groovy at all.'

Megan was constantly in demand to attend training camps and coaching workshops. Barker held workshops and clinics for the squad that prevented her from getting into flow. She was becoming exhausted and demoralized.

'I can't do any flow training now,' Megan said to me, when she came home from a camp and threw down her kit bag, frustrated. 'They are undoing all our hard work.'

I got up, hugged her and pulled her down on the settee.

'They can't ban a mental state,' I said. 'When you are in flow, they won't know. You can continue.'

'They stop me concentrating.'

'Flow will come back to you when you compete,' I said.

'I can't turn flow on and off like a tap,' she said. 'I have to use Barker's methods.'

I tucked some of her curls behind a seashell ear.

'It comes with the squad pay,' I said. 'I'm sorry about what they are doing to your training routine. Have you asked Gordon Barker to give you exercises in which you can practice flow?'

'When I asked him, he said that some people thought flow didn't exist. He said it hadn't been demonstrated to improve performance and therefore it was not relevant to my training.'

I was preoccupied with the perfection of her breasts.

'What's he like?'

'He's an old-fashioned bully,' Megan said. 'He likes to have his own way. He will select the team for the Asian Games. It's a national takeover of my personal performance, by a tyrannical bureaucracy. They suppose I lack motivation and need to be coerced into winning. I have always had freedom to train independently, but now that is gone.'

Megan was becoming aware of my hands and lay back on the settee, with me alongside her.

'The Australian Athletics Association are allied with the nanny state's push into sport and performing,' I said. 'The AAA has a commercial interest in exploiting performers and audiences for profit. They are opposing individualism and want to control what performers do and how much they get paid. Risk-out is pitching a re-write of sports rules to appeal to armchair sports collectivists, media presenters, advertisers and betting agencies.'

While I said this I undid her track suit jacket.

'Standing up to Barker won't be easy.'

'You are under his control,' I said. 'You have to do the prescribed exercises, use approved equipment, wear the squad uniform correctly. You must conduct yourself at all times by his rules. If this was Russia or China, you would be even more controlled.'

I struggled to take off her top, until she helped me.

'Barker's interference in my training is the last straw,' she said. 'Now Adamson is doing Barker's dirty work for him, I am being held back. It was bad enough not having Adamson in my corner on the flow issue, but now he is against me.'

'Could you quit Adamson?'

'He comes with my scholarship.'

'Has he been doing you any good lately?'

'No. I'll be better off without him.'

'Could you ask for someone else?'

'I can try.'

'That's decided then. Can you ignore Barker?'

'My bad,' she said. 'I wouldn't be doing my best for my country. National representation is an honour. But his coaching sucks. Why should I sacrifice my performance for his ego?'

I was certain Megan's body was perfect. It had been distracting me from the conversation. Now I took of the remainder of her clothing and she helped me off with mine. We lay together side by side, naked.

'Then perhaps you should quit the squad,' I said, kissing the end of her pert nose. 'The best you can do for your country is to follow the discipline that has brought you close to the world record.'

'Would I be able to compete if I wasn't in the squad?'

'The AAA has a bee in its bonnet about flow,' I said. 'It is powerful in controlling athletic events in Australia, to maximise revenues from audiences and tourists, by regulating events for profit. I haven't heard of other countries preventing their athletes from flow but the AAA wants to prevent Australian athletes gaining autonomy. They could demand to be paid. The IOC does not seem concerned.'

Megan's eyes were closed.

'How would that work?' she said murmuring.

'The IOC might let you compete as an independent,' I said. 'If the AOC suspended you, the IOC could overturn it.'

I was on top of her, kissing her breasts and down her body.

'How?'

'They could let you compete in the Olympics as an individual,' I said. 'In the past there have been athletes unable to compete with their national teams, who have taken part independently and won medals.'

I was gasping for breath but Megan was still asking questions.

'Why were they excluded?'

'Political transition, international sanctions, team violation of anti-doping rules, suspensions by national Olympic Committees and more.'

She held me then, making explorative squeezes and tugs.

She knelt over me and put me inside her, a wonderful feeling.

'Any cases of disputes with coaches?' she asked.

'Not so far, but the IOC could side with you,' I said, my voice distorted by ecstasy as she pulled and pushed. 'There have been cases where compassion has been applied, when an athlete has been victimised by their national committee.'

'If the AOC drop me, I wouldn't get my squad pay,' Megan said, twerking.

'Don't worry about money,' I said, gasping. 'When your mistreatment gets out, the media will pay you for interviews. Several sponsors want to use your name and images for clothing and footwear advertisements. You could crowd-fund your way to the Olympics. It's been done before. Can we talk about this later?'

I was finding talking difficult. Our emotions could not be expressed in the worn social language of romance.

'I am counting on the IOC to oppose the AOC,' Megan said. 'It would be good to be free of the Australian squad: it's so oppressive.'

'This is oppressive. I can't move,' I said. 'Would you crouch, please.'

I then resumed my favourite position behind her. I noticed we were being watched by a Currawong, an all-black bird with a lethal beak, seated on the veranda rail, peering in through the open door.

'Look out there,' I said.

'What's he want,' asked Megan, her voice muffled by bed clothes.

'It may think we're going to feed it,' I said. 'He may want some sausage.'

'Not more than me,' said Megan.

Soon after we climaxed together.

CHAPTER 42 INDEPENDENT

An irony of Megan's position was that to train by the methods that had won her a place in the squad, she would have to leave it.

'I don't want to be out of the squad,' she said. 'It is an honour I am proud of.'

'Aristotle said: ' *'He who has overcome his fears is truly free.'* You will do better as an independent.'

'People won't understand.'

'Ayn Rand wrote: *'It's the hardest thing in the world—to do what we want. And it takes the greatest kind of courage.'*

'If I win with flow at the Asian Games, they would have to let me use flow in the Olympic Games, wouldn't they?'

'They aren't likely to be bound by consistency. But the IOC could accept you.'

'If I have to, I will defy the AOC and appeal to enter as an independent.'

Miriam was a pole vaulter with Megan at the Institute of Sport and she was in the national squad. She had copied Megan's training in flow.

'Barker has threatened to drop me unless I stop using flow,' said Miriam to Megan. 'My improvement lately has been from flow, but I can't afford to lose my place in the squad.'

'I'm sorry. You should be able to use flow when you want to. I'm planning to quit the squad and enter as an independent.'

'It's risky.'

'Athletes in the past have run into flak when they pioneered a new technique. Some survived.'

'I'll hide that I'm using flow.'

'Good luck.

Megan trained with the national squad until the Asian Games. She sometimes diverged from Barker's training, doing flow exercises she had developed with me.

She was practicing her pole vaulting when Barker came across the field and watched her.

'What are you doing?' he asked.

'Good morning Gordon,' she said frostily. 'My performance goal is to equal my personal best of 5m20.'

'You are supposed to be doing laps now,' he said. 'I want you to stop vaulting and run laps. I will tell you when you have done enough.'

'I will do two more and then start laps,' she said. 'I am used to performing every day but your programme has only two performing sessions per week. It's not enough for me.'

'Too much repetition is harmful,' he said through clenched teeth. 'It can lull you into a false sense of security and you could hurt yourself.'

'To get into flow my method is to simulate competition and rehearse my performance,' Megan said. 'Some variation is good, so I don't become stale. Performing every day achieves the automaticity I need with my routines.'

Barker's voice went up a notch. 'I am aware your student friend Mr Chance has a theory about flow, but when you are training with the squad, you must follow my directions. If you do not, I will ask for a ruling from the squad's discipline committee. They will be concerned about your safety. You could be dropped.'

'Fuck you, bullying arsehole,' she thought. *'You are pretending the issue is safety because I have dared to challenge your control.'*

Megan said nothing and continued training at the university. She didn't attend Adamson's coaching.

'Where were you this morning?' he demanded.

'Working out.'

'Do you imagine you can do it by yourself?'

'Chance is helping me.'

'He has no qualifications in coaching pole vaulting.'

Megan shrugged.

'He's not coaching me. He lets me be do what I want.'

It was true. I didn't replace Adamson in his traditional coaching role, but I created a role advising Megan how to realize her dasein with phenomenalism. We consulted her digital model when planning training activities selected for potential to improve her performing.

Her results in competitions were good and she continued to hold her place in the national squad for the Olympic Games, to be held in Brisbane. She trained with the squad on her own terms, including using flow, in defiance of her coaches.

'Your training should recognise your importance as a performer, your goals and the training you want to do,' I said. 'Other conditioning could be harmful.'

'Fine-tuning my performance, by concentrated vaulting practice, is more important than running laps,' she said.

Megan had become more assertive, not only at the track but around the house and in bed. She seemed to have gained her second wind and was a force to be reckoned with. In bed she told me what she wanted me to do, where and for how long. I wasn't complaining: there was something very sexy about this precocious and appreciative girl. Our love-making had endless releasing, retreating, relaxing, reasserting. It was a negotiation with both of us winning.

I trusted Megan, to know what was best for her, with a love for her that was unconditional. She was under pressure and was sometimes irascible and exasperating, but always I gave her the benefit of the doubt. She was doing a very difficult thing and needed me in her corner to patch up the damage others were doing, keeping her returning to the fray.

As the Asian Games approached, Megan continued to defy Barker. She could be banned at any time and prevented from performing. The others were aware of the spat. She was careful not to confront him or antagonise him.

'We have seen the state's response to your performing in flow,' I said. 'You are showing independence to pursue excellence in defiance of authoritarian control. Barker could be waiting for you to perform badly. He would drop you from the squad. We need his cooperation with our experiment.'

I went with her to Seoul, my fare paid by my earnings from my article published in a sports magazine. On the day of the competition in Seoul, when Megan walked on to the runway for her first performance, Barker didn't come down to encourage her trackside. I talked with her, helping her to concentrate.

Megan was beautiful and epitomised everything I valued in a performer. Besides the extraordinary body I had come to know so well, she moved fluidly with the confidence of a cheetah hunting. Her gaze was alert, ready for utmost action. I watched her uncritically. There was no-one and nothing I would rather observe.

She started higher than the others and at her first attempt knocked down at 5m00. On her second attempt, her attention was riveted on taking-off powerfully opposite her marker, allowing the pole to pull her body up, swinging around. When the pole was straight she pushed down hard on it with her arms for maximum height and was pleased to see she was well-above the bar, passing over it easily.

At 5m10, her first attempt cleared. Another competitor got over too. At 5m20 she was the only one over and she was allowed to go on and attempt a new world record of 5m35, but failed by a hairbreadth. It was sensational and the audience were on their feet applauding.

'Your win vindicates our using flow,' I said to her as she wrote autographs for clamouring fans.

'The IOA could want me in the Olympics now,' she said.

I was proud of her independent stance. Barker did not congratulate her.

'He regards you as an outsider having the effrontery to win without him,' I said to her later. 'It happened in the 1924 Olympics in Paris, when a Jew was stigmatised by religious prejudice, but won the 100 metres. Barker's coaching does not respect you. He has his own agenda, to promote himself in the AAA and Coaches Association.'

'He doesn't care at all about my intentions or my success,' Megan said.

'We have taken a risk,' I said. 'You have performed brilliantly and they should require Barker to back off. A lot depends on the Coaches Association. Flow could put them out of a job.'

'The Olympics are 6 months away and we don't know what the AAA will do next. A lot can happen. They could investigate flow and find some reason to ban you.'

'After today, they would do better to find out about how to get other athletes into flow,' Megan said. 'You'll be in demand to conduct coaching workshops.'

My case study of Megan was going well. Her performing was almost certainly benefitting from flow. I had started writing up for a PhD, using Megan's performance improvement as evidence of flow's utility.

With Megan's success, vistas of applying the phenomenological approach to other events and in other fields opened up to me. It seemed to have most to offer in the 'classical' technology contexts identified by Persig (7). These were not all 'hard' technologies and included logical and reasoning methods. Education used a wide range of 'classic' technologies that could benefit from phenomenology.

Analysing, by phenomenology, performances in fields from sport to employment, required detailed attention to the technological processes and respect for the intentions of their creators. Deconstruction was necessary. The casual 'romantic' approach, deplored by Persig, was unable to imbue performers with the understanding and personal responsibility that Megan had embraced. There were many potential applications and I engaged with enquirers when I had time.

CHAPTER 43 MIND CONTROL

After the Asian Games, our return to Brisbane was greeted by enthusiastic media. We went to our place and Penny, Lily, Nick and Don brought drinks and food for a welcome home party. Megan recounted details of her winning performance and the conversation turned to discussion of the government's plan to regulate competition in sport, athletics and performance arts.

'The nanny state is seeking submissions for rule changes,' I said. 'They will have a fight on their hands with athletics. It has taken forever to grow the culture. Elite performances aren't a problem for anyone other than the investment companies who want to open up athletics to bigger audiences, media and gambling.'

'Collectivism has been creeping into competitions,' said Don. 'Running allows pacers in some events, cycling has teams and shepherding is allowed in some football games.

'The nanny state has been protective and benign, as the 'nanny' name suggests,' said Nick. 'Competitions have been redesigned for media coverage, audience participation and breaks for advertising. New controls are being considered that will benefit uncompetitive participants and prevent elite athletes from succeeding.'

'Athletics has become big business,' I said. 'The government is promoting huge stadiums for business corporations to invest and receive most of ticket revenue and other hosting income. Athletes and team managers would have performance-based earnings with employment conditions demanding and exploitative, as Debord predicted.'

'Professionalism changes the ethos of competition,' said Megan. 'Athletes whose living depends on being free of injury are less likely to take risks.'

'Professional sports people could train for 12 to 14 hours per day, while paid barely above minimum wage. The spectacle would have a few star performers, paid astronomical rates, for sensational publicity. Audiences are unable to discern that a competition is contrived and rivalry pretended, as part of a spectacle, with faked violence and imagined injuries.'

'Some of them could be happy with it as entertainment, ritual display and tribal confrontation. Not everyone is fulfilled by reading, movies and conversation.'

'We don't need the government meddling with athletics and sport,' I said. 'They have upheld individualism as a virtue. The philosopher Ayn Rand said:

'An individualist is a man who says: I will not run anyone's life – nor let anyone run mine. I will not rule nor be ruled. I will not be a master nor a slave. I will not sacrifice myself to anyone – nor sacrifice anyone to myself.'

'A nanny state takes away independence from individuals and makes them depend on the 'nanny state' collective,' said Don. 'A nanny state could delay natural personal development and maturation.'

'Nanny state overreach is unethical,' I said. 'State employees make their careers offering their services to vulnerable people who are unable to distinguish what they want, what they could have to give up and whether they would be better off.'

'Most of the services are beneficial,' said Megan.

'Not always,' I said. 'The nanny state pressures people to have screening for cancer, polyps, aberrant genes and to detect traits or genders unwanted in offspring. Treatments authorised and implemented by a nanny state have included electroconvulsive therapy, lobotomies, sterilisation, gender change and genetic modification. So far, few treatments have been compulsory, except by the Nazis, who conducted heinous forcible treatments, including injection of harmful substances. With a strong and revered leader, a nanny state could become a cult, perhaps not far in the future.'

'It's frightening,' said Megan. 'We don't have a despotic leader – yet. There is a power struggle in the AAA executive and the winner could run the AAA like a cult.'

'Existence of absolute rights of self-determination is an ideal I cherish,' I said. 'Whereas people may be required to give up their rights in certain contexts, such as: workplaces, disasters, pandemics and war, participation in sport is voluntary and has strict rules of conduct and dress, enforced by penalties. Freedom to compete is a basic right. I will oppose imposition of new rules by the nanny state that would prevent it.'

'The AAA should not attempt to control minds, at the bidding of the nanny state,' Don said. 'Mind control by the government is insidious.'

'Propaganda and advertising are accepted and penalties for non-conformance are increasing,' I said. 'Orwell's book '1984' had severe penalties for 'thought-crime' in a totalitarian society. That was fiction, but in the USA, McCarthyism was a real anti-communist movement. In the 1950s it criminalised pre-communist attitudes. Today, our government opposes growth of communism with capitalism. Communism failed as an ideology, but socialists are reviving levelling of individuals and elites.'

'There is some levelling in commerce, health and education, but not much in performing,' said Megan.

'I'll be doing what I can to stop it,' I said. 'Competition and elites are sacrosanct.'

The others agreed.

'We must oppose a nanny state takeover.'

Following Megan's success at the Asian Games, our activities were scrutinised by the university. Nothing was said directly, but it was evident that Megan's flow technique was unacceptable, as was my theory on which it was based.

I was required by my department head to hold a seminar to acquaint my colleagues with my research. A few of them had discussed my project with me and only a couple had indicated any opposition. But the room was packed with academics, who voiced many objections to the theory of flow. But they had no alternative explanation for Megan's steady improvement and success in competition.

Megan sat with me in the seminar but did not speak.

'You can tell your view,' I said to her before the meeting..

'They know our relationship and will assume my testimony is biased,' she said. 'It is better if I say nothing.'

I told the room that flow was unlike a performance enhancing drug, because it was invisible, innocuous, and difficult to attribute. The four basic psychological techniques of performance enhancement were: imagery, goal-setting, self-talk and physical relaxation. Flow was similar to these.

'Flow is a variation of traditional mental techniques,' I said. 'There is absolutely nothing to be concerned about.'

'Most athletes cannot afford coaching in flow,' said a Risk-Out spokesperson present. It was a campaign by academic intellectuals against elite performances, wanting levelling by the government. 'We want to exclude mental techniques that would require skill, effort and finance beyond the capability of recreational athletes.

'The AAA wants to reduce the exclusivity of elite performances. For example, the winning height in jumping can be changed from the greatest height reached, to an average of the last three heights cleared. An athlete's reliability would be more prominent.'

I hadn't heard this proposal before and was surprised the audience took it seriously because in my view it was ridiculous. Anti-elitism had many adherents on campuses who, as part of an academic elite, chose to ignore their own hypocrisy.

'I would contest that,' I said. 'Performers need time to get used to a venue. Rating them by average achievement could encourage performers to commence lower and delay knockdown. They shouldn't be pulled down by temporal lack of accomplishment.'

Risk Out did not contest this point and wanted regulation to protect sports players and athletes from risk. They said the flow technique was dangerous.

'I deny it,' I said. 'It's true that field event performers have more risk than runners and swimmers, who compete without an apparatus.

Jumpers, throwers and hurdlers can injure themselves on their equipment, as can skiers, skaters, cyclists, gymnasts, and horse riders. Pole vaulting has risks from spiked shoes, pole accidents, and from collisions with the box, the bar, the uprights and from landing off the mat. These are traditional risks. Use of our flow technique does not bring in new risks. Eliminating the risks would alter competition and the spectacle would be less attractive to spectators.'

'Obvious dangers have to be eliminated,' said the Risk Out speaker. 'Boxing without gloves and headgear has been stopped.'

'Testing of poles for stress fatigue has been adopted,' I said. 'Competitors can recognise many dangers and withdraw as they do in other walks of life. '

'Should competing with equipment in a trance-like state be allowed?' asked the Risk Out activist.

'No,' I said. 'Intoxication and addiction from drugs have evidence of harm and are banned.'

'Do you agree hyper-suggestion and hypnotic intervention could be dangerous?'

'Certainly,' I said. 'They are characterised by loss of control in a trance, but flow does not cause these. Nor is flow a condition mediated by a hypnotist. Flow is a psychological condition of arousal, not at all trance-like and without any therapist. Athletes in flow are fully engaged, hyper-sensitive to environmental threats and trained to automaticity to overcome unexpected events. Their heightened consciousness is safer than normal. Over-zealous regulation of substances banned as performance enhancing is magnifying abuse into a media spectacle.'

'Pole vaulting heights have increased and must be limited to prevent harm to the athletes.'

'That would countermand the evolutionary forces that had enabled elite performers to emerge.'

'If you are saying that flow is part of an evolutionary process, why should we allow new evolutionary processes that bring new dangers?'

'Flow has not evolved to be dangerous,' I said. 'but this has happened in another event. Javelin design was modified after Jan

Zelezny, a Czech, reached 105 metres at the Olympics, throwing dangerously beyond the throwing target area and endangering judges and other athletes. Flow has not endangered the public. A new javelin design was adopted. Zelezny reached only 85 metres with it, but he steadily improved and 20 years later his Olympic record had crept up to 98.48 metres. Perhaps they will change to another standard javelin one day. The choice of standard technology is arbitrary, but it has addressed real safety concerns. Flow is like a technology, the result of accumulated knowledge and application of skills, methods, and processes to performance, but it does not have real safety concerns. There is no need to regulate it.'

'The performing establishment wants flow stopped.'

'I wonder why,' said Michael who had come to support us. 'Their interest could be in media sensationalism, wanting traditional coaching to continue. This thinking would prevent adoption of flow because it is a better technique and has less need for coaching.'

'Nonsense!' said Barker. 'We want risks from using apparatus to be the same for every competitor. Competitors in an event should all use the same performance technique. In the high jump all competitors have used the Fosbury Flop since it replaced Straddle. High jump allows an open style. The alternative is nominated styles, like in swimming. It is divided into separate competitions for front crawl, breaststroke, butterfly and back-stroke. '

'Most performers will want to use flow,' I said. 'If it is denied them, they will quit and change to events that will allow it. It's incorrect to suggest that flow is elite, when it is an authentic technique anyone can take up to improve.'

My polemic had asserted that flow had no skeleton in its cupboard, had resulted in significantly improved performances and was a technique many athletes would choose. My parting shot was to question the objectivity of their criticism.

'Perhaps you are suspicious of the inconspicuousness of flow and its ready availability,' I said. 'You could think flow is just too good to be true. That is not sufficient grounds nor good reason to reject it!'

The chairman closed the meeting. 'I will report your intransigence, Mr Finething, to the Department's Disciplinary Committee. Unless you cease your investigation of flow, your enrolment in the PhD programme at this university could be cancelled.'

I was dismayed. I wasn't expecting such prejudiced opposition.

Afterwards, Barker came over.

'Megan McLean, your membership of the squad is terminated,' he said. 'You have received many warnings.'

'Why?' asked Megan.

'You have persisted in using flow, a banned technique. Am I correct in assuming you would continue to use flow?'

'Yes.'

He turned away. Megan no longer had the support of the AAA. Although we had been expecting it, it came as a shock.

Realising the prejudice, Megan and I found escape in our love-making, inviting, inserting, imposing, insisting, reaching mutual orgasm, forgetting everything else.

CHAPTER 44 TECHNOLOGY

The use of various technologies and techniques in athletics was regulated by the AAA. It defined flow as a technique and banned it from athletics competition.

Megan and I met with Barker at the AAA office, to request reconsideration of Megan's use of flow in the national squad for the Olympics.

Barker was at his desk, backed by national and association flags.

'Would the AAA please reconsider the ban on flow excluding Megan's participation with the squad for the Olympic Games? She has demonstrated her ability in winning the Asian Games, using flow and we request you allow her to use flow in her training and performance with the squad for the Olympic Games.'

'Not every technique has to be accepted when it wins,' Barker said. 'A new technique can upset the apple cart. We have to consider the effects on other competitors and on audiences. Prosthetic legs can run faster than natural legs. Should sprinters who have amputated healthy feet to medal be allowed to compete?'

'No,' Megan said. 'Voluntary amputation is sick 'Flow is not a prosthesis.'

'A Canadian sprinter with an artificial heart is winning,' said Barker. 'We can't allow every new technique. We can regulate to include competitors with natural body parts, or with standard and approved transplants, or with prostheses. Vaulting poles need to be identical for all competitors.'

'I disagree that a regulation allowing standardised aids would be fair,' I said. 'The horse that an equestrian rider chooses to aid her is not a standard horse. She rides her favourite horse. There is a bond between a rider and her horse, cultivated by long and careful training. On a 'standard' horse she would perform less well. She should be able to use a horse of her choice. For this reason a pole vaulter should be able to select any pole or poles.'

'That's a ridiculous analogy. A vaulter doesn't have a relationship with her pole.'

'She does. Every pole is unique. Her confidence in it and familiarity are vital.'

'It opens up a can of worms to allow poles to be designed for the athlete,' said Barker. 'It could end up with competition between androids. We must protect ourselves from an open slather of technologies. The individual human body is sacred.

'A performing pole is not a standard prosthesis that substitutes for something missing,' I said. 'Performers should be able to choose an accessory they most want for the task. The same goes for their technique. It should be up to them.'

'If a performer wins using a certain mental technique, is that fair?' asked Barker.

'Yes, if the technique is their choice,' I said. 'Standardising of mental preparation could be dangerous and could favour some athletes while disadvantaging others. Thought control is totalitarian science fiction. An athlete should be free to think what they like, without banning of a mental technique such as flow.'

'We think there are safety concerns and that is why we have banned it,' Barker said. 'We are opposing the flow technique to protect competitors who may be at risk.'

'Is there evidence of a safety risk requiring a ban?' I asked.

Barker stood up. 'There is subjective evidence,' he said. 'We will have to stop there as I have another meeting. Good morning.'

We left.

Megan had listened quietly. Afterwards she said to me: 'You were convincing, Their case for banning flow is weak and seems to be sour grapes. When other countries won't come in on it, they'll have to drop it.'

'The nanny state mentality is contagious,' I said. 'They expect their regulation of performing and sport to be awarded accolades by a public who won't notice the dumbing down of performances. It's the athletes who will suffer. Competitions will be distorted by unfamiliar requirements that prevent athletes applying their winning skills and requiring different performances.'

Don invited most of the physics department to his wedding. I talked with Megan about my project being blocked as we drove to the venue at the Botanical Gardens.

'Why do you think Don wants to be married,' I asked.

'He loves Sophia,' said Megan. 'Can't you see that?'

'Could it be that they are responding to nanny state incentives such as financial assistance with a home?'

'Maybe a little. Why are you so sceptical about their love?'

'I am sceptical about marriages. We love each other, but we're not getting married.'

'That's different. We are waiting for our careers to come good.'

We had reached our destination and turned into the Gardens.

Sophia was an educator based at the Planetarium. She was resplendent with her friends in their best attire, under an awning on the lawn. Instead of a reception, we went inside the dome and watched a presentation on objects in space, narrated by Sophia.

Afterwards we sipped drinks and ate finger food on the lawn beside the planetarium.

Megan and I chatted with Nick.

'That tree is a Melaleuca,' Nick said.

'A paperbark,' I said. 'How do you think it evolved to have its trunk wrapped in layers of paper-thin bark?'

'One theory is that in a bush fire, the bark insulates the inner trunk, stopping the tree being killed. The outer bark burns, leaving the tree coated with ash, which insulates it.'

'Do you believe it?'

'It's possible. The technology is the same as ablative shielding on the nose of the space shuttle to prevent it heating on re-entry. They used ceramic tiles, which flaked off, carrying the heat away.'

'Could they have got the idea from paperbarks!'

'Perhaps they had the idea of flaking the heat away first and then a paperbark showed it could work.'

'Sophia, your presentation was excellent,' Megan said when the couple came over.

'We are brought together by gravity,' said Don. 'Sophia's heavenly body is irresistible.'

'May the force be with you,' I said

'We will get married one day, won't we Chance?' asked Megan when they moved on.

'Let's see if theirs works out,' I said facetiously.

'That's not at all romantic,' Megan said. 'Maybe I wouldn't like being married to you.'

Our reality was that beyond the psychological involvement of our work, our relationship had ascended to intensely physical love which for both of us was the highlight of our days. It seemed romantic enough. Naked we touched each other, feeling the smoothness as we explored every part with our fingers and kissed them with our lips and tongues until we joined as one. We were urgent, as if it might not last

But more pressing problems appeared when I was called by the head of the Physics Department to present a summary of my research.

'Your data is not reproducible,' the professor said, without looking at it. 'Your theory is uncorroborated and seems quite unlikely. This department does its research in physics but flow is a concept in psychology. Mental preparation of athletes is of no interest here. I want you to end this line of enquiry. To investigate flow you need to re-enrol in psychology.'

It was a severe setback. I asked the head of Psychology if I could transfer.

'I can credit you with first year,' the professor said, 'but you need to study psychology for two years before commencing a PhD. Your theory cannot be readily tested by our usual laboratory methods. Measurement of athletes' physical performances is out of our league.'

'What can I do?' I asked Don. 'Having to do two years of psychology, in order to verify flow, when it is a respectable condition now, is too much. Even then, psychology may not be persuasive enough.'

'Mental conditioning is regulated in other fields because of ethical concerns: advertising, education and prisons,' said Don. 'Flow focusses intention on narrow ends and threatens competitors incapable of superior accomplishment. Competitions could be regulated to exclude it.'

'I suppose superior new techniques, like the Fosbury Flop, were resisted until athletes demanded that it be allowed,' said Megan.

'The stakes in achievement are being raised by hot-house methods like flow,' Don said. 'In the view of the nanny state, athletic achievement must not be faked by flow.'

'Flow has optimal achievement, not fakery.'

'We know that, but there are enough suspicious officials and pole vaulters to get it banned.'

Don's point was valid and my heart sank. From a collectivist viewpoint, flow would be elite, but its benefit could be widely available to individuals. Widespread adoption of flow in the community could bring achievement and enjoyment.

I thanked Don for his advice. Some members of my department accepted my findings and encouraged me, but others tried to meddle. I could not take my research any further at this university, despite my promising results.

I faced having to quit and find a job.

'If I write up my thesis, the most they will give me is a MPhil degree in physics,' I said, defeated, to Megan. 'My theory is worthy of a PhD but does not conform to the mould of academic disciplines.'

'I'm sorry. Perhaps your MPhil. can be presented in a book, or as a movie?'

'It's not graphic or visual enough,' I said. 'This is terrible. Where does rejection of flow by the university leave us?'

'My pole vaulting career could be over,' she said.

'Shit. They could try to stop you performing and your performing scholarship could be terminated. Your research is not under threat. At least you have that.'

Megan's research into motives for job seeking had been making progress.

'Job seekers are held back by performance anxiety,' she told me. 'With focus on their training, engagement and skills automaticity, they could 'flow' into optimal job achievement.'

'That's great,' I said. 'There's no problem with flow there.'

'Not so far,' she said. 'But the nanny state overreach could want jobs to go to the most needy.'

I paused, appalled at this new vista of collective employment.

'I want to help the needy but I also want employers to select the employees best qualified and prepared to perform each job. Applicants should have to compete.'

'I agree,' said Megan. 'The nanny state is trying to replace the culture of competition that worked well enough.'

'My life has prepared me to fight for my career, my partner and my community. The overreach of the nanny state has brought my progress to a standstill and I could be forced to quit my project,' I said. 'I took a risk in choosing flow as my PhD topic and I am being held back unjustly. I intend to fight for the right of flow to be used by Megan and performers everywhere.'

'Do you think we'll win?' asked Megan.

'It's a risk worth taking,' I said. 'It will be a battle but we won't be alone. It has been looming but I have drilled down to find the origins of opponents' anxieties and develop defences. I am confident that we will win but it may take some time.'

'I think you'll find opponents are out for themselves,' said Megan. 'Flow is good and they will not be able to stop it being used. I'm with you all the way.'

Risk Out led a campaign to standardize competition protocols, apparatus and training. Regulations and restrictions rewarded compliance and discouraged individuals from risk taking. The thrust was anti-individual and pro-nanny state. It was taken up by proponents of collectivism and idealism, under the influences of Marx's and Hegel's philosophies, having little interest in the ascendant individual human spirit Nietzsche advocated.

226

Risk-Out opposed elite physical performance and wanted to stop Megan performing because she was so much better than her nearest rivals. Their intervention was senseless standardisation. Poppy cutters infested sports arenas and workplaces vehemently opposing flow. Adherents deliberately performed below average,

Opposition to cerebration was a tradition, mainly in public when the ignorance of the mob persecuted thinkers with lies, ridicule, personal attack and even physical harm.

'STOP WINNING' was on banners and T-shirts worn on the campus.

'What can I do?' Megan asked when she had been criticised unfairly.

'Don't antagonise them,' I said. 'Feel sorry for them. Have compassion for them because they are losers. Remove yourself from harm. Keep away from them. Do what makes you happy. Don't waste energy fighting back. Gather a support squad.'

'Many athletes are opposed to Risk Out,' she said.

'We can gather support with an online campaign,' I said. 'I can publicize our concerns and wants on my blog.'

'I have been worn down by many small things,' she said. 'The anti-flow brigade has put me under stress in competitions. I have been having muscle spasms. I haven't been able to move fluidly. It could be the yips. Gymnasts call it the twisties. It could be serious. Some elite athletes have had to quit competing.'

'Continue,' I said. 'De-stress. We are going through a sickening phase of moralism, emanating from toxic nanny-ism. We have to hang on until the falsity is found out and expelled. I am writing up my research for a MPhil degree. One day I will be able to submit our results for a PhD. The findings are sound and I am not going to lose any sleep over the dismal falsity that has taken over. I am confident that it will not prevail.'

I weighed individualism against collectivism in people's souls and concluded that antipathy to flow emanated from competitors' collective envy of elites. I was conscious that Megan and I were hemmed in by hostile forces. When I was with Megan while she trained, in my research room at the university, or at home working on my ideas for my thesis, I escaped into flow, aware of my 'being there'.

'Risk Out reduces the competitiveness of those who think for themselves and gives currency to the thinking of those who allow others to dominate their lives,' I said.

'Excellence is not rewarded,' she said.

'Worse than that, the nanny state imposes negative feedback,' I said.

It was difficult for me to watch Megan train and perform at championships, because I was not an accredited coach and was denied access to competition enclosures. I couldn't talk with Megan during competitions.

Risk Out had devalued the individuality of athletics, replacing it with regulations and callous disregard for individual differences.

'The 'nanny state' is taking over,' I said. 'We could resist if our technique was attractive to the mob, but flow is equated with neoliberal selfishness and elitism. Regulations seek fairness by finding the lowest common denominator and sharing prizes. People want to be taken care of and it's hoped that anti-elitism will bring more kindness. What will happen in reality remains to be seen.

'Athletics and sport have enticed the masses with a spectacle of equality, boosted attendances at events, paid athletes suffering constricted playing conditions, unfair rules and moralities of zealots. The media have ushered the sporting lower class into a world in which they are exploited by capital.'

'What can we do?' asked Megan.

'Wait and watch,' I said. 'Their house of cards could come crashing down.'

CHAPTER 45 TEAM SPORT

One Saturday, I didn't have my usual game of social rugby and invited Megan to go with me to watch Australia play Wales at Suncorp Stadium in Brisbane. Megan could be interested because she had been born in Wales, a rugby-loving country and migrated to Australia with her parents as a child. Rugby games were under threat from levellers too and I thought Megan would be comforted seeing other athletes whose skills were threatened.

'Here he is now,' I said as Fred Emery, three metres tall and solid, a mate since school, emerged from the players' tunnel. He had given us tickets. Megan had met him previously. He was, playing in the back row of the Australian scrum.

He saw us, waved and loped across to the barrier. His face was ashen and he had a slight aroma of vomit. We guessed he had thrown up, as players sometimes did before a tough game, ejecting stomach contents that would burden their metabolisms during the coming ordeal.

'Who is going to win?' I asked him.

The giant gave a wry smile. 'It could go either way. We always have a tussle with the fishes.'

The Australian part of the crowd was chanting: 'WALES, WALES, BLUDDY GREAT FISHES ARE WALES.'

'Who's opposite you?' I asked him.

'A prick called Cowper. Watch in the first line-out. There'll be a bit of action.'

Fred trotted off to join his team at the other end of the field, opposite Wales. The players varied in height, from the scrum half, a one metre midget, to second rowers at three and a half metres.

Fred's tickets put us in a VIP box overlooking the centre of the field.

They kicked off. Play could have developed within the rules like grid-iron, with whole-team chess-like moves, but there were rambling rampages of broken field running, concerted by the scrum halves, who gathered and fed the ball to the backs who strove to penetrate the defence, in phases lasting up to 50 plays.

'It seems to be shambolic,' said Megan.

'The oval ball bounces and rolls unpredictably, so they carry it when they can,' I said. 'The set pieces, kick-offs, line-outs, scrums, mauls and penalty kicks are quite predictable. Fans get to see a diversity of skills.'

'Which team will win?'

'The more skilled, better-prepared and better-selected team always wins. There is an element of chance, but not as much as in soccer, where one goal is enough to win.

Wales dominated after receiving the kick-off, but Australia cleared with a kick to touch. It landed in front of us. We watched the forwards arrive for the lineout, with their cauliflower ears, flat noses and neckless statures. Fred was playing in his usual position of lock, at the back. Opposite him was Cowper. We could see by the set of their shoulders that the two were in a stoush.

Fred suddenly turned and punched Cowper in the face. The two of them traded a flurry of punches as the other players watched – they knew the rule was: 'third in, first sent off'. The two captains pulled them apart. The referee gave both of them a warning and the game resumed with another lineout.

Each team had eight giants in the lineout, attended by a robust and lightning fast dwarf. With the alacrity of circus acrobats, Fred's second rowers lifted him to their shoulders and the front row hoisted up the winger on to Fred's shoulders, to make a three-high-pyramid. Wales did the same and, as the ball passed overhead, the two wingers reached up precariously to tap it to the scrum half.

Wales used a professional foul to prevent the Australians pushing the ruck over the try line. A try would have been five points plus a two-point conversion kick, whereas the Welsh foul conceded only a three-point penalty kick.

Fred was England's kicker. His skills were legendary.

He walked back carrying the ball to the half way line, where the angle was less oblique. He teed it up, ten metres in from touch. He knelt and concentrated on his embroidery. His run up was 30 metres and had the precision of a long-jumper. The kicked ball rocketed aerodynamically without turning, or even wobbling, passing through the centre of the posts, still going up.

The kick to restart play was booted into touch. Fred caught a long throw-in and powered through the defence, breaking leg tackles and handing off body tackles. Wales slowed him down but they couldn't stop him before he got a pass away to a centre. As he fought free from the ruck to go in support, he was held. He replied with his fist and was in time to take a pass and dive over for a try.

They had scored in the corner and Fred carried the ball back, with a stiff breeze coming along the touch line. The crowd jeered as he bent to his embroidery. He polished the ball with a cloth and stooped to place it on the tee. The crowd had lapsed into an awed silence.

Somewhere in the stands a baby cried. Fred stood, turned, hands on hips and glared at the baby. The crowd laughed and were silent as Fred bent over, adjusting the angle of the ball.

Heckling the kicker was common, in inverse proportion to ability. No-one had heckled Fred so far this season. 'Hey wass, you've got a bluddy great arse, haven't you?' rang out a sing song Welsh voice. His words were repeated all around the ground. The crowd wondered if the message would penetrate Fred's meditative state. The giant stood up slowly from his crouch and turned to face the heckler.

'If you've got a big nail,' he said quietly, 'you need a big hammer!'

An uproar ensued as his words were repeated to the furthest corner. His kick sailed through the posts. Fred received a standing ovation, with stamping of feet.

After that, Australia had it pretty much their own way and the final score was 36 – 14. They had won with better team work...and Fred.

'What did you think of it?' I asked Megan afterwards.

'I enjoyed it,' she said. 'Compared with athletics, rugby has more drama, but less justice.'

'Rugby is less predictable.'

'Athletics is contrived to compare individual performances under equal conditions,' Megan said. 'Rugby is opportunistic.'

'There are some unwritten rules. Any rugby player who transgresses dangerously without being called for a foul is worked over by the opposing players, without penalty,' I said. 'Justice is fair.'

'Any athlete caught cheating would be disqualified, but it's rare. All sports are becoming more regulated, with officials aided by cameras,' said Megan.

'It's not accidental,' I said. 'It's the intent of the ruling classes to numb our lives with sameness, miring us in complex rules, arbitration and chance, reducing our enjoyment, increasing fearfulness, preventing individual skills.'

'Why?' Megan asked.

'To frustrate ebullience and promote misery,' I said. 'Rugby union is fighting to maintain player individualism. In every sport the nanny state is gaining ground, in the name of equality, even when there is none.'

'How does our misery benefit the ruling class?'

'Frustration is sublimated into consumption and profits.'

'It's totalitarian,' said Megan.

'Yes.'

'Rugby crowds want to see excellent performers,' she said.

'Doesn't everyone?'

'Not always,' she said, pouting thoughtfully. 'Reality TV features ordinary people in contrived situations. Rugby could go that way.'

'Viewers want unrehearsed performances in a fair competition,' I said. 'Players contribute in teams having equivalent skills, for example, a combination of speed and strength.'

'Rugby has unique team spirit,' Megan said. 'It will be a shame if rugby becomes like reality TV, with equal players pursuing appearance fees for their media-selected talent, without teamwork.'

'Soulless.'

'There are some punters in the crowd, but most fans are tribal.'

'Punters traditionally want to take a chance.'

'The fans want to see a stoush.'

'To stir their blood.'

'Yes, a punch up, to relieve their aggression.'

'It will be a disaster if they level rugby.'

'If the levellers get their way, rugby players will be restricted to a certain size and ability. It's happening in other team sports, in athletics, in swimming, in employment, in property ownership and even in shopping. The levellers claim restricting participants to a range of heights and weights will improve safety and participation.'

'Will rugby playing change?'

'Yes. Already they are gentling the game, to be like touch rugby, replacing resilience and tenacity with nimbleness and speed.'

'I gather you disapprove,' she said.

'I do, strongly. They are exploring new and unpromising worlds of human experience, where every participant is supposed to have equal ability. Rugby teams used to field specialists with a range of skills, operating as a cohesive unit. Today's game could be one of the last with a variety of plays. I asked you to come because I know you value diversity and this could be a last chance to see it in action.'

'I liked it that there were different specialties playing,' Megan said. 'I hadn't realised height was such an advantage in rugby. Where did they find those giants?'

'Clones are banned but are difficult to detect. Couples with tall strong bodies and genetic modification of their embryos are paired. Scrotal and mammary appendages are pharmaceutically shrunk.'

'Were there females playing?' asked Megan. 'I didn't notice any.'

'They don't get remarked.'

'How are players recruited?'

'Rugby clubs bid for options on babies, both male and female. They begin playing when they are 10 years old,' he said. 'It can be a rewarding career.'

'The specialists will be out of a job if levelling comes in,' said Megan. 'Teams will be composed of utility players. The variety of action in scrums and lineouts will be lost.'

'There could be reversion to unlevelled club rugby,' I said. 'The amateur game could make a come-back.'

'Audiences for levelled rugby would probably be larger,' said Megan. 'People prefer to see a contest between more equal physiques, like grid-iron.'

I knew that Megan was pressing my buttons, playing devil's advocate.

'I disagree,' I said. 'Audiences want to see specialised skills and a diversity of players.'

'Fans don't want a motley troupe,' said Megan. They want good-looking well-built players.'

'Will there be a position for Fred, with his embroidery?' I asked.

'Absolutely,' she said. 'People like to watch a circus of performers.'

'Levellers assume not,' I said, 'but they are misguided. People want brilliance, not samey repetition.'

'How very many are Megan's qualities I like,' I thought. *'She has been great company at today's game, showing interest and enthusiasm when many women would have been uninterested. She is wonderful. I can imagine me being interested in her forever.'*

Megan trained in isolation now she was out of the squad. When she competed at local meets, audiences were dismayed by her elite performances. Levelling had reduced the event to a farce.

'She's showing off,' said a trackside critic. 'It's style that counts now. She must be cheating.'

'She is reaching record heights,' replied another.

'The height cleared is only one criterion,' said the critic. 'She's pretty ordinary otherwise.'

Levelling affected everyone. I had striven to get ahead in my research, but it was more important now to be considerate of others, both at work and at home. I became assiduous in performing my share of housework chores and for the first time in my life I tidied up after myself.

CHAPTER 46 SWAN LAKE

Indoctrination of audiences by the spectacle had opened up athletics, rugby and other sports to commercial opportunities for mass media audiences. There was levelling and an influx of non-elite players.

Levelling had made inroads in performance arts too. Megan and I went to see Swan Lake by the Brisbane ballet company. The Minister for Levelling had imposed regulations and dancers' abilities had been adjusted by the government's Chief Handicapper. Her aim was to equalise individuals, by making ballet participation accessible to the whole population, by lottery, preventing the elitism of the past. We were curious how performances would be changed.

Megan and I sat together in the packed auditorium.

'Isn't it wonderful that the ballet schools will take anyone,' said Megan optimistically. 'All that is needed is good luck.'

'Ballet dancers have been an elite group,' I admitted. 'It will be interesting to see how levelling will affect the production.'

The handicapper had worked with the choreographer to dumb-down Swan Lake for first-time audiences of average cognitive ability. On a screen above the stage, a narrative of the story scrolled across. Because Megan and I had been assessed to have large brains, we were required to wear mental equalizers, tuned to a government transmitter. Our ear buds gave jarring chirps at regular intervals, to block critical thinking.

Suddenly I flinched.

'Ow! This equaliser is very annoying,' I said.

'It stops you overthinking,' Megan said. 'It wouldn't be fair to understand more than others and have an advantage.'

A line of ballerinas stretched across the stage. They were almost all in step, but their leaps and twirls were ragged, with frequent rests, about the same as could be accomplished by an untrained sample of the public. Many had weights around their ankles, their figures concealed by body padding and with their faces hidden by masks.

'They deserve credit for trying,' said Megan, as the audience clapped loyally.

'I'm not sure if they know what to do,' I said. 'They're not dancing in unison. They may not have practiced these routines.'

'It's good enough to convey the story,' said Megan.

'Ballet should preserve traditional forms,' I said. 'It should celebrate physical beauty and fitness. This is grotesque.'

'I agree it's below traditional performance standards, but it expresses equality exquisitely.'

'It lacks the novelty of popular entertainment,' I said. 'It has the appeal of a school pantomime, in which the novelty is familiar characters in stereotyped roles. Artistic interpretation is minimal.'

I despaired that ballet was being destroyed as an entertainment. A sharp ping sounded in my ear and my thoughts fled.

Four dancers linked hands across each other for the cygnets' pas de quatre. Their heights and widths varied unequally and they danced the piece with less automated precision than was traditional.

'This demonstrates levelling nicely,' said Megan.

In the two step, their rhythm was measured by the oboe, achieving a degree of synchrony in timing, but their footwork was clumsy and one slipped and fell over.

After that, the male and female principal dancers performed a pas de deux, but their athleticism was below average. When the male was required to lift the female, a stepladder was brought on to the stage. Her pirouettes were slow and the audience read a warning: SPINS CAN CAUSE INJURY. DO NOT ATTEMPT AT HOME WITHOUT SUPERVISION.

'Ballet is supposed to be uplifting, showing what dancers can accomplish through training,' I said. 'When not extraordinary, their attempts should be creditable.'

'We know that it was done differently in the past,' said Megan. 'In those days the dancers led privileged lives. Ordinary people were without opportunities to be nimble and graceful.'

237

'People now expect success to be easy,' I said. There was a brief scream from my ear device that gave me an instant headache. 'They need to see excellence in order to excel themselves, to escape their mundane lives.'

'Attention! Remain in your seats!' said the announcer. 'A dangerous prisoner has escaped and is on the premises.'

Six months earlier, the corps' male lead had defied the wearing of weights and had been sent for correction to the government's remedial institution. They had locked him in a cell, convicted of inequitable behaviour. He was irredeemably accomplished and sentenced to solitude so he could not inspire elite behaviour in others.

He must have escaped and now ran onto the stage, wearing tights, striding with pointy feet like a duck. He was tall and strong, wearing heavy ankle weights.

Without warning, he cut with secateurs the straps attaching weights to his ankles.

He gestured to one of the ballerinas to partner him. She stepped forward and he cut her straps too, peeling off her padding, removing her hood, revealing stunning looks and a classic dancer's physique.

Together they cavorted around the stage in longue jete', leaping higher and higher.

They were both in mid-air when an official walked on with a gun. Two shots rang out and the airborne dancers were felled mid-bound and lay lifeless on the stage. Stage crew came on and dragged them off. They mopped up the blood and the ballet proceeded.

'We apologise for the incident,' said an announcer. 'We hope you are enjoying the performance.'

I was thinking I would like to see others rebel, but my ear bud bleated painfully. The device must have detected my aberrant thinking.

A fictional ballet scene like the one above was told by Kurt Vonnegut in his original story: Harrison Bergeron (6). I am indebted to him and have adopted his staging because of the unsurpassable novelty of his original.

238

The possibility of another shriek in my ear made me cringe.

'Maybe the audience will benefit more with the performers levelled,' said Megan.

'When pigs can fly,' I said. 'Equal performance is an end, not a beginning. Levelling has no place in ballet nor in modern dance. Ballet depends for its attraction on excellence of technique. Making excellence disappear is a betrayal of individual fulfilment.'

'Shh,' said Megan, interrupting. 'Ballet is going to be for everyone – no longer exclusive.'

'Too much has been destroyed,' I said. 'The Nazis burned books and degenerative artworks. Levelling at the ballet is a microcosm of a totalitarian state.'

'Oh phooey!' she said. 'Many people enjoyed tonight's performance.'

Megan's optimism was endearing but differences between us were appearing with increasing frequency and threatening our harmony. I avoided confrontation but I felt vulnerable. We continued to agree on most matters.

CHAPTER 47 CHAIR RULES

After the tragic shooting at the ballet, the Chief Handicapper ordered his staff to prepare rule changes for levelling stage, sporting and athletic performances, to exclude elite dancers, permitting novices and amateurs to participate, with anyone able to compete with others of similar size.

In athletics, the jurisdiction of the AAA included control of athletic events, advertising, sponsorship, media contracts, fan ware and performance-enhancing drugs. Reginald Asquith was the elected Chairman of the AAA and responsible for levelling athletics. He had compiled a list of changes proposed for each event.

The Chairman appointed a firm of lawyers who, for a large sum of money, would draft amendments in precise legal language. He passed the proposals to each of the State associations. In Queensland Gordon Barker received the rules proposed for pole vaulting.

Barker informed the squad by email.

'Performers will be made equal in all the ways deemed important and no-one will have an advantage from different experience. They will not be advantaged by Body Mass Index, or by being smarter, faster, or better at performing than others. Competitors will carry weights in their belts that will equalise their performances.

'I will receive by August 2nd responses to the above, addressed to me and titled Competition Rules Submission with the names and contacts of the authors clearly stated'.

'I want the people's rights to be transparent and fair,' the Chairman told the state leaders. 'There must be procedures to consider everyone's views democratically.'

The lawyers drafted Amended Rules and sent them to the Chairman.

'Good heavens,' he thought when he saw the tomes stacked on his desk. He sampled a document. *'This is a complex proposal, written in legalese. I don't have time to check all this.'*

'How can I be sure these rules are democratic?' he asked Quill.

'The processes are sufficiently clear to people of exceptional intelligence, fit for public office, such as yourself,' said the leading lawyer, Quill.

The Chairman thought: *'This reminds me of a story: 'The Kings New Clothes' by Hans Christian Andersen. The king was duped to accept transparent clothes. It wasn't discovered until an ingenuous child voiced 'The King has no clothes!' I must beware my advisors, who could want to deceive me,'* the Chairman thought. *'My intelligence is exceptional and I can delegate these drafts and wise men will understand, while fools will be discovered. I'll be able to tell wise men from fools.'*

Asquith sought the views of the State Association. Queensland requested consultation by the lawyers with the Northern, Central and Southern performing associations.

'Athletes must not be empowered,' said Bender, the Northern Chairman. 'We leaders must keep control.'

'Why?' asked lawyer Quill.

'Because we know what is best for everyone,' said Bender.

'Do you mean best for our self-interest?' Quill asked.

'Exactly,' said Bender. 'If people have rights, they will expect performing to be run for their benefit, instead of for re-electing us, as they should.'

'For a consideration, we will omit people having any rights at all,' said Quill, smirking, with his hand out for a bribe.

When Chairman Asquith tried to check the words of the clauses, he could not interpret the complex structure of ideas and language.

'I doubt that I could ever understand this,' he thought. *'I cannot admit I lack intelligence to understand it, so I will pretend that these words are satisfactory. I want the amendments to be democratically*

prepared. These words must give the people rights. If I study the contents pages, I can claim I have read the document.'

To be on the safe side, he asked his Deputy, whose judgement he trusted, to read the draft through.

'Deputy Constance is loyal, honest and sensible,' he thought. *'If there is anything amiss she will tell me.'*

When Constance visited the drafting lawyers at their workplace, they handed her pages of the densely written amendment. She read and re-read the words, but they made no sense. She knew of the much-vaunted power of the document to detect intelligence.

'I must be unintelligent,' she concluded. *'There's not much future in admitting that. I will question what the Amendments will allow and discover if anything is missing.'*

She asked Quill: 'Where does this document allow people to have a say in a tribunal meeting?'

'In many places,' Quill said, pointing to various clauses. 'Here it's tacit, there implied, here it's sub-text and there it's *a priori.* Basically, people have a say in everything.'

'Is there the right to have a say actually enshrined in your proposed legislation?'

'Absolutely. We know what is wanted - we're constitutional lawyers.'

Constance could tell he was lying through his teeth.

'Oh my God,' she thought. *'The lawyers have been bought and are doing a whitewash job. If I go to the Chairman with this message, I will be shot. I must appear to understand and approve, or I will be deemed unintelligent.'*

She gave her approval without discovering that the lawyers had omitted the peoples' rights.

When the Equality Amendments were finished the Chairman and his entourage visited the law firm's offices to receive the completed work. He tried to check the clauses but they were written so abstractly that he was unable to see the practical implications. He could not admit it.

'Excellent,' said the Chairman, smiling. 'This will ensure our Nation has the best-ruled athletics possible.'

He announced he would carry the Equality Amendments in a Workers' Day parade through the streets of the City. The procession was led by a marching band, with acrobats, stilt-walkers, tumblers, jugglers and clowns. Local, state and federal politicians walked behind. When they reached the Parliament building, the Chairman walked to the front.

He presented the Equality Amendments to the Minister for Levelling.

'The intention of these Equality Amendments, sire, is to propose rules for performing that will prevent domination of events by elite individuals.'

'Good,' said the Minister, holding up the scroll. 'From now on we will be governed by equality. There are new opportunities, the same for everyone.'

'This is already being done in open-class handicapped sailboat races,' said the Chairman. 'Competitors strive separately to finish as quickly as possible and then each boat's time is adjusted by its handicap to find the winner. A good skipper who comes in last, in a bad boat with short waterline length and low sail area, can win on handicap.'

'Similarly in performing, each athlete's time or distance can be adjusted by a handicap to find a true winner. An athlete can win despite coming in last.'

After the meeting, Megan and I were at her parents' place. I knew that performing rules were being revised but didn't know what to expect.

'You seem to be sceptical of the rule changes,' said Michael.

'Could performing have weight categories like boxing?' asked Megan.

'Heavyweight boxers have an advantage but a heavy runner could be disadvantaged,' I said. 'Lightweight runners could have to carry weights.'

'Body shape is more important than weight,' Michael said.

'Performers in most athletic events have tended to be mesomorphs,' said Megan. 'Other types find it difficult to compete.'

243

'Could those with a record of high performance carry weights, as in horse racing?' I asked. 'Horse racing under handicap contrives that any horse can win.'

'Horse racing is cruel,' Megan said. 'Older horses carry more weight. A good horse has to carry more and more weight, until it's ultimately defeated by physical failure. Handicapping is not fair to horses.'

'TV audiences like close finishes.'

'Punters can second-guess the handicapper, winning by studying form, with the winnings of experts paid for by losers who bet naively.'

'There isn't much betting on athletics,' said Megan.

'It's increasing.'

'Race officials armed with the competitors' statistics would apply handicaps to each performer and work out an overall winner, ' I said. 'Would that be fairer? What do you think?'

'I think it's absolute crap,' said Megan. 'It wouldn't be as fair as accepting the unhandicapped results we are used to.'

'Unless there is a handicap system, individuals who are different could be penalised.'

'That's their tough luck,' I said. 'If they are different they have to accept the consequences. Should a tall basketball player be required to play on his knees? If he has a height advantage, he should be able to exploit it. Sport has held individuality sacrosanct and it shouldn't be changed now. Performance is what should count.'

'Performance is being taken over by freaks, as we saw in rugby,' Megan said.

'Useful freaks,' I said. 'They're not a problem. We need freaks for humanity to evolve as the environment changes. Diversity is good.'

'Levelling rules are regulating employment, limiting exceptional people,' said Michael. 'We are moving towards a handicapped society.

'The Government is committed to the spectacle controlling all types of competition: sport; performing; media access; financial services; access to medical care; buying; employment; access to services; and others.'

'Utilitarianism is taking over, doing the greatest good to the greatest number,' said Megan. 'It's a type of socialism I detest.'

'I call it a levelled society, with supposed equality,' I said. 'It's artificial, I don't like it and it will be bad for sport, bad for performing and bad for humanity.'

'We will oppose the new rules,' said Megan.

'You might not be able to stop them,' said Michael.

CHAPTER 48 OVERRULED

When the nation's athletes trialled the amended AAA rules, there was chaos. Tribunals met and opinions were offered, but the turmoil worsened. It was realised that the new rules had been imposed without athletes' agreement. The change from rewarding winners to consoling losers was a main difficulty.

'Is there any harm in rewarding people for trying?' Jack my supervisor asked me.

'Not in default of a winner,' I said. 'But consolation betrays competition. The tradition has been winner-takes all. Losers are wanting consolation prizes and sometimes they expect a share in winnings.'

'There is no getting around coming 83rd in a marathon,' said Megan. 'Awarding a 'consolation' prize doesn't fix it.'

'Consolation prizes encourage participation.'

'In education and employment, winning gets most attention. Neither losing nor consolation get much interest.'

'Deciding the winner is sometimes kept secret, to prevent contradiction and save losers' faces.'

'Sometimes they don't know who should win until they see performances.'

'The winner at pole vault is the one with fewest unsuccessful attempts to reach the winning height.'

'A competitor can opt to commence with the bar higher,' said Megan. ''She will make fewer jumps.'

'In races for high prize money, some horse trainers run their horses to lose in previous races, to lengthen the odds so they can place a bet that wins bigtime. Performers will downplay their abilities to influence handicappers.'

Qualification for competition entry could be an ordeal. I was sombre when I returned from a visit to the AAA office and spoke to Megan.

'Your gender identity has been challenged,' I said.

'What?' Megan said to me, aghast. 'How humiliating! Who was it?'

'One of the Asian Games performers.'

'The bitch.'

I was concerned by this allegation. Distance runners with high testosterone, like males, could be excluded, whatever their biology. A woman with high testosterone could be required to have injections. It was divisive and borderline athletes were unfairly ostracised.

This was cruel rejection and it hurt. The accusation dragged Megan and me down with flu.

Megan's testosterone tested normal.

Other rules of performing were changing too. Vaulting poles had evolved with a wide range of types. Under the new rules, performers were limited to only two poles each, restricted to certain lengths, with stiffness varying according to performer height and weight, to eliminate theoretical advantages. Megan could start with a short bendy pole and change to a long stiff one for greater heights.

Another change was reduction to only 30 seconds maximum time on the runway before starting a run up. It reduced Megan's ability to concentrate, making it more difficult to get into flow.

Clothing was controlled too. Women had to change their skimpy tops and bikini bottoms to one-piece, to appease calls for more modest attire from conservatives and religious leaders. The AAA implemented a one-piece uniform policy for jumping events.

'The zealots imagine that certain dress standards have to be maintained,' said Megan. 'A swimmer was arrested years ago for wearing a two-piece swimming costume. She was charged with indecency. The same prudery exists today.'

Many performers regarded rules of attire as unwanted interference

'Nanny state socialists should be more open towards sexual liberty and freedom,' Megan complained to me. 'They might support public nudity, or even licentiousness.'

'I wouldn't want that,' I said.

'Dress differentiation is a psychological boost,' said Megan to a reporter. 'We like to show off our bodies in distinct dress.'

She posed in a bikini for a photo and it appeared with a story about rules changing in social media.

The AAA requested comments on the new rules from the state associations, who made written submissions.

When the Tribunal had considered them and made changes, they distributed a 'final version' of the rules. When Megan and I read it, we were horrified.

'Performing is being over-regulated,' I said. 'Trackside camaraderie will be destroyed by too many arbitrary rules. Friendly competition will descend into back-stabbing. I am appalled at the changes proposed.'

'I want to be able to experiment with poles, refining my technique, but these rules have one-size-fits-all,' said Megan. 'Skill has been taken out and performing has become more mechanical. Pole vaulting used to explore the ambiguous edge between risk and certainty. Now, with only two poles, it's like changing from a floor shifter to a soggy automatic.'

'We can protest against the amendments,' I said.

'The new rules need a consensus of support,' said Megan. 'All we have is dissension.'

'The consensus should be that individuals are free to compete the way they want to,' I said.

'Are you sure people want to be free?' asked Megan. 'Freedom has responsibilities. Being condemned to be free forever is not everyone's idea of fun.'

'Why not?'

'Free competition is lonely. Freedom is inequality. It lacks community.'

'We are far from that,' I said. 'There isn't enough freedom for real competition. The new rules are a huge change for the worse and the objections we submitted have been ignored. We must meet with the AAA and reject the new rules.'

'They may be able to modify them.'

'They must redraft them.'

I contacted the police and informed them we wanted to hold a protest meeting outside the AAA offices in Brisbane City. The police licenced us to hold a meeting on the steps on a weekday at noon. Road and pedestrian traffic could not be disrupted and there could be no noise or violence. I gave them assurances.

'If there are any problems, we will end your meeting,' the police officer said.

It was a fine Thursday morning when AAA officials gathered on the steps outside their headquarters in the City Centre, defiantly facing a crowd holding banners and placards, with media journalists and TV cameras looking on. The Chairman announced there were new rules, which had been drawn up by a democratic process. He gave a long explanation of why and how the new rules had been prepared. He lied that all submissions had been considered.

'We at the AAA have prepared the new rules carefully and made necessary changes.'

The protesters shouted their opposition and brandished their placards.

'NO RULES CHANGE.'

'ATHLETIC PERFORMING MISRULED.

They chanted: 'WHAT DO WE WANT: NO CHANGE'.

Chairman Asquith spoke into a mike. 'We have had the old rules for a long time. Sadly, we are leaving that tradition behind to make progress. Today's world is fairer and we are changing with it. We are a democratic organisation. If there are any difficulties, we will be able to sort them out.'

A young man in the crowd jeered. 'You have ignored our submissions. The tribunal is a confidence trick! The changes are undemocratic. We demand the new rules are revoked.'

'We have made changes transparently,' said the Chairman. 'Our Equality Amendments are the very epitome of democracy. We have applied democratic principles in revising the rules as requested by the Government.'

'The Minister for Levelling is a fascist,' someone yelled. 'My grandfather fought against fascism! He died for democracy. Fascists have taken over. We want democracy!'

Someone shouted indignantly: 'There's no democracy here! We have no equality.'

A woman called out: 'Hey you, Chairman Asquith, your new rules suck.'

When people laughed at his red face, he turned away dismissively.

The first protester yelled: 'Resign you fascist bastards!'

Two policemen moved in front of him and held him by the throat.

The people tried to drag him back.

An independent politician, a woman, said loudly: 'Let him speak. He has a right to free speech.'

Two more police moved in and she too was silenced.

The people chanted: 'FASCIST SCUM. WE WON'T OBEY THEM.'

Startled and fearful, AAA officials tried to stare down the chanters.

'The Government is authoritarian and the Minister for Levelling is a fascist. Resign!'

The protestors continued chanting: 'WHAT DO WE SEE: NO DEMOCRACY.'

The Chairman realised that he had been misled. The Equality Amendments had not given the people a say, as he had instructed. The lawyers had duped him. He led the officials back inside the AAA building.

'I want the amendments revised immediately,' he said. 'The rules causing most objections must be put back to what they were.'

But, after receiving payment, the rascally constitutional lawyers had left town.

Megan said she would lead protests to the AAA State leaders, in a campaign to restore the rules, coordinating a large group of members for all track and field events. She withdrew her entry from the state championships.

At their party's national conference, the government discussed the new rules for sport, defending against allegations of totalitarianism. Conservatives wanted to respect individual rights but the socialist left wanted control by a strengthened nanny state. Individualism was part of the conservatives' core beliefs but the left had a dislike of elitism and wanted to open up sport to ordinary people. Improvements to the new rules were hurriedly proposed and approved in a vote.

Megan and I appeared in media presentations, marching in protest and disrupting a AAA meeting.

'The improved amendments are unacceptable,' said Megan. She had come out against levelling and was now the fiercest critic of the new rules of athletics.

Megan's boycott of the National Championships was copied by others and the event was cancelled.

For the Olympics in Brisbane, the old IOC rules would apply and Megan would compete as a member of the national squad.

Megan and I were united by frequent oral sex. We achieved intimacy that lifted us to new heights of understanding and passion. Cassius Clay and other boxers were reputed to abstain from sex before contests, fearing the indulgence would sap their body strength. Megan regarded sex as a fortifier. The one whose valour was diminished before Megan performed was me, from meeting her needs.

CHAPTER 49 OLYMPICS

'At last I can use my own poles,' Megan said, as we pushed a trolley carrying the long container from a bus into the Brisbane Olympic stadium. Other performers were doing the same, coming from the airport, from many countries. We had waited for our poles to be unloaded, using the time together to renew friendships and meet new people.

'Pole vaulters hang with their poles and with each other,' Megan told me.

She regaled me with a story about a guy who walked past a group of spectators at an athletics arena, carrying a long pole. One of the onlookers said to him, 'Are you a pole vaulter?' He responded, 'No, I'm German, but how did you know my name was Walter?'

As we edged forward in a line to go through customs, we talked with some others about the AAA rules debacle and how Megan's dispute with her coach had almost cost her place in the squad that went to Seoul.

'If the IOC had changed to those Australian levelling rules, I wouldn't have come,' said Dana, a tall Finn. 'They are ridiculous.'

'What difficulties would you have had?'

'I couldn't have performed the way I usually do,' Dana said. 'Deciding the winner from three jumps isn't fair to those of us who need several jumps to warm up.''

'I am surprised you would have a problem with levelling,' I said. 'In Finland there is a universal wage, isn't there?'

'Yes,' said Dana. 'But economic levelling is different from performance levelling.'

'That's right,' said Megan. 'The AAA is trying to equalise performances, not monetary prizes.'

'Thankfully the Olympic tradition is to award excellence,' I said 'The IOC has little interest in levelling. The Olympics has always idolised incorruptible individual achievement under transparent conditions, without apology to losers. The medal winners are the best competitors under equal rules for all. At the Paralympics, to be held here after the Olympics, there will be a range of ability levels.'

'Competition is exciting because it brings out the best in us,' said Megan. 'The huge audience worldwide encourages record performances never achieved before in human history.'

'The rules have to be transparent and fair. Although some nations have totalitarian governments, their athletes are not cowed and cringing, at least not while they are in the Olympic Village. If they are being over-controlled here, physically, chemically or financially, the methods must be concealed, or there would be complaints and boycotts. Coercion is uncommon. Defection is rare. Athletes are autonomous individuals. They inspire ordinary people to throw off their shackles and dare to be great.'

We had moved forward and the line had divided, so I was alone with Megan.

'Do we really dare anything?' asked Megan.

'Risk and success are inseparable,' I said. 'Athletes' risk failure and can lose their reputations, even suffering national disgrace.'

'Most athletes won't risk their health to win,' said Megan.

'When I see you hanging inverted on a slender pole shaped like a letter C, I recall it can break. You are reckless,' I said. 'Why does danger attract you?'

'I don't regard performing as risky,' said Megan. 'When I cross a busy street, I prefer to rely on my senses, rather than going to a pedestrian crossing and trusting drivers to see me and stop. I want to be independent and back my own judgement, rather than relying on a nanny state solution, such as a walk zone.'

'So what attracts you to performing?'

'I get a buzz from doing jaw-dropping vaults.'

'You also mentioned liking winning, being fit, meeting athletes and travelling to new places.'

'Public winning is important,' Megan said. 'Record breaking attracts me like a moth to a flame.'

'Does competing have a fatal attraction?' I asked.

'No. Moths usually turn away before they are burned.'

'Could you be burned?'

'The cloud on the horizon is that in time my abilities will decline and I will be forced into retirement. I must use my ability now or lose it. I imagine I am on the way up. Athletes often retire at a pinnacle of success, or when they lose their edge. I may do that.'

On the day of the competition, the pole vaulters emerged on to the oval from the tunnel to the changing rooms, one by one. They were similar in stature, lithe mesomorphs, long-legged and tall. They wore crop tops and bikini bottoms in their national colours, with skinny bare mid-riffs, pony tails, bare legs and brightly coloured shoes. They waved and jogged to the equipment area, to retrieve their poles from tubes in racks beside the uprights and mat.

Megan trotted out from the tunnel to a fanfare. 'FROM AUSTRALIA, MEGAN McLEAN.' Cameras and audience applause greeted her. Screens in the stadium and across the globe filled with her image, looking gorgeous and in perfect condition. She stood with the group than relaxed on a recliner, waiting for her turn.

In the centre of the oval, a flock of corellas, medium sized white parrots, swooped in and pecked at the grass, quarrelling and fluttering.

From where I was sitting in the stand opposite, I had a side view of the bar on its uprights and could watch performers' attempts. I could go down to the barrier to talk with Megan. Heats of the men's relay were in progress and she waited for the runners to get clear before crossing the track to me.

There were 15 pole vaulters. Within an hour all had cleared the starting height of 4.70m, except for one who succeeded at second attempt. The bar was put up to 4.85m. Megan commenced midway in the order, clearing the bar easily. Most got over. Four of them had second attempts. Two failed their third attempts and were eliminated. At 5m00 Megan equalled her personal best, achieved in

Seoul. Two women made their first jumps at this height. Only 6 cleared 5m10, including Megan on her second attempt. Two late starters cleared 5m20 at their first attempts, Megan succeeded on her second and went on with two others to 5m30.

It was down to three women: Tako Mogdeni, a Georgian, Lisa Hemming of the USA and Megan. The bar was at 5m30, world record height. Megan paused on the runway with her longest pole, taking all the one minute allowed.

She was still, seeming to concentrate, going into flow. When she powered forward, her run exuded confidence. This was her time, her place, her leap for individuality. I watched as the bent pole straightened until she pushed it away, using the impetus to curl her body over and around the bar, descending on her back and bouncing up from the landing pad, with an air punch and a yell of triumph.

The Russian rocked back and forth and then set off stepping high. She planted the pole hard but her grip slid down and she ran on under the bar and across the landing mat. She hurried to get back, starting again within one minute, to avoid a no-jump, but knocked the bar down.

Lisa Hemming stepped on to the runway, held the pole on her shoulder, brought her hands together overhead several times, until the crowd clapped in time yelling 'GO LISA'. 'GO LISA'. She set off holding the pole high and it lifted her with its C shape, flipping her inverted body up and over the bar. Her left side didn't get high enough, her left knee barely cleared the bar, her front brushed it and it fell with her.

Mogdeni and Hemming cleared their second attempts. The bar was put up to 5m35, which would be a new world record.

Megan beckoned to the stewards to move the uprights forward, so her stiff pole could take her forward far enough. Again she went through her concentration routine, getting into the heightened state of flow awareness she needed to respond to the changed conditions. Her take-off was good but her swing up and fly away were too early and she came down on the bar.

Tako's performance wasn't high enough, knocking the bar with her feet. Lisa cleared it to loud applause.

Megan's second record attempt had her mind focussed on her new goal and every fibre straining to reach the high speed she needed. This time she cleared the bar easily. She and Lisa had both cleared 5m35, her with 2 previous failures, Lisa with one and Tako had cleared 5m30 with her third attempt, getting the bronze medal.

Megan and Lisa now vied for gold and a new record. The bar was put up to 5m40. Tired after more vaults than the others, Megan rested as long as possible. The uprights were moved towards her. This time she came down too early and knocked the bar off. Hemming also failed. Then Megan brushed the bar with her feet and it fell. Hemming too failed in her second attempt.

Megan flowed into her third and final attempt, succeeding at 5m40 with aplomb, a new world record. She sprang up and raised both arms in victory. Lisa could not equal it and took the silver. Megan had won the gold and the record. She walked across the running track to me.

Megan threw her arms around me, shaking like a leaf and sobbing.

Her Olympic record was the first time in human history any woman had reached this height. It was a moment of triumph that would be known worldwide and never forgotten.

'You've done it,' I said, hugging her over the barrier, overjoyed.

'Thank you for everything,' she said, crying. She was noticing her surroundings now, as if for the first time, surfacing from her submergence in flow throughout the competition.

'They will say you had an unfair advantage using flow today,' I said, 'but your methods are well known and anyone can use them.'

'I couldn't compete without flow now,' she said.

'You won't have to,' I said. 'Your win today has put the last nail in the levellers' coffin.'

A reporter asked me to comment on Megan's win.

'I'm not her coach, just a friend,' I said. 'I helped her with her training.'

'Could you comment on her training?'

'She has developed her skills by diligent practice. Megan's success is a triumph for all those people who have done their best in competing with her, enabling her to reach higher than any woman has ever reached before.'

'What has been her response to the thrust towards equality in sport and athletics?'

'She has done her best, following the rules, with an unprecedented combination of mental and physical abilities.'

'I heard that she used your theory of flow in her mental training,' the reporter said.

'That's right, she did.'

'When will your theory be published?' the reporter asked.

'My MPhil thesis has been submitted,' I said.

'When do you expect it to be approved?'

'Soon. Megan's success vindicates my theory,' I said. 'I want to submit it for a PhD.'

Megan was awarded her medal, standing on the dais between Lisa and Mogdeni. She wept as the band played Advance Australia Fair and Australia's blue ensign fluttered. As I watched I recalled meeting Megan for the first time and recognising her drive to reach the podium she was on today. Her resolve was enormous and she had never failed to put her full effort into athletics, into living together and everything she did.

Megan addressed the assembly from the dais, flanked by the other medallists. Holding her medal, she spoke quietly to an audience that listened in silence.

'I want to thank my family and my coaches,' said Megan. 'I want to thank Chance Finething, for all his support. To reach the record height I first had to conquer myself, study myself by phenomenology, understand what I had to do and set my mind to control my body with flow. Chance was unfailing in his explanation of the philosophies of these techniques and his encouragement to meet the challenge.

'I want to thank the many athletes I have competed against in getting here. Obviously they could not all stand here today, but they

257

took part in good faith in a competition they regarded as fair. My success is a triumph not for me, but for all those who played a part, no matter how small, in preserving a worthwhile tradition, raising the bar and keeping it going up.'

The applause was rapturous, as Megan stepped down and mingled with well-wishers and reporters seeking interviews.

I went down and stood with her, holding hands. We had grown together, sharing with gentleness, fulfilling ourselves with giving to each other, our bodies glowing with health. Ours had been a unique coupling and I knew I had benefited enormously. It had turned out well and when I thought of our good fortune and how badly it could have turned out, I felt humble. I felt an overwhelming love for Megan. She meant everything to me.

PANDEMIC

CHAPTER 50 INFECTION

After her win, Megan and I celebrated at the Olympic Village with the Australian team. The Olympic Games had been a great success until, at the end, sickness struck. At the party, both of us developed headaches. Megan had a sore throat and congested breathing, whereas I had only a sore throat.

'I could have 'flu,' she said. 'Competing always pull me down.'

We left the party and went to our rooms. I gave her some Panadol. She felt nauseous and neither of us wanted food. With noses streaming and bouts of sneezing, we went to bed early.

In the night Megan became feverish and vomited. I called the Village doctor.

After two hours a doctor came, wearing a personal protection overall and mask.

'Sorry to have kept you waiting, but there is a new outbreak of a variant of coronavirus. Hundreds have been hospitalised in Brisbane.'

The coronavirus pandemic had started in 2020, with outbreaks that killed millions worldwide. There had been sporadic outbreaks since. Vaccination had reduced frequency and severity of hospitalisation but outbreak of this new variant in 2032 had health authorities renewing restrictions first imposed ten years earlier.

'Are people dying?' I inquired of the doctor.

'They are going into intensive care, like in a flu epidemic. It could be more transmissible than ordinary flu. It's fortunate the Olympic events are finished. This place could be a hotbed of infection. It's going to be difficult to contain it.'

She examined Megan and me, swabbing our noses and throats.

Two hours later she phoned.

'You are both positive for coronavirus,' she said. Megan needs to be in hospital. I have arranged for her to go into the Queen Elizabeth 2 Hospital. She'll be safe there.'

She called an ambulance.

'Can I go with her?' I asked.

'You can stay here, for the moment,' she said. 'You aren't so bad. Do not go out or see anyone. I'll arrange for someone to look after you.'

The doctor left.

I packed a bag for Megan. Then the ambulance arrived and they took her on a gurney and loaded her in.

'We don't deserve this,' I said. 'You vaulted brilliantly today. I am fortunate to have helped with training of an Olympic gold medallist and world record holder. We should be celebrating. I have experienced so much with you. You have enabled me to achieve my creative goal and make a difference.'

'It worked well, didn't it?' she said, lapsing into coughing. 'We aren't finished yet!'

'Goodbye love,' I said, waving as she left with the siren wailing.

I was anxious that I might not be able to contact her, nor check her progress. The paramedics gave me a phone number at the hospital. For the first time in my life I was in quarantine. I felt very alone.

'How necessary is quarantine?' I asked the doctor.

'Compared with strategies for controlling infections in livestock, such as slaughter of the herd, quarantine is a mild treatment,' he said.

'Are you saying extermination would work better?'

'No. We are kinder to humans. Quarantine for a week and vaccination should be sufficient.'

I was always sceptical of medical treatment efficacies. I wanted treatments and restrictions to have been tested. Experimenting on living humans was unethical, especially when they were ill. Their consent had to be obtained. Without empirical evidence, procedures and treatments were being derived from experience with other diseases, or inferred from theories, or even from hunches. I was suspicious, because the virus particles were small and the theories could not be verified by observation.

I spoke to Megan on the telephone.

'To confirm a cause it's necessary to observe physical contact taking place with a causal agent, a pathogen,' I said. 'One particle could be enough to infect a vulnerable person, yet someone with strong immunity can resist millions. A virus particle is too small for contact to be seen. Cause can only be inferred and it's unreliable. Consequently the effectiveness of precautions is uncertain.'

'Some restrictions seem to be overdone,' Megan said. 'The precautions are shots in the dark and likely to be over-cautious. Lockdowns assume the worst.'

'The Titanic of public health is threatened more by submerged pathogens too small to see than by the visible peaks of infected individuals,' I said. 'We are afloat on an invisible sea of infection.'

The invisibility of the virus reminded me of a famous historical misunderstanding in a different branch of science. I recalled that in 1667 scientists Becher and Stahl theorised that combustion was caused by an invisible substance 'phlogiston', present in fuels, used up in burning. The theory was accepted, until in 1770 Lavoisier showed, by weighing reactants and products, that the phlogiston theory was completely wrong. Combustion involved combination of a flammable substance with a previously unknown invisible gas, named by Priestley in 1774: 'oxygen'.

I was sceptical that, like phlogiston, empirical confirmation of the supposed processes of generation, transmission and infection of the coronavirus would take centuries to unravel.

'The aetiology of coronavirus could be as difficult to identify today as it was for combustion in 1667,' I said to Megan.

'The infection process has also taken a long time to understand,' she said. 'Following the pioneering of vaccination in 1853 by Jenner, Pasteur proposed his germ theory in the 1860s and it has dominated ever since. But the terrain theory proposed at the same time by virologist Bechamp was sidelined. He had related infection to weaknesses in people's immune systems. He advocated strengthening immunity by sunshine, fresh air, exercise, diet, clean whole foods, rest, hygiene, detoxification and absence of stress, anxiety and depression. The theories of Pasteur and Bechamp complemented each other, one explaining transmission of infection by germs and the other explaining resistance to infection by natural immunity. Bechamp's theory could explain infection in a coronavirus pandemic.

'Tracking and tracing of coronavirus confirms that the contagion can be transmitted. It may transmit less easily than health authorities claim. Many people do not become infected, even when they are in contact with victims. Are we to suppose the germs didn't reach them, or could it be they are more resistant? We don't know and cannot ignore Bechamp's terrain theory.'

'Coronavirus infection might be as complex as photosynthesis,' I said. 'The chemistry of photosynthesis took from 1450 to the 1930s to be understood. It might take 100s of years to understand coronavirus.'

'Is complete understanding necessary to control it?' asked Megan. 'We could get lucky?'

'In your dreams. We need understanding. Influenza is still with us, despite vaccines and research,' I said. 'We won't be able to eliminate coronavirus overnight.'

With only partial understanding available, I was reluctant to adopt restrictions, such as hygiene, sterilisation, masking, social distancing, lockdown, quarantine and vaccination.

'The assumption that virus infection can be excluded by a mask is misconceived,' Megan said. 'There can be millions of particles swarming in air, not only penetrating face masks but inhabiting our bodies, when they are numerous causing infections, unless resisted by immunity. A mask can even cause infection by reducing fresh air intake, reducing oxygen intake and exposing the wearer to higher levels of carbon dioxide. But a mask is effective in stopping spittle, at least some of the droplets, getting onto surfaces and thence into other people.

'Masking does not give perfect protection and reduces ability to exercise,' I said. 'Cringing precautions, lockdowns, partial hygiene and attempts at sterilisation, such as deep cleaning, could be worse than useless. They can reduce our natural immunity, allowing worse virus strains to evolve, weakening our resolve and making us defenceless. Masking is not a panacea and could even be harmful. The nanny state's excessive precautions could induce fear and learned helplessness, increasing infection rates.'

'Going without masks and allowing healthy people to encounter the virus could strengthen herd immunity and waylay infection,' said Megan.

'Restrictions that keep people at home, halt recreational exercise and cause learned helplessness, could promote infection,' I said.

'You need to rein in your scepticism,' said Megan. 'Experience from tracing sources of infection has revealed restrictions have been partially successful. There is evidence that lockdowns, hygiene, social distancing, sterilisation and masking have benefits. This could also be inferred from the sharp decline in influenza, which has fortuitously been reduced by coronavirus precautions. Models of virus transmission and protection technologies are becoming more confident.'

'Your learned optimism is a disease preventative (19),' I said. 'What would I do without you?'

CHAPTER 51 VACCINATION

Queensland was in lockdown and I was still at the Olympic Village in quarantine. Meals were brought to my room. I spoke to Megan online at the hospital every day. Her condition was improving.

'How much longer will this outbreak continue?' Megan asked.

'They say infection will spread until the population is immune, by either infection or vaccination,' I said to her. 'It took vaccinations to halt tuberculosis, polio, SARS and ebolla.'

'Would a vaccine be long lasting?' she asked.

'No. It wasn't for influenza because the virus mutates. Despite having been vaccinated, I almost died from influenza,'

'What happened?'

'After a long plane journey,' I said. 'I had trouble breathing and blacked out. When they woke me up, I was a basket case with flu. Since then, I have refused having shots but haven't had flu again.'

'Should the Government have protected you?' asked Megan.

'No; my jab was for the current variant. Viruses mutate unexpectedly. The Spanish Flu in 1918 may have killed more people than coronavirus. There have been other flu outbreaks, despite populations being vaccinated. Vaccination is not a panacea.'

'You seem to be suggesting deaths from coronavirus outbreaks are inevitable?'

'Malthus said human populations are controlled by disease, hunger and war,' I said. 'Pandemic diseases weed out the old, the unhealthy, the unfit and the foolish.'

'They also kill children.'

'A few of the weakest children would die anyway, unfortunately,' I said. 'Weak individuals are more likely to be casualties.'

'When populations grow, density increases and there is more transmission.'

'It is callous to regard deaths by disease as necessary. Compared with influenza, the coronavirus is more virulent and the need for restrictions is more compelling,' said Megan.

'I am not persuaded,' I said, bristling. 'I hope you don't expect me to compulsorily vaccinate? What gets done to my body is decided by me.'

'They say anti-vaxxers are traitors to the cause of herd immunity,' Megan said. 'According to zealots, vaccination refusal is a weak link in the chain of immunity.'

'There is no chain of immunity,' I said. 'Vaccination does not set up an impenetrable wall of virus resistance. The vaccines are inefficient technologies that only erratically stop individuals being hospitalised. To understand the venom against anti-vaxxers, look no further than how a spooked herd victimises someone who breaches a protocol. Vaxxers fear unvaccinated people more than they fear vaccine failure and side effects. They are irrational.

'Because transmission by germs is difficult to observe and control, artificial immunity from injection of vaccines has been the great hope,' I said. 'Complete confidence in the new vaccines is misplaced, because the coronavirus vaccines do not have Jenner's original vaccine technology, nor exhaustive trials. New vaccines lack rigorous testing. The presence of an unvaccinated person does not prevent herd immunity, the way one tiny crystal of impurity can weaken the crystal structure in a solidifying alloy. The last jab is no more effective than the first. The spooked herd exaggerates the danger from the unvaccinated.'

'The worry is that unvaccinated people could pass infection on,' she said.

'People need to protect themselves from people who are infected and unaware by distancing themselves and voluntarily isolating themselves, by staying at home and not going to work if they don't want to take any risk,' I said. 'Testing could be freely available and recent negative test results needed to access public spaces, transport, shops and workplaces.

'The concepts of 'spreader' and 'incubator' are weasel words suggesting that infected individuals could generate virus particles and distribute them on to an unsuspecting public. The intent is to create fear and ultra-caution. Is it likely people harbour and transmit virus particles all the time, with symptomatic illness detectable only when they are concentrated? A recent negative testing result could be demanded of suspect individuals.'

'Protection is a personal responsibility' I said. 'Compulsory vaccination or mask wearing are illogical. The *a priori* problem is that the vaccine doesn't always work. If the vaccinated people don't have confidence in it to protect them, it is illogical for them to demand that others vaccinate.

'Governments have found it easy to reach for new and potentially unreliable technologies to bolster their autocracy. Taking risks has more merit to a gullible public, than doing nothing. It's easier to mandate the whole population, when all but a few recalcitrant individuals would volunteer, without them causing problems. A logical response is for me not to accept vaccination. Society benefits when some individuals remain independent from the herd and enable testing of the non-vaccination option.'

'The U.S. Supreme Court in *Jacobson v. Massachusetts*, 197 U.S. 12 (1905) considered the case for mandatory vaccination,' I said. 'It ruled that the State of Massachusetts could compel residents to obtain free vaccination or revaccination against smallpox, or suffer a penalty of $5 (about $150 today) for noncompliance. The court's judgement relied on four criteria in deciding to compel vaccination:

1. There was a benchmark minimum number of consequential deaths (set at 500,000 by the defence during later prosecution of the tobacco industry).
2. The vaccination mandate was not shown to be arbitrary or oppressive. There were few arbitrary exemptions for those affected and treated, nor for others oppressed by it.
3. Other approved medications were available to reduce transmission of infection.
4. Vaccine safety and efficacy had been established for less than 100 years, (exceeded with the smallpox vaccine).

'The absence of these four conditions made mandatory vaccination unreasonable and therefore illegal,' I said. 'None of the four Jacobson criteria were present for coronavirus vaccination in Australia. If the governments of the US or Australia were to proceed with a vaccine mandate, it would be an unwarranted overreach, inconsistent with established public health policy and law (11).'

'The Jacobson criteria reveal that vaccination refusal has grounds for respect,' said Megan. 'Mandatory vaccination would be unlawful. They are wanting to vaccinate me, but I think I will refuse. If immunity is possible, wouldn't I have gained it from my illness?'

I changed the subject of our telephone conversation.

'What are you reading,' I asked her.

Megan told me about a novel she was reading set in Elizabethan England's literary circles, which had produced William Shakespeare.

'They talked a lot,' she said.

'So do we,' I said. 'A difference is their talk earned their livings.'

'I'll send you my invoice for you to pay,' she said.

'Do you charge by the word?'

'By the conversation. To get your money's worth, you have to keep me talking.'

We chatted then, about what we would do at home when we got out.

'I've had enough for today,' I said after some time. 'It's been fun. Bye.'

I ended my call to Megan. She was getting better in hospital. Coronavirus had affected her respiration and I hoped she wouldn't get pneumonia or any debilitating condition that would affect her athletic performance when she recovered.

I called Megan later that week.

'I'm almost recovered and they've said I will be able to go home by the end of this week,' she said. 'I want to take a break from performing until the pandemic is over.'

'It could be years,' I said. 'It will be difficult to recover your current fitness level.'

'Have you been vaccinated yet?' she asked. 'I have refused.'

'No,' I said. 'I'm waiting for more evidence that it's necessary. The case for mandated restrictions was not made in earlier virus outbreaks, with a couple of possible exceptions, such as polio. Voluntary restrictions were sufficient to protect people and what we have now is hysterical over-reaction that inconveniences many people unnecessarily.'

'Risks from vaccination are not hypothetical,' Megan said. 'According to some credible sources, deaths and hospitalisations from vaccination are under-reported.'

'Risks of the disease are exaggerated,' I said. 'The population has become squeamish and cringing. Compulsory restrictions can have effects exceeding those of the disease. Mandated vaccination, segregation, state-sanctioned discrimination, stalking apps, vaccine passports, restrictions on employment and public access, all go too far.'

'I agree voluntary restrictions would be better, but irresponsible individuals have to be controlled,' said Megan. 'I feel sorry for employees who have to run the gauntlet of the vaccination mandate for entry to their workplace. Entry to government buildings, such as libraries, should not require proof of vaccination. People vaccinated months earlier and reinfected recently can enter freely. It's ridiculous. Requiring a swab and negative test would be logical.

'The Government wants to take away our freedoms and will return them only by large personal sacrifices, including vaccination, as a precondition to going to work, or for travelling, or for receiving medical treatment,' I said. 'For people who are not infected, this is extortion. What is worse is that it converts a situation of omission, into commission of an offence, that applies force to people who are neither infected nor law-breakers. It's unreasonable to force healthy uninfected people to accept vaccination. We would not accept compulsory treatment for any other medical condition. It disrespects a person's right to decide.'

'Vaccination is not the end of it,' Megan said. 'Vaccinated people have to identify themselves and provide proof using online sites and mobile devices. Supplying the welter of passwords, cross-referencing and up-to-date identity documentation at the entrance to a restricted area, where trust had once operated, is humiliating, frustrating, disappointing and unnecessary.'

'Vaccination checks are reminiscent of civilian identity checks by the Gestapo in wartime Germany,' I said. 'Officials are not empowered to offer flexibility because they don't know the consequences of the procedures they are implementing, which might be inhumane. People who won't conform are turned away.'

'But an infected person could easily get past a vaccination checkpoint,' said Megan. 'The certificate of vaccination method is nonsense. If the concern is to keep infected persons out, everyone should be swabbed and tested on the spot.'

'Our vaccination rates are high and that is seen as a litmus test of trust in government,' I said.

'Isn't it because people are fearful?'

'Yes,' I said. 'Fear is being used to intimidate the population. Learned helplessness disarms immune systems. We are conditioned to tolerate or succumb to leaders' arbitrary idealism. Individualism is dead and the nanny state has been amplified as tyranny.

'Psychological harm from suppression of the community is large. People don't have a choice, whereas infected people who die can be unvaccinated of their own choice. The dead may have had more respect than the living. Consequences of economic hardship and poverty from restriction cannot be overlooked. Harsh restrictions may be justified to protect a minority, but financial and psychological damage by over-restriction of the majority are also important.'

'A few deaths by infection are too many,' Megan said.

'Endlessly authorities have appealed to the public: '*Do the right thing* or it will be harder for the rest of us,' I said. 'WTF is that supposed to mean?'

'The nanny state extols the virtue of 'doing the right thing', without saying *what* it is, nor why *everyone* should comply. Henry David Thoreau said:

'Disobedience is the true foundation of liberty. The obedient must be slaves.'

'There were big anti-vaccine and anti-lockdown rallies in Australia and I sympathised with those people. Their views should be respected.

'In my view *'Doing the right thing'* was more dangerous than the pandemic itself,' I said. 'It supposes that there is a 'thing' that requires action because it is 'right' and not to do it would harm others' enjoyment of their rights. Queenslanders do not have constitutional rights and there could be disagreement about what rights the thing would uphold or achieve.'

''Doing the right thing' is a weasel term, deliberately ambiguous,' Megan said. 'Benefitting others does not come naturally to any animal, except in kin groups, such as within human families. In evolution theory, altruism is confined to group selection, or kin. For altruism, individuals volunteer to sacrifice their own genetic inheritance to benefit relatives' genes. Here the concern is with 'doing the right thing' by strangers. With strangers, it's hard to be sure they will benefit from our unselfish act. Maybe after several generations, we could look back and say: 'Look how our 'doing the right thing' helped them have more children, causing us to have fewer.' That would be altruism.'

'It's not evident that 'the right thing' is actually right,' she said. 'It's simply unstated conformity and running with a herd spooked by coronavirus. We could be rushing like lemmings towards destruction. The lemmings who hold back, like me, provide a check and balance. Our example reminds herd members to ask: Why are we rushing? Could there be a cliff ahead?'

'Lemmings don't want to know,' I said. 'When an authority says run, they run.

'Doing the right thing' assumes reciprocity, a doctrine of Christianity and Kant's Categorical Imperative. Without definition, there is nothing to prevent unfairness and freeloaders taking advantage of those who obey.'

'Australians have inherited facets of individualism brought by settlers from the UK and other countries. Governments have managed the coronavirus pandemic with emergency legislation able to instigate border closures, quarantine and vaccination mandates. These measures were not subjected to all the usual democratic processes and consequently some people are aggrieved.'

'100 years ago, Russians attempted to improve society by replacing Christianity with Godless collectivism. 70 years later, 30 years ago, the Soviet Socialist state collapsed and despite ongoing suppression, Christianity was restored. In many countries, faith in a supernatural deity has re-emerged as a popular, or even the predominant, belief.'

'In Australia, secular principles are embedded in legal systems and government,' Megan said. 'Christianity is declining and the erosion of community and social traditions has created a vacuum filled by nanny state expansion and overreach. During the coronavirus pandemic, it displaced individualism with collective control. The spectacle was of government empowered to resist the disease at any cost to individuals, or to private businesses, with support from the public purse.'

'It's ridiculous to stop healthy people going about their business;' I said. 'It's levelling gone mad. Would it be logical to close all human traffic on public roads to prevent infirm drivers from causing accidents? No, of course not. Incapable drivers and vulnerable pedestrians would sensibly be banned from public roads, allowing other traffic as usual.'

'Frightened people want to stop infected people having contact with them, by identifying possible transmission routes and tracking each infection to a source, as if it can be stamped out,' Megan said. 'They want to deal with it, as if it was a terrorist bomb threat, by mobilising the population to catch a perpetrator or a chain of culprits. But it has been evident from the start that the threats cannot be eliminated, even by vaccination. There are too many transmission possibilities.'

'People are wrong to expect to be protected by unreliable technologies,' I said. 'The vaccines are far from perfect. Coronavirus will probably become endemic, like flu. People have to accept risk, the same as they do with other dangers, by taking personal responsibility.'

'Many people knowingly take risks,' Megan said. 'For example, they choose to live on the Brisbane River flood plain, because homes there are more affordable than where it is high and dry. They accept risks in their lives they can only partly prepare for.'

'They expect the nanny state to bail them out,' I said, 'or insurance if they can get it.'

'The nanny state's benefits are limited,' Megan said. 'Many people would withhold covid care to unvaccinated people. They are proposing that if an unvaccinated person goes to a hospital, treatment should be refused because they haven't subscribed to public welfare,' Megan said.

'Hospitalisation is not refused to other people living unhealthily, like diabetics and alcoholics,' I said. 'Why refuse treatment to the unvaccinated?'

'They say that non-vaccination is different, and hospitalisation should be refused, because the victim can affect others' health by transmitting coronavirus to them,' said Megan.

'Wouldn't refusing access cause more transmission?' I said. 'All coronavirus victims should be treated, to stop them transmitting. Hospitalisation would make vaccination unnecessary, by taking infection off the streets.'

'Is mandatory hospitalisation more acceptable to you than mandatory vaccination?' Megan asked.

'Yes,' I said. 'It is common sense to accept treatment when I have tested positive. But when I have tested negative, I have a right to refuse vaccination, whether my rationale makes sense to others, or not.'

CHAPTER 52 SELF-INTEREST

A condition of my quarantine at the Olympic Village was that I would be vaccinated, but I had refused.

'We may keep you here longer,' they told me.

Megan and I discussed online what to do. She had been quite ill but she had not needed ICU care and was recovering well.

'They want to vaccinate me after I complete my isolation period,' Megan said. 'My immunity might not protect me for long or against other variants.'

'I am not convinced the benefits outweigh the risks,' she said. 'With the current imperfect vaccines, getting back to normal with herd immunity is a fiction. Where vaccines have been used, there have been side-effect deaths. They have been few, but significant.'

'I agree,' I said. ''Health authorities cannot enforce vaccination. Those in positions of authority may find it acceptable to speak untruths - noble lies - for the sake of the common good. For example, they could say everyone must be vaccinated, which would be a lie. Plato describes this as part of the political process. It's a moral enterprise to demand equality where there is none and it abuses people's trust. Our government should tell the truth. When the state is morally derelict, its Government will collapse.'

'Vaccination is a collective action with dangers for individuals. Offers of lucrative insurance pay-outs for unexpected side effects have been used to induce people to be vaccinated, compensating them at community expense. The compensation is suspicious, because other medical treatments have not been supported by the community in this way.'

While we had been talking online, a nurse had come and taken Megan's temperature and blood pressure.

'Inoculation has momentum,' I said. 'GPs have been jabbing their patients at state expense for years, against: influenza, measles, mumps, polio, diphtheria, breast cancer, ovarian cancer, cervical cancer, prostate cancer and smallpox. Most people accept vaccination as a duty to the community, preventing infection of others and assisting eradication. It has not been compulsory.'

'Are you going to have the jab?' Megan asked me.

Behind me, an orderly wearing PPE was servicing my room, making the bed.

'My health is good, so I'll delay,' I said. 'Not all people can be driven by authorities like cattle. Vaccination hysteria has taken hold. People can judge others actions wrongly. If I was ahead of others in accepting a new and risky treatment, such as vaccination, my martyr's sacrifice could be esteemed by the majority as pioneering, which it is not. It would be subjugation. Conversely, if I defy the majority and delay, my truculence could be deplored as maverick freeloading. There is an all or nothing mentality and it makes me angry that the majority live in a make-believe bubble which can burst at any time. Those who extol the virtue of 'doing the right thing', without saying what it is, nor why everyone should comply, can bring more danger than the pandemic itself.'

'Aren't you concerned you could reinfect Megan and vulnerable people?'

'No. My infection and illness will have reduced my threat to them as much as any vaccination. The risk is small.'

'Is the situation dire?'

'No. I will not join a spooked herd who panic like suicidal lemmings.'

'Why are you angry?'

'None of the alternatives is attractive. The nanny state has invoked a spectacle of unreal images of contagion, with the public entranced, thoughtless, without conscience, atomised and unable to act for their own safety. They are kept watching screens like Netflix or TV and are exposed to advertising of products or subscriptions they buy but may not want. It is part of the same spectacle that keeps them slaving at work, consuming products they don't need. The spectacle prevents their participation in development of class consciousness that would prevent accumulation of capital by a few wealthy individuals. Debord (15) found the spectacle served capitalism. It is an attack on individualism by Marxist analysis and invokes a nanny state. He assumed the lower class was being exploited and blamed the middle class and their capitalism.'

'You are outnumbered by Marxists and that's why you're angry,' Megan said. 'The threat of mandatory vaccination is good reason to become emotional. There is a sanctity in the rights of individuals to accept or reject medical treatment and receive full disclosure of risks associated with any treatment, as well as the benefits.

'Some media have attributed anti-vaccination sentiment as the last noisy gasp of irrelevant 'freedom', the chant of 'misfits' and 'selfish' people. They have explained vaccination refusal as free-loader greed, wanting protection without contributing. But cognitive dissonance would prevent duplicitous free-loading, because believing vaccination is bad would be contradictory and without benefit.'

'I agree. Free-loader greed is a fiction, part of the spectacle,' I said. 'I am reminded of that by the kookaburras who visit our garden. They line up on a branch and deliver an infernal racket loud enough to wake the dead. It is much ado about nothing, territory staking without substance. Then they wing off inconspicuously. The totalitarians try the same strategy to stake their claims to seize anti-vaccination territory, hoping their noise will cover up their lack of reason.'

'Sensational media have raised a spectre of hospitals filled with unvaccinated patients and bodies piling up at hastily dug graveyards. Some of the dead people would be vaccinated and deserved better protection, such as no vaccination. Some dead would have liked to be vaccinated but didn't get it. Attributing deaths to wilful neglect is an assault on individualism. It's totalitarianism, indicated by arbitrary ideology, central power and fearful superfluous masses.'

Megan paused and when she continued, her voice on the phone was louder and higher-pitched.

'They have asked me: 'Are you really too self-centred to care about others' welfare, because an unvaccinated person can spread the disease further?' What should I reply?'

'I would say my first responsibility is to myself,' I said. 'Others should do their best to take care of themselves. They have no right to expect me to help them. I will help them as a second priority, when I am able. I would point out to them that I have recently been infected and still have lymphocytes in my body that would reduce transmission to others.'

'What if you infect your family?'

'I would have agency and be responsible, but no culpability, for deserting the herd,' I said. 'Herd members are denied self-interest. For them to demand allegiance from self-interest is totalitarian cherry-picking.'

'It is totalitarianism that I most object to,' said Megan.

'Fearful citizens should not expect governments to restrict others,' I said. 'People who are fearful should stay in their homes, not put it on others to protect them.'

'Deviating from the herd's mass vaccination is seen as dereliction of duty to the forces opposing the virus, like a chink in their armour, as if my defection could act as an Achilles heel and bring down all opposition to the pandemic,' I said.

'Could one person endanger the majority?' Megan asked.

'No,' I said. 'One defector could not betray the mass, but one defector could weaken the others' resolve when they are unsure. People have no right to demand others protect them. They must protect themselves. The herd wants compliance, but there are enough objectors wanting individual consideration to prevent a mandate.'

'Freedom and financial obligation, have been overlooked during the pandemic,' Megan said, with indignation. 'Media and politicians have let the virus wag the tail of the health and welfare dog. Pandemic treatment has usurped general health, security, food and shelter and lifestyle concerns. For many people hunger, care and debt are the real problems.'

Government disregard for ordinary people always made Megan angry. I turned down the volume on my phone to reduce her stridency.

'Our self-interest seems to be a tug o' war between individual freedom and a communal force, ruling over all human affairs, going forward into the most distant future,' she said. 'The spectacle has indoctrinated communities with continued economic growth, increasing demand for resources and insatiable consumer demand. None of these is sustainable in the longer term, but the spectacle regards them as investment opportunities. Individual freedom does not get a look in.'

I had experience of finance from my job in Canada.

'The spectacle has taken covid in its stride, funding government jobseeker payments by incurring public sector debt and by investors buying bonds,' I said. 'The Australian economy has hardly faltered. The government has kept the pandemic going as long as they can, but now they are lifting restrictions due to public antipathy.'

'So we won't need to have the jab?' Megan said.

'No,' I said. 'They are unlikely to make it mandatory and I would refuse. I hope you agree with me that it is in my best interest not to. If I were to agree to this, then I would be wide open to sterilisation, euthanasia, electroconvulsive therapy and thought control. I respect the rights of anti-vaxxers to control their bodies, even if their views seem illogical, or if incurring infection would change their minds. They have a right to be treated as humans and not vaccinated.'

'What if they try to force you by holding you in quarantine.' she said.

'That is illegal and would strengthen my opposition,' I said. 'More than opposing mob hysteria, I oppose totalitarianism.'

'Me too,' she said. 'Are there enough people opposed to compulsory vaccination to stop it?'

'I think so,' I said. 'There is a groundswell of opposition.'

'Simple people are alienated by high-handed government actions,' I said. 'Albert was a farm worker I knew in the UK, who deserted from his regiment in World War II. He was strong and physically fit. The army tried to train him to be a commando, but after repeatedly going AWOL, he could have been shot, but he was dishonourably discharged. He has died from old age, but others have inherited his spirit.

'I asked him 'Why did you desert from the army, Albert? Didn't you want to stop Hitler?''

''No,' he said, speaking with his West Country English burr. 'If Hitler and his lot had taken over, 'twouldn't have made any difference to the loikes of I. Us folk are poor farm workers at the bottom of the heap, having nothing to lose. I dursn't risk my neck for nothing. The war is caused by the higher ups. It's for them to be doing the fighting, not I.''

'His desertion was the best he could do for his family,' I said. 'He was dishonoured by the military but honoured by his family. His kind would have surrendered. Albert worked the rest of his life on the farm, skilfully and reliably. His earnings supported his wife, raising five children. It took courage to desert and face the derision. He had refused to be enlisted in the totalitarian cause because his duty was to his family. He deserved respect.'

'Would you have surrendered to Covid?' Megan asked me.

'I would take care of myself and my kin,' I said.

CHAPTER 53 TURKEYS NOT BEES

The next day was Nick's birthday. Megan and I met with him on Zoom from quarantine.

'Happy birthday Nick,' I said. 'What's your birthday treat?'

'I'm going to a movie theatre. I haven't been for over a year.'

'Nothing on?'

'Only mass entertainment,' he said. 'I have not wanted to support the spectacle, but now there is a good art movie showing.'

'What are you going to see?' I asked.

'Ghost Dance,' Nick said. 'Have you heard of it?'.

'No. I don't recall it.'

'If you had seen it, you'd remember. It's an old arty movie, exploring Jacques Derrida's philosophy of binary opposition.'

'It sounds like fun,' I said. 'Derrida was into phenomenalism. We've been trying to use it to deconstruct Megan's performing.'

'What have you found out?'

'Chance's negation has lifted my awareness to a new level,' said Megan. 'It's now existential.'

'Terrific. I too live in the moment,' said Nick.

'Are you fulfilling your human destiny moment by moment?' I asked.

'Yes, certainly,' said Nick. 'I want my end to come as a surprise to me. I'm only in this world for the ride, you know that. Why should I care where we're going?'

'The pandemic has new controls on behaviour that may take athletics where we don't want to go,' I said. 'We could be in for a nasty shock.'

'I'll be paid to perform what they want,' said Megan.

'That's unlike you,' Nick said. 'You used to be rebel. Is your allegiance now to yourself, or to the community?'

'Some of each, I suppose,' Megan said.

'That's what I thought,' I said. 'Your behaviour would be unusual if it was purely individual, or purely collective. People have a blend of individual and collective interests. The difference can be illustrated by considering two Australian species: brush turkeys and honey bees.

'Nick, would you choose your allegiance, between turkey individualism at one extreme and bee collectivism at the other?'

'Do I have to choose?' Nick asked. 'Couldn't my life have a blend of turkey individuality and bee sociality? I want to be a drone.'

'Haha. Queen bees are so huge being a drone would be exhausting. Let's suppose you have to choose for all humanity to decide its future.'

'Humans should prefer to live like turkeys,' said Megan. 'The life of bees is slavery.'

'I agree with Megan,' said Nick. 'I would prefer to be a turkey, rather than a bee.'

'Very wise,' I said. 'Honey bees are social insects. They live collectively, controlled by a single female reproductive, the queen, a few male drones and a majority of sexually inactive workers. Tasks of initiating, populating, feeding and defending a colony are performed by individuals of various castes. An individual's caste is determined by nurture with special foods, by grooming and by educational forays. Youngsters learn to forage from adult leaders. Bees live for only 60 days, within social structures having little tolerance for experimentation and deviation. To overcome disease, weather, famine and attack, an individual depends on the survival of the colony. The life of a bee has little individuality.

'Brush turkeys, by contrast, are, in the wild, solitary, with their own territories. They survive for about 10 years, mostly alone. They live freely in woodlands and in city suburb parks, without any social structure but a series of mates. A mature male builds a large nest mound, which is chosen by a female to lay her eggs, to be incubated by warmth from rotting vegetation. Chicks hatch and emerge from the nest without parental guidance or protection. He may use the nest again with other females. The life of a brush turkey has individuality.'

'I want to be more like a turkey than a bee,' Megan said. 'Bee workers are unable to reproduce but turkeys are polyamorous. Turkeys get some, whereas bees get none at all. That does it for me.'

We both laughed.

'In honey bees, the queen controls food gathering, reproduction and raising her offspring by producing substances fed to workers. In most human societies, mating, home building and education of the young are pursued by individuals having lives of about 80 years. Like honey bees, humans have designated roles in society with duties to perform. In some societies, humans appoint leaders to ensure public welfare. In brush turkeys, as far as we know, there are neither communal concerns nor leaders.

'I am all for turkeys,' said Megan. 'They don't need democracy and all that rigmarole.'

'Megan and I are more like turkeys because we're individualistic,' I said. ' Unfortunately the government administrators of our quarantine are a collective of busy bees. Nick, your environmental group is a collective, isn't it?'

'We act as a group rather than from individual interest; we have a common interest with shared goals.'

'Your involvement could change. The balance between individual and collective action can change. The Australian Athletics Association has tried to impose levelling, making competitions into collective events. The change has been unpopular with athletes because they prefer individualism.'

'Performers of athletic events are naturally close to turkey behaviour and mentality,' said Megan. 'But team sports have more like the collective behaviour of bees.'

'Humans are becoming isolated like turkeys,' said Nick. 'Life is increasingly lived alone, sustained by egos, enabling social skills to atrophy except for mating. Humans build bower-like homes to attract the opposite sex but they assign birthing, nursery and childcare to specialists, with education by state institutions, even having some children living away from parents in boarding schools.'

'Collectives reduce personal choice,' Don said. 'Interference in parenting by a nanny state collective is unacceptable. I want to be free of obligation to other people. This doesn't mean I am selfish or don't accept responsibility to help disadvantaged people. I want them to be independent, not obligated to me. I want to teach people to catch fish so they can feed themselves.'

'What if they are unable?'

'A weak turkey would be left to die, but humans have family, state or charitable care for the disabled.'

Through the window on the lawn outside was a family of Magpies searching for things to eat.

'Magpies live in families,' I said. 'They sometimes attack walkers too close to their nests and young. They are between turkeys and bees in sociality. They are beloved for their singing.'

"Bees hum,' said Megan. 'They don't know the words.'

'Ha-ha,' said Nick. 'Human lifetime monogamy is being replaced by serial monogamy turkey-style. Unlike turkeys and Dickens' orphans, humans help and remain in contact with offspring as they learn to survive through lengthy adolescence. Lone turkeys flourish in urban interstices, in remnant biodiverse communities, building nests opportunistically. The turkey lifestyle is being displaced and I think it's time for us to make a stand.'

'It's gotten pretty bad, I agree,' I said. 'Humans are acquiring bee characteristics. Humans live in densely populated colonies. There are trends against dimorphic specialisation, but increasing gender control of offspring, surrogacy, homosexuality, caste eugenics, population control and central control of birthing.

'Young humans are, like bees, nurtured increasingly in cell-like homes, festooned as encrustations around transport infrastructure. The young are conditioned by adult leaders to work outside the colony structure gathering nutrients. They learn specialised worker roles. The brain sizes of children and bees are different, but a study (18) has shown both species probably learn best by a buddy system, or apprenticeship, learning one-on-one with an adult.'

'How would bees deal with a virus threatening the colony?' asked Nick.

'Bees in the worker caste demand equality,' I said. 'They would require every individual to adopt the measures decided by the queen, without deviation, whether she demands exclusion, starvation, sacrifice or lockdown.'

'How would turkeys and bees deal with pandemic disease?' he said.

'Turkeys could do their own thing,' I said. 'They don't mind individuality. Even without vaccination, the risk of catching a virus while going to work or feeding, can be minimised by voluntary isolation. The risk is like the possibility of an oncoming vehicle crossing the centre divide on a public road. You could die, but with observation and caution, it's safe enough most of the time — unless you are unlucky.'

'What about if the chance of dying is great?'

'When fearful of catching it, they can choose to stay at home and starve,' I said. 'The road wouldn't be shut down preventing healthy living.'

'Turkeys take responsibility for themselves,' Megan said. 'They don't have central control by a nanny state.'

'Humans value central intervention especially for developing and administering vaccines. They have been of benefit in preventing and controlling polio, tetanus, smallpox and influenza.'

'Centrality in humans varies between countries,' I said. 'Chinese society is somewhat like a beehive, but in the USA turkey individualism is more admired and gun-toting is respected. Here in Australia, individual and collective orientations are not mutually exclusive, with elements of both individual and collective control present.

'If China is like a bee colony and the USA is like turkeydom, then Australia has facets of both.'

'Which way should Australians want human society to develop?' asked Megan.

'People I have asked want to be more like turkeys and less like bees,' I said. 'I am closer to a turkey than a bee. A turkey-like human would oppose pandemic restrictions and refuse to wear a mask. A bee collective would lockdown to exclude a virus.'

'Would human turkeys compel vaccination to protect the population?'

'No way. A dud vaccine could kill all of them. Their overriding purpose is for their species' genes to survive.'

'You are about as much like a turkey as a plum pudding,' Megan said. 'I know because I haven't heard you gobbling and you haven't started a nest for me yet. You need to lift your game if you want to be a radical turkey, not a conforming bee.'

'I gobble when I am pleased,' I said. 'A male brush turkey is fulfilled when a female deigns to lay her eggs in the huge nest he has built. She has made a careful choice from several nests. She is relieved when the egg-laying is over and he has controlled the temperature in the nest by adjusting the sand covering it.'

'Life's journey for a brush turkey is very different from a honey bee,' said Nick. 'A turkey lives on as long as it can, until it can no longer reproduce.'

He consulted his internet device. 'A bee collects and brings pollen to feed the queen's larvae in a colony of 30,00-80,000 individuals, in a hive producing 100 kilograms of honey each year. When, after a brief life, a bee is no longer able to work, the others finish it off.'

'The brush turkey parents have no parental duties to offspring and can give themselves over to pleasure,' I said. 'By contrast, a bee's life of toil raising young would appear tedious.'

Don arrived and joined in the discussion.

'It is a beelike tendency of humans to use elders to nurture children,' I said.

'The nanny state gives that role to teachers,' Don said. He was a teacher.

'State education raises bees not turkeys,' I said. 'Turkeys don't nurture.'

'Honey bees, caste as workers and reproductives, slave in the service of the state,' Megan said. 'They do as ordered. It seems relatively dull. After the nuptial flight, a termite queen grabs the nearest drone and they have it away and start a new colony. Humans can relate better to the solitary brush turkey, willing to forego bees' extensive nurturing duties, with the possibility of more than one mating.'

'Could it be said that nurturing of the young requires slave-like work in bees and humans?' asked Nick.

'The philosopher Rousseau would agree. He opposed education of children, a view that has been superceded. Educated humans oppose the slavery that bees accept.

Turkeys have adapted to centuries of climate change, by moving to more favourable territories or, when necessary, by adapting physically. Humans have renounced their earlier adaptation to climate and are attempting to control their environment by global action. Humans and honey bees are burdened with social technologies, such as beehives and food crops and are less capable of independent survival by adapting.'

'There are too many bees to seek survival alone outside a hive,' I said. 'They gather in collectives and accept slavery.'

'Chance, how did you become so adamantly opposed to what you call a nanny state?' Nick asked. 'Do you foresee humans becoming slaves?'

'Independent individualism is deeply rooted in many of us,' I said. 'The nanny state is over-protective and smothers healthy living. It is true but unfortunate that you can't save people from themselves:

'I predict future happiness for Americans if they can prevent the government from wasting the labors of the people, under the pretense of taking care of them.' Thomas Jefferson.

'The idea of protecting people is okay, but it's usually implemented corruptly, with faked paternal authority,' I said. 'The nanny state has expanded, way past the point of diminishing returns, growing media and entertainment under the influence of the spectacle. The nanny state allows the population to engage in purchasing fetishistic commodities having illusions held to be sacred, such as houses. Tribal sport is another example, giving poor people a false sense of wealth and empowerment, when really their conditions are shitty and not getting any better.'

'The nanny state enables the community to take care of needy people. It creates altruism,' said Don.

'If the giver gets a kick back, a vote, or even a mellow feeling, it's not entirely altruistic,' I said.

'Self-sacrifice is not a moral ideal, according to Ayn Rand,' said Nick. 'She argued that for any individual, the ultimate moral value is his or her own well-being. She believed selfishness is a virtue.'

'That is the battle line with the neoliberals,' Don said. 'Adam Smith's imprecation is to serve the community by pursuing self-interest. Darwin had survival as the purpose of selfishness. Species hold territory and food, without giving any away, except by tolerating others. The different species look after their own and most of their giving is to kin, which is not altruism. But the community needs to act as one to eliminate diseases such as coronavirus.'

'That is wishful thinking,' I said, 'Vaccination against flu has been available for years, but outbreaks occur every winter. We should stop the restrictions and go back to the way we were.'

'We can't go back,' said Don. 'Human survival in the evolutionary sense is not reversible.'

'We can try to contain coronavirus.'

'You mean by testing, lockdowns, distancing, masking, border closures, quarantine and vaccinations?'

'Responses should differ,' I said. 'When the herd is spooked, a diversity of tactics should be adopted, rather than mass application of technologies of uncertain effectiveness, such as vaccines.'

'By refusing to be vaccinated you have disenfranchised yourself,' said Megan. 'I can see why they have locked you up. Your turkey could wreck our bee-hive.'

'Bee-hives don't come into my picture of humans' future,' I said. 'I expect human bees to disperse to solitariness and become extinct. I want a society of strong independent turkey-like individuals.'

'Are you sure a turkey future would be better?'

'A human bee hive could succumb to hunger, disease or war. It would be too centralised to seed humans' evolving future,' I said. 'I see no future for my kind attempting to compromise with totalitarianism. The future will be inherited by survivors who have lived separately as individuals, their genes forged in the furnace of natural selection. Mankind did not cower from influenza, nor should it cower from coronavirus.'

'You seem to regard human destiny as a choice between selfishness or collectivism. But it's not as polarised as that. A nanny state could be a microcosm in which the best part of the human lifestyle is controlled to resemble hive-like conditions.'

'Living in a colony could have attractive features, but there could be bad with the good. Termites are social insects like bees and live in mounds. Termite workers amputate the wing buds of the young in the nest, to make them flightless. They give workers special foods to sterilise them.'

'That's appalling.'

'Humans could have those collective controls and castes sooner than you think. The tipping point could come when individuals lose their freedom to reproduce and defer to the state. Down with the nanny state. Down with bees. Turkeys forever!

CHAPTER 54 SPECTACLE

We were welcoming Megan home from hospital with a barbecue. When the group of friends gathered in our garden had eaten, I stood up and tapped on a glass with a fork.

It took a while to get their attention.

'I want to say a few words, to thank you for coming on this day which is important to us because Megan has at last been discharged from hospital, where she was treated for coronavirus. She is in good shape.'

There was clapping and a couple of whistles.

'Megan won the gold medal at the Olympics,' I said, 'but we caught the virus and I am still in supervised isolation. Neither of us would accept vaccination for philosophical reasons and as you see, my protective mask is now around my neck, thanks to your earlier agreement.'

'You believe in taking risks, Chance, don't you?' said Don.

'You know of my reckless youth, my student pranks when I did physics and my job troubles in Canada,' I said. 'I would not conform and took risks. I returned to Australia and went back to university to research risk taking by individuals. I was lucky to meet Megan, a champion pole-vaulter.'

They clapped or whistled.

'Of the two of us,' said Megan, 'Chance takes bigger risks. He brought phenomenology to my training and started me using flow, a psychological condition. The Australian Athletics Association opposes us.'

'Typical,' said Don. 'You are in a fight with the AAA. Why?'

'They have tried to stop Megan training in flow,' I said, explaining. 'The nanny state is trying to level athletics.'

'Really? Can they do that?' asked Don. 'Could your flow technique be upsetting the AAA because it is mind bending, like a performance enhancing drug?'

As usual, Don was playing advocate for the regime. It was irritating, but I knew Don was being fair in presenting the other side.

'There is no evidence for it,' said Megan. 'Flow does not use a substance. It is a psychological technique and impossible to test for.'

'Almost impossible,' said Don, correcting. 'Brains can be scanned.'

'We are being opposed by the capitalist spectacle,' said Megan. 'It has taken over athletics, sport, jobs, technologies, entertainments, coronavirus, climate change, everything. It keeps the lower class, workers of all kinds including athletes, in dull repetitive unhappy work, supplying products and media images they buy with their meagre earnings because there is nothing else to escape the tedium. The middle class invest in supply of the spectacle and employ workers to produce it as commodities, like Netflix subscriptions.'

'Is this Marxism?' asked Don.

'It extends Marx's theories. Guy Debord wrote 'The Society of the Spectacle' in 1967. It was a time of rioting in Paris. He identified worker alienation and middle class wealth as the problems causing revolutions earlier in Russia and in France. Conflict between the lower class and the middle class had been predicted by Karl Marx. Debord's update considered the role of television, advertising and the media in serving capitalised production. He described their alliance with industry and government as totalitarian in intent and coordinated by what he called 'the spectacle'.'

'I didn't know you are a Marxist, Chance,' said Don.

'I'm not. I want social reform to reduce worker and consumer alienation, without a revolution of the lower classes.

'I'm a worker for the athletics spectacle,' said Megan. 'I'm underpaid and required to perform with ridiculous new rules. I am alienated.'

'We are living within the spectacle,' I said. 'I am concerned that humans everywhere have fallen under the influence of appearances promulgated by the media that are determining societal evolution.

'The nanny state is central to the spectacle, with the middle and capitalist classes dominating the lower class, with the appearance of overseeing prosperity and development, when the reality is their exploitation of employees and consumers.'

'If you had experienced flow, you would know it is not harmful, unless you regard liberation as harmful,' I said. 'Levellers want to end all individual achievement, especially elite achievement like Megan's. They are trying to suppress individuality. But achievement in athletics, sport, purchasing, employment, education and artistic accomplishment is based on individual ability in competition.'

'You mean winner takes all,' said Nick.

'Competition can organise a wide range of demands.'

'The achievements of people outside the elite have been overlooked forever,' said Penny, Megan's sister, who was sitting beside Lily. 'Competition is harmful when it creates more losers than winners for no good reason. Many people have found the playing field tilted against them. Levelling has brought new people into sport and about time too.'

I fought to control my anger at Penny's poisonous words.

'That is so twisted,' I hissed through clenched teeth. 'Society depends on competition to decide who is best qualified to do things and have ownership. When the losers are not improving, they are better off trying something else.'

'That's your view, not mine,' said Penny. 'Nanny staters want allocation systems that are more humane. Everyone should get a turn in the spotlight.'

There was an awkward pause.

'Who are these nanny staters?' Megan asked.

'They're collectivists, conservatives and bureaucrats, opposed to excellence,' I said. 'They want big government and state control. They accuse their opponents of being undemocratic, unequal, socially irresponsible and non-egalitarian. Their policies are labelled as: socialist, communist, centralist, overbearing, autocratic, authoritarian, fascist or totalitarian. The nanny state is diffuse. Its unifying creed is profit and it is potent.'

'The nanny staters want entitlement to government benefits to be fair,' said Megan. 'It is a mad dream. They want the nanny state to intervene in domestic violence situations, in recruitment, in employment security and a universal wage. Some of their causes have hidden costs or intrude on individual liberty. I want them stopped before they take my freedom away.'

'Whoa!' said Don. 'I'm all for protecting people but I'm against government control. The way you describe it, the nanny state intends to be helpful.'

'When you are helped, you lose self-control,' I said. 'A nanny state can be conceived as benign and kindly but the hand that giveth taketh away. Karl Marx pointed out the ambiguous nature of work. A job that provides an income also probably wastes most of the worker's life in trivial activity. The philosopher Debord (15) called the situation 'the spectacle'.

'What is 'the spectacle?'

'It is not an imaginary or theoretical construct,' I said. 'It has the appearance of the legitimate industry of media and suppliers of entertainment and goods. When you go to the opera, ballet or to a symphony concert, your awareness and spirit embrace layers of visual images and lyrical sounds that absorb your attention. Bands tour nationally and internationally, with extravagant stage shows creating demand for their music with TV images and appearances. Spectacular events like the Eurovision Song Contest are staged by the media. Acts are commodified and marketed within the industry of the 'spectacle'.

'Debord's spectacle has commodities able to be sold and bought. The content is described generally as capitalist exploitation by a middle class, with alienation of the lower class, composed of workers and consumers.'

'Isn't there competition between performers in free markets?' asked Penny. 'For example, if Megan competes freely and doesn't like her rewards, could she find something else to do? Is there necessarily exploitation?'

I gritted my teeth. Penny was being a pain.

'Megan is being exploited as an unpaid entertainer. The Government discourages professionalism in athletics and encourages levelling. Winners get little more than losers, except for a few who are elevated to stardom, to attract audiences. The nanny state doesn't value Megan's training. Peer esteem is her only reward.

'Megan, Chance is all steamed up about levelling,' Penny said. 'I haven't noticed much levelling in my job. Maybe audiences don't value pole vaulting enough to pay anything.'

'Penny is jealous about Megan's gold medal,' I thought. *'Penny works for the government, in the communities' department, a garrison of the nanny state. Levelling would be endemic there. I will choose not to expose her bias. Her arguments were livening up the discussion.'*

Nick said. 'Maybe the nanny state is in other places, at the university, for example. What do you think?'

'It's at the university in a big way,' Megan said. 'Don't you agree, Don?'

Don nodded. 'The figurehead of the leftists is the nanny state. It's part of the Marxist spectacle.'

'Athletics is being levelled and I'm angry,' said Megan. 'In athletics they're trying to prevent competition, making it easier to qualify, so winning does not require talent. They're preventing me from training the way I want. The Government is regulating, trying to control everyone. The Government is bullying us.'

We refilled our glasses.

'Our barbecue has gone well,' I thought. *'People are interested and concerned about what is happening to Megan and I in athletics and our coronavirus restriction. I will try to get them involved in protesting with us.'*

CHAPTER 55 ACTION

We poured drinks and resumed our places in the semi-circle of our guests, to continue the discussion.

'How did you two come out against vaccination?' Nick asked when everyone was listening.

'I haven't told Nick my plan for where this meeting is going, but I have talked with him about it and he has sensed I have an answer,' I thought. *'Good ol' Nick. He is helping me get there.'*

'My week in quarantine at the Olympic Village was interminable,' I said, telling everyone. 'Being in solitary was paralysing. Quarantine nurses wearing PPE brought me food three times each day. They delivered it through the servery, sterilised and sealed, without opening the room to fresh air, except through a filter. The windows were fastened shut. I yearned to be outside in the open, with Sun and wind on my skin.'

'Why did they keep you there?' asked Don.

'After five days I had tested negative, but they wouldn't discharge me. I was desperate to leave. I wanted to visit Megan in hospital.'

'How much longer do I have to stay here?' I asked.

'Until the weekend.'

'I was missing Megan badly and was concerned about her health. When the weekend came I requested to be discharged.'

''Later on today,' they said, 'the doctor will vaccinate you.'

''I won't accept vaccination,' I said. Discharging me was possibly being delayed while they waited for me to change my mind. They could be trying to bully me into vaccinating. My risk of infecting others was small, having recovered from coronavirus, having spent a week in isolation and having tested negative. A side effect from vaccination was more likely.

'I decided to sneak out and visit Megan, returning before anyone would know. Repercussions from my defection were possible, but it would be worth the risk.

'I drove from the Village parking lot to the hospital and found a parking space labelled 'Medical Staff'.'

'When I walked into the hospital, I went to reception.

''I'm a doctor making a bedside visit,' I said.

''You are not allowed on the wards in civvies,' the receptionist said.'

''Can I borrow PPE?'

''They'll fix you up over there,' she said, pointing to a room with a sign 'Equipment'.'

'A nurse gave me a gown, mask, head cover, gloves and overshoes. I put them on and walked towards the lifts, with others similarly attired.

'Before I could enter the lift, I was accosted by two uniformed police, checking everyone.

''Where are you going, sir?'

''Floor 65.'

''Are you a doctor?'

''I'm a houseman. I'm visiting a patient.'

''Show me your medical pass.'

I searched my wallet and showed them my driving licence.

''This is not a medical pass?'

''It's who I am,' I said haughtily.

''If you don't have a medical pass, you can't go up to the wards. We are in a lockdown. You must leave this hospital now.'

I had expected less vigilant and less obdurate opposition. I began to walk towards the exit but doubled back to the other bank of lifts and entered one.

'I was a maverick, going against a spooked herd. When a herd is panicking, it is intolerant of solitary individuals not doing the 'right thing'. I tried to blend in with the herd. I went up to the 21st floor then crossed over to take another lift to floor 65, where Megan was in Ward J, room 17.

'I walked boldly along the corridor and opened the door of the room.

"Chance!' Megan was in bed. She put down the book she was reading.

I held her and kissed her.

"How are you?'

"I'm better but I am still quarantined. Are you discharged?'

"Not yet. I've walked out. I'm hoping they won't notice I'm gone.'

'Megan was relaxed. Her preoccupation with training had faded, releasing an inner self more attuned to others. For the first time, she had time to chat with me.

'Just then the door opened and a nurse came in.

"Why are you here?' she asked when she saw me.

"Everyone's got to be somewhere.' It was an Eccles line in the Goon Show.

'The nurse didn't smile and made a phone call.

"He's my partner,' said Megan.

'I explained my visit.

'The nurse said Megan was still in quarantine. She was recovered, but they wanted to keep her in isolation until the end of the week.

"You shouldn't be in here,' she said. 'You have to leave. Would you leave now.'

'Reluctantly I stood up and squeezed Megan's hand. Her face had good colour and her eyes were bright and soft. I had seen she was okay, which was the main purpose of my visit. We could catch up by phone.

"Goodbye love.'

'The words were inadequate and I kissed her lips, lingering, knowing it would void our quarantines.

"I have to report this,' said the nurse using her phone. 'Hello, security? We have an intruder on floor 65, ward J, room 17.' She turned to me: 'Wait here.'

'Five minutes later the same two police arrived.

"You!' one said. 'We told you to leave the hospital. What are you doing here?'

"I came to see my partner. She's a patient.'

"We told you to leave. I am empowered to impose a fine on you for illegal entry to this quarantine room.'

"I am not a risk to others, because I have been in quarantine and tested negative. Any risk is to myself and my concern. The quarantine is invalid because it assumes I am infectious, when I am not.'

'I told them about my quarantine at the Olympic Village.

"Where is your discharge form?' the security officer asked.

"I don't have one.'

'The police officer wrote an infringement notice and gave it to me.

"You will come with us. We will take you back to your quarantine.'

'I waved goodbye to Megan.

'When we reached the main corridor, I fled down a fire escape for three floors and emerged into a ward corridor. I went along to the lift, went down and out of the hospital. I found my car in the park, drove back to the Village and returned to my room. There was no sign anyone knew I had been away. I waited.

'I had wanted to see Megan, absconded, been caught and escaped.

'An hour later two security guards entered my room without knocking.'

'Are you Chance Finething?' said a guard. 'The Queen Elizabeth hospital has informed us you intruded there and left without permission. You have violated our quarantine restrictions and also the hospital's. You will be held in detention. Come with us now.'

'Where are we going?'

'To a police station.'

'But I have completed my quarantine requirement.'

'You have not been discharged. You must also pay a fine of $600 for breaching the quarantine order. You will be held in quarantine for two weeks.'

'I refuse to pay,' I said.

'After three days, they hauled me up in front of a magistrate who informed me I was in breach of public health regulations and I could only be released if I quarantined at home, monitored by the police.'

I paused and looked around the group of my friends.

'So here I am, in electronic custody,' I said.

'Are you going to pay?' Don asked.

'I have paid. It was the only way I could go home.'

'It seems unnecessary, since you didn't need to be in quarantine,' Nick said.

'It is totally unnecessary,' I exploded. 'It is a punishment for breaking a quarantine that I had completed. When they didn't discharge me after over a week, I walked out. I did the required time. They failed to discharge me.'

"Now you will come with us,' they said. 'You must appear in court before a magistrate who will hear your case. We are empowered to use force if necessary.'

'I had taken a risk and these were the consequences.'

My quarantine breakout story was interrupted by the metallic clatter of feet on our tank by the house. Half a dozen Sulphur Crested Cockatoos were visiting to feed on seed we had put out for them. They had landed in a tall tree and swooped down singly. Large and brilliant white, they voiced their harsh calls, the sound of tearing cloth, flicking up their yellow crests, strutting in a dignified group, like Vatican bishops.

'I was held at a police station,' I continued. 'After three days I was taken from my cell before a magistrate. She read aloud the testimonies of the village's and hospital's security officers.

"The charge is that you did leave quarantine without permission and intruded into another place of quarantine. The fine for these offences is $600 and you have failed to pay it within the maximum period allowed.'

'I read a statement I had prepared.'

297

'I am a free individual. Control of the virus pandemic by enforced quarantine reduces individual freedom. I have opposed it by passive resistance: declining to accept incarceration, ignoring mandated restrictions; and exercising my liberty at other times.

'I would willingly have isolated myself but have resisted enforced quarantine. Compulsion hijacks my volition and creates a precedent of learned helplessness that can reduce my resilience, can reduce my immune response and potentially cause me to become ill. My life is for me to maximise my health and freedom, rejecting unlawful control. I demand that you release me.

'The court ordered me to pay the fine and released me into home quarantine, under police supervision, for two weeks. Online delivery of food and other purchases to my home would be arranged at my expense.

'You have defied restriction orders and you must stay at home. Your partner may live there with you. You may have visitors, not more than six at a time, wearing masks.'

'Remote supervision using an app on my phone was a condition of my release. Parole officers use a GPS to check I am here, in enforced home detention.'

'That's how I came out against vaccination,' I said. 'I opposed unlawful compulsion and the conflict escalated. Megan resisted vaccination too, but completed her quarantine and is not in detention.'

CHAPTER 56 PLAN

'Megan came home from hospital yesterday and we asked you here to celebrate with us. Cheers,' I held up my beer can. 'Fuck 'em all.'

They laughed, in sympathy with me. I looked around the gathering, paused and drank from my beer can.

'I am socially controlled like a bee,' I said. 'I have wanted to live like a turkey but hardly anyone's doing it. The nanny state is winning the propaganda war with lies. Many people are angry: the restrictions have disrespected our humanity.'

'Could some precautions, like wearing masks be reasonable?' asked Don. 'Your refusal to wear a mask preserves your own freedom but jeopardizes the safety of others, near and far. You can take risks yourself but you shouldn't risk others' lives. Perhaps you need to value their lives more and accept minor inconvenience for their well-being, protecting them from the infection you could bring.'

'I am a turkey,' I said. 'I expect others to take care of themselves. If I was a bee, I would care about the other bees in the hive, but I'm not.'

'You don't seem to care about us?' Nick said quizzically. 'We may not like you as much now.'

'I expect to be devalued for not caring about others,' I said. 'Turkeys are used to being alone.'

'You're being cautious about the wrong thing,' Don said, 'overly cautious of vaccines and contrarian.'

'I have a right to be cautious and contrary,' I said. 'Crossing the road has dangers but I have no trouble deciding when to cross. Some risks are unacceptable, unless you're an adrenaline junkie. It is hard to know the benefit of a face mask when no-one knows if it could be fatal for one virus particle to get through, or whether it would take thousands. I need to know more about the risks. It's not good enough to always have to assume the worst. I have been detained unjustly.'

I had their full attention. They were used to my rants about social issues.

'Today will be different,' I thought. *'I have an action plan.'*

'My quarantine has ended and my detention will end in two days,' I said. 'I have a plan to oppose the unjust coronavirus restrictions with non-violent civil disobedience.

'I hope you will join Megan and me when we participate in a protest rally. I am not proposing an insurrection. I am not asking you to do more than protest legally against Government restrictions. Protesting is legal when protesters have a reasonable excuse. Ours is that although we have tested negative, our rights to access city streets, public transport and public amenities is prevented by police.

'The virus could be here for years,' I said. 'The infection rates, hospitalisation numbers, and mortality rates resemble strong flu outbreaks in the past. People are used to that. Our aged people have to die of something.'

'That's a callous view,' said Megan.

'Anyone who denies it is a liar,' I said. 'It is normal for old people to succumb to disease. Expending resources to extend their lives should be commensurate with past provision. When there was isolation in the past, it was voluntary. Oldies curtailed voluntarily their travel, entertainment and sociality. Dying was voluntary. Now the nanny state is trying to control it with lockdowns, bringing on premature death.'

'How is there more death?'

'People are fearful, are without visitors and can't live as well as they would normally,' Megan said.

'Forced vaccination as a condition of Access to loved ones, or to my workplace, would be by enforced vaccination, disrespecting my individual sovereignty,' I said. 'My body is my temple and access to it is under strict control by my mind or, if I am temporarily unable, by a trusted agent such as a properly appointed attorney under an advanced health directive. If I become mentally ill, they could authorize vaccination or even a lobotomy in the same way they could authorize ECT treatment. It is not acceptable.

'We are too old to be challenging laws like 20-year olds,' I said. 'At our age, we should be putting our energy into our careers and looking for advancement. But our opposition to totalitarianism is a higher priority. Protesting could be arduous for us, defying orders to disperse and even being beaten by the police. I am prepared to die opposing mandatory restrictions.'

There was silence.

'Me too!' chimed a couple of others loyally.

Megan held her hand to her mouth and shook her head.

'It mustn't come to that,' she said.

I told our friends details of our plan, to oppose Government restrictions.

'The Occupation of Brisbane will be an act of nonviolent non-cooperation and civil disobedience. The purpose is to end unjust restrictions that are preventing people pursuing their activities in public places. Unelected persons are imposing arbitrary authority. I want to resist totalitarian conditions of centralism, dictatorship, arbitrary ideology, atomism, surveillance and tyranny. The government has given itself a legal framework to prevent a popular movement of opposition, preventing gathering, preventing communication and preventing leadership. We want to oppose the government by passive resistance.

'We plan to walk through city streets unvaccinated, not socially distanced, nor masked,' said Megan. 'If there are enough of us, they will have difficulty stopping us and they will use violence when they have a chance of winning. Hopefully it won't come to that. I hope you will join us.

'It's not my aim to lead opposition to the State government,' I said. 'If leaders of our action group are prominent, they could be arrested and charged with insurrection. I am not leading this action: we can all be leaders. Our leadership will be dispersed, in loosely affiliated groups of non-violent dissenters.

'I will walk quietly through city streets ignoring the next lockdown. Restrictions of vaccination and face masks would apply to those tested positive. Others would be able to march freely.'

'Mobilising the population will happen tomorrow and the next day,' said Megan. 'Tomorrow, Wednesday, we will display our intention to oppose the Government by walking and rallying. On Thursday, we will walk in a legal protest and if they try to restrict us we will non-violently oppose the restrictions. We will defy the Police, who will lose public support if they become violent and injure unarmed protestors. Thousands of protesters will be arrested and they will clog the prisons, refusing to pay the fines, bringing the city to a standstill. The government would have to end restrictions or resign.'

'Bad government is better than no government,' Don said. 'How can we get good government?'

'A new government would be elected democratically,' I said. 'We won't accept another totalitarian government like this one.

'Leave now if you don't want to be a part of this,' I said. 'Those who remain, when you go home, prepare to join us on the streets tomorrow. The media will announce when our action has started, informing our purpose and where people can join in. We will each carry a placard: 'Freedom.'

The friends stayed, discussed our plan and agreed to take part in the protest.

'Thank you everyone for coming,' I addressed the exodus. 'It's great to have Megan back with us. Her situation in athletics is uncertain and she's wondering what to do next. A gold medal is not easy to follow. Thank you too for your interest in hearing about the spectacle and for sharing our concern about it. It is a force to be reckoned with. See you on Wednesday after 10am, on the streets, walking to the city centre.'

CHAPTER 57 RESOLUTION

My home detention ended the next day. I posted the notice below on my blog and sent copies to social and news media.

MEDIA RELEASE
Wednesday, September 24th, 9.00 am.
COMMENCEMENT OF PROTEST AGAINST CORONAVIRUS RESTRICTIONS
This media release announces the intended Occupation of Brisbane by citizens who protest certain Government coronavirus restrictions: civilians are unable to enter, without proof of vaccination, public buildings and places of employment, subject to employers' requirements. Travel for inessential purposes and to visit family members in residential institutions is also banned; schools are closed.

Demonstrate your rejection of these restrictions by walking with us to the city centre.

Because the restrictions have not had due legal processing, their implementation by police is 'reasonable excuse' for protest. Therefore, this protest demonstration is not illegal.

The protest is now launched and my involvement ceases except as a protester. There is no organisation. Tell others to walk and rally, today Wednesday 24th, 2032 from 10.00am, occupying the city centre on Thursday, from 12.00 noon.

Signed,
Chance Finething,
Citizen of Brisbane.

Megan and I and a handful of friends walked from our homes to an arterial road leading to the city centre and Parliament. We carried placards announcing: WE PROTEST VACCINATION COMPULSION and: WE CAN GO WHERE WE WANT. We carried a banner: OCCUPY BRISBANE WEDNESDAY AT 10 AM AND THURSDAY AT 12 NOON.

We were joined by other walkers and by the time the road joined a freeway, there were several thousand walkers. We followed a police car with flashing lights and we spread out and blocked one side of the highway. We proceeded like this across a river bridge and into the CBD shopping precinct, where others, alerted by media, joined us. We rallied in a city square, with speakers on megaphones. The atmosphere was festive: people were enjoying the sunshine.

When we walked to the Parliament, there were tens of thousands with us. We demanded to speak with the Premier and chanted 'Stop the vaccination mandate.' The Premier did not appear.

A journalist with a TV camera interviewed Megan and me, at the entry gate to the parliament building.

She asked: 'Why are you protesting? Wouldn't it be better to cooperate by getting vaccinated and wearing masks?'

'If our right to walk in the street is taken away or weakened,' I answered, 'is it possible that in future we could be sterilised, euthanized, conscripted into the military, aborted, refused abortion, forced to give blood, have our gender changed, have offspring genetically modified, or have a mind altering mental treatment administered?'

'It is unreasonable to expect people to accept vaccination when they distrust the vaccines and distrust the Government's intent,' Megan told her. 'The Government does not have the right to enforce a mandate that disrespects individuality. The Government is our government and it must allow us freedom. We are not threatening the government: we are disobeying it.'

Megan and I were arrested. We went passively amid non-violent protests. We were escorted to a vehicle and driven away to be imprisoned. Our arrest hardened the marchers' resolve.

By the evening of this first day, there were 30,000 walkers obstructing half a dozen roads around Parliament.

'Tomorrow we will show them we are serious,' I said.

Megan and I were locked in separate cells overnight and released the next morning.

On Thursday, Megan and I set off together at 12 noon. We walked under shady trees through boulevards, beside active transport pedestrians commuting to work. Under the trees, the light was greenish and cool.

When we tried to walk in the City Centre streets without a vaccination certificate, police told us to go home.

'Test us for the virus,' I said. 'If we are negative, we have a right to be in a public place.'

We walked ahead of a growing horde of all ages, some pushing children in strollers, answering our call to action. They wore jeans, shorts and T-shirts, many with slogans. They wore hats against the hot sun and carried water bottles. As they passed shops, offices and factories, workers poured out on to sidewalks to watch and clap. Many of them joined in.

We chanted: 'WE ARE ONE. WE HAVE THE POWER.

UNITED WE WILL NEVER BE DEFEATED.

We stepped to a sombre drumbeat. Our people were angry. It was a procession of individuals deliberately choosing to confront authority non-violently with concerted forward movement. Store keepers were boarding up their windows against violence and looting. The police had closed off the city centre and formed lines at barricades across streets, with vaccination cards or certificates on walkers' phones needing to be shown for entry.

The unvaccinated walkers came to a wall of helmeted police with riot shields. When those at the front were pushed forward from behind, police clubbed them to the ground. There was shouting and screaming but no retaliation. Those felled and injured were carried back with broken bones, concussion and bloody wounds by their friends and laid on the ground where they were cared for. Their places in the line were taken by others moving resolutely forward, with vaccinated protesters caught in the crush and police checking for vaccination became ineffective. The movement was swollen as bystanders joined in. Wave after wave pushed forward and were beaten down. The street was like a battleground with dozens of bodies. The Police were unable to deter the walkers. They frenetically arrested and removed them to prison, but the prisons soon filled to overflowing.

Megan and I avoided attracting attention. The Government were unable to arrest a leader. My re-arrest would have provoked more violence. Megan and I moved forward with the throng. We warded off the clubs when they struck us. I was felled with a cut on my head and Megan's arm broke defending herself against a police attacker. A first aid worker put her arm in a sling.

After several hours of beating unresisting protesters, the police became physically exhausted and disillusioned. The city centre was taken over by the rebels. By evening their challenge to Government authority had overwhelmed the police. The jails were full and the streets were thronged with walkers. The Police quit their posts and anyone could go to the city centre without being challenged. The Government had lost control.

200,000 protestors had resisted the government passively with civil disobedience. We had won. We had copied a similar protest, Ghandi's Salt March in India in 1930. It had civil disobedience, protesting British rule of the sub-continent. Police mutinied from their brutal task: opposing non-violence. The police gained respect for the protestors and deserted their posts.

Worldwide media attention was on our occupation of Brisbane. The focus of protest was lockdown of a City that had mandated vaccination for workplaces and had been overcome by unvaccinated citizens who, when they had tested negative, demanded access.

The people had risen in revolt.

The conflict was between those who asserted a right to be protected from the virus, by stopping others' rights to travel, work and engage in activities in the public space. A silent minority wanted to be absolutely protected by mandating exclusion of potentially infectious persons. The Government had tried and failed to act for the cautious 'haves' against the reckless and anarchistic 'have-nots' who threatened insurrection.

Peace emerged when the Government lifted their ineffective lockdown and focussed on maintaining order on the streets. They were called upon to resign. State leaders realised that transgression of free rights of the majority was a much more serious problem than a small part of the population demanding protection from coronavirus. They withdrew the police.

Peace returned to the streets. Megan and I were up all night, bandaging and supporting protestors and modelling peaceful behaviour. The police carefully avoided clashing with us. The Government made all restrictions voluntary. It was a victory for individualism. Widespread infection was forecast but most people were protected by their vaccinations. Vaccinations could be required by businesses, schools and hospitals. People testing negative, but without a vaccination certificate, could not be excluded. Unvaccinated people were urged to self-test and self-quarantine if necessary. A vigorous programme of tracing and testing at outbreaks averted spreading. Freeloading by hiding unvaccinated in a vaccinated herd was prevented by a regulation requiring people to display their vaccination status visibly by wearing a badge with an X.

In the morning, Megan and I went home. The protest had succeeded. Its opposition to the nanny state had been vindicated.

'You can go back to training,' I told Megan. 'The World Championships are in five months.'

'Is the pandemic over?'

'It may never be over, like influenza. Most things are going back to near the way they were before.'

'I don't know that I want to go to Europe,' said Megan. 'I want to finish my PhD.'

'Me too,' I said. 'It could take us two years. Then what?'

'It depends what you are going to do,' she said.

'I wonder what goal Megan would dare next,' I thought, *'with the advantage of her 'being there' existentially for her next performance in flow, striving to achieve and probably succeeding.'*

'I'd like to do something with you,' I said.

'Like start a family?' she said. 'Would that interfere with your work?'

I hesitated. I had been thinking recently I would like to have children. I wanted to pass on my learning to young people. Having children would be fulfilling.

'Not at all.,' I said. 'I would love it.'

CHAPTER 58 EPILOGUE

I had been a risk taker in my youth, but after several accidents at work, I became more cautious, with an individual approach to risk. When I met Megan, I recognised her as an individualist like myself. She was a dedicated pole vaulter. Like me, she was researching in psychology, our interests overlapped and we shared our lives. I had sought to help her improve her athletic abilities by phenomenological self-analysis and flow.

Megan's right to compete 'in flow' had been threatened by government, university authorities and the athletics association. They wanted to exploit pole vaulting, as part of a spectacle, in which its appearance was marketed as a commodity for profit. The images sucked out from real events the visible images, leaving them wasted. Our demonstration against the AAA and Megan's withdrawal from competition, had halted imposition of new levelling rules. Hopefully others would follow our example and resist intrusion of the capitalist spectacle into sport and other arenas.

Before the Occupation of Brisbane, the nanny state had been steadily gaining power, taking away self-determination. The spectacle took over pandemic management with images of medical chaos and catastrophic death. Investment for profit was helped by government funding and a fearful populace, creating expensive vaccines, treatment technologies, construction of hospitals, unpopular restrictions and welfare handouts. Our non-violent opposition to mandatory vaccination caused the lockdown and restrictions to be withdrawn and the Government to resign.

Non-violence is the greatest force at the disposal of mankind. It's mightier than the mightiest weapon of destruction devised by the ingenuity of man.
Mahatma Gandhi

The nanny state totalitarianism had been thwarted. Individualism was alive and well. We were fulfilled. The government, which had been intent on levelling, had used the pandemic to charge headlong towards totalitarianism, until we opposed them. They had retreated and now the new government was expected to keep capitalism on the tight leash of public good.

We had defied the National Government and its rule of fear.

A few people wanted me to run for election as their new State leader, but I declined. There were others more capable.

'If you ran, you would get a good following,' Nick said. 'Anti-fascism is flavour of the month.'

'I'm a disconnected anti-fascist,' I said. 'I am opposed to far-right, authoritarian and ultranationalist ideologies and their anti-liberalism, anti-communism, and anti-conservatism. I want to oppose the spectacle, with its central dictatorial supremacy, government control of business and labour and regimentation of society with suppression of opposition. My duty to the public good is to oppose totalitarian government. I don't need to be in the government to do that.

'I want a government to serve both individualists and collectivists,' I said.

I called for the national government to hold non-partisan elections.

'We must oppose the party spectacle,' I said. 'The party's over.'

'The politics industry is highly profitable,' Megan said. 'It will be difficult to stop it.'

'People can stop it taking over,' I said 'by passive resistance.'

'The same way we are stopping a takeover by the nanny state,' Megan said. 'We are claiming our freedom as individuals.'

'I am an individual and free,' I said.

'My freedom is being here,' she said, 'with you.'

'Perhaps we can join the herd again,' I said. 'The spirit of the desert is calling me.'

'Me too,' she said. 'At last we can be free.'

'Knowing our kind will inherit the Earth.'

BIBLIOGRAPHY AND REFERENCES

1. Knox, M P, Time is Gold, Novel Ideas, 2020.
2. Heidegger, M. Being and Time, 1927, Must Have Books, 2021.
3. Brymer, G. E., 'Extreme Dude: A Phenomenological Perspective on the Extreme Sport Experience', PhD thesis, Wollongong, 2005.
4. Arendt, H. The Origins of Totalitarianism, 1951
5. De Beauvoir, S. The Ethics of Ambiguity, 1947
6. Vonnegut, K, Harrison Bergeron
7. Persig, R. Zen and the Art of Motorcycle Maintenance, 1974
8. De Tocqueville, Alexis de, Tocqueville, Alexis de, 1805–1859, Democracy in America.
9. Foucault, M. Nietzsche, Genealogy, History, in D F Bouchard, Ithaca: Cornell University Press, 1977, p153
10. Foucault, M. Discipline and Punish, 1975
11. COVID-19 Vaccine Mandates Fail the Jacobson Test, Epoch Times, December 30, 2021.
12. Nietzsche, F. Thus Spake Zarathustra. 1883
13. Burns, P. 'Albert Einstein's Theory of Happiness', Medium, November 12, 2021
14. Debord, G, The Society of the Spectacle, 1967
15. Mark Fisher.s Marxist Supernanny, https;//youtu.be/F2GPXGsS
16. McLuhan, M. Understanding Media, 1964
17. Fisher, M. Capitalist Realism – Is there no Alternative?, 2009
18. Richardson, T and Franks, N Teaching in Tandem Running Ants.
19. Seligman, M. Learned Optimism, 1991

www.ingramcontent.com/pod-product-compliance
Lightning Source LLC
Chambersburg PA
CBHW070100120726
47909CB00002B/448